EUPHORION THE YOUNGER

BY

STAVROS STESOPOULOS

TRANSLATED FROM THE GREEK

BY

OLIVER THOMSON

With special thanks to my wonderful wife Jean

and to the long-suffering

Lesley, Jim and Madeleine at Sparsile

Contents

TRANSLATOR'S NOTE

To make life easier for the reader I have taken a few liberties in my spelling of Greek names. Where a name is already quite well known like Piraeus, Sophocles or Aeschylus I have stuck to the conventional English spelling, but for the less well-known I have been more authentic, making them end in -os not -us or -on not -um (e.g. gymnasion)and so on.

For the assistance of readers I have included at the back of the book a list of all the characters who make an appearance and indicated whether they were real people (the vast majority) or fictional (just a few of the main characters, but even they are based on historical evidence - for example the parents of the two principal characters certainly did exist). For each character I have appended a brief cv and dates.

FOOTNOTES

Readers can ignore the translator's footnotes if they wish, but they are often quite amusing, and for the benefit of travellers to Greece and Turkey they clarify the real places mentioned in the book which may now have different names, identifying the location and the modern name if they have changed. They tell you if the buildings featured have survived and can be visited.

PREFACE

This remarkable novel, written by the young Greek writer Stavros Stesopoulos who died tragically in the Smyrna massacre of 1922, has now been translated into English for the first time. Though first published in Athens in 1920 it still has that youthful freshness which brought to life the events of 2500 years ago. So Stesopoulos may have seen a copy of a contemporary document, fragments from the memoirs of Euphorion, which were lost during the siege of Smyrna, but provided unique insight into some of the most dramatic events that form the background to this tale of war, love, crime and political intrigue

Nearly all the characters in this book were real people and all the main events are true or at least vouched for by contemporary historians like Thucydides. The hero's life and adventures coincide with the most glorious episodes of ancient Athens but sadly also with its arrogance and eventual defeat. They also provide the solution to one of history's great unsolved murder mysteries.

Map 1

MAP SHOWING ATHENS AND ELEUSIS IN 470 BC
TO DELPHI
TO MARATHON
ATTIKA
Euphorion's Estate
Temple
Cave of Persephone
ELEUSIS
Megara
Sparta
THE SACRED WAY
Akademos
Sacred Lake
Kimon's Villa
Ceramic Agora
market
ATHENS
Akropolis
Kynosarges
R. KEPHISOS
The Long Walls
Harbour
ISLAND OF SALAMIS
Salamis City
Psyttaleia
PEIRAEUS
Bay of Phaleron
TO SOUNII
Mount Hymettos
Map 1

Map 2

MAP TO SHOW THE FIRST THREE VOYAGES OF EUPHORION
MAKEDONIA
Amphipolis
BLACK SEA
Byzantion
Thasos
Proconnesos
Imbros
Kyzikos
Troy
Lemnos
Lesbos
MAP TO ILLUSTRATE THE FIRST
THREE VOYAGES OF EUPHORION
THE YOUNGER; First
Second   Third xxxxx
PERSIAN EMPIRE
Skyros
Chios
Notion
Ephesos
EUBOIA
Thermopylai
Delphi
Tanagra
Thebes
Andros
Ikaria
Maiandros
Myous
Miletos
ATHENS
Korinthos
Tenos
Samos
Aigina
Mykonos
Kythnos
Paros
Delos
SPARTA
Naxos
Amorgos
Melos
Phaselis
R. Eurymedon
Krya
Rhodos
Map 2

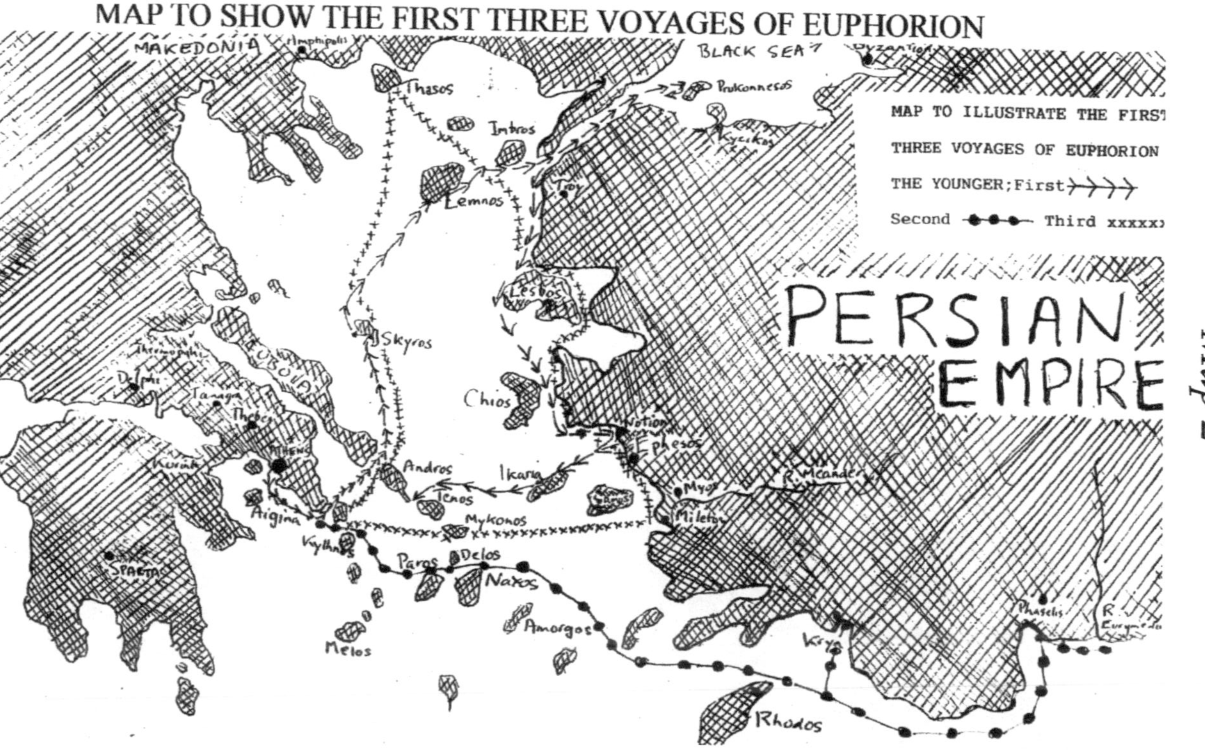

CHAPTER ONE

THE FIRST ONSLAUGHT

'YOUR FATHER WAS A REAL hero, Phori,' my grandfather used to say to me from a very early age and I suppose much of my life has been dominated by the idea that I must live up to that image. My name is Euphorion, Phori for short, and my father was Kynegiros, the man who won everlasting fame by grabbing the prow of a Persian galley on the beach at Marathon, then holding on till his arm was hacked off.

That was five years before I was born. And though I have had my full share of adventures in both war and peace I have never, at least in my own opinion, done anything quite so obviously heroic. So I am not, I hope, writing this out of personal vanity, but as a warning to future generations, for people like myself who had some modest success in warfare often became so addicted to it that there were dire results for our glorious city. But perhaps you should be the judge of that.

To start at the beginning, I was born seventy years ago in Eleusis[1], the small town fourteen miles from Athens along the Sacred Way. It was the same year that King Darius of Persia died, and as I've said, five years after his unexpected defeat by the Athenians at Marathon, where my father had fought so bravely. My grandfather, Old Euphorion, had a small estate near Eleusis, mainly planted with olive trees and vines, although the area is mostly flat and therefore more famous for its corn.

This great fertility was probably the reason why Eleusis was a great centre for pilgrimage and the Mysteries performed in its great temple were respected throughout Greece, even by the Spartans.

I must confess, however, that in my young days I just took it for granted that crops would come up in the spring and parents would have children, never dreaming that gods would step in to make matters better or worse or that we should express our gratitude to them when the harvests of any kind were good.

Though this book is primarily meant as a record of my own modest exploits, my friends, my enemies and my loved-ones, I must, if you don't mind, give a brief explanation of the events five years before my birth which had a huge influence on my own career and the lives of my fellow Athenians. For my life has coincided with both the greatest successes and some of the worst disasters of our wonderful city. And to understand this I need to start with the Persian Wars and some of the political in-fighting that followed.

Unfortunately the success of General Miltiades, who was the real architect of our victory at Marathon, led to a great deal of jealousy and the old guard were reluctant to give him too much credit. This was one of the reasons why they made so much fuss of my father, who by that time, had lost his arm and was no threat to the establishment. In fact, according to the historian Herodotus[2], who was a great admirer of Miltiades, my father actually died of his wounds, but my birth five years later shows that at least that part of his account is inaccurate.

The trouble with Miltiades was that he came from an extremely ambitious family; his father, Cimon senior, had been a champion chariot driver at the Olympic Games and he himself as a young man had served as a mercenary in the Persian army, making himself offensively rich in the process. He had also learned new-fangled military tricks which horrified the old guard, especially the idea of our bold troops pretending to retreat so that the enemy would rush into our trap. That sort of thing was simply not done.

But even worse, Miltiades had acquired certain traits of oriental luxury and sexual liberalism that horrified the old guard even more. Shortly before the war he had made himself dictator of the Greek colonies of Kallipolis [3] near the entrance of the Black Sea, so he was used to getting his own way and had a huge grudge against the Persians for driving him out.

Consider the dire position that Athens faced in that fateful year. Our own army was about nine thousand strong at the most and pretty amateurish. We were faced with an onslaught from a Persian army at least five times that size, much more professional and much better equipped. Of the other cities that might have come to our aid most of them were so frightened that they would rather surrender than fight. The only city that should have helped was Sparta, which did have an excellent army, but the Spartans disapproved of our style of government and were probably quite happy to let us be destroyed. The only thing that might persuade them to help us was if there was something in it for them.

So as a forlorn gesture Miltiades sent a messenger Phidippides,[4] a cousin of my father's noted for his stamina, to run all the way to Sparta to ask for help. His run there and back was around a hundred and fifty miles and he managed it in two days, so it just about killed the poor man, but in vain for the Spartans wouldn't make a move till the full moon was over and by then, as it turned out, it was too late.

On top of all this we had other problems to make our position even more dangerous. For a start the city in those days did not have fortified walls, so there was no question of us surviving a siege. Then there were our generals, most of whom had little front-line experience, particularly the top one, Kallimachos, who was a decent enough man but old-fashioned and lacking initiative.

His one big idea was for our soldiers to march out of the city and die gloriously with no expectation of victory. We had one more problem, the fact that we were supposedly a democracy, the first one in the world, and committees are never very good at running wars. But, as it happened on this occasion it turned out surprisingly to be a blessing. Miltiades was one of those rare generals who could also talk. So the old guard could not prevent him making a speech at the assembly, in fact they probably never expected him to come up with a plan that would win support. But he did. Basically he told the old guard that they were all very brave, but it was just plain stupid to commit mass suicide by marching out of the city against a much bigger army. Nor would that save the lives of their wives and children.

His idea was not to sit and wait for the Persians to arrive at the city gates, but for our entire army to head off eastwards and lie in wait for them in the hills above Marathon. Naturally the old guard thought it was far too risky leaving the city undefended, but Miltiades was a smooth talker and could speak from personal experience about the Persian mentality, for he had spent so long as a mercenary in their pay. So, amazingly, he won the vote.

Thus for four days and nights our army waited quietly in the hills and watched as the huge fleet of Persian ships packed with soldiers anchored in the bay at Marathon. On Miltiades' orders they made no move as the gorgeously dressed Persian troops disembarked, so confident in their ability to defeat us that they left half their army on board the ships. Even with only half their troops they hugely outnumbered us, though you have to take the statistics of Herodotus with a pinch of salt. Certainly their cavalry must have looked very forbidding, but Miltiades used all his powers of persuasion to dissuade Kallimachos from launching a suicidal attack and abandoning our strong position in the hills.

My father often talked of the feelings of the ordinary infantrymen as they watched the mass of gold-trousered Persians forming up on the beach below as they prepared to attack. Though the Athenians cracked jokes about them being soft and effeminate this was just to boost their own confidence, for although this may have been true of some of the leaders the ordinary Persian soldiers were seasoned fighters and by no means cowardly.

Eventually they were ready with a mass of mounted archers to charge up the hill against us. Miltiades' strategy was to let them do this and for our centre to fall back pretending to be in a panic, which as father said was not too difficult. Thus the Persians would be lured into a trap and our two wings could then close in behind them as they pushed recklessly forward. Then we could cut them off from their companions and kill off fair numbers as they became disorientated in the rough terrain.

The plan worked perfectly and the Persians lost five thousand men hampered by the rough ground, whereas no more than a couple of hundred of ours were hit by their arrows.[5] Then the surviving Persians surged back down to the beach in disarray and got in the way of their own reinforcements. One of the stories that emerged from this was of the mountain god Pan,[6] the one with goat's feet, well-known for giving people a fright in lonely bits of countryside. He scared the Persians witless and caused a stampede. Up to that time Pan hadn't received much attention in Athens, but afterwards there was a grotto built for him on the north side of the Acropolis in gratitude for his assistance at Marathon.

The Persian high command was little concerned with casualties and did not take this initial mishap too seriously. Mystified by the tactics of Miltiades and more concerned about the anger of their short-tempered King Darius, they dithered and let their cavalry re-embark, perhaps intending to attack our undefended city before our victorious army could get back. It was at this point that my father committed his legendary act of gallantry, clinging to the ornamental prow of a beached Persian galley in spectacular fashion, though in all honesty it can have had little tactical value. Even if he had managed to hold back the ship for another minute or so, our men, by the sound of it, were too exhausted to try storming a fully manned ship. Besides, we had already won an unexpected victory which, if not conclusive, had achieved a huge moral advantage.

In addition Miltiades had the foresight to send our infantry back to Athens at double time in case it was attacked. Thus, when the Persian fleet headed round to Athens and their leaders saw our troops back near the city and ready for another fight, they decided enough was enough and headed home.

Thus it was that my father became for a few years one of the most famous citizens of Athens, and certainly of Eleusis, a role later taken over by his brother, my uncle Aeschylus,[7] when his plays became popular. The Persian invasion had been halted and their king lost interest in the campaign, so the huge army turned back to base, boasting it had given us all a good fright.

It was in this atmosphere that the people of small towns like Eleusis started to refer to themselves as Athenians. And I was born into a community where fighting the Persians was the highest calling to which a young man could aspire. Athena, our city's own special goddess had many years ago helped kill the Gorgons, had given us the sacred olive tree and the skill to build ships. Now, with the help of Miltiades, she had helped us to survive an onslaught from the biggest army in the world. But we still had many dangers to overcome and in that I was eventually to play a part.

Meanwhile the old guard did their best to minimise the contribution of Miltiades to our unexpected victory. General Kallimachos had died gloriously on the field of battle and even though he had been reluctant to accept Miltiades' strategy he was given all the credit. Miltiades, on the other hand, was too clever and unscrupulous to be popular with his fellow officers, too rich, dissolute and arrogant to please the city fathers. Disgusted by their lack of appreciation of his remarkable victory, he headed off on a personal whim with a fleet of seventy ships to conquer the island of Paros[8] in revenge for it having taken the side of the Persians. After a twenty five day siege he gave up trying to capture the city and ravaged the hinterland instead.

Soon afterwards he was accused of attempting to rape one of the virgin priestesses and was wounded in the leg while trying to escape. Rightly or wrongly he was taken back to Athens in disgrace, flung into prison and died when his leg-wound went septic. Nevertheless his memory and his children lived on and were to play a significant role in my life years later. It was a tragic end for a great man and, after all, molesting priestesses in captured cities was not normally seen as a heinous offence, especially in a place like Paros that had sided with the Persians at the Battle of Marathon.

However, it seems to be a fact of life that great men like Miltiades always seem to take a step too far, and the temptations of untold wealth when fighting the Persians were to prove too much for several other fine leaders over the next few years. Some people say it's because the gods get jealous if a mere mortal is too successful. But why should gods be jealous? Now that I am old I realise that some of the less talented and more cautious of our generals tended to be envious of those who took risks and pulled off unexpected victories. So they got the gods involved in taking sides, just like they used to play off the exceptionally beautiful goddess Aphrodite against the less beautiful but more sensible goddesses like Hera.

---

1. Eleusis, now known as Elefsina, is these days a suburb of Athens reached by a freeway and dominated by oil refineries, but the ruins of the temple precinct survive next to the Archaeological Museum. Translator.

2. Luckily copies of the History of Herodotus written soon after these events have survived to the present day and give a very readable account of this exciting period.

3. Kallipolis is now known by its Turkish spelling as Gorbolu or Gallipoli and in 1915 was the scene of the campaign conceived by Winston Churchill to attack Turkey. Unfortunately Turkish opposition was stronger than expected and Allied losses were considerable, including many Australians and New Zealanders. The old Greek city was destroyed by an earthquake but the whole peninsula is now a historic park.

4. There was a later legend that Phidippides also ran back from Marathon to Athens with news of the victory, a distance of twenty-six miles, so when the Olympic Games were revived in 1898 it was decided to run a race to celebrate this feat, The first marathon was won by an Athenian water-carrier called Spyros Louis who ran it in 2 hrs, 50 mins, 50 secs.

5. The official figure was 192 as recorded on the Funeral Mound or Tymbos which still stands on the site of the battle famous for its crops of wild fennel. The date of the battle is now recorded as 490BC so Euphorion was born five years later, in 485.

6.   The god Pan had goat's horns and goat's legs, and was the patron of shepherds and the mountains. He created the concept of panic that was named after him. He was also a great player of flutes or pipes and later patronised theatre critics, hence 'panning'. He was also a part-time sex god best known for his seduction of the Moon goddess Selene.

7.   Aeschylus, the son of Euphorion Senior, wrote some ninety plays of which seven have survived and are still performed. He is regarded as the father of tragic drama.

8.   The island of Paros lies around a hundred miles south east of Athens, near Naxos. It sent troops to help the Persians both during the Marathon campaign and the Salamis one ten years later. It became famous for its marble, much prized by sculptors and it is now a popular holiday resort.

CHAPTER TWO

THE SECOND ONSLAUGHT

I WAS ONLY FIVE YEARS old when the Persians mounted their second big invasion of Greece, but I still have vivid memories of the ordeal which my family and many others suffered at the time. It is also important for my story because yet again the politics of the period were to have an impact on my later life. Just as before Marathon ten years earlier, the old guard in Athens had their own cautious ideas for defence, but it was an upstart nobody who came up with the idea that was to save all our lives. And this new upstart, Themistocles, along with his family, was to play a part in several of my later adventures.

'He's a rogue, Phori,' said my father, referring to Themistocles, who had fought near him at Marathon. 'He's spent all the family's money, but he knows how to line his pockets with more.'

At that time I was too young to be told of Themistocles' other rakish activities but in due course heard the rumours of his many youthful escapades. This was all in stark contrast to the favourite general of the old guard, Aristides.

'Now there's a real man,' my grandfather old Euphorion would say. 'He always puts his country first and never has anything to show for it.' At this point my father would wink at me but nod in agreement with the old man.

Later I came to appreciate these two rival leaders, each remarkable in his own way, yet complete opposites. Themistocles was to all appearances idle, pleasure-loving, sly about his sources of cash, self-indulgent but occasionally brilliant, whereas Aristides was hard-working, conscientious, ostentatiously prudent about money, austere to the point of being martyrish but totally lacking in humour and new ideas.

'The only thing they both have in common is Stesileus of Kos,' my father would say mysteriously, and in those days I had no idea what he meant. Only later did I learn that it was common gossip that the two men both fancied this handsome youth from the island of Kos. It wasn't so much their interest in this lad that caused any shock as the fact that two such important men should have this element of jealousy to add to their political rivalry.

Their other great disagreement was over their contrasting preferences for fighting on land or sea. Aristides was typical of the old guard; he had led his clan at Marathon and had the sort of dogged mind that you expect from an infantryman. He admired the Spartans, despised fancy tactics and instead preferred straightforward slogging it out on land, even allowing the Persians to have a fair fight rather than trying to beat them by guile. Themistocles on the other hand only cared about winning and would cheat if it meant fewer casualties. He also preferred fighting at sea where devious tactics were more common and a psychological victory could sometimes be achieved before the real fighting began.

So about the time I was born Themistocles became chief magistrate and began pushing for a huge expansion of the Athenian fleet with extra dock facilities to be built at the Piraeus. To pay for this he used up the extra silver that had been found recently in the new seam at Mount Laurion. According to gossip he also sold the timber from his own estates to the shipbuilders at a handsome profit. As some cheeky poet commented,

'Well known he was an able man to be

But with his fingers apt to be too free.'

Themistocles even picked a spot in the new docks to build a temple for the goddess Aphrodite for she's the one sailors love best, especially the men at the oars. For what can they think about all day but a real or imaginary sweetheart, and Aphrodite always has the figure to keep sailors happy.

Of course Themistocles was a former pupil of the Kynosarges Gymnasion, a school for boys who did not have pure Athenian blood in their veins, where I later became a pupil myself. There he had made a feature of his unwillingness to learn music and his general lack of discipline.

However, he did make a point of learning a few tricks from the philosophers, and he was one of the first politicians to get the knack of fancy talking to the assembly, so that he could score points off Aristides and win support for his new fleet. In fact Aristides seemed such a bore by comparison and suffered so much from a smear campaign that he was sent into exile. Everyone remembers the famous story of the Athenian voter who was so tired of hearing how virtuous Aristides was that he voted[1] for his exile just to relieve the tedium.

So with his rival out of the way for a year Themistocles was able to pursue his master-plan for expanding the navy. Within three years he had built up a fleet of two hundred triremes, fitted out all three harbours at the Piraeus to provide berthing for them and trained the crews. What's more his triremes were state-of-the-art with eighty one oars each side, three rows of twenty seven. With their reinforced waterline rams they could do considerable damage, but also carried around twenty soldiers, including half a dozen bowmen to pick off the enemy officers. Now for the first time it became fashionable for the Athenian toffs to join up as trireme captains. Even Miltiades' son Cimon, another tearaway like his father, decided life as a trierarch[2] was more glamorous than the cavalry. So he left his favourite tavern, tossed his saddle off the Acropolis in a ceremonial act of resignation and learned to thrash his crew across the Aegean.

Thus, even as a five year old, I was aware both of the excitement and sense of impending doom as we heard at last that King Xerxes, the new ruler of Persia, was on his way to attack us with a massive army. It was so big, they said, that he had to build massive floating bridges across the rivers and used up the granaries of several cities every time he stopped for the night. He even dug a new canal to get his ships safely past the stormy coast at Athos.

All Persians had a reputation for cruelty, but Xerxes had already shown special talents in this direction. Amongst the gossip picked up by Herodotus there was the story of a rich man called Pythios. He had entertained King Xerxes very lavishly on his way through Sardis but then had the effrontery to ask for one of his favourite sons to be excused military service. Next morning the boy concerned was to be seen neatly cut in half, with one piece of his body left on either side of the gates of Sardis as the great army marched out. No wonder my nurse Psyche, a silly but rather loving slave girl from Thrace, would say to me, 'Don't be naughty, Phori, or I'll send you to Xerxes,' and this was enough to ensure my obedience for a good half hour.

All this time the huge invading army came nearer and nearer to us and soon there was not a grain of food left north of Thebes. As the Persians approached each city they demanded earth and water as a token of surrender, which none of the cities were brave enough to refuse. Thebes and Tanagra both gave up without a fight and still the Persians kept coming.

Meanwhile Themistocles and his fleet had sailed north to join up with the Spartans who were, for once, in a cooperative mood, but not for long. My one-armed father was to his disgust assigned as a guard for the Mount Laurion silver mines and his brother, my uncle Aeschylus, was part of a small shore detachment in the Pentelikos mountains. The rest of our family, including my brother and myself, were taken by our mother across to the island of Salamis, clutching the eight drachmas provided by the state for each family. Since neither Athens itself nor townships like Eleusis had defensive ramparts, Themistocles had ordered the entire populations to be evacuated to the relative safety of hills or islands. So we left our yellow corn-fields and camped in the rocky creeks of Salamis, waiting for disaster.

Many things I didn't then understand but learned later from my father or heard them from Herodotus himself. At about this time

King Leonidas of Sparta was the first person to stand his ground against Xerxes and for me that was the start of a lifelong admiration for the Spartans, though it was to be sorely tried in later years.

When I grew up it was fashionable to be cynical about Leonidas, to imply that he was a narcissist desperate to prove his own heroism, letting three hundred of his followers be killed in the process. But it has always fired my imagination as it did then to think of those gallant troops holding the narrow pass of Thermopylae[3] against such a huge army. That was until they were betrayed by the wretched Phocians who showed the Persians a track round to the rear of the pass so that they could attack the Spartans from behind. After that he stood no chance.

My other boyhood hero was Scyllias, the diver who swam ten miles, mostly under water, to tell the admirals what the Persian fleet was doing. That to me had all the excitement of one of the old stories of Odysseus which I listened to in the nursery.

Luckily for us the Persians were struck by disaster when two hundred of their ships were sunk by a sudden squall off the coast of Euboea. We all know it can happen easily enough for warships, particularly Persian ones which have little free-board and are prone to capsize once water gets into the bilges through the oar holes. For Xerxes' vast force the losses were barely noticeable but it was a bad omen. By contrast the Athenian flagship was seen to have an owl perched on her yard, a sign of good luck, and there was also talk of the pet dog of general Xanthippos which swam gamely after his master's ship when it had been left inadvertently behind on the jetty. So the omens for us had improved.

Meanwhile I and my family had walked up from the miserable ferry that goes over to Salamis[4] and set up camp in a small creek from which we could just see across the sea to Eleusis. The women were weeping a lot of the time, except for our nurse Psyche. She kept swearing at the Persians in her strange Thracian accent and complained that Athens didn't allow slave women to help crew the triremes.

We had a reasonable supply of dried fruit and bread to keep us going, and the slaves made tasty pancakes for us on an open fire, but my lasting memory is of the swarms of stinging insects which followed us everywhere. During the second evening on Salamis we saw an ominous glow over on the mainland. Our elders gasped that it was our own little town of Eleusis in flames. The huge old temple of Demeter and the hilltop fort of our city had been torched by the invaders and our homes reduced to ashes. My mother surprised me totally, for she was very proud of her home, by saying without the slightest sign of a tear, 'What does it matter? We have each other.'

'I'll burn the bastards,' said our faithful slave Psyche, despite the fact that she might have been just as well off as a slave to the Persians.

We couldn't see Athens from our position but we heard soon afterwards that it too was on fire. A few volunteers had stayed behind to defend the Acropolis but all had been massacred and the entire city laid waste.

That night I slept badly, as I think did most of the others, We had all watched those distant voracious flames and been stunned to expect that we had no homes to return to and probably no fathers or husbands still alive.

Suddenly I heard Psyche give a cry. 'There's a Persian ship coming. We'll all be crucified,' she wailed. But the ship seemed to turn away from us at the last minute and we then saw that it was the leader of a long column of ships. Frustrated by our narrow field of vision, and with nothing else to do, we started to clamber up the banks of the creek to get a better view. Eventually we found ourselves on top of a small cliff from which we could see the whole stretch of water between Salamis and the mainland.

To our left there were two lines of ships which we thought were our own and on our right, approaching in six columns, was a much larger fleet which we took to be the Persians.

'We'll all die,' wailed Psyche, losing her usual optimism.

'Keep quiet, Psyche,' said my mother.

From where we stood the sea looked greasy and calm and the oared galleys were like hundreds of water centipedes with their legs moving slowly across the surface. As they came closer to each other we could see the Athenian ships were forming into a kind of arrow pattern, as if to cut across the six columns of the Persians, but nothing made any sense and for what seemed like hours there was no real action. Then the centipedes began to butt each other or to slice off each other's legs. We could see that several ships on both sides were damaged, some even sinking, some locked together, yet we could not make out what was happening.

'There's another Greek one sinking,' said Psyche.

'No it's not, it's Persian,' countered my mother.

'There's one on fire,' said one of the children. As a five-year-old I had little idea of what it meant to be on a burning wooden boat, that was a fear that came into my life much later, but for us children playing around and tossing small rocks into the sea it was all a great game.

Far over to our right we saw a small new group of Greek ships coming round from what I later heard was the island of Psyttaleia.[5] This must have been Aristides' squadron, for it is recorded that he had been ordered to seize the island and capture three of Xerxes' children who had been left there for safety, just as we had been left on Salamis.

None of us knew it at the time, but our priests had ordered that these children should be sacrificed to the god Dionysus, no doubt thinking that this would drive the Great King into a frenzy or perhaps even make us feel a bit better. Anyway we never knew about it till much later, so it is hard to say how we would have reacted, but having just seen our homes go up in flames and knowing that many of the garrison soldiers would have been crucified, it is probable that we might have had little sympathy for those Persian princelings.

'There's another one sinking,' said Psyche, pointing. 'It's Persian.'

'Yes it is,' said one old man who had come with us and seemed to have some knowledge of ships.

'And another,' said my mother. 'Maybe we have a chance,'

An hour passed and it was still hard to make out what was happening, for a wide stretch of water was covered with ships in various states of disrepair.

'Some of the Persians have turned,' said the old man excitedly. 'They're going the other way.'

There was a vague hint of confidence coming back to our group and as it turned out this was justified. For the tactics of Themistocles in persuading the Athenians to let their city go up in flames and trust to wooden ships, not stone walls, had paid off. By coaxing the other Greek fleets to wait and fight with us at Salamis he was able meet the Persians if not on equal terms then at least without being hopelessly outnumbered. It came out afterwards that he had also played one or two other tricks.

He had written a letter to Xerxes, pretending to turn traitor, a pretence which in his case was quite credible, and warning him that the Greek fleet intended to retreat. This induced the gullible Xerxes to detach a portion of his fleet to head south to cut off the supposed Greek retreat, while his remaining fleet was lured into the narrow waters between Salamis and the mainland, expecting to chase the Greeks as they fled. In effect this was just what Themistocles wanted, for in narrow waters the Persian superiority in numbers and speed would count for less. Then his trick of driving a watery wedge between one half of the Persians and the other spoiled Xerxes' carefully orchestrated formations.

Sometimes it doesn't take much to cause confusion and misunderstandings at sea. I suspect the Persian captains were too used to following orders and once separated from their admirals they were at a loss what to do. I don't know at what point Xerxes heard that three of his children had been sacrificed to a Greek god. As a father now myself I can hardly bear to think of his reaction. But if he had not been so over-confident in victory he would have left them at home. Such is war. Besides he had dozens of children.

I think it was also a fact that the Persian ships were designed as armed troop carriers rather than fighting ships, their main aim being to put their passengers ashore and fight on land, whereas the new Athenian triremes, designed for sinking or seriously disabling enemy ships at sea, carried only limited numbers of soldiers and did not have to get involved in land battles. Anyway, to celebrate we had a feast of pancakes and sardines, for food was one of my main interests in those days, and we waited to see what would happen next.

Three days later the ferryman came across to tell us it was safe to go back to the mainland. But what we might find left of our homes filled us with dread.

1.	Votes for exile were normally at this time scratched on recycled scraps of pottery known in Greek as ostraka; hence the word ostracism.

2.	Trierarch means captain of a trireme,

3.	Visitors to Thermopylae will find that the pass is no longer narrow as the River Sperchelos has deposited some twenty meters of mud over the area and pushed out the shoreline several hundred yards. The name Thermopylae means hot gates and came from the hot sulphur springs nearby

4.   The island of Salamis which at one point is just over a mile from the Piraeus is nowadays a popular holiday resort for Athenians and others. A full description of the famous battle won in the nearby narrows by Themistocles can be read in the History of Herodotus. Curiously the name Salamis comes from the Semitic word 'shalom' meaning 'peace' and dates from the days when the island was settled by the Phoenicians.

5.   The island of Psytteleia is still uninhabited but on it stands one of the largest sewage treatment plants in Europe.

CHAPTER THREE

MY FIRST MEETING WITH KORE

I MUST GIVE SOME ACCOUNT of the next five years of my life for two reasons, though in other respects I was just an average youngster. One was my first acquaintance with the family of high priests at Eleusis and their daughter Kore who was to be the most important person in my adult life, though it was to be many years before the difficulties of our relationship were finally overcome. The other was the final stage of the war with Persia since many of its events and the people who took part were to have a considerable influence on my career and the adventures in which I later became involved.

But first I will dwell briefly on the return of my family to the ruins of Eleusis after the Greek victory at Salamis. My father was kept on duty guarding the silver mines at Laurion[1] so he did not return till well after the rest of us. Despite the general relief that the Persians had retreated it was a miserable home-coming and even as a young child I was sensitive to the devastation that surrounded us. I can still remember the stench of burnt corn and the charred wood of our ancient olive trees. All the crops had been removed or destroyed by the vengeful invaders. Our own house was a blackened shell and the little town was in ruins.

The only part of the town that the Persians could not destroy was the deep dark cave that was known as the gateway to hell. The facade of the great Temple of Demeter stood like black broken teeth while the priests howled and shook their fists towards the east. Luckily for us there was one underground granary that the Persians had not discovered, so we did not starve. However, we did have one problem for most of our clothes had been lost or ruined during the war and our linen crops had been trashed by the Persians, so we would have to wait for a new linen crop to grow and dry before we could weave new tunics. Meantime the slaves just patched what we had

My mother, Phasia, was a very practical person. She had to be to cope with a frequently absent one-armed husband, and she bustled about trying to make us comfortable in the remnants of our old home, helped by the loyal but constantly grumbling Psyche who, in a crisis, behaved more like a member of the family than a slave. It helped that my uncle Aeschylus had been relieved of his duties fairly quickly and being part-time choir master of the temple had some influence in the town. I can remember his grey-bearded rather pawky face, always hovering between laughter and rage, as he went off with the male slaves to scavenge for roofing materials. I have always thought of him as old, though at this time he was perhaps just over forty and had yet to achieve fame as a writer of plays.

'I'm angry, Phori,' he'd say. 'Mad angry, as Ajax was when he thought a flock of sheep were the sons of Atreus and slaughtered them all for insulting him. That's how angry I am with the Persians.'

It was at his suggestion that my mother volunteered with a group of families to go and help with the urgent repairs in Athens, even though we hadn't finished repairing Eleusis, far from it. Themistocles, fresh from his victory, had asked for all the older men, women and children to help build the new city walls in case there was a further land attack by the Persians. In fact he faced strong opposition from the Spartans who objected to the idea of Athens getting new city walls, so he had to prevaricate with them to give us time to put up the makeshift defences. Cut stones from ruined palaces and temples were manhandled to make the front and back of the huge circular walls which soon stretched four miles round the city and we children just tossed rubble in between the two walls to make them a solid structure. At that age it was fun.

Our family was working on the west side, not far from where a captured Persian general lay rotting in the sun. He had been chained to a rock as punishment for attacking our city and had taken ten days to die, but at the time none of us saw any need to pity him. To my childish mind all Persians were utterly evil and all Greeks, specially Athenians, totally good and it was to be many years before I realised that things weren't quite so simple. Meanwhile to keep us entertained while we worked the city sent out a number of choirs who sang songs about our recent victory. One of them had a chief choirboy called Sophocles,[2] a lad who was later to cause mischief for our family and cross my path on several occasions.

To me the whole episode of wall-building was a further childish adventure and the bakers brought sweet honey cakes to keep us going, much to the disgust of Psyche who thought we should always have vegetables.

'At least the Persians haven't stolen all our honey,' said my mother. 'The bees of Hymettos[3] saw to that.'

By the time that Themistocles had kept the Spartans talking for about three weeks the new city walls were high enough to be defended and it was too late for anyone to say they shouldn't be built. So we could go home to Eleusis and finish our own repairs. I remember we were offered a lift in a cart that had brought in a load of olives from some estate that had escaped the looting.

That night we camped beside the cart about six miles out along the Sacred Way. The stars were shining and my uncle Aeschylus was in one of his most jovial moods. Despite the protestations of my mother he launched into one of his favourite stories, supposedly to help send us to sleep. It was about Kekrops, the first man to live in what is now Athens. Unfortunately for him he had three disobedient and silly daughters. They were told not to open a certain box, but of course that's exactly what they did, and out came a serpent called Erechtheos, a wicked creature born after the evil god Hephaestos raped the good goddess Athena. The girls were so horrified by the creature they'd let out of the box that they jumped off the Acropolis to their deaths.

'Stupid story,' said Psyche, shivering nevertheless, though she was far from being in awe of Aeschylus or any of the male heads of our family.

'Anyway,' said Aeschylus unabashed. 'The good news is that Kekrops taught us all how to grow olive trees and founded the twelve towns of Attica. We should be grateful for that.'

I mention this because it was one of many stories he told us so that our heads were filled with a strange mixture of history and legend which even in later life I found hard to separate. That evening we had a supper of mashed beans which allegedly was the favourite dish of Hercules.

The next day we resumed our journey back to Eleusis. Though the fields were still black with ash the farmers were beginning to get back to work and rescue the odd olive stump that had survived the fires. Soon with the autumn rains we would be able to re-plough the land and sow barley for next spring. To our delight also my father Kynegiros returned home from Laurion soon after our arrival and with his customary vigour which more than made up for his missing arm, he cajoled the slaves to clean up our vineyards and start clearing the rubble from the sacred temples nearby. Unlike his brother, the choirmaster, he still had a full head of hair with no trace of grey. He was also even-tempered though from time to time he did rant at the wanton destruction inflicted by the Persians.

Yet even though I'd never known him any different I could not help finding it unpleasant when he was in an affectionate mood and inadvertently touched me with the stump of his right arm. I felt guilty for feeling squeamish, for I think I really loved as well as admired my father but somehow the stump reminded me of sharp knives and blood. Yet the gory corpses of Persians caused me no worries at all.

It was my uncle as choirmaster who was our main contact with the other great family in Eleusis that was to play such an important role in my later life. Since time immemorial the Eumolpid family had been hereditary priests of Eleusis, in fact some said they had once been kings. Psamos, a man of about the same age as my father, was the current high priest and though his temple had been destroyed he had managed to hide most of the sacred objects before he left his post during the Persian invasion and this was a source of great joy, for the worship of Demeter, goddess of fertility, was one of the most popular in all Attica.

Psamos had married a stocky, smiling woman called Gaia who had apparently been very much courted by my uncle Aeschylus, but in the end she had plumped for Psamos and the role of high priestess. So we occasionally teased him on the subject, but so far as I know they were still friends and of course as choirmaster he was close to both of them. They had three children, two boys who both died young of some mysterious illness and a daughter Princess Kore who was about a year younger than me and destined to play a major part in this narrative. It would be very much exaggerating to suggest that we were childhood sweethearts, for apart from anything else, as the potential next high priestess of Eleusis, she was precluded from such frivolities and was regarded as of divine status.

For the time being she was the only girl in our neighbourhood, so we treated her with the disdain that boys tend to feel for little girls who try to act like boys. Certainly at that age she had few inhibitions as she jumped in our wake from one shattered pillar to another, picking the red poppies and big daisies which soon began to sprout from the ruins. I remember she had long brown legs and could run pretty well as fast as any of the rest of us.

One unusual feature of our situation, which I did not appreciate till much later, was that it was far from normal for children to be allowed to play in the temple area. In fact I and my brothers with Kore in pursuit were probably the first in five hundred years because never before had the temple been roofless, the doors hacked off their hinges and many of the priestly officers still away with the fleet. The vast hall of the Mysteries, now open to the sky, with its cracked columns and blackened walls nevertheless made a deep impression on me, sufficient to make real for me the legend that each year the beautiful young priestess Persephone would be snatched away from the earth above and dragged down a dark tunnel to Hades far below.

We could still see the entrance to the sinister tunnel, but even then dare not trespass within ten yards of it. Nor did I ever then imagine that at some point in the future little Kore would take over that dreadful role. Besides at that age I naturally did not yet understand the importance attached to fertility, both the human kind and for the crops and animals, which was why the ordinary people of Attica set such store by the goddess of Eleusis and the priests who served her.

Meanwhile more good news arrived from the front. Pausanias, the regent of Sparta, and brother of the dead hero Leonidas, had led the combined Greek armies to a great victory at Plataea. As usual some Athenians tried to play down his success, suggesting that like all Spartans he was more concerned with propitious omens and the advice of his priests than with military tactics. Aristides as the senior officer from Athens who took part in the battle certainly took this line. But my uncle Aeschylus and even my father were more inclined to admire the Spartans than listen to city gossip.

Pausanias had certainly led the campaign well, even if he was excessively pleased with his own performance. Mardonios, the Persian general, had been killed along with many thousands of his crack troops despite their golden uniforms and wicker shields. The remnants of the Persian army had headed off home. The Greek cities of the north had been recaptured and any Greek leaders who had surrendered too easily to the Persians were condemned and sent into exile.

To cap it all, one of our own sea-going generals, Xanthippos, the one whose faithful dog had jumped into the water when he sailed for Salamis, won another great land and sea battle against the Persians at Mount Mykale[4] east of Samos. The Persian sailors had beached their fleet to avoid fighting at sea, but our infantry landed and attacked them so vigorously that the local Greeks from Samos were encouraged to fight for us instead of against us, thus turning the tide. Xanthippos was one of our more unassuming heroes; he came home to the family farm and lived quietly with his dog. More than can be said for his ambitious son Pericles whom, as you will see shortly, was to play a major part in both the ups and downs of my own career.

Thus by my seventh year our world was safe again. The little owls were nesting once more in the hollow olive trees at the far end of our estate. Young Kore was still just a playful hoyden, not yet a priestess, but our days of childish scampering near forbidden places were coming to an end. The walls of the Temple were rising once more and hid its mysteries from the gaze of all but the initiated. My father was of course one of them, as was his brother Aeschylus who spent a lot of time rehearsing the choir and composing new songs in his favourite iambic beat. My own playground shifted to the old rock fortress where I spent hours scrambling on its modest cliffs and thus acquired a lifelong aptitude for climbing which was to come in useful later in my career.

---

1. A rich vein of silver was found in Mount Laurion (now Lavrio) some forty miles from Athens in 483 BC and it played a major role in funding the expansion of the Athenian navy. More recently Lavrio has been mined for cadmium and other rare metals.

2. Sophocles, the future playwright, became the bitter rival of Euphorion's uncle Aeschylus; seven of his plays survive including the well-known Oedipus trilogy.

3. Mount Hymettus is eight miles from Athens and rises to some 3,300 feet. Its thyme honey is still famous.

4. The ruins of the harbour at Mykale now lie two miles inland on the Turkish coast due to the silt carried down by local rivers

including the Meander. Mykale is called Samson's Mountain by the Turks.

CHAPTER FOUR

THE FALL OF HEROES

AROUND THE BEGINNING OF MY tenth year our family moved for the winter from Eleusis into Athens where we had a reasonably large town house in the ceramic[1] quarter. This was partly because my father was now tending to spend most of his time on jury duty and even Aeschylus fancied extending his repertoire to write plays for the big theatre by the Acropolis walls. I had hardly seen much of Kore during the final months in Eleusis, so I was barely conscious at the time that this was going to be quite a long parting. Anyway I was coming to the age where it was proper for me to see less of females and concentrate on my training as a cadet for the army or navy.

The main reason for dwelling at any length on this period of my life is to reflect on the strange ups and downs of our leaders, the heroes who so often ended up as villains. In particular those who won great battles seemed so often to turn almost overnight from popularity to hatred. And the result of all these vagaries was to have substantial influence on my own later career.

You have already read that Miltiades, the hero of Marathon, had become the villain of Paros and died soon afterwards. Next it was the turn of Prince Pausanias, the victor of Plataea, one of those members of the Spartan royal family who strutted gallantly in his great red cloak, impressing and annoying at the same time.

His main problem was that he was still officially just a regent with no expectation of taking over the throne of Sparta, since it was just a matter of time before his nephew came of age. Thus he wanted to make the most of his brief period in power and add still more to the glory and booty that he had won at Plataea. It is of course well-known that Spartan officers are not allowed to possess money, so when they acquire it accidentally in their wars the unaccustomed wealth often goes to their heads. Pausanias wanted as much as he could get and was soon suspected of taking bribes. His greed and exceptional vanity soon made him an uncomfortable general so far as the Spartan establishment was concerned.

In addition, his arrogance annoyed many of the officers in other contingents of the Greek army, for it was always Spartan soldiers who got the best billets and Spartan horses the best stables. After a number of successful sieges, still desperate to prove that he was indispensable to Sparta, he tackled Sestos[2] near the entrance of the Black Sea and there his career began to unravel. He suddenly started wearing exotic eastern clothes, he was drinking too much and he clearly believed that he had a god-given right to any woman he fancied. In the case of Kleonika, a virgin from Byzantium,[3] he went so far as to blackmail her father to hand her over to be his mistress, but when she at last agreed and came to his bedroom she accidentally knocked over a lamp, and he woke up suddenly thinking he was about to be murdered and stabbed her to death.

Pausanias seems to have been unnerved by this accident, and fell into a deep depression and neglected his duties. The Athenians who had for some time been unhappy serving under him, chose this moment to force him out of Sestos, a humiliation for the Spartan establishment which was too much for them to bear. They summoned him back to Sparta and, fearing for his life, he hid in a small temple where the authorities bricked him up and left him to starve. Three weeks later, desperate for something to drink, he crawled out covered in lice and his own excrement, bribed with a mug of water not to die on holy ground. So much for great men and the Spartans, whose reputation for fearlessness is legendary, are without doubt afraid of great men. They cannot stand individuality and were so worried that more of their royal princes might succumb to similar temptations that they decided to take no further part in the Persian wars.

The case of my third fallen hero was rather different. Themistocles had been a brilliant general on land and sea, but he wouldn't let anyone forget it. His constant thirst for adulation grew irksome, especially for those who had played their part in his victories, but received less credit. He had always been arrogant, quick-tempered and greedy for cash, but after Salamis his wealth became increasingly ostentatious. Athens of course had a method of getting rid of people it didn't like, scratching the name on a scrap of pottery, as had happened with Aristides, so now it was the turn of Themistocles.

The tipping point came when he built a temple to the goddess of wisdom beside his own front door. Rightly or wrongly he was assumed to be claiming a monopoly on wisdom and a huge pile of potsherds was the result. For him, however, exile was by no means the end of his career. As we shall see, after trying life in other Greek cities he eventually decided to leave Greece altogether, and was received with open arms by his old enemies the Persians who heaped him with honours and riches. Thus he lived on and some years later was to be the focus of one of my strangest adventures.

I have devoted some time to explaining the fate of these three flawed heroes because their careers formed the background to my youth and in many ways created the circumstances which directed my own extraordinary if somewhat less famous adventures. It also has to be said that their fall from grace opened the way for a fourth hero, who was to be my commander and inspiration during the early years of my military career. This was the former play-boy, Cimon, son of the great Miltiades, who as we have seen had ostentatiously given up the cavalry to become a dashing trireme captain just before Salamis. By the time I went to school he had risen up the ranks and when I later had my first taste of war he was commander in chief.

After more than ten years of war against Persia the Spartans and Athenians had a totally different attitude towards bringing it to an end. The Spartans did not trust their own kings, especially if they were far from home, so they had no desire to keep fighting to win revenge, nor to liberate the unfortunate Greek cities in Asia Minor which were still under Persian domination. The Athenians on the other hand had got a taste for war, especially being on the winning side, and new men like Cimon wanted to make their fortunes.

To liberate fellow Greeks seemed as good an excuse as any, even if those liberated soon found that the liberators were just as oppressive as the Persians had been. So to make up for the lack of Spartan help Athens founded a new league and asked all the members to send money to Delos to pay for more ships. It was a dangerously ambitious scheme full of false temptations and invitations to pride. It was also to shape the pattern of my life and that of many of my fellows.

Of my teenage years there is less to be said. I was no better or worse than the average in the gymnasion. If I excelled in anything at that age it was at rock climbing, for after my childhood scrambles on the cliffs of Eleusis life in Athens gave me plenty of opportunity to try different routes up the Acropolis. One of my favourites was up to the ruins of the Erechtheon, still a roofless shell since the Persians had burned it, but soon they started to rebuild the place for the sacred olive tree, the salt water spring and the lamp that would never go out. There was a little cave as well where the lizards scurried out of the sun and a small shrine to the fashionable new god, Pan.

My father was very busy after our move to Athens so parental supervision was more lax and only Psyche noticed the odd scratch and bruise which I acquired on these jaunts. I persuaded her to keep quiet.

One of my other slightly guilty pleasures in those days resulted from living by the ceramic quarter, for on my way home from school I often stopped to watch as the vase painters sketched my favourite heroes from the myths on the wonderful red jars and bowls.

'Too young to be looking at that sort of thing,' the potters would sometimes say to me, winking, but it was several years later that I found out why they were sniggering, for I understood by then that many of the pictures portrayed chasing women or little boys. One side of school that I enjoyed from the start was learning to read the poems of Homer. I was fascinated by the adventures of Odysseus which made me thirst for similar experiences and, though the language was old - fashioned and sometimes hard to understand, I loved the rhythm of his poetry. Much more, to be honest, than the rather complicated verses of my uncle.

Meanwhile our new hero Cimon had not only humiliated the Persians but was doing great work attacking the Aegean pirates who had sometimes sided with the Persians against us. His only rival for command of our fleet, the dog-loving Xanthippos, had retired exhausted, for there was no doubt, as I later discovered for myself, that you had to be really fit to sail in the triremes. With around two hundred men spending most of the day at the oars there was no room for proper hygiene and the stench could be sickening even when the sea was calm. The damp, dirt, heat, uneven diet and lack of sleep meant that older captains in particular often suffered from fevers and rheumatism, and if they were in command their judgement could become unreliable.

Cimon was still relatively young and fit. What's more he had no money worries as he had a share in the family gold mine. Thus when he began the siege of Eion[4] at the mouth of the River Strymon he was the talk of our school. It was a difficult siege because the Persian commander, Boges, knew his job, but in the end they ran out of food and Boges set the town on fire rather than surrender. He killed his own wife and family, hurled them down into the fire, then jumped after them himself. So Cimon became in our eyes the new hero of Athens, but like so many Greek heroes he too was later to become a target for jealous rivals. Meanwhile he enslaved all the surviving population of Eion, very useful for a man who needed cheap workers to dig his nearby gold mines.

---

1.   The Kerameikos district of Athens still exists close to where the road to Eleusis passed through the walls. It was the potters' quarter, centre of one of ancient Athens most important export industries; hence our word ceramic.

2. Little of Sestos survives. It was the home of the beautiful maiden Hero whose boy-friend Leander used to swim across the strait to see her, a feat famously copied by Lord Byron, but fatal latterly to Leander. It is now in Turkey on the peninsula of Gallipoli.

3. The Greek colony of Byzantium was renamed Constantinople which was in turn reconfigured as Istanbul. Pausanias had captured this city from the Persians earlier.

4. The site of Eion, later renamed Chrysopolis or Gold City, lies at the mouth of the River Strymon east of Thessalonika. The ruins of the Persian fort can still be seen. A few miles inland are the ruins of the Athenian colony of Amphipolis built by Cimon to support his gold mines. The Persian King Xerxes allegedly had nine young men and nine young women buried alive here on his way to Thermopylae. Cimon's siege took place in 476 BC.

CHAPTER FIVE

THE STRANGE ARTS OF WAR AND PEACE

WHEN I WAS FIFTEEN MY father succumbed to a terrible cough and died within a few days. My mother and I both sat with him till the end. Apart from losing an arm he had, I believe, fully recovered from his ordeal at Marathon, but his months in the dark tunnels of Mount Laurion guarding the silver mines had not helped. At that age his death was a great loss to me, partly perhaps because it meant that I would never be able to prove to him that I too could be brave, a need which had worried me since early childhood when I first learned of his great exploits. In a way the fact that I now also felt a slight sense of relief contributed to a feeling of guilt.

As he lay dying he summoned me to his bedside and almost apologised for not having explained to me earlier that it was a family tradition for the men folk to be initiated in the Mysteries at Eleusis. At the time I had only the vaguest idea of what they were all about, but though I was slightly embarrassed by what seemed a rather old-fashioned ceremony, I was by no means averse to seeing the daughter of the chief priest, my childhood friend Kore, so I agreed to his request. He took off his gold signet ring and pressed it onto my finger, then patted my hand.

I have to say that after my father's death my mother seemed to bear up remarkably well, putting on her special yellow gown and her fig-leaf garland to say her fare-wells, but Psyche, our slave, surprised me by bursting into tears and blaming it on the onions. My uncle Aeschylus was clearly much saddened by his brother's death, but was also still on a high for he had recently won first prize in the theatrical competitions for his new play called 'The Persians',[1] which of course glorified the role of Athens in their defeat.

Meanwhile having learned to read and write and being able to recite the first three books of the Odyssey by heart I had moved to a new school. As was a family tradition I went to the Kynosarges Gymnasion just outside the city gate, not because like many of the other pupils I had some non-Athenian blood, but because the two alternative schools, the Academia and the Lyceum, were both thought by our family to be rather snobbish and elitist. So at Kynosarges I spent every day practising the javelin, discus, running and wrestling.

At fifteen I was above average height and reasonably strong. Running in particular came easily to me for the regular fourteen-mile walks to Eleusis had helped develop my stamina. Riding I enjoyed, but not as obsessively as some of my friends. I preferred javelin-throwing to twirling the discus which seemed a waste of time. What I liked least was standing and waiting for the javelins to land, then taking them back for the older cadets who took delight in making us stand right beside the target. To be honest I never totally overcame my fear of a javelin in full flight.

It was at this time that I first met one of the senior cadets who was later to play a significant role in my own career and in the fate of our city. This was Pericles, who at eighteen had finished his training at the more snobbish Academia, but had been asked to help out at the Kynosarges. At first I regarded him as a sadistic bully who stretched us to the limit and taunted us with his sarcasm. He had an aloof, aristocratic manner – his father was the dog-loving general Xanthippos – and a rather odd shaped head which earned him his nickname of Onionhead.[2] Even in later years when I became one of his senior lieutenants I was never totally at ease in his company.

'Son of the hero of Marathon,' he would say to me sarcastically. 'Run and get that javelin, Euphorion. Run, I said.' And no sooner was I back and panting on my mark than he would make me throw again. So as he kept this up for hours on end my aim became less accurate, but he still persisted remorselessly with the drill.

It was partly because of Pericles that a number of us went to extra oratory classes with Anaxagoras of Clazomenai,[3] nicknamed 'The Brain'. This minor celebrity of the day came from one of the islands and spoke with an odd accent. His piercing stare contrasted strangely with his shambling physique and he was utterly unimpressed by military prowess or wealth.

He took a deliberate delight in challenging everything we stood for. But he could also explain many things that the rest of us found incomprehensible, like what caused rainbows. He had even predicted that a stone would fall from the Sun into the Aegean Sea and it had. Much later he was condemned to death by the courts for saying that heaven was made of stone. His reply was that all men are condemned to death.

'Who is Apollo?' he'd ask with a twisted smile.

We'd all look blank.

'Speak out,' he'd snarl.

'The Sun God,' one of us would answer nervously.

'What's the Sun, then?'

'A god,' someone answered.

'No, it's a hot round ball. How can it be a god? What does it give us?'

'Light.'

'And heat. Is it not just a huge rock like red-hot iron that goes round the earth once a day? But it doesn't have a body like a god. Or a brain. What makes it move?'

We looked blank again.

'What makes a discus spin? Does it go faster if it spins?'

Pericles who had already attended these groups for a couple of years, would smile superciliously and take the old man on with an argument. That was what mattered to him, learning to beat one argument with another, ready for the day when he would be able to outwit every other speaker in the assembly to get his own way.

Even Pericles, however, was somewhat subdued when a famous former pupil came to visit our gymnasion, for he was always anxious to impress the authorities. This visitor was the great general Cimon, acknowledged now as the successor not just of his father Miltiades, but of Themistocles too, for by this time the victor of Salamis was in disgrace. Cimon watched us at javelin practice and then addressed us, thrusting his red cloak over his shoulder as if he were a Spartan and flicking his legs with his swagger stick[4] as he talked.

'Soon many of you will be out in the triremes or serving with the land garrisons,' he said somewhat pompously, rapping his leg with the stick. 'The Persians must be killed or ejected from every part of Greek soil, every island and every city on the coast of Asia that has ever been Greek. They are a cruel and decadent people. Most of their satraps are effeminates, ordered about by their wives or their eunuchs. They believe in evil gods. I find the best thing is to kill them.'

He laughed and slapped his sword with his stick.

For teenagers who had lived as children during the last great war it was naturally a very impressive performance and for me this man was a living hero. Yet perhaps it is just in hindsight, but even then I think I sensed a certain hollowness in his words. As you know all talk is exaggerated when there's a war on, and at that time most of us still believed that the Persians as a race were irredeemably bad, so it seemed right that Cimon really enjoyed killing them.

As Cimon left with a flourish of his red cloak he gave us each a silver drachma, as if sealing our loyalty and adulation for the future.

'Save it till you hire your first trireme crew,' he said and waved as he rode off round the walls to his villa. The one person visibly unimpressed was Pericles, who came from an even more snobbish family than Cimon and probably already saw himself as a rival. 'Clever operator,' he said under his breath. ' Easy if you own half a gold mine. Buys all the best crews. Buys popularity.'

That evening I described Cimon's visit to my mother and she too was less impressed than I expected. 'Strange man,' she said bitterly. 'I used to be friendly with his wife, Isodike. She was once a lively girl, but now she's like a mouse, while that man cavorts around with his own half-sister. She,' my mother spat out the words 'behaves like a Spartan woman and you know what that means: not so different from a Corinthian whore. And her husband Kallias the torch-bearer is one of the finest men in Athens. Cimon was always a boaster and a waster. It's scoundrels like him that end up generals.'

As it happened I later found out that Kallias had made most of his money as a slave trader and amongst his other contracts he was the chief supplier of slave labour to the silver mines of Laurion. It was also rumoured that he had become so besotted with Cimon's half sister Elpinike that he bought her from Cimon, who it seems had married her for a while, thus helping him pay off all the fines inherited from his father Miltiades.

Just a few months later I saw Cimon again and the element of showmanship was even more obvious. He had just captured the island of Skyros,[5] reputedly a nest of pirates who robbed both Greek and Persian ships without scruple. Those who survived the attack were all being sold off as slaves and the island was to be replanted with veterans from the Athenian fleet. But in addition Cimon had searched the island for the tomb of Theseus, the legendary hero of Athens who was supposed to have died there.

Surprise, surprise he found an appropriate tomb with an extra-large skeleton that could only be Theseus. So Cimon put the tomb with its contents onto his flagship the Salaminia and sent messengers ahead to make sure there was a big crowd to watch his arrival at the Piraeus. I and my school-friends stood on the rocks at Acte as the huge ship was rowed at a stately pace into the harbour with music playing and Cimon himself in full armour on the foredeck. It was impossible not to be thrilled.

Soon the huge sarcophagus was manhandled ashore and the procession headed up to the city, where Cimon had ordered a feast at his own expense. As Pericles pointed out he had managed to dredge-up half the Persian treasure from Eion and collected pirate gold on Skyros, so he did not even have to use his own money and could throw handfuls of small coins to the children.

In normal times Athenian women hardly ever left their homes except for funerals and a few religious anniversaries, but on this occasion many did make an appearance. One in particular I noticed, a very striking dark-haired lady who welcomed Cimon with a passion I'd never seen in public before. A bystander pointed out that it was Cimon's half-sister and ex-wife, the voluptuous Elpinike of whom my mother had shown such disapproval.

I also recognised one other woman, Gaia, the skeletal wife of the high priest of Eleusis, who was officiating with him at the reburial of Theseus. She was the goddess Demeter's embodiment on earth. Behind her stood a young girl holding a goblet and for some moments I failed to realise that it was my childhood friend the Princess Kore. Her face was somehow different and she had grown long legs since I had last seen her. Anyway she was preoccupied with helping her parents and did not see me. I was also far too embarrassed to try to attract her attention.

As it turned out it was not to be very long before I saw Kore again, for the time was approaching when I should fulfil my promise to my father and undergo initiation into the rites of the Earth Goddess, an experience I somewhat dreaded, for my generation was already beginning to ask cynical questions about some of the old-fashioned gods.[6] After all we had gone through two wars during which the interventions of the gods, if there were any, had been very unpredictable if not downright antagonistic, except for the panic-causing Pan. Who still believed in an old man with a thunderbolt sitting on top of Mount Olympus? Yet the Earth Goddess Demeter was different because she loved the earth and the earth gave us our food, so that seemed sensible enough.

In my father's place it was my uncle Aeschylus, as ex-chorus master of the Mysteries, who sponsored my initiation. So as was customary we all met in the market place on the 15th of the month Boedromion, the anniversary of Theseus' victory over the Amazons. I was still too young for full induction but I would at least complete the initial ceremonies. Several other cadets were there from my school, including Pericles and another boy a year ahead of me, who was also to play a significant role in my own and my family's story. This was Sophocles, who was nearly as supercilious as Pericles, and I had taken something of a dislike to him since first coming across him during javelin practice. This dislike was apparently reciprocated and, as will become apparent, he turned into a real thorn in our family's flesh.

So that evening we gathered in the market place and the booming voice of Psamos the high priest of Eleusis summoned us to order accompanied by a thundering of drums and strange howling that seemed to come from the earth itself.

'Take away any who are defiled,' he shouted.

'What does that mean?' I protested to my uncle.

'You'll soon find out,' he replied.

'Take away any who have not atoned for their sins,' came the voice of Psamos. 'Those who are pure will go to the Elysian Fields whilst the rest will wallow in perpetual filth and ignominy. Those who are pure will find happiness in this world and the next.[7] Take away those who have not atoned for their sins.' He repeated it four times.

'Take them away,' echoed the crowd, also four times.

To my surprise there were two youths in the procession who appeared to freeze at this moment and skittled off into the surrounding crowd. Eventually when Psamos had continued this chanting for what seemed like an hour it was time to move on. The procession headed off through the city gate over the boggy ground towards the beach at Phaleron, where old General Aristides leaned over his farmyard wall as we passed, looking ancient and emaciated. He was one of the few great men who had not succumbed to riches and had never courted popularity. Yet now he was a somewhat pathetic figure.

Once on the beach Psamos led us all into the sea up to our thighs and we poured water over each other with bowls. It was cool and pleasant. Then in turn, for a donation of ten drachmas, we each collected a piglet from a huge sty near Aristides' place and took them to a makeshift altar. There Psamos and Kallias the Torch-bearer with a practised flick of the knife sacrificed the animals to the Earth Goddess Demeter.[8] Not a sight that I particularly enjoyed.

After sleeping most of the next day we all gathered again carrying torches and wearing garlands of myrtle, with Kallias the Torch-bearer leading the way. By midnight we were crossing the little bridge over the Kephisos where by tradition a crowd would gather to shout rude comments about the passing priests and new initiates. It was strange to see the contorted faces in the torchlight as normally prudish citizens of both sexes shouted obscenities as we passed and laughed outrageously at their own rather feeble jokes.

'There's a right little Hermes the Phallus,' cried one.

'Why was Kleisthenes called the rumphole of Athens? Because he was a rump hole.'

'Do you always do it from behind?'

'A Persian eunuch could do it better than you.'

'Like little boys, do you?'

And so it went on. We all had to take it in good part and covered the last few miles to the Sacred Lake where the reflections of the torches in the water, the swooping of bats and the perfume of myrtle and wild garlic made for an eerie atmosphere. There we stopped to remove our tunics and went in for the ritual bathe, the women going off to the other side. It was pleasantly cool after the ten-mile hike and I soon found myself swimming almost alone in the middle of the lake, which was not deep. Then quite suddenly I saw in front of me the face of Kore, daughter of Psamos the high priest. She bounced out of the water like a jumping trout with her wet tunic stretched against her brown skin. For some unaccountable reason I felt disturbed and clumsy and she laughed at my awkwardness.

'You can know nothing of the Mysteries, Phori,' she said. 'Not till you become a man.'

I was gratified that at least she remembered who I was, albeit I was annoyed that she was abusing her status as the high priest's daughter to make mock of an old friend.

'I'm not sure that I really want to,' I said as cuttingly as I could manage, treading the brackish water to preserve some modesty, but the memory of her sprightly form emerging from the torch-lit lake remained with me for many days and nights to follow. To be honest, despite some scepticism about Demeter the Earth Mother, I was slightly curious about the Mysteries, though I was still too immature to understand anyone having anxieties about fertility, whether agricultural or human.

Early the following evening we at last arrived at Eleusis, which had been substantially rebuilt since my last visit. That night there was singing and dancing for many hours and I watched with mixed feelings, sometimes catching the odd glimpse of Kore as she led the reels or threaded her way under the archway of torches. I almost wished I had not come at all, since the final stages were still forbidden to me. From a distance I saw Kore going to the Sacred Well for water and coming back with a huge vase perched on her head the way the slave girls did it, yet she could still manage a fetching little wiggle of her hips as she made her way back.

As the procession entered the Hall of Mysteries I slipped away and revisited some of the cliffs of the fort which I had clambered over as a child. Far below I could see the entrance to Persephone's cavern and now the initiates were changing into clean clothes, a sign of their purification. They poured pigs' blood and barley beer into the chasm which supposedly led down to Hell. The idea of Persephone going down into the depths of Hades for six whole months merged in my mind with her earthly reincarnation, my Princess Kore, disappearing into the vast hall, one minute laughing, the next crying, and I wondered if I should ever again be able to talk to her as an ordinary person.

1. The Persians first performed in 472 BC is one of the seven plays of Aeschylus which have survived. It has an element of anti-Persian propaganda.

2. Pericles was nicknamed Onionhead or Squillhead, squill being a pointed type of onion

3. Anaxagoras (510-428) was one of a number of pioneering philosophers who tried to analyse natural phenomena like the stars and lightning. He was born in Clazomenai, the ruins of which are now at Urla near Izmir in Turkey.

4. The Greek word for a swagger-stick was bakteria which was picked up by later scientists to give a name to stick-like microbes seen under the microscope.

5. Skyros these days is perhaps more famous as the burial place of the British war poet Rupert Brooks who died after being taken off a troop ship on its way to the Dardanelles in 1915. It has a small airport and several good beaches.

6. The use of the word cynical here is strictly speaking an anachronism since the group of philosophers known as Cynics or dog people was not founded till 444 BC. But there is no other word in English that quite conveys the meaning.

7. It has to be said that the Greek religion did not generally place a lot of emphasis on the afterlife. Hades was an underworld with absolutely no light to which both the good and the bad were transferred after death. This is why the Eleusis sect was popular as it did provide some post-mortal happiness for its members.

8. Demeter the Earth Mother survived the end of the old Greek religion to become identified with the Virgin Mary and the old rites of spring performed in Eleusis turned into Easter.

CHAPTER SIX

POLITICAL GAMES

IN MY LAST YEAR AS a cadet at Kynosarges a number of our group were chosen for the junior team to race for Athens at Olympia. This, as I soon discovered, was not just an occasion for sporting rivalry between the cities of Greece but a lot of underhand dealing between the rival politicians and their tame spies. This time it was to see an off-course tournament between the factions of the two bitterest rivals in Athenian politics, the now ageing Themistocles and his ambitious successor Cimon. For me, though I did not appreciate its significance at the time, it was to be the occasion for my first sight of the wily spy Aristodikos of Tanagra who was to play such a sinister role in several of my subsequent calamities.

I was tired and stiff after the long cart journey from Athens, but the approach to Olympia was both delightful and intimidating. With its lush green forests of oak and pine, and the fast-flowing rivers it was not surprising that this was a place chosen by the gods. It was where Zeus had staged his coup against the old god Chronos and taken over as the king of the gods. So it was here that three hundred[1] years ago the Spartans had the vision for an all-Greek games in honour of Zeus. Or so they claimed, for there were at least three other versions of the story, including the one that said it was Hercules who founded the games. Having won all the races himself, with his usual modesty Hercules said the only prize should be a wreath of olive branches. But of course he was doing all this for the universal good of the human race. So they said.

Anyway a vast new temple to Zeus had just been started and there was a new hippodrome which had the basic circuit ready for the chariot races though the banks of seating were only half finished. The new baths complex was however all ready and this was where we underwent the ritual bathing before the contests began. We had oil spread over our bodies and then we rolled in the dust before washing ourselves in the cool water of the River Kladeos which was diverted through the bath house for our benefit. Then we all competed stark naked and I sometimes felt a little inadequate when surrounded by so many muscular wrestlers and discus throwers.

Toughest of all were the competitors for the pentathlon who had to do five tests: running, wrestling, boxing, jumping and discus-throwing; good luck to them. Officially no women were allowed during the games, but it seems there was the odd exception for, despite the rule that any women who appeared would be thrown from the cliff above, Cimon's exotic sister seemed able to flout all the rules with impunity. The same gruesome punishment applied to any competitor or his sponsors who tried to bribe the judges. So much for the sacred forest of Zeus. However, I was here to represent my own city, so personal feelings had to be set aside and despite myself I did feel a certain pride.

For a while I was preoccupied with preparations for my own race, the half mile, where I was relieved to come in a respectable fourth after two Spartans and a Theban; at least I was the best from Attica. After that I had more time to look around the huge stadium where each city was showing off to the others with colourful tents, chariots, arms displays and the like. Hundreds of naked competitors lined up to do the different events, their skins glistening with oil. But the biggest attraction was the competition both on and off the field between the two wealthy rivals, Themistocles and Cimon, both of whom had entered their horse teams and both of whom, despite representing the same city, seemed bent on heightening the tension and displaying the acrimony of their relationship. Their two tents were the most lavish, with splendidly ornate furniture and gold tent trimmings, their riders were the most splendidly dressed, and their entertainment side-shows the most elaborate. Pindar, the grovelling poet from Thebes, was writing slavish doggerel about both teams, so that whichever won he would still be paid for his efforts.

Alongside Themistocles, as well as a retinue of gold-clad Persian slaves, were three of his sons, all a few years older than me, but already famous for their drinking and brawling in the streets of Athens. They were great ones for knocking over the stalls of the bread-women or bragging about their conquests of boys, beating slaves or buggering Persians. I could remember their silly catcalls during the performance of my uncle's Persians play, despite the fact that it cast their father in a good light.

Now they were ignoring the formal proceedings to indulge in a drunken party whilst their father made sure the crowds were entertained by his tame magi[2] singing incantations and some Asian fire-eaters. He often boasted about how he had tricked King Xerxes by pretending to be a traitor and to spy for him so that he could outwit him at Salamis, but now it was hard to work out whether he was just lying or believed retrospectively in his own imagined cleverness.

Cimon had not brought his children but instead was supported by his exotic half-sister Elpinike, one of the very few women attending the games, dressed in her usual way like a Spartan, and flaunting her presence in a way no normal Athenian woman would have dared. So the comings and goings between rival tents continued and I began to realise that what I had naively thought was just a contest between athletes was also an excuse for doing deals between cities, swapping colonies with each other, and supporting political cliques

It was about this time that I first spotted Aristodikos, though it was to be some years later before I began to understand the scope of his activities. For the moment he struck me as a suave, beautifully dressed, thin-lipped man in his mid twenties and I learned he was a member of the ruling clique at Tanagra,[3] a small city near Thebes, one of those that had surrendered meekly to the Persians. Now he was scheming to get his wretched little clique of oligarchs back into power, but he needed allies and was thus making himself useful as a spy and go-between for conservative elements throughout Greece. I had noticed him in deep conversations with Cimon, then shuttling to the Spartan tent, then back to Cimon's.

Soon there was a rumour going round the entire stadium that Themistocles had taken a huge bribe from a satrap. The rumour was to follow us all back to Athens and soon crowds were gathering in the marketplace demanding his ostracism. Whether Themistocles had really been acting as a double agent or just bluffing we will probably never know, but even if he was he had certainly saved Athens from Persian conquest. And even if he was innocent then he certainly became a traitor later. Most likely at this point he was just being framed by Aristodikos.

It was only later that I connected his behaviour with the campaign against Themistocles and later still that I heard how he had been rewarded. Cimon had arranged for the Athenian garrison of Phyle[4] to allow the Tanagra oligarchs a safe passage so that they could retake control of their city in a surprise coup.

Cimon was now the undisputed leader of Athens but was not content just to have Themistocles ostracised. He had him impeached, deprived of his citizenship and all his property on a trumped-up charge that he had been plotting with the disgraced Pausanias to betray Greece to the Persians, an idea that seemed far-fetched to me even at that age. Cimon was still so jealous of the old man's prestige that when his family managed to slip out of the city undetected he had the guard commander executed for negligence. That incident filled me with considerable horror since, as a cadet, I was regularly on city guard duty on that section of the walls. And why should a rich man like Cimon be so alarmingly desperate for popularity yet utterly cold-blooded in dealing with those who stood in his way?

As it turned out Themistocles was lucky to escape with his life after his impeachment, for he was pursued all over Greece and hounded out of every city where he tried to seek asylum[5]. In the end after an arduous trail through the mountains he found a merchant ship whose captain took a hefty bribe to ferry him across the Aegean to the relative safety of Anatolia. Even then things went wrong for by an unfortunate coincidence his ship blundered into an Athenian fleet led by none other than Cimon, who was in the process of punishing the island of Naxos[6] for daring to reject the supremacy of Athens. It took all Themistocles' legendary powers of persuasion to cajole an Athenian boarding party to turn a blind eye to his presence and let his ship complete its voyage. Thus Themistocles made his escape to reach Persian territory and his career there was to provide the scene for one of my later adventures.

Meanwhile, as I learned later, Cimon taught the people of Naxos a very severe lesson for trying to be independent of Athens. Their city had barely recovered from its earlier pummelling by the Persians and he now completed its destruction and exacted huge tribute in gold. The wretched Naxians had paid dearly for even half defying the Persians and now paid all over again for defying Athens. All they wanted was to live their own lives free from interference by either Persians or Greeks, but the truth is perhaps that they were too successful to be popular, for their island had everything, a good supply of fresh water, fertile soil, and the blessing of the gods, for this island had been the home of Zeus. My first visit there was to come a few eventful years later.

---

1. The ruins of Olympia are still substantial and a major tourist attraction. The accepted date for the foundation of the games by the Spartans is 776 BC, some three centuries before Euphorion's participation, but even then there were numerous other versions of who really founded them and when. They were revived in 1896 after a long gap since AD 393.

2. The magi were the priests of the Persian religion, Zoroastrianism, founded by the prophet Zoroaster (Zarathustra) so it was natural that Themistocles should have some in his retinue.

3. Tanagra was a small independent city on a hilltop near Thebes, famous for its aggressive politics and its splendid painted figurines. Scant ruins of the town remain but the figurines can be seen in most major museums.

4. Remains of the once almost impregnable rock-top fortress of Phyle still survive, offering fine views over the routes north from Athens which it once guarded.

5.   Asylum or asylos is a Greek word meaning inviolate and often used to refer to people protected from robbery or women from forced marriages.

6.   Naxos, also once known as Dionysia, lying south east of Delos, is the largest of the Cyclades and had a history as a successful base for commerce as well as having excellent farm produce. Subsequently it was conquered by the Romans, then the Venetians, then the Turks before at last coming back to Greece. It is now a popular holiday destination and there are still relics of its illustrious past.

CHAPTER SEVEN

MY FIRST CRUISE

JUST AFTER MY SEVENTEENTH BIRTHDAY I embarked on my first training cruise in the trireme Ariadne.[1] I had already served for six uneventful months in the city garrison, the first posting for most cadets, and then done a further three with the infantry on the Megara frontier, but I had seen no real action. However, my first sea trip was a revelation. Even the smelliest streets of the foreigners' quarter beneath the Acropolis, where the cesspits were untended year after year, were as fresh as a hillside olive grove compared with a trireme which never seemed to lose its stench. The nearest a trireme got to hygiene was for all the crew to go to one side so that she would tilt and they could aim their excrement into the water without splattering too much over the hull. In theory the ships were supposed to beach most nights, but that was by no means always possible, depending on the distance between ports or islands and the strength of the wind.

The diet was better than I expected, for Cimon as chief general paid close attention to feeding his sailors well. We had reasonable quantities of lentils, dried fish, dates, figs and watered-down wine, plus whatever we could pick up on the way. Under sail with the wind behind us we could cover fifty miles a day and nearly as many if we kept the men rowing and had no head wind. Our oar-masters did not use the lash as freely as their Persian or Corinthian counterparts for our oarsmen were mainly free men, some of them even citizens, who amazingly volunteered for such back-breaking work.

The trierarch on my first voyage was Ephialtes, an extremely ambitious member of a once prominent family, just a few years older than Pericles, who was by this time serving as lieutenant on one of the other ships. He had a piercing gaze and huge self-confidence so that sometimes he even over-ruled his own ship-master on technical issues like navigation and sail-setting. He had a ruthless, analytical streak, but clearly regarded a sea career as just a stepping stone to political success. I did not know it at the time but he was destined to be the victim in a tragedy which played a key role in my life. For the time being I felt as if he looked down on me from a great height and had no desire to encourage humble cadets, let alone exchange a friendly word. Behind it all there seemed to be an underlying bitterness which I could not fully understand.

My immediate supervisor on board was Kleistes the oar-master, a rough-tongued little man, but he knew everything about triremes. Naturally as the junior cadet I was his first choice for unpleasant tasks like shinning up the mast or to scrub sea-slime off the beak, and initially I resented this somewhat for to be honest I still had a certain fear of deep water, but I came to respect his knowledge. Steadily I grew more at ease with life at sea. And though my function on board was as a soldier I was given a few days at an oar just so I would know what it was like. It was desperately arduous, especially on the top benches, and I had severe blisters and an aching back to prove it.

'You've got about as much sense as Aphrodite's left buttock,' Kleistes would say by way of encouragement to me or 'You're knotting that rope like the legs of a Corinthian whore.' He was harder on the cadet officers than he was on his oarsmen, for we were the scum of the earth.

One good thing about spending some time on the oar benches was that even the slaves were friendlier to me than the officers. There was a strong camaraderie down in the depths of the ship as we all just had to keep rowing, whatever the aches and pains, for if you stopped your oar would be rammed by the neighbouring oars and would most probably hit you hard in the stomach. Initially I felt awkward speaking to the slave oarsmen for cadet officers were supposed to keep aloof and I felt guilty about having superior conditions compared with theirs. However most of the ones near me seemed to bear no grudges and I began to relax in their company.

'You get five drachmas a week, don't you?' I said to one. 'I get nothing.'

'But your family has plenty of money,' he replied. 'My wife would starve if I didn't do this job. As it is we often have only acorns to eat.'

One of the other things that made rowing bearable was the flute player,[2] for every trireme had to have a good one with plenty of puff to play loud enough to be heard above the swish of the oars. Ours had a double flute and was great at keeping the right tempo for the oarsmen and a decent tune to keep our minds off the pain.

During our first week at sea we completed a number of evolutions and practised obeying formation signals from our general Cimon, returning to the Piraeus each evening. Then we made our formal departure from the home port and covered sixty miles to the island of Ceos for the night. There Cimon's fleet astrologer sacrificed a nanny goat and blessed our expedition as ordained by the gods. Next day we sailed due north with the wind almost dead behind us to Skyros, the island recently captured by Cimon, where new colonists from Athens had now begun setting up home.

It was a barren, rocky place whose former inhabitants, mostly pirates, had all been killed or forced to leave. There was a round fort above the harbour where we moored, sterns to the jetty, and we could see the escarpment from which the famous Theseus[3] had jumped or been pushed to his death.

The next morning the wind had dropped and we had to row north from Skyros with Kleistes in a foul mood.

'You're rowing as well as a nursery of Theban catamites with hangovers,' he shouted and for once fingered his whip as if he meant to use it.

'We've just been overtaken by a pod of baby dolphins,' he added sarcastically.

As junior cadet I was at that moment busy aft cleaning the officers' armour. When not at an oar I spent a lot of my time cleaning things, partly I think because Ephialtes our captain was less rich than most trierarchs and had to borrow money to fit out the ship, so he was especially keen to make a good impression. Unless he did so he perhaps felt he stood little chance of further advancement in the fleet and in turn his political career would also be blighted. So the *Ariadne* had to be the smartest, fastest ship in the fleet.

'I hate cadets, Euphorion,' said Kleistes. 'You know how I hate cadets. Get up to the top of the mast and tell me when you see Lemnos.'[14]

I did as I was ordered, with some trepidation as the ship was rolling from side to side and the top of the mast swung out over the water in an alarming fashion, but when the island was still just a faint blur in the distance the wind picked up again and Kleistes ordered me back down to the deck.

'Pull on the starboard halyard,' he yelled. I still found the mass of ropes very confusing, but gradually I began to acquire a mental picture of how the sail worked. It was the height of a large house and square, with six halyards to haul it up the mast and four sheets to pull it to one side or the other to catch the wind, not to mention umpteen brailing ropes to adjust the sail area. To my shame it was to take me weeks to tell one rope from another.

Now the sail began to fill and the oarsmen were allowed to rest on their oars as we picked up speed towards Lemnos. Suddenly the world seemed a better place; the sun glinted happily off the blue-green sea. Two hours later the sail was down again and we were rowing astern onto a gentle, sandy beach, with an anchor out at the bows to help haul us off again in the morning.

'The smelliest women in the Aegean,' said Kleistes. ' But I don't care. I love them. Lovely udders too. ' He cupped his two hands in front of his chest and jiggled them, then he hoisted his tunic as if ready for action.

I remembered some of the strange stories about the women of Lemnos. They had insulted the goddess Aphrodite and she made them smelly in revenge. So their husbands all deserted them, but the women then killed all the men except for one. I was amazed to find myself in such a strange place, albeit we had as yet seen neither men nor women since we arrived on this beach.

Once the ship was secure we were all given a few hours shore leave, so we soon had a roaring fire and cooked a swordfish which had been speared by one of the soldiers. Then there was goats' cheese, garlic and onion, the staple trireme diet. Afterwards most of us strolled up the little river which ran down to the beach. Soon we came to a small village set amongst olive groves laden with fruit. Beyond that were plum orchards stretching up into the hills.

'Great place for prunes,' said Kleistes. 'Best in the world, but don't eat too many.' He winked and walked over to a smiling young woman who had a little stall laden with goods.

'Always buy some Lemnian earth when you land here,' he said. 'It's the best poultice you can get. In case you're injured,' he added optimistically. 'And it's good for boils and blisters as well.'

He handed over a few obols[5] to the woman.

'The priestess can only dig it out one day a year,' he explained. 'It's worth every obol.'

While I was enough of a pessimist to have nightmares about a javelin-strike, I was too embarrassed to copy him and buy some of the stuff.

'Right,' he said. 'Now it's time to go and try some of the smelly women. They're cheaper than the mud.'

This I found even more embarrassing, as I had no experience of whore houses and was, to be quite honest, enjoying the experience of visiting this strange place more than enough without seeking additional excitement, or as I thought even more likely, extra humiliation.

'I'm on the sunset watch,' I said. 'Got to get back to the ship.' So I headed back down the river, to some sneering from the other cadets and a huge grin from Kleistes.

The following morning we set off at dawn, hauling the trireme back into the sea using the anchor rope. Then it was a slow journey as we had to row most of the way through the narrow straits of the Hellespont with the wind against us. Our captain Ephialtes was, as usual, impatient with our lack of progress and took it out on Kleistes who was somewhat subdued after a late night on Lemnos. I thought the captain was out of order berating his own shipmaster in front of the entire crew.

'For the sake of Poseidon, Kleistes, get your men in order. This ship will be a disgrace to the fleet,' he snarled.

Kleistes beat his drum faster for the oarsmen. 'In, out, said Zeus to the swan,' he intoned. 'In, out, said the Bull to Europa, In out, said the Theban to the catamite.' So he kept on and raised the odd faint smile from some of his fitter oarsmen.

'Over there see the ruins of Troy.'[6] said Ephialtes, now in a better mood and pointed to a bush-covered mound surrounded by a few hovels. It was nothing much but for me that glimpse of the Dardanian shore, the scene of so many famous deeds was a real thrill. There long ago my Homeric heroes Odysseus and Achilles had besieged the wicked Trojans,[7] just as we were now heading to fight their successors the Persians.

That evening we beached on Prokonnesos,[8] an island in the small sea between the Aegean and the Black Sea, and when we awakened next morning it was to hear the alarm sounded for an unidentified ship coming from the direction of Kyzicos.[9] Here our drill for hauling our ship off the beach by the anchor rope paid dividends, for we were afloat within minutes.

'She's Persian,' muttered Ephialtes, his blue eyes alight with excitement. 'Full speed, oar-master.'

Kleistes brought in the third tier of oarsmen and gradually stepped up the tempo on his drum till we were skimming across the sea faster than I had ever seen before. Meanwhile the Persian warship had altered course to head for the shore and so did we to cut her off.

'Stand by to ram,' snapped Ephialtes.

'Standing by to ram,' acknowledged Kleistes.

'The angle's too fine,' snapped Ephialtes. 'More speed.'

Kleistes increased the tempo of his drumming and screamed obscenities at the crew. Luckily I was not on an oar that day, for I could see the grimaces of pain as Kleistes beat his drum even faster as we curved round to ram the Persian almost at a right angle. I could see why Ephialtes preferred this tactic, for it avoided the risk of ramming her oars from the rear, dangerous since unless our crew got in their oars smartly we would suffer nearly as much damage as our victim.

By this time we were within a few hundred feet of the Persian. At the last minute when he saw we were going to ram him amidships the Persian tried to veer away and Ephialtes all but shot past his bows, but Kleistes, reacting quickly swung the steering oar across and we hit him six feet or so behind the beak. There was a searing shudder as our beak dug into the hull of the Persian and we drove the whole ship in front of us with our momentum.

'Backwater, starboard side only,' ordered Ephialtes and I could see he was enjoying himself immensely.

Now we could see a gaping hole in the Persian ship's side. A number of their forward oarsmen seemed to be badly injured and she was starting to list as water poured into the hull. Her crew were cursing and shaking their fists at us. There was smoke rising in her stern where a cooking fire appeared to have been upset.

'Hard astern,' yelled Ephialtes. 'Stand by to ram again.'

Having rowed back about two ship lengths we reversed direction. By this time the Persian was no longer moving and it was easier for us to ram her amidships, closer to the softer part of the ship's underbelly. She began to sink rapidly but Ephialtes stopped only long enough to pick up one Persian officer from the water, leaving the rest to drown, for it was unlikely any other Persian ship would venture out to rescue them. The dripping Persian prisoner was interviewed for about ten minutes with a knife at his throat, then on Ephialtes' orders he was tossed over the side. By that time we were only a few hundred yards off Prokonessos but whether he made it to the shore we did not wait to see. I have to confess that at that time I felt only pride in our achievement and it was not till many years later that I began to question our behaviour. For the time being I greatly admired the ruthless efficiency of Ehpialtes and in those days there seemed nothing wrong with allowing Persians to drown. All I felt was that I would never be as skilful and effective as he was.

---

1.   Much research has been devoted to the design of Greek warships and how they managed to function with three banks of oarsmen on both sides; hence the term trireme. Recently there have been trials with reconstructed full-scale replicas.

2.   The flutes played to keep the oarsmen happy were rather like the drones of bagpipes that could be played quite loudly and relied on circular breathing. It was said that the goddess Athena gave up flute playing because her cheeks became too red and spoiled her good looks.

3.   Theseus was a legendary figure best known for rescuing the hostages from the labyrinth of Minos on Crete and then betraying his mistress, Minos' daughter Ariadne, who had helped him to escape but whom he deserted on Naxos, the subject of the Strauss opera Ariadne auf Naxos. Once he became King of Athens he seems to have become arrogant and unpopular; hence his exile to Skyros.

4.   Lemnos is a flattish, once volcanic island in the northern Aegean now well known for beach club holidays.

5. An obol coin was 1/6th of a drachma which was then the basic daily wage of a trireme oarsman.

6. The ruins of Troy, as most people accept, were discovered and excavated by the German grocer Schlieman, and can be visited at Hisarlik on the south side of the Dardanelles.

7. Given the fact that Euphorion had grown up to fear and hate the Persians it is not surprising that he took the side of the Greeks against the Trojans.

8. Now known as Marmara and a part of Turkey famous for its marble and with a ferry service to Istanbul.

9. Kyzikos was a Greek town later deserted after several earthquakes. The ruins are at Erdek by the Sea of Marmara in Turkey.

CHAPTER EIGHT

THE ATTACK ON EPHESUS

THE DAY AFTER OUR SINKING of the Persian warship the *Ariadne* received new orders from Cimon, who was waiting with his flagship further down the Asiatic coast. So we headed back down the Dardanelles and beached for the night not far from the mound that had been Troy. Regrettably I was on guard duty and had no chance to explore the ruins but from what I heard they were pretty scanty. And naturally our obsessive captain was in a hurry to be in the next battle.

The following day we made good progress southwards and joined up with several other ships from the fleet as we approached Lesbos, another island I was fascinated to visit for the first time. I had never been a huge admirer of the poetry of Sappho, but I was certainly aware that the Lesbians[1] were a very talented people and Agamemnon had said they had the prettiest women in the whole Aegean. As we drew nearer I could see it was a rich and beautiful island with blue-grey mountains rising above the lush green meadows. Though, like most of the islands, it had been conquered by the Persians, we were told that its main cities had survived almost intact, but I saw no proof of that, for we just beached briefly for the night before heading on southwards.

By comparison Chios,[2] which we reached the following evening after an easy sail, seemed a much less attractive island with dark brooding mountains cut by steep valleys with dried-up waterfalls scarring the rocks. It was, however, a popular stop-over for our crews because they were all universally fond of the mastic gum which was a Chios speciality. It was sweet to chew and Kleistes, who was something of a hypochondriac, swore that it was good for several ailments and he always took some home for his wife. This was our last overnight stop before the mainland town of Notion,[3] recently recaptured from the Persians and our rendezvous with Cimon ready for the assault on Ephesus. It had a reasonable harbour so we did not have to beach our ships but instead tied up, sterns to the jetty.

I must admit I had an uneasy night's rest at Notion for I realised that the next day I would have my first experience of a land battle. Dark visions of the death of Hector haunted me and reminded me of those horrid hours standing in the javelin target area at Kynosarges.

'Let's see how a son of the hero of Marathon reacts to cold steel,' said Ephialtes, as if reading my mind, a trick which later helped his career in politics. By this time we were rowing in line-ahead just outside the harbour of Ephesus[4] which was formed by a natural bend in the river Kayster. Ephialtes had summoned the officers and cadets to the stern for a briefing.

'Our spies report there is a garrison of no more than a hundred genuine Persian troops,' he said. 'The rest are renegade Greeks or Lydians from other cities who've evicted the Ephesians, but are unlikely to put up much of a fight. We have three hundred fighting men on the fifteen triremes plus a couple of hundred citizen oarsmen in reserve. The problem of course is the walls.' He paused, then. 'General Cimon has ordered a scouting party, six men each from the two leading triremes, so I want volunteers.'

I was not aware of volunteering, but perhaps I did half nod my head in an effort to appear enthusiastic, or to avoid appearing cowardly, and that was enough. To my surprise the man in charge of our shore patrol was none other than my one-time senior cadet, Pericles, who was second in command on the *Cassandra.*

'Cover your faces with mud,' he said, when we landed that evening on a beach about two miles from the city. 'Anyone who makes a noise, I'll cut his throat,' he added.

There was only a small crescent moon hanging over the dark slopes of Mount Koressos, as we picked our way up river to the walled city. When we arrived at about midnight there were a few torches burning near the turrets, but otherwise little sign of the garrison, though they must by now have been aware of the enemy fleet nearby. On the other hand the walls looked formidably high and hard to climb.

Pericles kept us moving as we skirted the entire circuit of the walls looking for the weakest point. He impressed me with his knowledge of the stars, for he used them to keep a sense of direction as we wandered over rough paths in a huge circle. At one point there were a lot of dogs barking and we could see several sentries peering down into the darkness where we were standing near the river. I remembered the famous saying of the philosopher Heracleitus the Obscure who lived in this very city. 'You never step into the same river twice,' and I wondered if the great man was still alive.

'That must be the acropolis,' said Pericles quietly, sketching on a slate which hung from his belt. 'Up there is the huge temple that Croesus[4] paid for. Silly man. Obscenely rich, but Darius fried him to teach him a lesson.'

I was just beginning to get accustomed to our monotonously silent patrol when to my horror I tripped over a living human body which cursed me in an unfamiliar accent of Greek. Pericles was at my side in a moment, doubtless ready to fulfil his earlier promise of throat cutting.

'Drunk,' he whispered after catching a whiff of the man's noticeably pungent breath. 'Gag him and bind his hands. Take him with us.'

The man was just sober enough to grasp the meaning of an unsheathed dagger and was soon stumbling along in the middle of our column. He was short, somewhat overweight and dressed like a beggar.

'Tell us, drunkard, where is the weakest part of the city walls?' asked Pericles menacingly.

'I am a Greek,' said the man, albeit speaking in an Ionian dialect that was almost like a foreign language. 'No need to threaten me. The weakest section is south of the acropolis where the walls cross the river.'

'Right, back to the fleet,' ordered Pericles, marking the spot on his slate. So before dawn we were back on the beach and Pericles was briefing the senior officers. Our prisoner who was by this time nearly sober was quite happy to discourse on various ways of getting into Ephesus in return for a hot breakfast. I asked him if he had heard of the philosopher Heracleitus.

'I am Heracleitus,'[5] he replied, apparently delighted that anyone had heard of him. 'Sometimes unjustifiably known as The Obscure. Since the Persian conquest all my pupils have left me. Neither the Persians nor the renegades listen to me and I am too old to fight. Times are very hard,' he added with a touch of self-pity which disappointed me in such a great man.

After a short rest we headed back towards the city and the fleet stood off in case of surprise attack. Then at nightfall with Heracleitus still in attendance we moved forward in two sections, one under Pericles, the other under Ephialtes. As junior cadet I was the ladder carrier and near exhausted by the time we reached the wall by the acropolis.

'You first, Phori, up the ladder,' whispered Pericles who unfortunately had heard me boast in the past about my fondness for climbing, which I had done mainly to make up for my self-perceived inadequacies in other aspects of military drill. 'I'll be right behind you,' he went on. 'When you get to the top turn right and spear any Persian who comes at you from that side.'

I nodded, strapped my spear behind me and started up the long ladder. I was deeply afraid, but as much of humiliation as anything else. It was dark but I could just see well enough and when I reached the upper rungs of the ladder I could only feel the parapet with the tips of my fingers. Luckily I managed to find a toehold in the wall itself and scrambled clumsily over the parapet seconds later, followed very quickly by Pericles. I turned right and there was a sentry coming towards me with a curved sword. This was my first chance to use my spear in anger and if there had been more time to think I would have had an attack of nerves, but I managed to wing him and that was enough. He sagged moaning in a corner of the parapet.

'Your aim's no better than a Megarian brothel keeper's', said Kleistes who had now also joined us and he quickly finished off the wounded sentry.

'This way,' said Pericles, beckoning me to follow and our whole section stumbled down a steep stone staircase into the dimly lit city below. There was a smell of stale cabbage and burnt olive oil. In what felt like half an hour, but was really much less, we reached the central square, dominated by the vast bulk of the famous temple of Artemis[6] that was already a hundred years old. There, surrounded by torches, was a statue the height of three houses, a massive goddess with twenty huge breasts hanging down. At its base sat three half-naked women, one old, one fat and one serenely beautiful. They looked dazed as we rushed past. As I learned later they were all women of rank and virtue who had to act as prostitutes one night each year to raise funds for the temple. Such was the cost of maintaining the great feasts of Artemis.

Our objective now was to reach the governor's house before the alarm spread. But when we found it the house was guarded by two gold-clad sentries with bows and swords, who had now already had time to summon the rest of the guard, about a hundred fully armed Persians who would be the end of us. Happily by this time one of our party had let the main force under Ephialtes through the gates and they overcame the garrison with relative ease. I was about to join in the fray, but there was no resistance left and I did not have to face any more of the curved swords. However, I made a gesture by prodding a couple of the Persians who were attempting to escape and felt I had done my bit.

'My throat's as dry as Artemis's udders,' said Kleistes, wiping his sword.

'Follow me,' shouted Ephialtes who now assumed command of the whole force. 'To the governor's quarters.'

The governor when we found him was, I am bound to say, a tall dignified man, but Ephialtes ran him straight through with his spear. From the next room was brought a short fat Persian swathed in gold and with his head completely shaven.

'Make sure the eunuch isn't carrying a dagger,' ordered Pericles, pushing the man against the wall with his sword so that the blade sank several inches into his yielding stomach without piercing the cloth. 'Unwind him.'

This turned out to mean gripping one end of the man's golden wrapping and twirling him round till it fell off. A small dagger clattered to the floor and with the garment removed I saw for the first and I am glad to say last time in my life what it meant to be a eunuch.[7] This was not the kind of heroic warfare I had read about in the Odyssey and the excitement of my first siege began to ebb. The acrid smell of human fear mixed with over-sweet eastern spices and perfumes as we searched the rest of the headquarters. Those still alive, both men and women, were herded into the central compound. When they saw that we had put out the sacred fire of their temple they were distraught; they wailed and tore their hair and clothes.

Ephialtes meantime had called a meeting of the leading Greek families in the city and began an inquiry into who had betrayed it first to the Persians.

'Croesus King of Lydia[8] conquered our city first,' said one old man. 'Then Darius conquered it from him and burned him to death. The chief family has always been the Artemids and they advocated surrender both times.'

'Who is the head of the Artemids?'

'Apollinaris,' said one of the crowd.

'Step forward, Apollinaris,' ordered Ephialtes.

A white-haired old man stooped with age was pushed forward by the other Greeks of Ephesus. He could never have been a very impressive figure, but in this final humiliation he did preserve some vestiges of dignity.

'Throw him from the top of the citadel,' said Ephialtes with no sign of hesitation, a characteristic which I was to notice marked out all the more successful commanders, specially those who wanted to get into politics.

'All I wanted was peace,' said the old man. 'Is that wrong?'

I was one of the section which led the man up to the top of the acropolis rock. Of course I had been taught to despise totally anyone who would surrender his city meekly to the Persians. We Athenians had been willing to fight to the death at Marathon and Salamis to avoid such a fate, so we had the right to be contemptuous. But I cannot say that I enjoyed thrusting this cringing old man to the ledge above the temple. We had to draw blood before he finally toppled over, to bounce from outcrop to outcrop before he landed near the feet of the huge stone goddess.

Still, youth recovers quickly and so did the Greeks in Ephesus. Soon the artisans began to emerge from their shacks and found that they had regained what we amusingly called their freedom. Sometimes they even cheered us, so I recovered myself and enjoyed some of the perks of victory, at least the good food and wine. But within days the Greeks whom we had supposedly saved from servitude were beginning to curse us, for with men like Ephialtes in charge we Athenians could be just as greedy and oppressive as the Persians. Naturally Ephialtes was notching up his share in this victory to boost his political credentials back home. So neither they nor we were sorry when we re-embarked for the long voyage home.

1.	Euphorion was of course completely unaware of the meaning subsequently attached to the women of Lesbos which was all due to an unreliable interpretation of the female poet Sappho's slightly erotic but beautifully written verses. She had been happily married, had a daughter and was extremely warm-hearted.

2. Chios is the fifth largest Greek island and lies only 4 miles off the coast of Turkey.

3. The now vanished Greek town of Notion was 30 miles south of Izmir.

4. The ruins of ancient Ephesus including the famous temple of Artemis are to be seen in Selcuk near Izmir, Turkey.

5. The drunkard may well have been lying about his name for according to other accounts the philosopher Heraclitus had actually died a few years before the siege, in 475BC.

6. The goddess Artemis, known as Diana by the Romans, was reputedly the sister of Apollo and a major patron of virgins, wild animals and hunting.

7. Eunuchs or castrated male slaves were highly prized by the Persians for positions of trust in government and noble households.

8. Croesus, the last king of Lydia, was supposedly the richest man in the world and had conquered many of the Greek cities on the Asiatic coast. Despite his conquests and his wealth he was defeated by the Persians in 548 BC and condemned to death by burning.

CHAPTER NINE

THE FRUITS OF VICTORY

OUR VOYAGE BACK HOME FROM Ephesus was pleasant and leisurely. Even Kleistes seemed to allow his oarsmen an easier time, just reminding them in his own inimitable fashion that the faster they rowed the sooner they would see their wives and mistresses.

Similar banter was noticeable amongst the officers and cadets, most of whom had at least one female alleged to be waiting breathlessly for their return. So I felt out of it and began to persuade myself that the Princess Kore was waiting for me, though in rational moments I knew perfectly well that she was not. She was after all the daughter of the high priest and priestess, destined to inherit their mantle and if she married at all it would be to a member of the priestly hierarchy. For the time being, however, I consoled myself with the fantasy and it was enough for me to hold my head up amongst the rest of the crew.

During our crossing we stopped one night at Ikaria,[1] a long rugged island where we enjoyed the hot springs and restocked the ship with olives and figs which were in plentiful supply there. We also took some octopus and porgy[2] fish from a local fisherman who offered us his whole catch for next to nothing. Then it was on past Tenos and a brief diversion to the little town of Karystos on Euboea, the first Greek city to rebel against the Athenian League. It was one thing to fight the Persians who I had been brought up to believe were evil people, but altogether another matter fighting against other Greeks, even if they did refuse to pay their taxes. Luckily when we got there the siege was all but over and none of the other

Euboean cities had come to her aid, so we just turned round and headed home.

The following day, like all home-coming sailors, I was conscious of a surge of joy as we first caught sight of the Temple of Athena black against the red sunset on Cape Sunion, with the Piraeus just a two hours' row to the west. It must be said that I jumped ashore from the *Ariadne* with a great deal more confidence than when I'd left a few weeks earlier. Though I'd certainly not achieved any unusual heroics I hadn't made a fool of myself in battle; at sea I'd only succumbed once to nausea in a choppy crossing near Lesbos, I'd coped with the discomfort and stench of a trireme, and held my own with my fellow cadets for most of the time.

Thus I waved goodbye to my shipmates on the jetty and headed up the main street of the Piraeus noting that several buildings in the dockyard were being rebuilt. I stared somewhat furtively, but with rather more interest than four weeks earlier, at the beckoning prostitutes waiting to welcome home the fleet, though to be honest I was equally excited by the fresh-baked smell from the baskets of the bread-women, since I had not tasted decent bread for a month. I felt I was looking with fresh eyes at everyone, the sausage sellers with their dangling displays, the pushy shield salesmen outside the huge workshops of Lysias, the birdmen with their twittering cages, the girl slaves swinging their hips as they balanced the morning water jars on their heads, the children of the Piraeus[3] scampering around the dockside puddles.

My mother Phasia was certainly glad to see me back though she said I had lost too much weight, but Psyche for some reason did nothing but scold me.

'Silly fool going to war on a ship,' she said. 'Why can't they leave all these people be? We don't need any more war.'

The more I tried to explain things, the more incoherent were her responses.

'I suppose you'll want a pancake,' she said. 'With sardines and anchovies.'

'That would be wonderful.'

Two days after my return all the officers and cadets from the fleet were invited to a feast held in General Cimon's garden near the Academia. His villa was beautiful, with an avenue of plane trees and a small stream leading down to the Kephisos had been dammed to make a pool surrounded by purple and blue anemones. At the gate there was one of those statues of Hermes with an exaggerated phallus, garlanded on this occasion as if to emphasise the connection between the general's virility and his success as a commander.

Despite his liking for rough sports and heavy drinking Cimon was also a bit of a snob, and it was clear even to me that he regarded Ephialtes, my captain, as a bit of an upstart compared with some of the other ships' commanders, sons of the old guard, but he could not ignore the man's talent as a leader. Yet I felt there was a tension between them and wondered if it boded ill for the future. Certainly their styles were very different: Cimon, rich, complacent and obviously enjoying himself, whilst unsmiling Ephialtes always looked as if he despised pleasure and was disgusted by a display of hereditary wealth.

As was normal at such feasts there were no officers' wives present, not even Isodike, Cimon's own long-suffering consort, but two ladies did make an appearance. One I recognised as the general's statuesque half-sister Elpinike, according to my mother and fleet gossip also his some-time mistress, a rumour to which her immodestly Spartan style of robe, more revealing than the Athenian fashion, gave some credence. She reminded me of the stories of the Amazon[4] female warriors, who reckoned that upper clothing interfered with their aim as archers. She flirted provocatively between her half-brother and her husband Kallias the torch-bearer, who was more of a diplomat than a soldier. Later I saw her with her arm round Ephialtes, which I thought would do his promotion prospects more harm than good, but you never know. I have to say that Ephialtes completely ignored her as if fawning females were no more than his just deserts.

The second lady was almost as exotic but rather younger, Astria of Salamis, the general's current mistress. On this occasion she was dressed as a Maenad[5] with only wolf-skin pulled loosely about her body and a snake hung round her neck. As if in a drunken trance she wove her way through the trees to the haunting music of a piper, her mind apparently not with us but amongst the gods, as is the way with Maenads.

Cimon welcomed me to the party in a manner which suggested that he could not remember who I was, but didn't wish to admit it in case I was the son of somebody influential. Stuttering over my name he introduced me to the painter Polygnotos who took one glance at me and moved off. I knew that Cimon had brought the great artist down from his country seat on Thasos to produce some massive murals emphasising his own heroic role during the Persian wars. According to gossip the painter had also been bribed with a weekend with Elpinike, resulting in his famous painting of a half-naked Laodike, a long dead Trojan princess, that bore an uncanny resemblance to the general's half-sister.

As the evening wore on Cimon had his tunic hoisted immodestly high and was playing Kottobos, one of the favourite games of officers relaxing after a campaign. I had tried it briefly at Ephesus, and it consisted of flicking small quantities of wine at various different targets such as bald heads, open mouths or oil jars at the other end of the room. It always caused a lot of raucous laughter and most people found it mildly amusing, even the normally pompous prophet Astyphilos, who was predictably well rewarded for advising Cimon on the right moment for his attacks by such obscure methods as examining the entrails of a dead goat.

Meanwhile we had plenty of good wine and superb pieces of lamb grilled over olive twigs and tamarisk. For me it was a revelation to mix for the first time amongst the ruling elite of Athens. I enjoyed it all apart perhaps from the sight of Sophocles fondling a young waiter in the bushes. Not that I'm prudish, but he struck me as greedy and I wasn't surprised to hear that his mess-mates had presented him with a cockerel, the customary award for such men who preferred boys.

Towards the early hours I said my thank-yous and weaved my way back home, jumping the streams with alacrity and still excited even as I picked my way along the filthy streets past the ceramic quarter. There a few guttering torches flickered above the deep open drains in which the night excrement of Athens flowed sluggishly down to the city wall.

The next day it emerged that our family had suffered a more than minor disaster. For the first time in several years my uncle Aeschylus had failed to win first prize in the drama competitions and this had instead been awarded to the precocious young Sophocles. Like most of my fellow cadets I enjoyed a visit to the theatre, though to be honest I really preferred comedy, but out of family loyalty to my uncle I had to support tragedy.

Naturally as teenagers we were used to the coarse humour of the market place, but it was different to see a chorus of two dozen men and women emerging from opposite sides of the stage to join in a vaguely obscene dance. Sometimes they would display a clay phallus of which the females made mock, with endless jokes about old men in love with unattainable young boys, or brothers sleeping with sisters or male slaves making up to their mistresses or female slaves to their masters. Tragedy was more serious stuff and of course my uncle had begun his career as a temple choirmaster. I liked the sound of his poetry but it could be a little on the heavy side. However, it was unfair that he had lost the first prize to Sophocles who had completely ignored the rules. Aeschylus had never been allowed more than two actors at a time and Sophocles had won by using three. The old man was deeply mortified and threatened to leave Athens altogether, especially when Sophocles started adopting airs and became quite insufferable.

'You'd think he was Thespis[6] himself, the original actor,' said my mother, who was very fond of her brother-in-law.

'He's forever trailing around some boy or other.' I added. 'Usually an actor or a singer. Apparently Pericles reprimanded him for being so indiscrete about it when he was in Ephesus.'

'I have no more prejudice than the next man,' said Aeschylus. 'But I don't hold with mixing such things with one's duty as a citizen.'

'Quite right,' said my mother.

'But he's a Spartan-hater like all your fancy new democrats,' said my uncle, for he like Cimon was an admirer of all things Spartan. 'For me the Persians have always been the enemy, the Spartans are our allies.'

'What about the Thebans?' I asked. 'They betrayed us.'

'True, but the only reason the new brooms like Pericles want to keep fighting the Persians is to outsmart Sparta. That is madness. We should leave competition between Greek cities to the Olympics and stand together against the magi-loving[7] barbarians.'

I knew what Aeschylus meant for I had seen Sophocles sucking up to Pericles and Ephialtes very obviously tagged along. The three of them practised their fancy speech-making and made mock of Cimon's less sophisticated[8] approach. They all imitated the fashionable philosopher Anaxagoras who attacked everything that was old-fashioned. Change was what the younger set wanted and above all for Athens to be the prime city of Greece instead of Sparta. Hatred of Persia was becoming secondary to that ambition.

'All my life I've said there should be respect for the achievements of the past,' said Aeschylus. 'These so-called philosophers are just upsetting people as a means of lining their own pockets. Protagoras,[9] he's just a trouble-maker finding fault with the old religion. Damon's[10] a good musician but I don't trust him at all. Herodotus is nothing but a gossip and a picker-up of old stories, hanging around Sophocles who is I grant you pretty bright. I don't like it.'

'We have to move with the times, uncle,' I said, though I had some sympathy with his point of view.

'We always seem to want to bring down our greatest men as soon as they get to the top,' he said. 'You watch. The next one to fall will be Cimon.'

I wondered how long it would be before he was proved right.

---

1. Ikaria, the island ten miles south of Samos, was famous for the longevity of its inhabitants and named after Icarus, the man

who fell into the sea there whilst trying to fly and therefore only had a very short life.

2.   We think of the porgy fish as bream.

3.   The song known as the Children of the Piraeus became one of the best known modern Greek songs when it was given new words 'Never on Sunday' for a film starring Melina Mercouri.

4.   These ladies of course gave their name many years later to the largest river in the world because the Spanish conquerors saw female warriors there.

5.   The name Maenads was given to female worshippers of Bacchus, the god of wine, and they became notorious for their extravagant behaviour, overindulging the refreshments which were an official part of their ritual dances. They seemed to have mixed the Egyptian drug nepenthe in their wine.

6.   Thespis, from a town in Attica, now known as Dionysus, was a singer and the first professional actor to go on tour with props in a cart. His name was picked up by the acting profession.

7.   The magi or priests of the Persian prophet Zoroaster are sometimes more familiar as the three kings who came to see the baby Jesus.

8.   The word sophisticated is something of an anachronism here since the first sophists did not appear in Athens till a few years after this event, but no other term quite fits.

9.   Protagoras was a humble porter from Abdera in Thrace but was spotted by Democritus, who also came from Abdera,when seen carrying a huge pile of firewood perfectly balanced on his head, so he became the first teacher of philosophy or sophist to be paid, and was commissioned by Pericles to draft a constitution for one of the Athenian colonies.

As an atheist he taught that the soul dies at the same time as the body. His sponsor Democritus became a hermit sitting in a cave trying to understand how nature worked, but was regarded by his neighbours as insane, so they summoned the famous doctor Hippocrates to cure him. Hippocrates pronounced that Democritus was sane but the neighbours insane.

10. Damon was Pericles' favourite musician and poet but also a keen student of government and methods of disciplining the populace.

CHAPTER TEN

PLOTS AND MYSTERIES

A WEEK AFTER THE FEAST I was sent on three months guard duty at Mount Laurion as part of my training, the very place where my father had commanded twelve years earlier. As it turned out it was to provide me with a further piece in the puzzle that was to bedevil my career for the next ten years.

'You're Kynegiros's boy,' said the overseer when he met me on my first morning in the new job. 'Good soldier he was, even if he was single-handed.' He laughed at his own joke, his eyes twinkling in a dirty, wrinkled face.

It was our job to drive the wretched slaves down the ladders to the dark tunnels of the mountain where they hammered and clawed at the rock, then carried the debris to huge pans called washeries where it was sifted. After that the ore was melted and turned into the famous silver coins stamped with an owl. There were more than ten thousand slaves working there, many of them at this time Persian prisoners of war, but some also Greek renegades.

The tunnels in the summer were tepid and clammy with so little air it was hard to draw breath. And they smelled about as bad as triremes. Several of the slave-miners in my group had developed dreadful coughs and could barely crawl along the corridors, doing pathetically little work, but I had to get the most out of them that I could and moved around different tunnels urging them on. It was a different story when I did duty at the furnaces because there the main problem was to stop slaves sneaking away with small lumps of silver stuffed in their mouths or other ingenious hiding places.

Gradually I got to know some of the Greek-speaking slaves by name and this was how I began to put together a more detailed picture of my future adversary. One of the miners called Pedipeus had been there for eleven years, the longest so far that anyone had stayed alive in that hell-pit.

It turned out that he had been a senior magistrate in Thebes and shared in the blame for surrendering the city to Xerxes. He paid the penalty for this when captured by the Spartans after the Battle of Plataea. Though I had been brought up to despise any Greek who appeased the Persians I could not help feeling sorry for this tall, distinguished-looking man who had fallen so far from such a position of power and wealth.

'Young man,' he would say. 'We were foolish, but we weren't bad. We were led on and betrayed by a man much more base than us. He's not a prisoner in the mines. Oh no. Naturally he didn't appear like us to fight at Plataea and run the risk of being arrested. In fact I've heard he still mixes with the great and the good.'

'Who was he?' I asked.

'I can hardly bear to speak his name. Aristodikos of Tanagra. He told us we could outwit Xerxes by pretending to surrender, but so far as he and Xerxes were concerned it was no pretence but the real thing. He was just a coward out for money and an easy life.'

At that time the name Aristodikos rang only faint bells with me but after searching my mind I remembered the shadowy go-between whom I'd seen shuttling amongst the rival camp sites at the Olympic games.

'He should be here instead of you, then?' I said.

Pedipeus shrugged and hit the rock savagely with his axe.

'Isn't it ironic that his name means best judge?' he replied.

Apart from three other Theban dignitaries my squad of slaves included a child murderer and a former priest of Zeus who had profaned the temple with some dreadful act of lechery. The rest were just prisoners of war. Their average expected life-span once they came to Laurion was about six years. It was not a posting that I enjoyed, even if the huge number of little silver owls was helping to make Athens the richest city in Greece.

At the end of my three months I was posted to do frontier duty at a small fort near Mount Geranea[1] where the road from Athens to Megara met that from Sparta to Thebes. It was late autumn by this time; the fort was quite high above sea-level and very draughty, so it was unpleasantly cold standing on watch in nothing but a linen tunic. Luckily the ever-thoughtful Psyche had secreted a woollen cloak, doubtless knitted by herself, into the bottom of my kit-bag.

Along with five other cadets I was one of a garrison of around a hundred. I was surprised to find that the deputy commander was none other than young Sophocles who was barely two years ahead of me in the rankings, but of course had made himself well-known by his victory in the drama contest.

'This is the crossroads between two different kinds of Greek,' he announced pompously, 'the Ionian and the Doric. We speak the same language but disagree on lots of things: politics, religion, architecture, poetry and death. Our brief is to check all travellers using this route and in particular keep an eye on Megara.'

I should explain that the city of Megara[2] on its two rocks was an ally of ours; it had sent twenty triremes to help us at Salamis and three hundred infantry to help at Plataea. So we didn't want the anti-Athens party there to stage a coup. Such is the fragility of friendship between Greek cities. You see we Greeks are a race —but not a nation. We had more or less managed to stick together when faced with invasion by the Persians, but once that threat receded the various cities were back to their bitter rivalries.

We quarrel over our colonies, over trade, over borders and most of all over our style of government. Naturally we Athenians think we have the best, not just a republic[3] but a democracy. There are others that are republics but just run by a few families of oligarchs. And then there's Sparta, not a republic at all, the only city that still has kings, but a strange kingdom at that, for they trust their kings so little that they have two at the same time. I know this must all seem strange to anyone but a Greek, but that's the way we are.

So for the next three months we patrolled the roads above Megara, monitoring troop movements from Corinth and Sparta, our most dangerous rivals, and it was on one of these patrols that I had my second encounter with the mysterious Aristodikos of Tanagra. A group on horseback had appeared from the south, and judging by their long hair and red cloaks most of them were Spartan officers, but amongst them was the sinister figure of Aristodikos. The duty officer, it happened to be Sophocles, held up his hand and asked them their business.

'We are on an embassy to meet general Cimon,' said one. 'I am Kleomenes, sub-regent of Sparta.' The man looked tanned and fit, holding himself with the arrogant poise of a typical Spartan warrior. The other Spartans showed their seals, but Aristodikos kept in the background, acting as if he was just one of their servants.

'What's the news from Sparta?' asked Sophocles.

Kleomenes smiled rather superciliously. 'Argos tried to dispute our leadership, but we dealt with her. Your man Themistocles was part of the trouble. He stirred them up, then escaped. He may have been a great leader once, but now he's senile and should die gracefully.'

'You Spartans don't encourage the old to stay alive, do you?' said Sophocles, and for once I felt some sympathy with him, for the Spartans were proverbial for putting out the weak to die, both old and young.

Kleomenes smiled. 'What use are the weak? Anyway with your permission we must continue on our way. We are due in Athens this evening.'

Sophocles waved them through, then when they had gone turned. ''Why is Cimon meeting with Spartans?' he asked, not expecting an answer. Nor could I think of one, but it reminded me of the strangely secret conversations at Olympia and of the connection between the sudden downfall of Themistocles and the spectacular rise of Cimon.

Six weeks later I was home on leave and my mother reminded me that I was now old enough for full initiation into the Mysteries. While by no means enthusiastic I was still haunted by my last sighting of the Princess Kore and curious to see her again even if closer contact was forbidden. 'It made a great difference to your father,' said my mother. 'It was easier for him to accept his disability and the inevitability of an early death once he realised he would go to a better life hereafter.' She blinked back tears and my compliance was assured.

She was herself an assistant in the female rites of Thesmophoria,[4] so she had her own convictions, a decent woman who praised selflessness and had little admiration for power or military glory.

'You know what your uncle says,' she went on, dipping her bread in wine, as she always did at lunchtime. 'Hell is a great lake of mire with an eternal flow of filth; heaven is a grove of myrtles and apricot trees. You will be a better person if you accept the Mysteries and give yourself to the Earth Mother. One day we will all meet again in heaven.'

Thus once again in the month Boedromion[5] I listened to the herald in the market place of Athens and handed my ten drachmas to Lampon, a friend of Pericles who happened to be treasurer for the day. That evening we set off as before to the Phaleron[6] beach and with men and women on opposite sides waded into the sea to wash away our sins.

'Pride, greed and cowardice, these are the worst sins,' intoned the high priest Psamos from a small hill above the sands.

'What about lust?' muttered one of the other new recruits, screwing up his eyes to see the women on the other side of the bay.

I did the same, but they were really too far away for modesty to be offended. For an instant I thought I caught a glimpse of Kore, but whoever it was quickly disappeared beneath the water and afterwards I began to doubt if it was her at all. I floated on the gentle swell staring up at the huge empty sky and the water lapping at my ears cut off the coarse humour of some of my fellow bathers.

That night there was the usual party on the shore, where we enjoyed watered down wine, dried fish and dates. There was a large crowd, several hundred, all excited by the events of the afternoon. The citharas[7] and drums beat out a bewitching rhythm and soon we were winding round the bonfires in an endless reel. Psamos had a special wagon so I looked for Kore near it and eventually found her sitting morosely by a small fire. She was wearing her official yellow robe as the personification of Persephone with a yellow ribbon binding her long brown hair. Her legs were tucked beneath her and she was chewing a piece of dried fish.

'It's you, Phori,' she said, tossing a bone in the fire. 'You're cleansed from sin?' She sounded rather doubtful and raised her elegant eyebrows.

'I am,' I said. 'Officially at least.'

'Does it feel good?'

'I think so. Come and dance with me.'

'I mustn't touch a man till the Mysteries are over,' she said.

'We can dance without touching then.'

She looked suddenly unsure of herself, but got up and threw her fishtail into the fire.

Then suddenly she grinned, and hitching up her yellow robe into her girdle, she skipped off round the fire with the flames glinting on her long brown legs. She trailed one hand behind and I almost grabbed it, then remembered that I must not.

'Persephone, Kore, Persephone, Kore,' chanted the crowd as we all twisted round the fires in opposite circles, swerving whenever there was a risk of touching anyone of the opposite sex. For two hours we kept on dancing and I had to use all my wits to keep close to Kore as she dashed on, sometimes changing direction suddenly, but always I had to avoid touching her and often her smile flashed past me, her impish eyes glinting in the torchlight. Sometimes she and the other girls did cartwheels with scant regard for modesty, yet we all kept on moving to the music. It was nearly dawn when one by one we lay down exhausted and laughing on the scrub grass of the dunes.

Then I heard Kore say, 'You'll not see me again till the spring,' and she disappeared.

The rest of us slept where we lay till the afternoon when the procession began to wind along the Sacred Way. There were the usual rude jokes when we crossed the sluggish stream of Kephisos.

'Look at that one's funny beard. His mother must have been raped by a goat.'

'Ask him how Zeus did it with a swan without getting pecked.'

'Here comes Hermes of the midget phallus.'

There was a young man, I think, though it might have been a girl, made up as the god Eros, complete with golden wings and a bow and arrow.

'Keep moving,' he/she shouted in a high-pitched voice. 'I am Eros,[8] god of lust, favourite son of Aphrodite. She made me love girls and boys alike. Keep going. You've only seven more miles to go. You pathetic worshippers of Demeter. Better me and promiscuity by far.'

He was booed by most of the onlookers but kept at it. Such was the competition between different gods in those days.

Amongst the crowd I noticed my old nurse Psyche yelling with the best of them, but luckily she didn't see me. Then came the second bathe in the sacred lake and the last seven miles to Eleusis, where for the first time since I was a child I was allowed to enter the temple precinct, now handsomely rebuilt. Psamos led the way past the dancers at the fountain and his wife, playing the role of the Earth Mother, sat on the Mirthless Rock waiting for her daughter.

All that day we had to fast and it was not till sunset that the ceremony began. The choir sang the song written for them by my uncle:

'Blessed is he who sees these things before he dies.'

It was so dark inside the temple, with only one torch to light it, that it was hard to distinguish the entrance of the cavern that led down to Hades. By this time I was quite light-headed with hunger, more than ready to take any oath required of me. Then suddenly there was a loud roll of drums and a door opened so that what seemed like an intense beam of light fell on Gaia, priestess but also for this one night a goddess, just at the very moment when her daughter Persephone — Kore of course — tore herself from her mother's arms and ran off through the door down into the cavern beyond, the entrance to Hell.

Now I understood what she meant by saying I would not see her till the following spring. It was her sacrifice for the fertility of next year's crops and for babies as yet unborn.

'You have escaped damnation. You are a mystic now,' said Psamos to each of us in turn as we went back into the cool night air. Outside there was a long table with cups of the sacred drink of mint and barley beer[9] which I drank down thirstily, the best and worst drink I'd ever tasted. The other initiates began to joke and relax after the tension of the long ceremony, but I was bewildered. There are still some secrets of the Mysteries which I have not revealed and will never do so, but perhaps I can reassure you that the very fact of secrecy perhaps matters more than the secret itself.

For me I was still trying to wrestle with the fact that the girl I knew as Kore was for many people a goddess who disappeared underground for half the year.

She had said that it would be next spring before we met again. As it turned out it was to be three springs.

---

1.   The highest peak of Mount Geranea, now known as Makryplagi, rises to over 4,000 feet.

2.   Remnants of ancient Megara survive including its famous tunnels but it is now mainly industrial.

3.   Republic is of course a Latin word meaning public things but the Greeks tended to use the word polis, the word for city, in

this connection, hence politics. Democracy on the other hand is a genuinely Greek word meaning rule by the people.

4.   The Thesmophoria festival was also all about fertility and the earth. So only women took part, but their husbands had to pay for it.

5.   Boedromion means much the same as September.

6.   Phaleron, now Faliro, is these days three hundred yards further away from the sea, but has a fine maritime museum that includes a reconstructed trireme.

7   The cithara was a stringed instrument similar to a lyre or lute and played with a plectrum

8.   In some versions Eros was a much older god even than Zeus, in fact the fourth after Chaos, Gaia and Tartaros, but in other versions he was the son of Aphrodite and Ares. By this time he was associated as much with homosexual as with heterosexual love.

9.   Some people allege that this special beer called kykeon had psychotropic properties due to traces of acacia or phaleron grass or N.N-Dimethyltryoptamine and this induced those who drank it to have visions

CHAPTER ELEVEN

THE NINE WAYS

DURING THE FOLLOWING WINTER WHICH was long and harsh I was back on frontier duty, mainly at the rock-top fort of Phyle on the road to Thebes.[1] Nothing much happened there apart from the odd vulture swooping down for its supper, but I was present when yet another of those strangely secretive Spartan groups passed through, accompanied yet again by the unsavoury Aristodikos.

The least pleasant thing that occurred that winter was back at home where an incident between my family and that of Kore made any possible friendship between us even more unlikely than it already was. This was caused by my uncle Aeschylus, who had been increasingly tetchy since losing his theatrical crown to the young upstart, Sophocles.

He seemed moody and depressed. His wife, one of my favourite aunts, had died a number of years ago and he was rumoured to have had the odd affair, though I was not aware of the ladies concerned. My mother knew nothing of such goings-on and would have slapped the face of anyone who suggested it. Our slave Psyche, who had turned down numerous offers of marriage to other slaves so she could stay with us, was rather more cynical about him and always dusted or scrubbed rather ostentatiously around his writing space as if she disapproved of such frivolities.

Anyway what happened was much more serious. It turned out that after a drink or two the old man had made a pass at his old flame Gaia, the high priestess, aggravating the offence by doing so in the holy period just after the Mysteries. Luckily her husband

Psamos was a man of considerable self-control and my uncle had been his choir-master for many years, or the penalties might have been much more severe. He was inclined to suggest it must have been a misunderstanding, though Gaia herself was still outraged, a situation made worse when my mother took Aeschylus' side and blamed Gaia for either lying or leading him on. Thus the scandal persisted and to calm things down it was put about that Aeschylus had broken his vow of secrecy about the Mysteries and must leave Attica for a number of years. This was very unfortunate for his new play, Agamemnon, was in rehearsal and he would thus never see it performed, let alone stand much chance of regaining the coveted first prize from Sophocles.

I rode over for the day to see the old man off. For all his eccentricities he was loveable in many ways, with his chubby face, bald head and jerky mannerisms. My mother was in tears, still convinced that Gaia was a trouble-maker.

'I'm sorry, Phasia. It really was my fault,' said Aeschylus. 'I should have remembered that Gaia had no sense of humour.'

'And I don't know if her daughter's much better,' added my mother to my astonishment.

'Where does she disappear to for six months, that's what I'd like to know,' added Psyche, but no one took any notice.

So my uncle and I set off for the frontier, he to catch a merchant ship that was sailing from Megara to Sicily, where he had a number of friends, and I back to my post at Phyle. 'Look after your mother, Phori,' were his parting words. 'She's a good woman. So is Gaia for that matter, hence probably my downfall.'

Once back at Phyle[2] my military duties kept my mind from brooding too much about the now strained relationship between my family and that of Kore, as the months slipped past to spring when Persephone was due once more to emerge from the underworld. It was a harsh winter, particularly up in the hills. We had a couple of skirmishes with brigands to alleviate the monotony and I was also distracted by a last minute conversation with my mother.

Aeschylus, she said, as head of the family had taken it upon himself before his departure to begin negotiations for me to acquire an appropriate wife. This was a girl called Zoe whom I had never met, but she was the daughter of Myronides, one of the up-and-coming generals who also had a large farm not far from our own at Eleusis. It can be understood that while I had had youthful yearnings for the unattainable princess Kore, I was a typical free citizen of Athens who would not query the wishes of his elders, so the suggestion of an arranged marriage was perfectly normal.

Just before the end of my posting at Phyle there was one further incident which contributed to my awareness of the clandestine operations conducted by some senior Athenians and the ubiquitous interloper, Aristodikos of Tanagra. I had been assigned to escort a special party which was crossing over the border to visit the famous Oracle of Delphi, and by a strange coincidence not only did it include my future father-in-law General Myronides, but of course Aristodikos, acting as guide through the dubious territory of Boeotia. It turned out that the expedition had been masterminded by our chief general Cimon, for one of the problems of a military man in a democracy is that he sometimes has to use odd tricks to get his own way. What he wanted was a new batch of Athenian colonists to settle in Eion to replace their predecessors who had unfortunately all been massacred by a local tribe. It was a township founded by him on the Strymon River[3] in Thrace and just happened to be close to his family gold mine. The reluctance of Athenian citizens to move house to such an apparently dangerous outpost was understandable, as was his unmentioned desire to have a garrison near his gold mine. So to persuade the assembly to make a favourable decision Cimon had offered to consult the great priestess of Delphi and obtain what was supposed to be a totally unbiased view from the god Apollo himself.

It took our party two days to thread through the hills to the shrine of the god. The slopes of Mount Parnassos[4] were bright with yellow gorse yet the sky was often black with thunderous clouds above the misty peaks. Our road twisted backwards and forwards along cliffs and over ravines where a stumbling horse would have little hope of survival. Luckily there was a small inn by the road that served us lentil and chickpea soup: at least it was hot.

'This is the crossroads where King Oedipus killed his own father,' said Myronides, who had been this way before, and indeed it was a bleak and unforgiving spot even in the spring. I have to say that it was several years after this trip that my uncle's rival Sophocles revived this legend with a series of plays about the wretched man who made love to his own mother. But Thebans do tend to be odd.

Eventually we saw our road ahead twisting its way uphill to a beautiful temple which was silhouetted white against the blue of the mountains. We passed several small but elegant buildings which were the treasuries of various Greek cities and arrived at the entrance hall of the temple built on the spot where the famous monster Python had been killed.

We were kept waiting for two days before our leaders were allowed to consult the oracle and I suspect, in retrospect, that this was all part of the plan to increase our awe of the occasion and make us so frustrated that we would be glad to accept any answer. The one relief from boredom as we kicked our heels was to see the two huge paintings produced by Cimon's tame painter Polygnotos. I was particularly intrigued by his 'Siege of Troy' which yet again included a scantily dressed Trojan princess who bore an uncanny resemblance to Cimon's feisty sister Elpinike with whom Polygnotos seemed also to be obsessed. She even appeared quite gratuitously in the other huge picture of Odysseus on his way to Hades. Then at long last, after Myronides had presented a bag of gold coins, our leaders were admitted to the shrine itself, whilst I had to wait outside with just a rather awkward view of the proceedings, hampered both by the angle and by the fact that there was very little light.

At first only the quiet voice of the duty priestess gave us any sense of direction. At the end of the temple it merged into the rock-face and I could hear water trickling from a spring. There was also a strange, rather unpleasant smell which someone described as sulphur. Then I made out that there was an elderly priestess, clad immaculately in white, sitting with her eyes shut on a three-legged stool beneath which curled a snake. We were motioned to wait in absolute silence and this lasted for about an hour, with no movement except for the occasional puff of putrid gas from this strange spring. Then at last Myronides was beckoned forward.

'Tell me, Pythian,'[5] he asked, reading from his brief. 'Is it right for Athens to send a new colony to Eion?'

For a moment it seemed as if the priestess of Apollo had not even heard the question for she seemed to be in a trance and some said it was the fumes of the spring that had this effect. Then suddenly her eyes flickered open and for a second she fixed us with a beady stare. Then her eyes closed again and there was a pause. Her mouth opened, but we could hear nothing intelligible. Myronides was about to turn and go, but the junior priestess motioned him to wait.

Again the chief priestess spoke and this time it was not only audible but chanted exquisitely in hexameter verse, just like Homer.

'Tell the people of the Owl to send two hundred families to where the nine roads meet,'[6] she said, then slumped forward apparently exhausted.

There was no question of further elaboration, for the younger priestess ushered us out, smiling benignly and closing the vast door behind us with a clump. It was cold outside and there was no temptation to linger in Delphi, so we collected our horses and were soon on the road back to Phyle. I was beginning to think that the whole episode had been like a charade.

Then I heard Myronides ask Aristodikos if he understood what the oracle had said.

'Yes,' replied the Tanagran. 'Cimon will be very happy. It just happens that he has already selected a site for the new colony at a place called The Nine Ways.' He shrugged his shoulders meaningfully and Myronides raised his eyebrows as we crossed the foothills of Parnassos once more.

Thus it was that I learned some of the special techniques of democracy, indeed discovered that it was not all that different from oligarchy,[7] nor so very far removed from tyranny. It was one or two people manipulating a state for their own personal glory, and though I was then still programmed to be ambitious, I hated the idea of trickery and bullying. I had also learned that oracles very often give affirmative advice to supplicants who bring gold coins.

---

1. Thebes, the home of the famous or infamous King Oedipus, lies some thirty miles north of Athens and had from ancient times been one of its greatest rivals. So this was probably the reason it sided with the Persians in the recent wars. Today it is primarily a market town and ruins of its old fortress the Kadmea survive. The history of Oedipus owes a great deal to Sophocles but even more to Sigmund Freud.

2. Phyle is known as Fyli and the remnants of the fort's massive stone walls still stand on a remote crag above Motorway 6.

3. The River Strymon now called Struma rises in what is now Bulgaria.

4. Mount Parnassos is a limestone outcrop over 5,200 feet high and these days a popular ski resort in winter as well as a site for bauxite mining.

5. Pytho was the old name for Delphi, given to it, according to legend, because Apollo killed a serpent (Greek word python) here which rotted and left a terrible smell. The games here were called the Pythian Games.

6. By an odd coincidence Eion or Amphipolis, as it was renamed, was also the place where the Persian King Xerxes buried four young boys alive to ensure good fortune for his invasion of Greece.

7. The translator points out that all three of the words used here, democracy, oligarchy and tyranny were invented by the Greeks, not to mention also demagogy and monarchy. Democracy meant rule by the people, but it should be borne in mind that people in Greek cities did not include women, slaves or foreigners. Oligarchy meant rule by the few and generally speaking lived up to its name. Tyranny was simply a nasty word for monarchy, usually reserved for self-made monarchs or their unpleasant children. Similarly demagogy tended to be reserved for democrats who made too much effort to please the masses.

CHAPTER TWELVE

MY SECOND VOYAGE

TWO WEEKS LATER AFTER A short leave in Athens I received my first appointment as a ranking officer with the fleet and my twentieth birthday[1] had passed. As I walked out towards the Piraeus I could see the changes in the city. Cimon's new Temple of Theseus was rising rapidly on the hill above the marketplace. In its main portico the huge paintings by Polygnotos glorifying our war against the Persians covered several walls and some of the valiant maidens depicted bore, as usual, an uncanny resemblance to Cimon's half-sister Elpinike. Naturally he too figured prominently in the battle scenes. Cimon had also planted an avenue of plane trees for shelter and repaired the main water supply, a very popular move. It's much easier being a politician if you have a family gold mine, not to mention a hoard of Persian treasure.

As I said goodbye to my mother she told me she was planning my wedding to Zoe for the autumn, a thought which gave me a mixture of pleasure and concern, for I'd only met her once very briefly and could hardly remember what she looked like. As I reached the port area I had never seen the three harbours so busy, with more than two hundred triremes being made ready for sea. Some were still ashore on the slipways being painted with pitch or having new planks added to their sides. Others were moored in sixes beside the jetties, connected to one long causeway so that stores could be easily loaded.

Everywhere dockyard artisans were busy, repairing the leather pads which protected each oar hole from chafing, mending halyards, stowing sails, touching up the different lurid faces which decorated each venomous prow, adjusting the linkage of the twin steering oars.

I had heard rumours that Cimon was experimenting with a new wider deck for triremes and now saw evidence of this, for many of the ships had been fitted with extra space to carry more men-at-arms. There were also quite a few of the Assembly inspectors snooping round to check that trierarchs had not skimped on fitting out their vessels. A long queue of donkeys laden with stores stood waiting patiently as I headed down the jetty to look for my new ship, the *Hecuba*, the trireme to which I had been appointed fourth mate. There were baskets of olives, tall jars of oil for the ships' lamps, double-handled water jars, stacks of barley-cake and honey, wine, dried fish, piles of spears and shields, neat stacks of newly oiled oars.

Eventually I found the *Hecuba* moored on the Akte side of the Zea harbour, fifth out of a set. Looking head-on at the six ships I could see six frightening tooth-filled mouths and twelve angry painted eyes reflected in murky waters of the harbour. Sharks and sea dragons were the favourite models, but *Hecuba*, named after the luckless queen of Troy, was different with a tearful face shrouded by painted flames.

I reported for duty and found that my former mentor Pericles had been promoted to trierarch. I was filled with a degree of dread since, despite his nonchalant pose, Pericles was a very demanding officer and very hard to please.

'Welcome aboard, Euphorion,' he said, bleakly acknowledging me. 'Take charge of the loading parties. I want this ship fully manned and ready for exercises by dawn tomorrow. We have only two days for training before we're off with the fleet at the end of the week. I'll leave you to it. I have business back in the city.'

I knew already that Pericles had a mistress as well as a wife, which was not unusual even at his age, and that he was also becoming heavily involved in the politics of the Assembly. But I was surprised yet again by his casual ruthlessness. He treated the professional sailors with considerable disdain and the oarsmen, except those who were voting citizens, with absolute contempt. Even with fellow officers like myself he was generally aloof. His mind, it seemed, was always on more important matters.

'By the cleft in Aphrodite's buttocks it's Euphorion,' came a voice behind me. It was Kleistes who had been transferred as ship-master to the *Hecuba*.

'Ephialtes must have given you a good report,' I said. 'He and Pericles are very close.'

'All trierarchs are much the same to me,' he replied. 'Mad dogs that you have to control.' He winked and turned to start testing all the halyards and loose timbers ready for our voyage, while I carried on getting the stores on board.

'We have been assigned to sail to Delos,' said Pericles the following morning. 'To pick up money from the Treasury for the fleet wages and repairs. So we set off a day ahead of the rest and meet at Knidos[2] in two weeks. That means we have only one full day for training and I mean to make every minute count.' And of course I knew that he did mean it.

That day we spent ten hours at sea and he made it tough for all of us. We practised speed runs, ramming speeds, sudden stops, frequent shipping of all oars on one side or the other until the oarsmen were utterly exhausted and then still more. Surprisingly for a man who enjoyed using expletives for the mildest of topics Kleistes kept totally cool, cajoling the crew with patience and great skill. There seemed a grudging respect between him as a professional seaman and Pericles the politically ambitious amateur.

Thus when we cast off from the jetty at Zea the following morning we were a tired but reasonably proficient crew and swept past the eyes of Cimon's flagship without catching a crab. As third watch-keeper my station was above the beak with my spear aloft until we were clear of the harbour entrance. Though I say it myself I felt an impressive sight.

Our course was due east and after an hour or so we picked up some wind for a run past the southern tip of Keos which gave the oarsmen a well-earned rest. The third tier rowers were particularly tired for they had the longest and heaviest oars, and though they got extra pay for the privilege they had to be fitter than the two lower tiers. Thus by early evening we made it to Kythnos[3] and Kleistes took us stern first into a sheltered cove on the far side of the island where we could beach for the night. Above us the yellow hills were covered with broom and tamarisk.

'Steady on your oars,' yelled Kleistes as we backed gently onto the sand with our anchor out at the bows so that we could haul ourselves off again quickly next morning. 'Steady, I said, you bastard offspring of Argive brothel keepers.'

Even Pericles managed a brief smile and rewarded the crew with two hours shore leave in shifts, though I knew he always had an ulterior motive, usually to win supporters for his political ambitions. There were hot springs just half a mile up from the beach and most of the crew bathed in the warm bubbling water and soothed away the aches of the previous two days. Then we returned to the ship with bags of fresh figs which we'd picked from the largest fig trees I'd ever seen. We also bought some of the tasty cheese which was a speciality of the local farms.

The following day the wind was coming from the north-west as it often does and we were able to use the sail again to make rapid progress to Delos. By afternoon, however, *Hecuba* was dipping and rolling with the waves to the point where the sea was spilling through the lower oar holes and we had to shorten sail. Matters grew even worse when we approached Delos and Kleistes told Pericles that he could not enter the harbour in such dangerous sea conditions.

'Nonsense, ship-master,' said Pericles abruptly, treating even his most senior officers with disdain.

'It may be,' replied Kleistes. 'But the currents outside Delos[4] harbour are very tricky. It's your decision. You have to pay the treasury for the ship if we sink her, but I only lose my job.'

Pericles paced up and down the poop deck snorting disapproval about the over-cautiousness of ship-masters. But then he suddenly relaxed, smiled icily and said, ' Find us a patch of clear water then and put out the sea anchor. We'll wait till the wind drops.'

It was a most uncomfortable night. The oarsmen cursed each other and groaned with the cramp as they tried to doze on their benches. Some were seasick. The officers, including myself, lay in the limited shelter of the upper deck, getting up for alternate anchor watches and to keep an eye on the restless crew below.

By dawn the wind had died down a little so we weighed anchor, and as we rowed towards the harbour I appreciated Kleistes' comments about Delos. It was a very small island with a rocky shore on all sides. The neighbouring island of Rheneira, where they bury their dead, was only half a mile away and the narrows in between were full of swirling currents which made the trireme buck this way and that. To add to this the wind seemed liable to sudden changes of direction, so even on this milder day Kleistes had some difficulty in getting through the narrow harbour entrance. As we eased up to the jetty I noticed that he and Pericles avoided each other's eyes and busied themselves instead with the details of our arrival.

'Euphorion, you take charge of the Treasury platoon,' ordered Pericles. 'Sign for the money and get it back here quickly. I don't want to be stranded in this harbour.'

So I gathered a party of ten men and as we landed I was at once conscious of a strange unworldly atmosphere on the island, the holiest spot in the entire Aegean Sea. The Treasury was the central collection point for taxes from all the islands that had joined the confederacy with Athens, but it was quite a small building, designed just to hold large quantities of gold and silver. It stood beside a most ornate temple of Apollo and the sacred lake where Apollo was supposed to have been born, well-guarded by the sacred geese and swans. The famous horned altar of Apollo, which was one of the wonders of the world, stood nearby and two large quaintly carved stone lions guarded a huge statue of the god, naked but for a metal loin cloth. Beyond it was an avenue of phallus statues stretching towards the hills. Above rose the rocks of Mount Kynthos[5] among which I could just see the dark cleft known as the Grotto of the Gods, the holiest place on this holy island.

Conscious of Pericles' impatience to be on his way I had no wish to waste time, but inevitably the treasury priests were in no hurry to hand over our silver and made as much fuss of the paperwork as if they thought we were Persians in disguise. So I had no choice but to stand and observe the island's other activities. In stark contrast to the priestly area where we waited was the famous slave market next door, the busiest in the Aegean, a useful place for triremes to sell off old oarsmen and replace them with younger ones. I could see several rows of slaves for sale, men, women and children, some who looked Asian, some African, most just standing around naked so that merchants could inspect them easily. Service in the temple and slave dealing seemed to be almost the sole occupations on this island for it was too rocky and windy to have fruit trees or reasonable crops. Even the fishermen seemed to prefer other island bases nearby. There were just a few piglets and goats around, but it was clear that their main purpose was to supply the sacrificial altars of the temple, not food for the populace.

At last three boxes of gold and silver coins as well as silver ingots were released and I organised my men to get them down to the harbour, but it was no mean task. There had to be 4,200 silver drachmas[6] per month for each trireme crew, that's to say one whole silver talent for each ship and just under a drachma per day for each man, so the weight was considerable, about two tons of silver to be transferred along the dock. Pericles glared at me as we at last re-boarded the *Hecuba*.

'You've taken your time,' he said harshly. 'I've wasted nearly a day here already. Consider that an official reprimand.' And he turned away from me abruptly.

I was mortified by such a public rebuke, which I felt was most unfair. I supposed that I had been too considerate, too reluctant to offend the priests and other treasury officials, but I should have been more conscious of the fanatical urgency of my commander and bullied them to hand over the money more quickly. A wink from Kleistes behind his captain's back was no consolation. That night I found it hard to sleep for thinking that I had let down both myself and my family and that a career which might have been quite promising was now so soon doomed to failure.

1. For purists this makes the date 465BC, the same year that the Great King Xerxes of Persia was murdered in his bed by one of his own guards, a story retold in Handel's opera 'Serse'.

2. Knidos was a small Greek city built mostly on an island, but connected by a causeway to the mainland of what is now Turkey near Datca.

3. The beautiful island of Kythnos some 56 nautical miles from Athens is known for its fine beaches and thermal springs.

4. Delos, an island almost in the centre of the Cyclades, became a holy island in prehistoric times and is now a World Heritage Site with a number of surviving monuments.

5. Mount Kythnos is only about 360 feet high but its summit provides an excellent panorama of the fabulous ruins of Delos. It also provided a popular name for girls: Cynthia.

6. There were six obols in a drachma and 4,200 drachmas in a talent, Half a drachma was the subsistence rate per day for men on jury duty or at the Assembly and oarsmen in triremes got 21 drachmas a month. One of the commonest trading coins was the four drachma piece known as the owl as it had a picture of the iconic Athenian owl.

CHAPTER THIRTEEN

THE GREAT BATTLE

WE LEFT DELOS AT FIRST light with Pericles still in a foul temper and headed south east for Naxos. The island's main city had been destroyed by the Persians twenty years earlier and had never recovered, nor had its people really ever quite decided whether they wanted to support Athens or one of the other great cities like Sparta or Thebes. Despite their wealth they had sent very few ships to help us at Salamis and had been savagely punished for rebelling against the Confederacy.

I saw now with my own eyes the evidence of how brutally Cimon had suppressed them and replaced many of the native Naxians with his own retired soldiers and sailors, many of them from among the poorest and toughest denizens of Athens. Back home they thought themselves too good to work as potters or blacksmiths, since such humble tasks were best left to immigrants, but once given plots of ground they could style themselves landowners.

However, they tended to keep the rebellious streak that characterises the badly paid lower oarsmen, so even when given these new opportunities on a plate they were still unreliable. And since they were too proud for manual labour they tended to employ Naxians to do all the hard work, so they failed to make as much profit as they should have done from their new status. Mostly they just sat about the harbour and gossiped about old campaigns or thought of mosaic patterns for their new patios.

Above us as we back-watered up to the beach rose Mount Zia,[1] the highest mountain on any of the islands. This was the very shore, I remembered, where Theseus the hero of the Cretan maze had abandoned the princess Ariadne and she had cried herself to death. I must admit I felt not much better after my reprimand from Pericles, especially since he refused all leave for the crew, as if punishing every one of them for my tardiness the previous day. Perhaps, however, I did him an injustice for he wanted a very early start the next day. Besides, we had to guard our precious cargo of gold. So two nights later after one last stop on the newly freed island of Astypalea we joined up with Cimon's main fleet in the anchorage of Knidos.[2]

The flagship *Salaminia* was in pride of place at the jetty and Cimon immediately summoned a meeting of all his commanders. My bad luck, if that is what it was, almost now turned to good, for Pericles had vindictively doubled my guard duties, so instead of relaxing ashore I was busy mustering all the trierarchs onto the *Salaminia*. Thus I was able to observe the general at close quarters and heard some of his briefing to the senior officers. With his stocky athletic form clad like a Spartan's in a red cloak he came straight to the point. He was dividing his fleet into three flotillas to launch a major attack on the Asian mainland. Ephialtes in the *Ariadne* was to lead one group to capture a line of Persian-held Greek towns along the coast from Miletus. *Hecuba* was part of the second group designated to attack the rich city of Phaselos[3] on the mainland just north of Rhodes. The third group would be his own to deal with any Persian reinforcements.

As it turned out our special task turned into an anticlimax for Phaselos surrendered to us almost without a fight. Its Persian garrison was in no mood to face a long siege and its Greek inhabitants had been under Persian rule for so long that all they cared about was avoiding the destruction of their city. So with the help of some local merchants Pericles negotiated for the garrison to leave unscathed if they paid a fine of ten talents and not a drop of blood was shed.

It was only later that I heard that Cimon, far from being pleased by this outcome was quite the reverse: he had expected the Persians to send major reinforcements to save the city and had been using it as bait for a major battle. Thus thwarted he sent us to besiege another city for the same purpose, this time the walled citadel of Krya[4] further down the coast. There the fires of Beelzebub burned all night and the citizens had no Greek blood but were Phoenicians, a fanatical bloodthirsty people who provided most of the ships and the sailors for the Persian fleet. They were likely to fight to the bitter end and it was said that they'd even sacrifice their own children to put their god in a better mood when things were difficult.

A day later we had landed near Krya and were preparing to storm the citadel with orders to spare nobody, young or old. I have nothing against killing Persians or Phoenicians even in cold blood, for they left a dreadful imprint on all our lives, but I did not particularly relish the thought of taking part in such slaughter myself. For Pericles was the sort of captain who often sneered at Cimon behind his back, but always wanted to demonstrate an excess of enthusiasm in every campaign, so that he could make even more of a name for himself. If Cimon needed a massacre to make the Phoenician navy angry enough to fight, then Pericles would deliver one.

Pericles, with his uncanny knack of knowing how to make the best use of other people, naturally remembered that I was a bit of a rock climber so he picked on me to lead the scaling of the ramparts. As it turned out the lower areas were of natural rock which was not too hard to climb and my party of twenty managed to drag three ladders up through a fissure to a ledge which proved high enough for us to reach the parapet. Thankfully I was so busy organising the climb that I didn't have time to brood about the dangers that might await me at the top, so I was slightly less frightened than otherwise might have been the case. As it turned out I was the first up and luckily there was no sentry anywhere near us, so my party all got into the town before the alarm was raised. By that time we had opened the gates for the main group, including Pericles himself. He set an example by impaling the Phoenician commander on his bedroom door.

'I think you should rape the women, if you can stand them,' he said with ice cool nonchalance. Luckily our hoplites were far from fussy and obliged. Call me a prig if you like, but I only managed to kill one Phoenician, a thin young man who actually made an effort to fight me, and I was too inexperienced to rape anyone.

'Squeamish, Euphorion?' sneered Pericles. 'Do things in the interest of the state.' He snatched one of the gold-clad women of the governor's harem, pushed her with the point of his sword into an alcove and flicked aside her robe. Then lifting his own tunic he made enough of a show of raping her to impress his own followers and reduce the woman to convulsions. There was no pleasure in it for him, but then Pericles was largely above ordinary human pleasures; what he wanted was power. Just like Ephialtes.

The rest of our troops were more effective at raping and at least a dozen of the wretched women who were violated threw themselves from the battlements in their distress, others just cried in corners, but as the seamen and hoplites dragged away their booty they took time to follow Pericles' final order which was to set the city alight. As a demonstration of ruthlessness and as a dire humiliation of the Persian empire it was all that Cimon could have asked for. Now it was a question of waiting to see if the provocation had worked. If it had, then we would shortly be faced with a much more formidable enemy.

The next ten days were spent in a leisurely cruise along the coast of Pamphylia, liberating the odd town without difficulty, whether the inhabitants wanted to be liberated or not, but not indulging in any further brutalities as we waited for the news of Krya to reach the satrap. It was then not long before some fishermen came alongside with news that a large Phoenician fleet was mustering at the mouth of the River Eurymedon[5] with the Admiral Ariomades from Tyre in command.

As originally instructed we now linked up with Cimon's main fleet which had been waiting off Cyprus. We passed lines of high cliffs where the mouths of rivers were in mid air and the water spouted down into the sea. Then as we neared the river Cimon ordered our leading ships to hoist Phoenician pennants which we had captured at Krya and some of the officers donned gold cloaks to make themselves look like Persians. By this deception we were able to get rather closer to the enemy before we were identified and some of the Phoenician ships were still at anchor as we prepared to attack. Half our fleet was detached to drive the Phoenicians onto their own shoreline while the rest, including *Hecuba*, went to tackle those that made it out into the open sea. The Phoenicians had a reputation as skilled seamen and showed it, but on this occasion their admiral, not surprisingly, seemed confused.

Cimon now ordered us to sail round them at speed in an ever-decreasing circle, so that they were forced into a smaller space. Then at a prearranged signal we all turned inwards at ramming speed and headed for the nearest enemy ship. I held my breath as Hecuba caught a large Phoenician with four banks of oars just behind her mast. There was a dreadful jarring as our beak dug into her at the waterline and she started to heel over as we back-watered, their unlucky crews still chained to their benches so they stood no chance of escape.. Within an hour most of the Phoenician ships were sinking or beached. So Cimon had achieved his objectives.

The next day Ephialtes and Pericles were both ordered to head up river with ten triremes leaving the rest of the fleet to round-up the remainder of the Phoenician warships. We beached west of the estuary and then rowed up the river which was narrow and fast-flowing. The Persian troops who had been with the fleet were ahead of us making for Aspendos,[6] a formerly Greek city famous for its salt pans. There were tall pink birds squawking beside the crusty white banks and beyond them fertile fields of corn and vineyards.

It was not long before we began to overtake the fleeing Persians, still half a mile short of the walls of Aspendos, and they seemed badly demoralised, whilst we were still exhilarated by our victory at sea. Throwing spears into the backs of retreating Persians is not as demanding as having to look into their eyes and face their weapons, so even I managed to wing at least two of them. I reached the city's walls with enough sweat on my brow and enough blood on my sword to be respectable.

It was a further week before we finished the mopping-up operations which included burning around two hundred beached Persian triremes and organising transport for several thousand prisoners of war, most of them to be sold into slavery. Both Pericles and Ephialtes made no attempt to hide the fact that they were recouping all their expenses on fitting out their triremes by grabbing significant personal booty. I took a roll of red silk for my mother plus a few gold and silver coins for myself. Cimon was immensely rich already and I'm quite sure added considerably to his tally, but for him at this point the winning of a double victory on sea and land was more important, for now he could rank himself as at least the equal of his old rival Themistocles, his own famous father Miltiades and many previous heroes of Athens.

Apart from my small share in the booty I came away from the Eurymedon with some additional mental baggage, though I was not really aware of it at the time. I had seen death and destruction on a massive scale, including atrocities committed as part of declared tactics. I had found out that Persians were human beings like ourselves, mostly just obeying orders. I had been brought up to believe that they were evil vermin, but now I realised that they must now think that we were evil vermin too.

---

1.   Mount Zia, the Mountain of Zeus on Naxos is 3,000 feet high. The sad fate of the Cretan princess Ariadne deserted here by Theseus is the theme of the Strauss opera 'Ariadne auf Naxos'.

2.   Ruins of the ancient Greek port at Knidos can be seen in Yazikoy on the south-west coast of Turkey.

3.   Ruins survive of the Greek — and later Roman — city of Phaselos which was situated near the modern town of Terikova near the Olympic National Park in Turkey.

4.   The Lycian city of Krya or Carya has long since vanished but its site is believed to be near modern Fethiye in Turkey.

5.   The River Eurymedon is now known as the Koprucay. It rises in the Taurus Mountains, is fed also by a number of underground springs and flows down to the Mediterranean through a series of dramatic gorges which are now popular with white-water rafters.

6.   The surviving ruins of the once great Greek city of Aspendos, including its remarkably preserved theatre, are now mainly from the Roman period as it was severely punished for refusing to surrender to Alexander the Great. They are about 25 miles east of the modern Turkish town of Antalya some 10 miles up the River Eurymedon/ Koprucay. The Aspendans were famous amongst other things for sacrificing pigs to the goddess Aphrodite.

CHAPTER FOURTEEN

MARRIAGE

OUR VOYAGE HOME FROM THE Eurymedon was not unpleasant and we spent two days on Kos,[1] the island that the sea god Poseidon had picked up and flung at a giant. It was a benign place where the grasshoppers clacked all day, the larks were effortless in the sky and the trees sagged with juicy apples and pears.

When we arrived back in Athens we strutted around the city like peacocks for several days, enjoying the admiration of the populace, but soon the elation wore off. This was especially true for Cimon now he feared the backlash that seemed to affect all successful generals in Athens, the suspicion that they had lined their pockets and might at any moment try to turn themselves into tyrants. So he made a great fuss about spending his money on public works, finishing his temple of Theseus, building a new aqueduct to the Fountain House, laying out a new park and pandering to the taste of the lower orders by putting up obscene statues of Hermes. He recruited an entourage of artists, including the sculptor Pheidias who was always caked in marble dust whilst he worked on a huge new Zeus. Then there was his tame war painter Polygnotos who was still infatuated with the great man's half-sister, Elpinike, and kept inserting her somewhat incongruously in his huge battle scenes.

Both the two successful captains Ephialtes and Pericles were now trying to convert their military achievements into political careers. And, as I had seen, they had the advantage of having been taught to make clever speeches that could win over the populace. I was to find out years later just how potent and dangerous this could be.

Meanwhile I was past twenty and my mother was making plans for my marriage to Zoe, a pleasant girl whom I had now met a couple of times, albeit without any serious conversations, let alone physical contact. As it happened, since the excitement of Eurymedon I had been conscious of a rapidly increasing desire for a bed-mate and was beginning to think that my earlier affection for Princess Kore had been just a teenage fancy that was anyway doomed from the start by her priestly status. I suppose also I should have mentioned that I had indulged in a highly inefficient coupling with a peasant girl on Naxos – at the time I had tried to put it out of my mind, for I felt I had deserted her just the way Theseus had famously deserted Ariadne on that self-same island. I should also say that despite the fact that many of my comrades in the fleet had succumbed to the temptations of available young males I had never felt more than a momentary urge in that direction even on the longest voyages.

Thus I readily accepted the idea of marrying Zoe, the choice of my family, a girl of impeccable pedigree and from my very limited acquaintance with her, pleasant looking and healthy. It seemed she was as willing as I was myself to become the partner of someone she barely knew, but had been selected by her parents no doubt after discreet research into my background.

How she felt about me I don't know and never thought of asking, for it was all part of normal process in which no strong feelings had to be involved. Psyche my old nurse came to live with us as housekeeper in the family town house near the ceramic quarter[2] and my mother tactfully moved back to Eleusis. The house was comfortable enough with a good deep cesspit which helped it to smell good even in the summer. Like most Athenian houses it had no outside windows, only ones that looked onto the inner court, and it was single-storeyed with a flat tiled roof. As usual there was a master bedroom while the rest of the quarters were divided between male and female. The main door opened outwards into the alleyway to make it harder for strangers to push their way in and it was usual for a slave to ring a bell when people went out to stop wayfarers from being knocked off balance by an unexpected door-opening.

Financially I had no real problems. Our country estate at Eleusis produced around five hundred jars of olive oil and nearly as many of wine, so I had a reasonable income without much effort apart from the occasional call-up to the fleet. But as one of the better-off citizens in due course I would have to pay for fitting out a trireme and that would be serious money.

So married life was very pleasant. Zoe had been brought up in the women's quarters where she heard little of the arguments of the men-folk in her family, and had been taught the main purpose of her life was to breed the next generation of men. She seemed to accept her lot without a grumble and, though I don't think that I was passionately in love, I certainly found great pleasure in doing my bedroom duties, even if her naivety meant that we could not really have an intelligent conversation about life outside the home.

Psyche looked after us both well: she would serve us dried fish, barley bread to dip in wine and fruits in season, goats' cheese as well occasionally as some lamb which Zoe and I both enjoyed. Psyche had a trainee slave girl who fetched water each morning and also went to the market for fresh figs and honey. Zoe was an excellent weaver – she brought her own weighted loom – and made cushion covers and other things for our home. She could play a few tunes on the lyre and hardly spoke in those days unless someone asked her a question. She also looked very sweet as she sat coyly in our hip bath while Psyche tipped jars of water into it. And despite being a general's daughter she seemed quite distressed when the time came for me to go back to the wars.

It has to be said that Psyche really had very little respect for any other women except my mother and regarded my having a wife just as a necessary evil. She believed in the old story of Pandora,[3] that women were inflicted on men as punishment for stealing fire from the gods. Her attitude reminded me of the lines of the poet Simonides,[4] that woman is a mixture of an untidy sow, a lying vixen, a promiscuous bitch and a sex-mad ferret, but I found Zoe totally different. She was utterly devoted, uncomplaining and listened attentively to all my war memories.

As I have indicated the Battle of Eurymedon had crushed the ambitions of Persia for at least a generation, but that did not mean the end of warfare. Now it was the ambitions of Athens, the richest and most successful city in Greece, that excited envy and had to be protected by violent means, intimidating or suppressing even our fellow Greeks if they showed signs of disapproval. I was still too proud of our achievements to see anything wrong with this, but I had begun to question who exactly was benefiting from it all.

This became evident when I once more became ensnared in the machinations of Cimon. As I mentioned earlier he had made sure that the Delphic Oracle blessed the new colony near his gold mine at Eion, but it was still causing problems. Thousands of colonists had been lured up there by the idea of a quick fortune in the gold mines of Mount Pangaeos[5] only for many of them to be slaughtered by the cannabis-crazed Thracians. Their wives had only been spared to be carried off and sold as slaves in Macedonia. So the onus was very much on Cimon to mount a new expedition to protect his colony. By this time I rather fancied getting my own trireme or at least a second in command, so I began to hang around the assembly and make a few contacts.

Rather appropriately, the man I latched onto was Cimon's son Lakedaimonios, his name reflecting his father's passion for all things Spartan. The son was very different from the father, an unambitious trierarch in his late twenties, more at home chatting with the intellectuals than the fighters. He tended to mix with a small crowd at the Agora that included the ubiquitous philosopher Anaxagoras. So I joined them for the odd session, sipping diluted wine and listening to the great man.

'The sun is not a god,' he'd say suddenly to shock us all, drawing in the sand with his stick and taking a good swig of the wine kindly paid for by Lakedaimonios. 'Consider the huge rock that fell from the sky on the Hellespont,' he went on. ' I saw it myself. It made a hole half a mile wide and covered an even bigger area with its debris. No one had ever seen that kind of rock before, so it must have come from a star or the sun or the moon. The sun I believe is a rock, probably as large as the entire Aegean Sea.'

'That's not possible,' commented one of the young bloods in the group.

'Yes it is,' replied Anaxagoras after another swig of wine. 'It's perhaps five hundred miles wide and extremely hot and it revolves round the earth once a day, so it must move very fast.'

'Sit down and make yourself comfortable, Phori,' said Sophocles who had also joined the group along with his latest boyfriend.

'Now tell me why is it hotter in the summer than the winter?' Anaxagoras stared round the group but clearly expected no one to answer.

'Because the sun comes nearer in the summer,' came a familiar voice and I saw that Pericles too had joined us on his way out of the assembly. This was just one of his many ways of practising as a speech-maker.

'Not a bad answer,' admitted Anaxagoras. 'But why does it come nearer?'

This time not even Pericles could think of a witty response.

'You are all highly competent people,' went on Anaxagoras. 'You can manage cities or fleets or armies. I couldn't even manage a small farm. I kept forgetting to plough the fields or prune my vines, so my crops came up at the wrong time and my vines grew weak. But I am destined to think, to tell people why we are born and why we die.'

'If the sun is not a god, what is a god then?' asked Sophocles, who like Pericles preferred to keep the attention focussed as much as possible on himself, regularly asking questions when he was not the least bit concerned with the answer.

'Consider the earth is like a huge round plate with Greece at its centre, Persia on one side and Italy on the other, then if there are gods they too should be in the centre.'

Several of the group nodded knowingly, though I don't know why.

'Gods are the essence of man. We are the first people in history to have freedom of thought.'

'But not freedom from hunger, eh Anaxagoras?' whispered Pericles. 'Would you like some supper tonight?'

Anaxagoras nodded with alacrity, but otherwise pretended to ignore the invitation. 'A god is always present in a man,' he said. 'And a man is always present in a god.' Then after a brief hesitation, 'Time is getting on. We should adjourn this discussion till tomorrow.' And he walked off quickly, following Pericles in the direction of his home and his supper. This gave me the opportunity to tackle Cimon's son and I managed to persuade him quite easily to take me on as his first lieutenant. 'We can discuss the movements of the stars,' he said. 'The skies above Eion are often very clear. Come and try some of my new wine.'

Thus I told Zoe a week later that I would not see her for a month or two and found to my surprise that she was quite tearful.

On the eve of our departure to rescue the colony at Eion there was one of Cimon's famous garden parties for the fleet officers, hosted as ever by the elegant Elpinike and her husband, the torch-bearer Kallias. Cimon himself was in a back room showing off his latest purchases of red vases with obscene pictures. Certainly they came from the lurid end of the ceramic quarter which did good trade with outrageous pictures of copulating fawns and gods misbehaving that seemed to appeal to wealthy male collectors. Soon I had had my fill of the party atmosphere and slipped away through an olive grove towards the road.

Near the entrance of the garden, standing alone by a small fountain, I saw a woman in white with long dark hair. She had changed a lot since I last saw her, but I recognised her at once as Princess Kore. She no longer had the simple joy of girlhood; she was paler and her eyes showed suffering, yet she was even more beautiful than before. She took a step towards me and there was a kind of suppressed energy.

'Kore,' I said. 'The last time I saw you, you were descending into Hades.'

'I have done that twice since then and come back twice too, more or less. You have seen death too, I hear?'

For the first time I felt a pang about the massacre at Krya. 'Yes, I have,' I said.

'I hope you see life too, then,' she said and turned away. Then looking briefly over her shoulder, 'I hear you've married. I hope you'll be happy.'

'Wait.' I pleaded, not knowing what to say.

She shook her head and disappeared into the darkness.

The following morning I joined my new ship, the *Athena*.

---

1.   The island of Kos is now a popular holiday destination just a few miles off the Turkish coast near Bodrum. It has a long and remarkable history for it sent a contingent of troops to aid the Greek side in the siege of Troy. It was also the home city of the pioneering doctor Hippocrates who devised the Hippocratic oath.

2.   The famous potters quarter of Athens, the Kerameikos, was centred round the little River Eridanos which had a silting of rich red clay. These days the river is largely hidden in an underground culvert. However the district of Kerameikos still survives and the excavations needed for its new metro station unearthed a number of ancient ruins with many artefacts now housed in the Kerameikos Museum, as well as around a thousand human burials, probably attributable to the plague that hit Athens when our hero was in his forties.

3.   According to Greek religion Pandora was the first woman on earth, rather like Eve in the Old Testament, so in the same way she took the blame for nearly everything bad in the world, but especially the misbehaviour of the male sex which had succumbed to her wiles. Pandora opened box = Eve picked apple.

4.   Simonides, the poet from the island of Samos, had also founded a new city whose name he adopted for himself, but was a noted misogynist.

5.   The gold mines in Thrace, including at Mount Pangaeos, which rises to 6000 feet, had a long history. Even quite recently a company appropriately called Eldorado aimed to open a new mine on the Perama Hill. Greece certainly needs the money.

CHAPTER FIFTEEN

COMMAND AT LAST

LUCKILY, DESPITE A SEVERE ATTACK of nerves, I made no obvious mistakes when we cast off in the trireme *Athena* along with the rest of Cimon's fleet that morning, for Lakedaimonios was a rather over-anxious, irritable trierarch, as if living always in his father's shadow. What is more it was my first voyage without the caustic advice of Kleistes, who was still on the *Hecuba*. Soon we were rounding Cape Sounion and heading for an overnight stop at Skyros. The old pirate base was looking a lot smarter than it had on our previous visit. Now stocks of timber and pitch, dried fish and dates were all stacked up neatly by the harbour for replenishing visiting ships and the new colonists had made little gardens amongst the rocks by their cottages.

From Skyros our course was northwards and the following night we anchored off Neae.[1] Then after a good day's sail the next day using Mount Athos as a landmark, we passed Eion on our way to Thasos. The reason for this was that the islanders of Thasos had decided that they wanted a bigger share from the nearby gold mines and had banded together with the local tribesmen to make life difficult for beleaguered Eion. Naturally this also involved a threat to Cimon's main source of income, his private gold mine nearby. Thus our mission was to search out the Thasian fleet which was rumoured to be much the same size as our own, but was lurking somewhere behind the island.

Thasos[2] was in many ways the most beautiful island I had seen so far on my voyages. Its steep sides were covered almost entirely in trees which came right down to the shore. This plentiful supply of timber as well as its fine wine, its silver and gold mines had made the islanders wealthy and perhaps a little greedy. I'd heard the dreadful story of King Tereus of Thasos who'd married a princess from Athens. They had a son together but the adulterous Tereus raped his wife's sister Philomela and cut out her tongue, so she couldn't tell anybody. The resourceful Philomela then wove a tapestry which explained the ghastly deed to her sister, who promptly served up her little son to the boy's hungry father on a platter. To follow, she turned herself into a nightingale, her sister into a swallow and her husband into an ugly hoopooe. Hence the generally unsavoury reputation of the Thasians.

When we eventually caught up with the Thasos fleet they tried to avoid a pitched battle so Cimon adopted his favourite tactic of sailing round them in ever-decreasing circles until they began to get in eachothers' way. The bluff worked, for Cimon was anxious to avoid too much fighting himself, as he wanted to keep his crews intact. Half the Thasos fleet surrendered and the rest scuttled back into their harbour.

My captain, Lakedaimonios, had been more hesitant than usual, perhaps inhibited by having his father watching from his flagship, but I flatter myself that I made up for his deficiencies and the *Athena* acquitted herself well in this action. However, it turned out that defeating their fleet was one thing, but to capture their city was a much more daunting task. It stood on a rocky outcrop by the shore with good strong walls and the surrounding area too steep for the easy landing of troops. Above it loomed a huge temple of Apollo and this was supposedly the birthplace of the goddess Demeter, so it was held in great respect.

Cimon was well used to sieges but this one was particularly difficult and I was more than relieved when no one called on my rock-climbing skills, for I am sure that any attempt to scale those walls would have ended in death. In fact it was the death of one of our trierarchs who went too close to the walls that led directly to my next extraordinary adventure. I was unexpectedly summoned to report to the general on his flagship.

Thus a tender collected me and I climbed on board the *Salaminia* where I was ushered into Cimon's cabin. It was the only ship in the fleet that had such a cabin and it even boasted several of his risqué painted jars on a shelf. There were two other senior trierarchs standing there with him and at the back, looking quite out of place, stood the sinister figure of Aristodikos, who always seemed to appear when least expected.

'Wait a minute, Euphorion,' said Cimon and turned as if to finish his business with Aristodikos. 'Tell King Alexander[3] that I insist on his co-operation or no more gold,' he said. 'One week to make up his mind.' And Aristodikos was dismissed, presumably to head off to Macedonia with his message for the gold-loving king. Then Cimon turned to me. 'You will have noticed, Euphorion, that we lost a trierarch today. Most unfortunate. Now it's not that you're the most experienced candidate, but I want someone discreet for a special mission.

'Thank you,' I said, stunned and delighted.

'I'll give you two days to work up with your crew and then you'll be sent to a secret destination on your own. Carry on.'

I was then rowed across to my new command, the *Medea*, amazed that despite Pericles reprimanding me I had still been promoted so soon. As I stared at the sun-spattered blue sea, I thought this is a thing I love, the blue, the saltiness, the gentle swell, the friendly dolphins, the challenge of mastering water and wind, the power to visit every island in the world. A huge sea eagle was circling far above, surveying the tiny humans far below.

A few minutes later I was climbing a little self-consciously onto the deck of the *Medea*. The last thing on my mind was my little wife to whom I had said I would be away for a matter of a few months. Now it might be much longer, but at that moment it was my career that mattered. Zoe would be busy at her loom in our comfortable Athens home whilst I faced unknown dangers across the sea. And for the first time in my life I felt important.

1. Euphorion may have made a mistake here for according to Pliny the island of Neae rose out of the sea after an earthquake and may not have been there in 465BC.

2. Thasos lies off the Macedonian coast of northern Greece, has always been rich in minerals and is now a popular holiday resort with fine beaches and many medieval monasteries.

3. King Alexander I of Macedonia died in 454 BC and was a remote ancestor of Alexander III, otherwise known as the Great.

CHAPTER SIXTEEN

A SECRET MISSION

FOR THE NEXT TWO DAYS I was allowed to practise manoeuvres with my new crew whilst the rest of the fleet began a blockade of the city of Thasos with the objective of starving it into surrender. Then I received my secret orders, which filled me with considerable surprise, for they were to deliver a letter to Mnesiptolema, the priestess of Didyme in the Asian city of Myos which was still in Persian hands. It would mean a journey of some three hundred miles just to get there, but at least I would miss the tedium of a long blockade and I would be able to enjoy my first command without feeling constantly under the critical eyes of senior trierarchs. In addition Pericles, who was present at my briefing, handed me a small package for delivery to Miletos. 'You'll be passing there anyway,' he said.

Naturally I didn't refuse and the following dawn *Medea* left the fleet on a south-easterly course. By midday we were passing Samothrace[1], an island about the same size as Thasos, which amazingly — according to legend — had once been submerged by a huge flood. Since then its people had become very pious and were well-known for giving refuge to escaped criminals and other asylum seekers.

Meanwhile I was still relishing the joy of independent command and as we rowed at a steady pace with little help from the wind even the seagulls and dolphins seemed to respond to my orders. Luckily I had spent some time in this area during my other cruises, so I could sense that my shipmaster was steering us in the right direction. However, I felt that every eye was on me, waiting for me to make some silly error or show lack of confidence in what I was doing. Two of my junior officers had been in the year behind me at Kynosarges, but were a cocky pair who already thought they knew everything and would be quite happy to see me make a fool of myself.

By the evening, despite my misgivings, we had covered another thirty miles and made it as far as Imbros where we half beached for the night with two anchors out at our bows. So I began to feel a little less insecure. At least we got fresh water and the seamen rested, though I slept poorly, constantly worried that our anchors might not hold or we would be stranded too high on the beach or that the oarsmen would mutiny or desert. None of these things had ever worried me when I was not in command.

The next day we headed due south down the Asian coast towards Lesbos which I had visited before and which made navigation easy. What's more there was a useful off-shore breeze to help us on our way. So we were able to enjoy a pleasant evening moored in the harbour of Mytilene and I actually took the risk of letting most of the crew have some time ashore.

Next morning we continued southwards to the narrow strait between Chios and the mainland for another event-free night at anchor. Chios is a mixture of rocky outcrops and fertile orchards, so we restocked with fruit and olives and some red mastic for the last stage of our voyage. From this point onwards we were mostly in Persian-held waters close to the mainland so we kept a double watch, but luckily no Persian ships ventured out to challenge us.

Thus after another two days, one under sail and the other mainly rowing, we made it at last to the mouth of the River Meander.[2] I had decided to leave my errand for Pericles till my return journey, so we had passed by the horrific ruins of Miletos, so ruthlessly destroyed by the Persians twenty years earlier. It was still only partially rebuilt, for all the inhabitants had been killed or enslaved. Now only a strip of coastline was back in Greek control, but the area inland known as Magnesia belonged to Persia and my destination was the regional capital. Thus after a night beached near the mouth we prepared to row up the river, a frustrating task since it was famously far from being in a straight line.

Luckily the potential long ordeal for our oarsmen was avoided, for suddenly an ornate barge appeared from nowhere and its coxswain gestured to come alongside. Mnesiptolema had sent him to pick me up and there was a suitable place where the *Medea* could be beached to await my return in a few days. I was far from sure of our safety but accepted the ride up to Myos and left my ship-master in charge. It turned out to be sensible for the river soon became very shallow and at least the barge could cut some of the corners; so my crew were spared rowing in that airless atmosphere.

Thus after a couple of hours we came to a small neat city on the north bank of the Meander. It was surrounded by date palms and the buildings were ornate in a style more Asiatic than Greek.

'Princess Mnesiptolema is expecting you,' said the barge-master and I was ushered onto a jetty, then led through two large stone halls with beautiful mosaic floors and past a large statue of Apollo in the Ionian style. Finally I entered the temple of Didyme which was dark and cool, and sitting at the far end was its priestess dressed in long scarlet robes. She was a woman perhaps a few years older than myself with a beauty which I can best describe as aggressive.

'Thank you for coming all this way to visit us, Euphorion,' she said in perfect Greek. Then as my eyes grew accustomed to the dim light I saw that sitting behind her on a golden throne was an old man in exotic eastern robes. 'My father the governor of Magnesia,' she said.

Now, at last, the truth began to penetrate my stupid skull, which had been so preoccupied with my sudden promotion that I had failed to remember what had been common gossip. Despite the robes and the bulging signs of obesity I now recognised the old man as our former chief general Themistocles, the man exiled from all the cities of Greece and made a governor by his former enemy the Great King of Persia. And of course I remembered that his daughter had been given the well-remunerated post of high priestess of Didyme, the Asian version of Apollo.[3]

'Welcome, Euphorion, or may I call you Phori?' said the old man. 'I knew your father well. We were quite close at Marathon. And how is my old friend Aeschylus? I hear, like me, he ran into trouble with the authorities in Athens. Pity, for he stood up for me rather well in his Persians play. Ironic. I was the city's best general and he was its best playwright and we're both turfed out. Never mind, we live very comfortably in Myos.'

He smiled at his daughter.

'It's an honour to meet you, Themistocles,' I said, handing over the package from Cimon. ' I was only five years old when you won Salamis.'

'Strange,' he went on. 'The Athenians couldn't abide me becoming rich, but the Persians encourage it. Now I am master of four great cities instead of one. Anyway if you'll excuse me I will go next door and study this message from my old rival Cimon. Everything he knows he learned from me and that he cannot stand. I expect he just wants to pick my brains. Perhaps you will join me later for supper and bring me up to date with the latest gossip from Athens. Meanwhile my daughter will show you round Myos, though of course my three other cities are even bigger and richer.'

I wondered that a man of his great achievements could not resist these odd little displays of vanity. 'I even have my own oracle,' he added. 'It will prophesy anything I want for a small consideration.' He winked and shambled out.

Mnesiptolema smiled and took me out into a small courtyard surrounded by date palms and sweet ciceley, then ordered a slave to bring us wine. It was undiluted, remarkably cool, sweet and flavoured with some spice like myrrh which made it seem pleasantly strong.

'The good thing about the cult of Didyme,' she said, 'is that the devotees are mostly very rich and generous in their donations to the temple. And as I'm sure you know the family of Themistocles all like money.'

'Don't we all,' I replied affably, relaxing now after six arduous days of responsibility and wakefulness. 'It makes life more pleasant.'

'Yes,' she said. 'So many Athenians seem to despise pleasure. I can't think why. Plenty of slaves, fine silks to wear, good food and beautiful horses. I was just a child when we had to leave Athens, but I'm told it was dreadfully dull even then. Just a smelly little house even for an important man like my father. I prefer it here.'

'I can understand that,' I said without hypocrisy as the scented air and wine went to my head. Long days at sea with nothing but the odd diluted cup of second pressing made me more susceptible than usual, though in retrospect I felt my behaviour was highly irresponsible.

'I haven't met many Greek men recently,' she went on. 'I miss that side of things. My husband is my step-brother, since I really didn't want to marry a Persian. I'm sure you understand.'

'Indeed I do,' I said, but I didn't.

'He's away in Sardis now on business. Have some more wine.' She flicked her fingers at a slave girl, pointed to our cups, then dismissed her with a wave. 'Come here and look at the city.'

I followed her up some steps to a small rampart where the palms waved gently behind us. Momentarily I remembered Zoe and then forgot her again.

'I am priestess of Apollo Didymaios, but I also belong to the Maenads so I worship the Phallus,' said the priestess with cultivated archness, looking me straight in the eyes. 'It is the age-old custom of the priestesses of Magnesia to give themselves once a year to the first man they meet.'

She paused and then went on in a half chant as if she was leading a service. 'It is in honour of the earth mother and thus we celebrate the rebirth of the world. As you know when Osiris[4] was murdered his distraught mistress Isis could find every piece of his body except the one that mattered most. But to that specially valuable part which was missing she chose to give the greatest honour.'

She paused again significantly, then brushed her hand quickly down the front of my tunic. 'As in days gone by I hereby anoint the living memory of Osiris.'

It may seem that Mnesiptolema was mixing her cults here, but in those days it was not unusual for fanatical ladies to concoct mixtures of god stories. I have to admit that I found her fervour compelling and she produced one of those alabaster bottles which I believe some married women keep, at least I have been told so. She lifted my tunic and splashed some liquid over me.

'The goddess, the priestess and the harlot are all one,' she went on, loosening her scarlet robe so that it fell back from her shoulders. 'I have two though Artemis has twenty, but mine are more beautiful.'

She leaned forward and the combination of wine, perfumes and flesh like Pentelic marble convinced me that it would be sacrilegious to interrupt such a holy ceremony. Our mouths met in a joint prayer to Isis as she searched for the missing part of Osiris. And when she found it she showed it reverential respect for several minutes.

'Blessed be Eros,'[5] she intoned, then in her normal voice 'You've been at sea a long time, Phori.'

To this day I'm not quite sure what she meant, but I felt I had performed my part of this foreign ritual very adequately and could not be faulted in carrying out the diplomatic mission entrusted to me. I had simply done my duty as an Athenian officer.

'Praise be to Phallus,' she concluded. Then she added practically, 'Now my father will be ready for his supper.' She repinned her robe and went down to the courtyard while I followed in something of a daze.

We then partook of one of the most exotic meals I had ever tasted, including some red-band fish deliciously cooked with oil and cheese. There were several different kinds of fresh fish and meat which I hardly recognised, vegetables with delicious spices which were totally new to me as well as three or four different aromatic wines. We spent an hour or more with Themistocles who rambled on quite happily about himself. He laughed loudly at my description of Aristides as a poor old man living with his two crusty sisters on a pig farm at Phaleron. He also seemed aware of some business between Cimon and King Alexander of Macedonia, but that meant little to me at that time.

'The only thing I miss about Athens is the theatre,' he said. 'I so much enjoyed your uncle's work. As for Sophocles I only saw one of his plays, the Ajax, and I thought he was trying to be too clever.'

'Have you a message to go back to Cimon?' I asked.

'I do not know why he thinks I should help him,' he answered. 'But I'm glad to say I think he's playing with fire.' He laughed at his own joke and passed me a sealed package. 'Don't lose it. See the satrap's seal? Don't let it fall into the hands of Greeks or Persians. Now off with you. Salute the owl for me. I shall never see Athens again.' And he turned away.

Mnesiptolema seemed to have rather lost interest in the proceedings, but kissed me perfunctorily by the little pier where the barge was waiting to take me back to the Medea. I never saw her father again and Mnesiptolema only once in the far distance.

Meanwhile I must pause for a moment and report on events of which I was not personally a witness but were significant in my life. By the time I had become a fledgling trierarch my former mentor Ephialtes had been elected one of the nine generals and had taken a fleet round the Aegean to intimidate any of the island states that might have contemplated rebelling from our league. In fact no blood seems to have been shed. However his real ambitions were non-military and it was becoming clear that he wanted to be the effective leader of Athens. He had a long-lasting grudge against those noble families which had become wealthier or more powerful than his own and was determined to destroy as many of them as he could, in particular the family of Cimon, his one great rival for supreme power.

Thus he made use of Cimon's absence during the Thasos campaign to stir up public opinion against the old guard and began taking them to court on charges of petty incompetence whilst in office. Many of those charged were supporters of Cimon and in due course he began his attack on Cimon himself, accusing him of embezzlement after the Amphipolis incident. Cimon was so rich and had so many fingers in his gold mine and other affairs that he was not a difficult target, so it was just a matter of time before he would face ostracism and exile.

Relentlessly Ephialtes began weeding out all the rich aristocrats from the upper assembly and destroying the political influence of the old guard. Then with an easy majority in the main assembly he passed a succession of reforms that allowed poor citizens to be paid for doing jury duty or attending assembly, thus ensuring that he had plenty of votes on his side. So Ephialtes was now the most powerful man in Athens, with Pericles as his second-in-command. Whether they genuinely believed in democracy or were just using a populist approach to help their own careers no one really knew, perhaps not even the man himself. The only real problem for Ephialtes was that his enemies and rivals were out of office but they were not dead. So there were many bitter men looking for revenge and a return of their good fortune. And he also had a very ambitious second-in-command snapping at his heels, Pericles.

---

1.   The rocky island of Samothrace is most famous for the statue that was found in its ruined temple, the Winged Victory, now in the Louvre Museum, Paris. In ancient times it was a base for mystery cults related to the main one at Eleusis. The island is little developed and popular for camping holidays and climbing as its Mount Fengari rises to 5,000 feet.

2.   The River Meander, now known as the Buyuk Menderes, is south of Izmir in Turkey. Very prone to silting it gave its name to wandering rivers all over the world. Only the ruined temples of Myos or Myous survive as the town was abandoned after a plague in ancient times.

3.   In this area the surname given to the god Apollo was Didyme, due to the great sanctuary dedicated to him at the town of Didyma, now Didim in Turkey. Ruins of the temple survive near the Meander.

4.   I think it is unlikely that Euphorion would have heard of Osiris for at this time he was strictly an Egyptian god. The confusing legend that he was a product of one of the chief god Zeus's one-night stands was invented later when Egyptian religion became

quite fashionable amongst some Greeks. Mnesiptolema with her wide range of contacts was clearly aware of the story that he was killed by his evil brother Typhon, who chopped up the body and threw all the bits into the sea (or the Nile said some) apart from the genitals. The wife of Osiris was Isis who got her revenge and was herself later worshipped also by Greeks and Romans as the goddess who first produced corn.

5. According to the poet Hesiod, Eros was the fourth god of the Kosmos, but the Asiatic Greeks were more inclined to turn harlots into goddesses, whereas in Athens it was quite a fashion to prefer the god Hermes as a symbol of male virility. Liddell & Scott's *Greek-English Lexicon* coyly translates the phallus as 'membrum virile' an emblem of which was carried in solemn procession during the Bacchic orgies as a symbol of the regenerative power of nature. Such a cult was to play a significant role in Euphorion's very last adventure.

CHAPTER SEVENTEEN

AN EARTHQUAKE AND ITS CONSEQUENCES

SO MUCH HAD HAPPENED DURING MY trip up the Meander that I nearly forgot to deliver my other message, but luckily I remembered just as we were about to pass Miletos.[1] That once beautiful city was near the entrance of a lake at the mouth of the Meander so the journey did not take long. The package from Pericles just had the name Hippodamos on it and the address of a tavern.

Nevertheless as soon as I entered the tavern I saw a very strange excitable-looking young man holding forth in one corner and instinctively guessed that he was the sort of person to whom Pericles would be writing. He took the letter, glanced at it, gave me a bright smile and said. 'Perfect symmetry, that is worth crossing the sea for. Everything perfectly in place.'

I had no idea what he was talking about, but assumed that he was yet another of those travelling philosophers who were becoming so fashionable and came to Athens for free meals.

'Tell Pericles I'll be in Athens before the winter,' he said and offered me some wine.

It was at least a year before I learned that he was not a philosopher at all but a kind of architect who planned new cities, and Pericles even at this early stage in his career was already planning to rebuild Athens as the greatest city in Europe.

Meanwhile I refused the wine having had something of a surfeit of it in Myos and was in a hurry to rejoin the fleet. Apart from one nasty storm when the water started coming in through our lower oar-holes we had a good crossing from Miletos, passing Cape

Mykale and making it home with only three stops: Ikaria, Mykonos and Kythnos. The summer must have been all but over when we at last came alongside in the Piraeus and berthed next to my old ship the *Ariadne*.

'Ship your phallic oars up your backsides, you crowd of Samian pig-farmers,' came the familiar shout of Kleistes from Ariadne's deck. I don't think he'd recognised my ship. 'One scratch on my outriggers and I'll have you all sent to the silver mines. Ah, it's you, Phori, I might have guessed.'

We in fact came alongside fairly smoothly and I noticed that the flagship *Salaminia* was also back in harbour, but deserted except for one sentry. So I would have to go back up town to deliver the message to Cimon. By chance it was one of the Mystery days and across the bay at Phaleron I could see a crowd of initiates washing away their sins in the sea. I wondered if Princess Kore was there with her father, the high priest.

An hour later I was weaving my way through the busy streets of the port and up the road to Athens. Before going home I felt I had to deliver Cimon's message.

'Thank you, Euphorion,' said the great man, touching his nose to remind me that this was a secret. 'Not a word. Anyway come back for the Mysteries party tonight. My sister is hosting it here as usual. And I have another job for you.'

That evening I quickly called home to see Zoe, who to my surprise seemed angry and hurt rather than pleased to see me, especially when I said I was going out again.

'It's business really,' I said. 'You shouldn't complain.'

'I'm not complaining,' she said with tears in her eyes. 'I've just spent the entire summer weaving and spinning and worrying about you, but you barely ask how I am before you go out again.' She put down the hedgehog skin comb she used for her wool.

'How are you?' I asked guiltily.

'You don't care,' she said. In a way she was right. The house seemed small after the spaces of Thessaly and the palaces of Myos. Zoe too seemed small compared with Mnesiptolema and Elpinike.

'Your career is what matters,' she went on resignedly. 'I shouldn't have shown any distress. Do you want supper before you go?'

'Yes, but quickly if you don't mind. It's half an hour's walk back to Cimon's.'

Psyche came in with the supper and gave me a surprisingly hostile look, considering she was supposed to have been my nurse, not Zoe's.

'I wish I could go to parties like that,' said Zoe.

'This is for the Mysteries. You could come if you were initiated.'

'This is your favourite eel stew with beetroot gravy,' said Psyche grudgingly as if she disapproved strongly of my behaviour. 'With figs and broad beans to follow.'

Half an hour later I set off through the dark narrow streets thinking it was time I sent Zoe off to live in the farm at Eleusis. It was important for me at this stage to be close to the hub of things, but there was no need for her to stay in the city all year. It was not that I had any desire to take a mistress or be unfaithful, nor did I really feel any guilt about my meeting with Mnesiptolema, when after all I had been on duty, but I have to admit that I thought of Zoe more like my house and my orchards, normal features of the life of an Athenian trierarch, things to take for granted.

As usual anyone that mattered was at Cimon's party, including General Myronides, my father-in-law, the rising stars like Ephialtes and Pericles, plus the leaders of the younger group like Sophocles. I was one of at least a hundred serving trierarchs and there were at least the same number from the new intake of initiates to the Mysteries. In fact it seemed that to belong to the Mysteries was quite helpful for a political or military career.

'Have you heard about the earthquake?' was almost the sole topic of conversation as we sipped Cimon's excellent wine beneath the rustling plane trees.

'Near Mount Taygettos. Sparta is all but destroyed,' said one of the guests.

'The Messenians have seized the chance to revolt. The Spartans will be slaughtered,' added another, showing more signs of complacency than of sympathy.

I noticed there was a red-clad Spartan envoy in deep conversation with Cimon and that ever-present go-between Aristodikos of Tanagra. They must be the source of the news.

I should explain that Mount Taygettos[2] above the River Eurotas overhangs the somewhat scattered city of Sparta, and as I heard later the earthquake had caused a landslide that engulfed a significant part of the town, killing a number of the ruling class, whereas the slave-class of Messenians and helots had been relatively unscathed. This natural catastrophe seemed to the underclass like a gift from heaven, for despite a huge numerical advantage they were normally too timid to show any sign of rebellion against their hated masters. But now the earthquake had tipped the balance more in their favour. The Spartans themselves, of course, did no work but depended entirely on the despised helots for food and every other service.

'This could be a great opportunity for democracy,' said Ephialtes, who was in a group with Pericles and the free-drink-following philosopher Anaxagoras of Clazomenai. I was to think later that it is amazing how democrats in one city assume that all other cities should be the same. 'The Spartans have no work-force left,' went on Ephialtes, warming to his subject. 'So they lose their power and Athens is left the unchallenged leader of Greece. And we can insist on helping to install democracy in every city that does not already have it.'

'Oligarchy[3] is deeply pernicious,' said Anaxagoras. 'Almost as bad as tyranny.'

Pericles nodded his approval. 'Let Sparta fall,' he said and Anaxagoras clapped his hands. The group of sculptors and architects moved over to join them. Myron, who had a large statue workshop near the ceramic quarter, was delighted, for the Spartans were notoriously devoid of interest in the arts. They thought art bred vanity and corruption amongst their warriors and perhaps they were right.

At the other side of the garden, however, different views prevailed.

'We cannot let Sparta fall,' said Cimon in a loud voice and those with a more conservative frame of mind began to gather round him. 'That would make Greece like a man with one leg and the other lame.'

The elegant Elpinike squeezed his elbow in approval. Myronides nodded his head. Aristodikos and the Spartan envoy began quietly circulating, flattering the other officers and preparing the ground for a rescue mission to help the Spartans put down their wretchedly treated peasants.

'To take advantage of one state's weakness would be to betray all we have fought for,' was the suave line. 'After all, our own slaves might revolt as well and where would we be then?'

None of these arguments had any appeal for Ephialtes, who had always been a Sparta-hater just as he was a hater of all aristocratic groups, but maybe he thought that if he let Cimon have his own way it would be a final nail in his coffin, for whether he was on the winning or losing side in Sparta he would be wrong in the eyes of the massed ranks in the assembly. And Cimon would be finished.

Soon I grew bored with all the political manoeuvring and mingled with the new initiates, wishing them luck on the Sacred Way. Psamos and Gaia were there but there was no sign of Kore. Besides I felt that I had no right even to look for her. I had allowed myself to commit impious lechery of the kind that ruined the great Miltiades and now also been callous to my own wife.

I stood in line to thank Cimon and when it came to my turn he said, 'Come and see me in two days. I'm putting together a special force. You're a wall climber and I want you in it.'

I thanked him again and set off home, but just as I came to the gate a familiar figure emerged from behind a tree.

'You're not coming to Eleusis this year, Phori?'

'No, Kore,' I said, totally at a loss due to her sudden unexpected appearance. 'But I hope the Mysteries go well,' I added lamely.

'It's never a good time for me,' she said. 'I hate the autumn and having to disappear. How's married life? Are you happy?'

She seemed to be treating me like a complete stranger, yet I sensed she was just as much at a loss as I was myself.

'What is happiness, as Anaxagoras keeps asking?' I replied, reluctant to imply that Zoe had completely replaced her in my mind. It was because she was a priestess that I had not been able to advance my relationship with her, so it certainly wasn't my fault. Yet I still felt a bit guilty. 'I don't know,' I said. 'I suppose I am most of the time.'

'I am destined to marry the god Poseidon. It's the family tradition.' She shrugged her shoulders and I sensed a slight hint of self pity.

'That's confusing religion with real life,' I said.

'But they are confused.'

I found myself looking at her again, the face I could never remember when I wanted to, the tall beautiful woman who was still like a child, not quite a goddess, not quite human. Yet utterly different from the straightforward uncomplicated Zoe.

'Keep safe, Phori,' she said and vanished into the trees.

I could not help feeling that something had gone very wrong with my life, but I didn't understand why. Perhaps I was just tired.

An hour later I was back home. Zoe murmured gently as I lay down beside her. She turned and clung to me, tears trickling against my face.

'I'm glad you're back from the sea,' she said and I was glad too.

The next morning I heard there was a row going on at the Assembly so I headed in that direction. It was soon obvious that the new breed of officers led by Ephialtes were mounting a verbal assault on the older guard led by Cimon.

'Gold was seen to change hands,' was the theme. Cimon was accused of abandoning his siege of Thasos and bribing the Macedonians to let him keep his gold mine going.

'Lies, lies,' shouted Cimon's allies, perhaps sensing that the crowds were planning the downfall of yet another Athenian hero.

'We have witnesses,' came the reply.

Then one of Cimon's minions read a formal announcement. 'Thasos will fall within the month. We fully expect to take a hundred talents in gold the moment the walls are breached and Cimon assures me all this gold will come straight back to Athens.'

The crowd murmured approval. Ephialtes let out a mocking laugh, and Pericles who seemed to want the approval of both sides made a bland speech urging reconciliation. Yet it was clear that Cimon had come very close to losing his position as chief general. He still had enough friends at the Assembly who knew how lavish he was with his wealth, but Ephialtes had growing support and the situation might soon change, especially if Cimon made any kind of mistake.

When I called on him a day later there was certainly no sign of the great man losing any of his confidence or convictions. He was sitting on his portico drawing with a stick on a and map of the Peloponnese.[4]

'King Archidamos is here in Sparta,' he said, pointing at the centre of his map. 'He's young and inexperienced, but he's done quite well so far, suppressing the main group of rebels. Mantinea here,' he pointed to a mark in the sand, 'has promised help. Argos here cannot be relied upon.' He snorted in disgust before going on.

'The Argos crowd may even seek to take advantage out of sheer jealousy. There have apparently been several massacres of Spartans in this area near the city where the earthquake did the most damage. These helots[5] are utterly without scruple once they see an opportunity for freedom from Spartan control. No respect for man, woman or child. We cannot allow that kind of thing to spread to other parts of Greece. We may not like it, but we must help the Spartans.'

'I heard the earthquake was their own fault,' said one of Cimon's senior officers. 'They killed some helots who'd sought sanctuary in the shrine of Poseidon. Strange that such a superstitious people should make such an obvious mistake.'

'They have always known that they have to be utterly ruthless with the helots. One sign of weakness and it's the end.'

'So when do we start?' asked one of the keener junior generals.

'The area where we have been asked to help is Mount Ithome,' replied Cimon, indicating another mark in the sand. 'The Spartans acknowledge that we're better at sieges than they are, and a large group of helots are holding out in a fort on Ithome, one of the highest and hardest to climb spots in Greece.[6] That's why I've asked some of our best climbers like Euphorion here to join our special force. We leave the day after tomorrow.'

There seemed general agreement amongst this group at least that the Spartans would be grateful for our help, but I noticed the strange Aristodikos having an animated conversation with Myronides at the back of the portico.

'Euphorion,' Cimon called. 'I want you to organise a platoon of engineers. There's plenty of timber down there, so we'll only need to carry tools, saws, nails, ropes and a few long ladders. We need carpenters and more good climbers. Take this money and get down to the craft quarter to buy what you need. By the way,' he said speaking again to the whole group, 'In order to get the agreement of the Assembly for this expedition I had to let Ephialtes pick all the men for the other regiment. Troublemakers I expect, but I'm sure we'll cope.'

The others laughed and I headed off to bargain for supplies at the stalls in the craft quarter. At the tannery stalls near the Acropolis I played off one against another until I had a whole ass-load of leather thongs for holding scaffolding together. Then it was off to the stalls of the metalworkers for grappling hooks, axes, wedges and big nails. In the end I had eight ass-loads and found Kleistes to act as my assistant. He would bring ten ships carpenters to meet me at the Delphic Gate at dawn the next day.

That evening I spent with Zoe who seemed strangely tetchy and lacking in understanding of the importance of my mission. I lectured her on the duty of a soldier's wife to support her husband in his patriotic duties. She apologised one minute and the next started ranting about the stupidity of war. I put down her sudden changes of mood to a very sheltered upbringing.

Next morning I met Kleistes and our eight ass-loads of supplies had been transferred to two large horse drawn carts, and so we set off to join up with Cimon's main army near Megara.

Soon we were at the isthmus of Corinth where the crazy old dictator Periander had thought he could build a canal. We could see the huge temple of Apollo and the menacing fortress high on its rock above the city. We didn't place much trust in the Corinthians – 'Never trust a Corinthian,' said Kleistes. 'All they want is other people's money or other people's bodies, no matter which sex.'

Cimon had made use of Aristodikos to act as an emissary to ensure us a safe journey through their lands, for the Corinthians were always very wary of strangers and like to take a fee from people crossing their precious isthmus. Then it was on to Nemea, famous for its Games which were nearly as grand as those at Olympia and the place where Heracles killed a lion as one of his twelve labours. From there it was steadily uphill to Arcadia and Mantinea where the River Ophis circled round the town like a moat. Here amongst the hills were many dense forests of oak trees and the high meadows were full of cattle such as we hardly saw in Attica.

We seemed to keep going uphill until we came to a narrow mountain pass, and we were guided through it by a small Spartan platoon whose officer eventually pointed out to us the rock-top fortress of Ithome. It was hard to believe that anyone could be living in such an inaccessible spot, but we were informed that eight thousand slave-helots had sought shelter in its walls. In addition they had an ample supply of water and apparently enough food to last a year. So our only chance was to take the place by storm.

King Archidamos made a brief appearance at our camp, a man no older than myself, but even more arrogant in his posture than the average Spartan.

He spoke to us somewhat patronisingly, implying that he had only asked for reinforcements because Athenians were more accustomed to the somewhat despised techniques of siege-craft, whereas Spartan warriors were gentlemen who fought only against their equals. It was no wonder that rumours were soon circulating that some of our troops, the ones under Ephialtes, were muttering that they quite sympathised with the helots who had to slave away all their lives for these red-cloaked masters.

Within three days my group were ready to start the siege, but I decided to do a solo reconnaissance of the rocks below the citadel in order to assess our chances. It took me over an hour to climb a narrow gully where the stream at that time of the year was no more than a trickle. In some places the sides were so close that even where there were no footholds I could lever myself up by squeezing my back up one side and pushing with my feet on the other. With ropes and grappling hooks I was confident that I could bring up my whole platoon this way as well as our ladders and other equipment. All I would then have to do was find a way through or over the walls of the citadel. These, as I had expected, were quite rudimentary on this side of the fortress, for the occupants clearly regarded their natural defences as all-but impregnable. Then all we would have to do was fight our way to the gates and let in the main army.

I had now reached the base of the man-made walls where they joined the top of the cliff. With only a narrow toe-hold and a drop of several hundred feet beneath me I edged slowly along to where the wall seemed lower. It would be difficult but not impossible for Kleistes and the rest of my men, so I was feeling intensely exhilarated at the prospect of a famous victory, something even to compare with my father's feat at Marathon. I crept along to a slit which appeared to go through the wall and would let me see what was on the other side. It did —and I could hear voices.

Carefully placing my feet in case I slipped I put my eye to the aperture which I think was probably a drain. After the bright sunlight outside it took me a moment to adjust my vision to the shaded area inside the walls. Then I saw there was a girl no older than Zoe sitting under a tree with a small baby at her breast. The baby sucked hungrily and sometimes the girl smiled, sometimes pushed her breast to help the baby get at his food. Two other children were playing beside her, and beyond in a courtyard were more children and a couple of women, one very old, the other quite young. One of them was peeling acorns which must mean they were very short of food.

I don't know how long I clung there but it was at least a few minutes. The urge for military glory suddenly tasted sour in my mouth. Almost not caring if I fell I edged back to the top of my gully and began the laborious descent back down in the fading light. I still feel half-ashamed at my huge dereliction of duty, but by the time I regained our camp I had decided not to go back up that gully. I know that I could have brought about the capture of that fortress and would no doubt have become a famous general as a result, but I didn't. I reported back to Cimon that I could still find no practicable route for troops to assault Ithome. It was a lie.

As it happened even Cimon's enthusiasm for helping the Spartans seemed to have somewhat waned, and amongst the troops generally there were murmurings that we were fighting for the wrong side. So how much my decision really affected the course of history[7] I am still not sure. But I think my report was perhaps a turning point, and though I perhaps thus saved the lives of a few helots I may also have caused the deaths of thousands of Athenians and Spartans. For, as Thucydides pointed out, the Spartan king dismissed Cimon and his whole army from participation in this war and caused such huge loss of face for our general and our city that it led to a major rupture between Athens and Sparta. That rupture in turn began a process that led inexorably to a long and disastrous war.

---

1.   Miletos was for many centuries an important Greek port in Asia Minor but it was stranded inland by ever-mounting tons of silt washed down by the Meander and its impressive ruins are now six miles from the sea near the Turkish town of Balat.

2.   The Taygettos range rises to over 7,000 feet and lies on a geographical fault line between two continental shelves. One of its defiles was used by the Spartans for throwing down disabled children so that they could keep their master-race pure and strong.

3.   Oligarchy or government by the few was the opposite of government by the many, the hoi polloi, and was becoming increasingly popular amongst the smaller cities where the rich wanted to hold onto their privileges at all costs. Tanagra was the typical breeding ground for this type.

4.   The Peloponnese, shaped like a maple leaf with three fingers, was later called Morea for that reason. It was allegedly named after a king called Pelops, son of the constantly thirsty Tantalus.

5.   The Helots were so called because their ancestors were citizens of the city of Helos in Laconia which refused to surrender when attacked by the Spartans. The entire population was enslaved and made a permanent slave under-class to do all the manual labour for the Spartans. Helos is now the small village of Elos on the coast near the mouth of the Eurotas River.

6.   Mount Ithome is now surmounted by an abandoned monastery and is some 2400 feet above sea level. It is passed by the Kalamata-Pylos road.

7.   In the words of that shrewd observer Thucydides (Book 1 Chapter III): 'The first open quarrel between the Lakedaimonians (Spartans) and the Athenians arose from this expedition... and the instant they (the Athenians) returned home, they broke off the alliance which had been made against Persia and allied themselves with Sparta's enemy Argos.'

CHAPTER EIGHTEEN

TWO DEATHS, ONE MURDER

WHEN I ARRIVED BACK HOME in Athens there was a strange silence about the house, so I thought Zoe must have taken my advice and moved out to Eleusis. But then I found Psyche skulking in the kitchen.

She looked at me as if I was a naughty child. 'She's dead,' she said abruptly. 'Of a fever a month ago. And the baby was still-born.'

I felt my legs lose all their strength. Zoe, a child. She had said nothing about being pregnant before I left, but she must have known. So much about her behaviour began to make sense, but more than that my total ineptitude as a husband. Nor had I ever appreciated the excitement that fatherhood might mean until this moment when I realised that I had been close to it, yet irretrievably lost it. Zoe, for whom I had been too immature and thoughtless to feel proper love had become part of my life and I had often thought of her when I was away on campaigns. Her soft body and gentleness had gone. I had no chance to make amends for the misery I had caused her in our final days together. Now I was a widower at the age of twenty-three.[1]

'Men,' muttered Psyche contemptuously. 'I suppose you'll want something to eat now.'

I shook my head.

'I'll get it anyway. There's some pigeon pie and green beans. Not that you deserve it.'

I'm ashamed to say that a few minutes later I did eat the supper she served me. She was just a slave who loved me and despised me, knew what I was like but still felt a duty to look after me. I should have treasured that too.

I soon realised that more had changed in Athens than my own domestic circumstances. Whilst we had been away Ephialtes had hurried back from Sparta, spreading news of our rebuff by the Spartan king and stirring up opinion against Cimon for exposing us to such humiliation. Together with Pericles he had persuaded the Assembly to reduce even further the influence of the old guard in Athens, so Cimon's position as chief general was now in serious doubt. The two rising stars were far more skilled than he was at making persuasive speeches. What's more they made the new style of politics extremely popular with ordinary Athenians by paying them to attend meetings or sit on juries.

Soon subtle rumours were circulating that Cimon had bought off the King of Macedonia, that he was in secret talks with Sparta, that he was planning to make himself a dictator. It was just a matter of time before someone started to scratch his name on a potsherd and the pile would rise and rise, just as it had for his old rival Themistocles and so many great men before him. I caught a glimpse of him once before his ostracism and saw a marked change in his bearing: there were the beginnings of a paunch and grey streaks in his hair. Sad, but at least he still had his gold mine and his estates in Thrace for a pleasant enough retirement. As it turned out he was not destined to be there all that long, but at the time it just seemed that as usual the Athenians were turning against yet another of their ablest leaders.

For the time being my mind was taken off both this and my personal grief when I was recalled to the army. Despite the failure at Ithome I still had a reasonable reputation for siege work, and at the age of twenty-six was offered command of ten triremes in a fleet of forty being sent to capture the port of Naupaktos[2] on the Gulf of Corinth. In charge was my father-in-law Myronides who had been very cool towards me since the death of Zoe, but was too much of a professional to let that hinder our relationship during a campaign. The whole idea of capturing this city was, of course, a way of getting back at Sparta since the objective had been to resettle it with thousands of helot refugees from Ithome, thus depriving Sparta of its servile work-force. Our plan to evict the current population was justified by the fact that they were notorious pirates.

This was the first time I had sailed round the Peloponnese and it took five days before we at last entered the Gulf of Corinth on the other side. At that point Myronides split his force into three: one flotilla to keep guard at the entrance of the gulf, the second to watch out for the Corinthian navy and my own detachment to conduct the assault on the target.

When we arrived within a few miles of Naupaktos I took a small party ashore to look round. It had an impressive natural harbour where the pirates could moor the ships they had captured until a ransom was paid. Not only did these Lokrians capture merchant ships at sea, they even entered other cities' harbours and cut out their prey, so all Greece would be well rid of them. However, their nest was guarded by a well-fortified rock so I decided on a night attack. To be honest while I have a distinct dread of being attacked myself at night, I find I am less of a coward attacking other people under cover of darkness. Certainly in sieges you can take your time at night and so long as you keep silent you have a reasonable chance of getting in.

On this occasion we found the walls were of fairly rough construction and ill-maintained as you might expect with a pirate community. There were plenty of gaps in the stone where we could push in nails or knives to give us a foothold. I had Kleistes with me and we had hauled ourselves up onto the ramparts within an hour of starting, then pulled up fifty more men before we were spotted. By that time we had killed the two nearest sentries and barred the door of the main guard barracks, which we set on fire. Most of the rest of the pirates were asleep, many I think the worse for drink, so panic set in and we had a fairly simple job overcoming them. It was then only a matter of opening the sea gates, lifting the harbour boom and our ten triremes rowed in to complete the capture. We had lost only three men.

The following evening when all the prisoners had been sorted out we bedded down in the hovels of the Lokrian pirates. The floors were thick with goats' dung, alive with ticks and stank of human waste and rotten vegetables. Kleistes managed to organise a reasonable supper of smoked fish and onions, but I for once had little appetite.

'Tasty stuff, as Chronos said when he finished off his daughter's buttocks,' laughed Kleistes, as I tried to settle down for the night.

In retrospect I felt afterwards that I had shown more than my usually low level of courage that day, mainly because I was still ashamed of my dereliction of duty at Ithome and partly because this time I was in charge and dare not show hesitation in front of my men. Kleistes commented that I had been mad, which I took as a compliment and even Myronides gave me grudging approval. Yet, excited as I was, I felt strangely empty and still had the memory of Zoe's last tearful frown as I tossed on that foul Lokrian mattress. Kore too came briefly into my mind and vanished again almost immediately like the fruit bowls of Tantalus. And I'm ashamed to say that once or twice I even found myself recalling the greedy white body of Mnesoptolema.

After two days mopping up we left a small garrison in Naupaktos and sent messengers to Ithome to tell the helots they could move in whenever they wanted. Then we set off on the long journey home, much of it against the wind, so we had a long demoralising row while much of the time I gave myself over to morbid thoughts of my domestic failure.

As we approached the Piraeus we gave the hostile island of Aegina a wide berth. In the far distance I could just see a glint of gold above the Acropolis where Pheidias had nearly completed his massive new statue of Athena with her helmet coated in pure gold. Below stood the ostentatious new temple of Theseus paid for by Cimon, who doubtless expected people to come and worship the old hero, even though what he really wanted was to be worshipped himself. This was a city to be proud of and I had played a part as champion of the oppressed workforce of Sparta. I did not even think at that time what disasters might result from the insult which I had helped to inflict on the vanity of the Spartans.

If I expected a hero's welcome I was soon to be proved wrong. Even as I walked up to Athens from the docks with Kleistes I found myself envying the fact that he was returning to a wife and children, whilst I had nothing. All that was left to me was to pursue my career and perhaps also fight to have the good name of my uncle Aeschylus restored.

I arrived at the Assembly expecting the odd word of congratulation on my little victory, for the news had gone ahead of us, but instead I found only a shocked silence which I could not at first comprehend.

Then I saw a group of people standing around a body which lay in a pool of blood and rushing towards it was a first-aid party with bandages, some of the priests of Asclepius,[3] who undertake that role in the city.

'Who is it?' I asked.

'Ephialtes, two minutes ago,' someone answered.

I saw Sophocles standing a few yards away and went over to him. 'Who did it?' I asked.

'No one seems to know. I was just outside the Assembly talking. He'd just finished making a speech.'

'One of these damn helots from Ithome,' muttered a bystander, no doubt a pro-Spartan.

'Rubbish,' said Sophocles, who was on the liberal wing.

'A hired assassin,' said someone else. 'Paid for by Cimon, I wouldn't be surprised. Money can get you anything these days.'

'Warmer perhaps,' said Sophocles. 'But who saw it happen?'

'He was walking through the crowd,' said a priest. 'But now nobody's admitting to have been in the crowd or seen anything.'

'Odd,' said Sophocles. 'Crowds don't just vanish.'

'Cimon had reason enough to want revenge,' offered an elderly member of the assembly. 'It was Ephialtes who caused his downfall, no?'

'It's not Cimon's style,' I offered. 'Not a street corner job like that with a paid-up thug.'

'You could also argue that Ephialtes was standing in the way of Pericles,' said Sophocles mischievously. 'But of course I wouldn't do that,' he added, winking. 'Maybe he pinched someone else's lover. That's more likely.'

I had seen plenty of badly injured men in the past few years, but there was something unnerving about a talented, vibrant man like Ephialtes lying helpless in the middle of a public square. I moved over to where he lay with the priests mopping his wounds. He was still trying to speak, yet surprisingly nobody seemed to be listening. I leaned towards him to see if his ramblings made any sense to me.

'Best jud..,'[4] he said, his face twisted and sweating. Not long afterwards he died. I cannot say that I had ever warmed to the man for I'd often seen him take the lives of enemies whom he regarded as expendable, but this was an ignominious death for one who had striven so hard and had so recently achieved the supreme ambition of his career. I wondered who might have been guilty of this crime and was astonished that so many of the witnesses seemed to have melted away into the back streets behind the Agora.

Though I had never thought of Ephialtes as a friend, I could not help admiring him, He was a ruthlessly ambitious man whose ambitions coincided conveniently with the ambitions of Athens to have an even greater empire, but he did have many good qualities and he did not deserve to be knifed to death in the middle of the assembly.

---

1.   If Euphorion was twenty-three the date would be 462 BC.

2.   Naupaktos still has a small picturesque port. It was for a time renamed Lepanto and was the scene of the famous naval battle won in 1571 against the Ottoman Turks by Don John of Austria with a fleet of mainly Spanish ships. The Venetians built the city walls and it has a massive citadel. To the west in marshland lies Missolonghi, site of a major rebellion against Turkish rule in 1824 and the place where Lord Byron died of a fever when he came to support the Greeks.

3.   Asklepios, the Greek god of medicine was supposedly the human son of Apollo with a woman called Coronis, but he was intensely jealous and suspected that another man had fathered the boy so he killed her with a flash of lightning, and kept the baby. Asklepios grew up to be a brilliant herbalist and doctor, including the Argonauts as his patients. He was promoted to godhood after his death.

4.   Anyone reading this account in English is at a disadvantage, for what we think Ephialtes was saying was aristos dic... which means 'best' and something like 'judge' or 'justice.' This ties in with a comment attributed to Aristotle.

     For those curious as to the present location of this murder site the market place or Agora has now been extensively excavated and can be reached from the Monastiraki metro station.

CHAPTER NINETEEN

RESCUING MY UNCLE

I HAVE ALREADY INDICATED THAT since my domestic happiness had been snatched away it was now one of my aims with such willpower as I had left to help my uncle Aeschylus to regain his good name and return to Athens. Luckily as it turned out this happened to coincide with the desires of Pericles who, with the exile of Cimon and the death of Ephialtes, now emerged as the leader of the Assembly. In fact it was quite remarkable how quickly after one leader had been exiled and another murdered the crime was forgotten and a former rival slid effortlessly into their position. Certainly Pericles made a fine emotional speech to the Assembly calling on the Furies to destroy the mind of the assassin, but he suggested no practical methods for identifying the culprit or bringing him to justice. In the meantime I puzzled over the possible meaning of Ephialtes' last words and the rumours that Cimon might have been behind the plot.

Later that month Pericles invited me to his office to discuss the repatriation of Aeschylus. 'We've got big plans, Phori,' he said. 'You remember you met my town planner in Miletus and brought back his message? He's here now and we are turning Athens into a spectacular city with the world's greatest temple on the Acropolis dedicated to the Virgin[1] Athena.'

'I didn't think you believed in the gods,' I said. Lampon, who was both a priest and his secretary, looked shocked.

'That's immaterial,' he replied. 'The citizens need a focal point and this city has to have the biggest temple in all of Greece. Besides Athena is the goddess of wisdom and I certainly believe in that.' He paused and then went on, 'Since we have liberated all the cities around the Aegean we are now the capital of a large confederacy and Athens has to look the part. Only Sparta and Corinth are still holding out against us and thanks to your capture of Naupaktos we have placed a wasps' nest between the two of them.'

I began to gather just how ambitious he was and how long he had been planning this great scheme of his. I was just one of many who had been used. I had thought naively that my expedition to Naupaktos was just to find a safe home for the helots of Ithome. No, his real motive was to irritate our two closest rivals. The helots would be expected to pay back their debt to us by encouraging rebellions round Sparta and Corinth.

'Anyway,' Pericles went on. 'I had a special reason for asking you to come to see me today. I have gathered together here all the best architects, sculptors and painters to help beautify the city. We also have most of the best philosophers, but we have lost one of our greatest playwrights and poets who as it happens is Aeschylus, your uncle.'

He paused. 'What about Sophocles?' I asked.

'Sophocles is brilliant,'[2] he replied. 'But he needs competition and Aeschylus is the only man alive capable of that. I have sent two messages to him in Sicily asking him to return to Athens, but he has ignored them both. I think you are the only person who can persuade him and bring him home. If you will agree to go to Sicily, I can let you have two transport ships for six weeks.'

I needed very little persuasion for it was exactly what I wanted myself and besides I was curious to see Sicily. However, I had no experience of oarless ships so I would need help.

'Can I have Kleistes as my ship-master?'

'Of course you can. And tell Aeschylus we want him to stage the greatest trilogy of all time to celebrate the end of the Persian Wars. That'll bring him back.'

Three days later I was excitedly preparing my two ships for sea with Kleistes as usual swearing obscenities at our crews. Initially we followed the same route as my previous voyage round to the Gulf of Corinth but then had to decide whether to hug the coast past Corcyra[3] then to the heel of Italy or risk cutting straight across the Ionian Sea. Kleistes sniffed the wind and recommended the open sea route, a distance of more than three hundred miles without sight of land. In all my career at sea so far I had never been out of sight of land for more than a few hours except at night, so the prospect of such a long sail was new to me. But Kleistes argued that we could use the prevailing south wind to head westwards, that the skies would be clear enough for us at night to use the Little Bear so we could make Syracuse in three or four days whereas the coastal route would take double the time.

'Of course neither of us will get any sleep,' he said. 'But this wind should hold or Aphrodite is a Megarian brothel keeper.'

So we headed west into the unknown and I learned to appreciate Kleistes' skill as he watched the stars at night or during the day climbed down the side of the ship to feel the temperature of the water or look at passing bits of seaweed. Luckily the weather stayed favourable. Three days later we spotted our first seagull, then that evening saw the distant shores of Sicily. Within an hour we could see the towers of Syracuse and turned southwards to pass Cape Odysseus, hugging the coast for the last sixty miles to Gela.[4]

When we landed after eight days at sea I was amazed at the ornateness of the buildings and the lavish surroundings in which the Greek colonists of Sicily appeared to live. It was explained to me that since their war against Carthage they had such vast numbers of slaves that they could devote far more labour to their public buildings than the Athenians even at their most extravagant. And their merchants were extremely rich.

In due course I found my uncle rehearsing one of his plays in the theatre. He greeted me unconcernedly as if I'd just crossed the street to see him. Then he turned to roar abuse at his chorus for singing a wrong note.

'Don't tell me you've been ostracised already,' he said eventually.

'No,' I said.

'How's your mother?'

'Well,' I said. 'She sent you her love. Pericles is now in charge and he's desperate for you to come back to Athens.'

'What's wrong with Sophocles? Has he run out of ideas?'

'No, but he gets complacent when you're not there to provide some competition.'

'And what about the absurd accusation of Gaia and the high priest?'

'No one takes that seriously,' I answered, surprised that he no longer appeared to take any of the blame for harassing his one time sweetheart.

'I'm getting a bit old for long sea voyages,' he went on. 'What did Sophocles produce last?'

'His Ajax. It was good but...'

'Well, give me time to think about it. It just happens I do have a trilogy nearly finished. By the way, who killed Ephialtes? Not that I'm surprised. Cimon would never stoop so low, of course. Good man, just like his father. But some of the Tanagra set, you can never tell what they might get up to.'

'You seem to know all that's going on even here in Gela,' I said, somewhat taken aback.

He shrugged. 'I'll go and start packing,' he said,

Two days later we were leaving Gela harbour with Kleistes muttering dire consequences unless we were across the Ionian Sea by the end of that month. In fact the wind had become quite unpleasant by the time we saw Zakynthos again and our ships were leaking so badly that even some of the rats disembarked there. Thus a whole month had elapsed before we rounded Cape Malea again and turned northwards at last towards Athens.

Aeschylus had suffered a lot from seasickness but bore it stoically[5]. However, at this point he made a special request.

'Could you drop me off at Eleusis, Phori?' he asked. 'So I can make my peace with Gaia and Psamos.'

I agreed, so we altered course to come round Salamis and a day later tied up in the tiny harbour of Eleusis. Astern of us there was an imposing four-decker which looked distinctly Persian.

'What's going on?' I asked.

The harbour master winked. 'A certain famous Athenian general has died in Magnesia,' he said, tapping his nose. 'And his daughter has brought his ashes back to Attica for burial.'

At that moment I looked across at the strange Persian ship and saw the statuesque figure of Mnesiptolema as she came ashore carrying an ornate jar with great reverence. As she stepped onto the jetty she was greeted by none other than the high priest of Eleusis' daughter, my childhood friend Kore. It was strange that there had been two women in my life who were both priestesses, yet they were so different from each other. Somehow I felt ashamed.

---

1. The Greek word for virgin is of course 'Parthenos'; hence the name of the temple. It is strange that humans have a tendency to expect their gods to be virgins. It was ironic that Pallas Athena aka Minerva had Zeus for her father, but on this occasion her birth was not the result of one of his frequent one-night stands, but of taking a small cutting from his brain.

2. Sophocles was rather more interested in the seamy side of life, things like incest. Hence his plays like Oedipus the King which later provided some helpful hints to Sigmund Freud.

3. Corcyra/Kerkyra is now known as Korfu. It was the location in ancient times of one of the bitterest battles between oligarchs and democrats. More recently it became the favourite seaside home of Kaiser Wilhelm II.

4.   Gela in Sicily was founded by Greeks from Rhodes and Crete. It is still a major city with a surviving acropolis, but it also has industrial areas including oil refineries.

5.   Technically the word 'stoically' is another anachronism for it was nearly a century after this time that Zeno of Cyprus founded a sect whose members were nicknamed stoics because they always met in the stoa or portico that surrounded the Athenian market place. Zeno had also been a sailor and acquired some of his tolerance after being shipwrecked near Athens.

CHAPTER TWENTY

SHIPWRECK

THERE IS NO DOUBT THAT Pericles was delighted that Aeschylus had come home, despite the fact that the old man was a touch conservative in his politics. Even Sophocles, who had now become seriously wealthy with his family's sword-making business, showed some deference to him, so the two poets began to accept the fact that neither should always have a monopoly of the prizes at the theatre. In fact when my uncle's Agamemnon was staged in the new theatre of Dionysus beside the Acropolis he got a warm ovation. Even the less poetic amongst us enjoyed the idea of Clytemnestra killing her husband[1] in his bath and, like all good revenge stories, it kept on leading to another death.

I was surprised that during my absence in Sicily there seemed to have been no progress in finding the murderer of Ephialtes, puzzled too that my uncle seemed to have heard some gossip on the subject that he would not pass on to me. All sorts of rumours about Cimon and oligarchic plots still haunted the city, but Cimon was of course still an exile and unable to defend himself.

I had spent a lot of time at sea recently and was still feeling no little self-pity at the loss of Zoe. The fleeting glimpse of both Mnesiptolema and Kore at Eleusis had unsettled me, and for the first time in my life my eyes lingered unnecessarily on the women of the brothel quarter. They were all sorts and colours and did good business whenever a trireme came back into port or just before it left again. Some also ran restaurants with hare soup, lamb kebabs or eel stew and Euboean pears. They sold jars of oil or unguents that some men took back to their wives in alabaster bottles. I tore myself away to the stalls where Boeotian pedlars sold cat-skins, cheep cloth from Megara, mandrake for bringing on strange fantasies, provocative statuettes of Aphrodite Porne, goddess of whoredom and second-hand red vases with lurid illustrations of gods fornicating with mortals. My mind was tempted by these images, which I tried and failed to suppress.

Towards evening on my fourth day back home life was really beginning to pall when I had a message to report fully kitted to Myronides the next morning. So I picked up some clean tunics from Psyche, collected my armour and a book of the Odyssey, then headed back to the Piraeus. Luckily the dockyard had given the *Medea* a good scrub and renewed the huge date-fibre rope round her hull which kept her in trim.

'There's a Corinthian fleet of about fifty triremes waiting for us off Aegina,' explained Myronides to the assembled trierarchs. 'They feel threatened by Naupaktos. They don't like the fact that Megara has come over to our side. We have about seventy triremes and may get reinforcements from Samos and Lesbos, but we must be careful. We head south before noon, so you have three hours to get your ships ready. Twenty ships are needed to blockade Aegina itself and my land army will be marching west to defend Megara.'

I was glad to see *Medea* had almost finished taking on provisions, mostly dried fish, bread, wine and fruit as well of course as fresh water which was consumed in huge quantities by the oarsmen, especially in warm weather. The last replacement leather thong was being fitted and several new oars loaded, so I felt a degree of possessive pride. Kleistes cast off and we slipped away from the jetty to lead a column of twenty ships on the starboard wing. As we reached Aegina we re-formed into five columns of ten triremes each, rowing beautifully in unison over the flat green water of the gulf. Myronides had given orders before we left port, that on spotting the enemy fleet we should charge at its weakest point and divide it in two. So when the look-out shouted that he could see the Corinthians, as lead ship *Medea* had to start the attack.

Gradually Kleistes worked us up to ramming speed and I concentrated on getting the angle right so we would hit the fragile centre of the Corinthian flagship. As we came within a hundred yards of the enemy they seemed to be moving slowly and I wondered if I had miscalculated. The next trireme behind me had fanned out to ram the ship astern of my target. Our oarsmen were now sweating and breathing heavily, so I knew they could not keep up this speed for long. I told the man on the steering oars to ease off two points. If the Corinthian ship turned towards us then we would have to be ready to ship all the oars at the last minute, one side or the other. In fact she left it too late to turn, and with only a slight change of course we prepared to ram through her port oars.

'Stand by to ship port oars,' I yelled. The third tier of oarsmen did so a second later, followed in quick succession by the middle layer. The bottom oarsmen kept rowing till the last few seconds and then followed suit, as they had been trained to do. The Corinthians had however lost momentum by their last minute turn, so just as they began to ship their oars we sliced into them about four feet from the hull. Our speed was such that we were still moving when we knocked into her stern oars and had smashed most of the rest. I reckoned that at least fifty oars were beyond repair and at least as many oarsmen badly winded or otherwise bruised.

We fended off then with the port oars backing water, eased off about seventy yards and then rowed forward again to smash her amidships at the waterline.

This we managed successfully and Kleistes already had grappling hooks out ready for boarding. As trierarch I had to set an example, but I have to admit that I always dreaded boarding an enemy ship, for it brought one very close to sharp blades of one kind or another.

However I was even more afraid of disgrace, so I leapt across, waving my sword and shouting to the men. Luckily we had the psychological advantage and almost as soon as I had killed their oar-master the rest seemed to surrender without much reluctance and the ship was still almost seaworthy, so a useful prize.

My men pitched twenty or so dead bodies into the sea. I put Kleistes in charge of the captured ship with a skeleton crew and instructions to patch the hole and get her back to the Piraeus.

'That's easy enough, as Zeus said when he raped the lovely Europa,'[2] said Kleistes and saluted as we shoved off.

The red orb of the setting sun was just beginning to slip behind Aegina and there was a touch of cool air as I stared round at the rest of the fleet. It was clear that at least half the Corinthians were disabled or captured and the rest were in the distance heading back home. Myronides sent orders for half our fleet to pursue the Corinthians, but my flotilla was to escort the captured ships back to base. We rowed a few miles to gain shelter opposite Megara. I delegated anchor watches and curled up exhausted in my corner of the quarterdeck to snatch a few hours sleep.

That night I was to suffer the worst disaster of my career, and in retrospect I should have taken more precautions to avoid it. It was to be several years before at length I found out what had caused our change of fortune. That only became clear on my way back from Egypt when I found Kleistes chained to the oars of a Spartan galley. The ease with which we had beaten the Corinthians had made me complacent and I had underestimated their resilience. Kleistes too had fallen asleep and his small crew had been overpowered by the Corinthian prisoners who had battered their way out of the hold and thus got back their ship. As he told me himself, we should have killed more of them.

They then managed to get enough good oars working to sweep round in a circle and ram *Medea* and her unsuspecting crew. It must have taken a huge effort, but perhaps they felt guilty for their poor showing the previous day. My two watch-keepers had either dozed off or were not keeping a proper look-out. Even if they had been, it would have taken us twenty minutes to cut the anchor and get the oarsmen ready to move. The impact of their attack almost rolled us over and certainly caused severe damage beneath the waterline, so I awoke to find the deck tilting over and water pouring into the bilges. At that moment the sail-yard swung round and hit me on the head, knocking me into the sea.

Naturally the Corinthian trireme made no effort to pick up survivors, nor did any other ship in our group manage to prevent her escape, but I discovered later that most of my men were picked up by some of our own ships, though I knew nothing of it at the time. I had briefly lost consciousness, and to add to my problems in falling I had collected a large splinter of hardwood in the fleshy part of my thigh. Thus I came to all alone in the cool, black water. I remember still the feeling of sheer horror as I looked up at the night sky and there was no sound but the slush of waves. My leg felt too painful to move and I had no idea in which direction was the land. My only solution was to tread water gently with one leg and my arms, hoping that dawn would bring help. It struck me that I might be caught in the Salamis current which would take me eastwards, but I wasn't sure.

I think I passed out again and when the sky began to lighten there was no sign of any ships, but to my relief there was a stretch of low shore perhaps about half a mile away.

By this time I was feeling very cold as well as tired, but the sight of land gave me the courage to make my other leg move and I started to swim towards the shore. It was hard going, but I found a routine that I could cope with, two hundred strokes swimming followed by a short rest treading water. I had perhaps repeated this pattern six times and was beginning to grow depressed again when I suddenly sensed the current was helping me and I could hear waves breaking on the shore. I made one further effort. I was getting stupidly careless with my swimming and several times spluttered on large mouthfuls of salt water through breathing at the wrong moment. My leg was throbbing violently and I was nearly resigned to the idea of just sliding back into the gentle water when I felt a tendril of seaweed pluck my arm like an old friend.

A minute or so later I saw a small rock in front of me and looked down to see crabs scurrying on the sand below. Gratefully I stumbled ashore on a narrow beach beneath a low cliff. Every muscle aching I just fell naked, face down on a patch of tepid sand and enjoyed the stillness.

Having been quite impressed over the previous two years by the ideas of Anaxagoras I'd come to think it was stupid to believe that our lives are managed by a dozen or so gods messing around with us, whilst they live in luxury on the top on Mount Olympus.[3] Yet for the previous six hours I had frequently asked Poseidon for help, or at least to stop hindering my survival. Then, in the last few minutes, I felt as if perhaps Demeter or Athena had been on my side. But then as I still lay there I began to feel cold again, sick and feverish with no will to move further up the beach, nor could I think of which god might help at this particular stage. There were none that owed me any favours and none I felt I could ask for without gross hypocrisy.

For perhaps four hours I lay on the beach dozing, still feeling cold but no colder, for the sun had begun to shine quite strongly. My mouth felt swollen with thirst, my stomach sick and my leg extremely painful when I tried to move. I admit I lost faith in Anaxagoras and was willing to beg any of the gods for a drink of water. But now Apollo the sun god showed no mercy and seared my salty skin.

As the sun grew brighter I had turned my head so my cheek was on the sand and I could look along the beach at crab level. Suddenly I saw a woman strolling along followed by a dog. She was throwing a stick into the sea for the dog to fetch and paddling herself in the shallow water, in no hurry at all to reach the spot where I lay.

At last she saw me and came over slowly, perhaps thinking I was dead. As she came closer I recognised to my great surprise that it was Kore, the priestess of Eleusis, so I realised that I must have drifted several miles up the coast before I came ashore. She did not immediately recognise me: my hair tousled with salt and sand, my leg crusted with blood and grit as I still lay stomach down to hide my nakedness. My situation reminded me of the famous scene in Homer's Odyssey when the hero is washed up naked on the shore of Phaiacia and the Princess Nausicaa finds him while playing ball with her friends.

'Phori,' she said suddenly smiling. 'You look like a piece of flotsam. Did you fall off your trireme?' Her dog was sniffing me suspiciously and she came round to see my wounded leg. 'That looks nasty,' she said.

"I've lost my ship,' I said pathetically, remembering for the first time that though I was still alive I would now be in disgrace.

'Well what does that matter? You soldiers are always fighting and where does it get you? Never mind. You've got quite a fever and that wound needs cleaning. Can you walk?'

I was shaking uncontrollably and feeling very pathetic. To my astonishment she unclipped her girdle, half unwound her robe and held it out for me to wrap myself in it beside her.

'Don't be modest, since I'm not either,' she said. 'We'll share it,' she added and wrapped us together, pulling me upright beside her so that I felt her warmth and putting her arm round me as we stumbled up the beach followed by her disapproving dog. There we came to a path which led up through the cliffs to the temple of Eleusis.

---

1. Clytemnestra, Queen of Mycenae stabbed her husband Agamemnon when he returned after ten years from the Trojan Wars. While he was away she had taken on a lover called Aegisthus. In revenge she was in turn murdered by her two children, including Electra who also provided some ideas for Sigmund Freud.

2. Europa was a lovely Phoenician princess with whom Zeus, king of the gods, as usual became very briefly infatuated. To facilitate the seduction he transformed himself into a handsome bull and gave her a ride all the way to Crete, where he transformed himself back to a god and, despite her vow of celibacy, had his evil way with her and fathered King Minos of Crete, allegedly constructor of the famous labyrinth at Knossos.

3. Mount Olympus or Oros Olympos has a number of peaks, the highest known as Pantheon or Mytikas being 9,800 feet above sea level. So it is hardly surprising that no ancient Greeks thought of climbing it. Thus they could let their imaginations accept that this inhospitable rock had a charming residence on top where the twelve chief gods could live and drink nectar all day. The first recorded ascent was in 1913 by two Swiss mountaineers

aided by a local goat-herd, Cristos Kakalos, who proved there were no gods in residence.

The date for the above events seems to have been 458BC when Euphorion was twenty-seven.

CHAPTER TWENTY-ONE

SURVIVING DISGRACE

FOR ABOUT THREE DAYS I lay dreaming feverishly in the healing quarters at the temple of Eleusis, conscious occasionally of my wound being bathed and of soothing oils on my sun-burned back. In that period I was vaguely aware of Gaia being more attentive than Kore and I could understand how my uncle had risked his career for her, if that is what had happened. Kore was conscientious in her nursing, but rarely smiled and avoided my glances.

Several times I suffered the indignity of sudden diarrhoea: I think they had maybe dosed me on squirty cucumber, and I was deeply embarrassed by the smell and weakness of my body. My misery was made worse by the recurrent nightmare of my stupidity in letting my ship be sunk by a captured enemy whose powers of recovery I had grossly underestimated. I had nothing to look forward to in Athens but disgrace and humiliation.

When I was feeling strong enough to walk I went to thank my rescuers. Kore herself was nowhere to be found, but Gaia and Psamos smiled graciously.

'We would have done the same for any human being,' said Gaia.

'You've recovered quickly,' added Psamos. 'My mother nursed your father in this very room after Marathon. The only thing that makes me sad is that now Greeks are fighting Greeks instead of just Persians.'

'Your family has always fought to protect Eleusis and your temple,' I said.

'Yes, it has. But only when we were attacked. I think Athens is becoming too greedy. But I suppose that's just an old priest talking. Anyway may the Earth Mother bless you. Your fine payable to the temple is ten drachmas. Since you lost all your money in the shipwreck you can bring it on your next visit.'

'I will. Please thank your daughter Kore for her help to me.'

'Certainly,' he said staring at me in a way I found hard to interpret. 'Tell your uncle Aeschylus we were asking for him,' he added with what I thought was real sincerity, which pleased me considerably. 'Good luck.'

I was somehow deeply disappointed that Kore had not bothered to see me off, but of course there was no reason why she should. The only indication that she might be nearby was the presence of her dog. I later heard that his name was Poseidon, and he seemed intent on encouraging my departure by snapping at my ankles.

Within an hour I was on the road to Athens, but found that I was still rather weak and after a couple of miles I accepted a lift on a hay cart. The driver tried to make conversation, but I was morose at the thought of having to report my negligence to the navy commissioners. At the Dipylon Gate I thanked him and went the rest of the way by foot. Even in the short time that I had been away I was amazed at the amount of new building that had taken place. The city walls were being strengthened and extended in two lines down to the Piraeus. The new marble porticoes round the market were growing rapidly and everywhere there were masons chipping at huge lumps of marble brought down from the quarries of Mount Pentelikos[1]. One of them I recognised as old Sophroniskos, a stone carver who had worked at Eleusis and he greeted me.

'I thought you were dead, Euphorion,' he shouted.'Glad to see the rumours were untrue. See, I've got my son working with me now,' he added pointing to a tousle-headed youngster covered in marble dust but with a mischievous grin. 'Meet Captain Euphorion, Socrates.[2] He commands a trireme.'

'Did command,' I muttered, but acknowledged the boy waving to me with his mallet. It was to be many years before I saw that boy again, spouting rebellious ideas to his cronies in the market place.

Meanwhile I approached the office of Pericles with considerable dread, but I thought I might as well get my ordeal over. To my surprise he greeted me quite warmly and was already well aware of the sinking of the *Medea*.

'You won't let it happen again, Euphorion,' he said more as a statement of fact than a threat. 'Double anchor watches day and night, that must be the rule. We live in an age when you can take nothing for granted. People like the Corinthians will stoop to anything to gain some small advantage. Glad you're alive anyway,' and he waved his hand in dismissal so that I left his office convinced that I should support this man for the rest of my life.

My interview at the fleet office was much less pleasant. The duty inspector asked me coldly and without a trace of sympathy the full sordid details of the loss of the *Medea*. I was glad to hear from him that most of my crew had been picked up by other ships, but the skeleton crew on the Corinthian prize had disappeared with the ship. That meant that Kleistes was either dead or a prisoner of war.

'Of course you realise that you'll never again be given command of another warship,' said the inspector finally.

'Not even if I pay for it out of my own pocket?' I asked, not really wanting an affirmative answer.

'I doubt it, even if you pay for two,' he replied rather sarcastically.

As I left the office I met General Myronides, my sometime father-in-law who now had a double grudge against me. I'd cost him both a trireme and a daughter, so I expected little sympathy. His own wife had also died quite young, as was not uncommon for Athenian officers' wives who hardly ever left their homes and had little fresh air or exercise. Myronides was too mean to have a mistress or a new wife, so he just slept with his slave girl, a rather unattractive Cretan with a solid eyebrow right across her forehead and thick brown legs. Luckily at this point he was too busy for idle chatter and just shook his head grimly to me as he passed.

When I reached the market square there was a hint of panic in the atmosphere, for there was a rumour that a Spartan army was on the move. Nikomedes, the Spartan king's uncle, had crossed the isthmus of Corinth into Boeotia and was encouraging armed uprisings by the oligarchs in several cities, thus ejecting the democrats who tended to favour the Athenian alliance.

Worse still it was rumoured that Theban agents were bribing him to attack the half-finished walls between Athens and the Piraeus. With most of our fleet still away in the Gulf of Corinth and half the troops still helping the Egyptian rebellion against Persia our own city was extremely vulnerable. Just the small cadet garrisons at Phyle and Geranea lay between us and the Spartan army.

That night all available officers were asked to report for duty in the agora and when I did so, still feeling far from fully fit, I was shocked to see that most were just the very old or the very young. Even the politicians like Pericles had their armour buckled on and were getting ready to join the ranks. The man himself stepped onto a dais and said, 'This is an emergency. We're calling out all the reserves in case of attack.'

'Form up in divisions for numbering,' shouted Tolmides,[3] the duty general.

As I still felt well below my normal level of fitness I could not say that I was out of place amongst the frail old men and young cadets who were beginning to trickle steadily into the square. There were quite a few tradesmen as well, some potters, their hands still brown with clay and blacksmiths in their aprons.

'Everyone can join except that lot,' said one elderly wag pointing at three criminals who were nailed to planks outside the gate and looked close to death.

By early evening we were ready to march from the Acharnian Gate where the ceramic quarter had spilled out beyond the walls and hundreds of the poorer potters lived in brick hovels above their workshops. Many of them specialised in the garish paintings of sexual misdeeds, especially those of the gods, that appealed so much to the new rich.

Pericles marched with us showing no particular sign of his political rank except that he was accompanied by his ubiquitous secretary Lampon and his butler Euangelos, neither of whom these days left his side for long. Prominent also amongst the ranks were a number of Cimon's old set, including the old warrior Euthippos and a number of other die-hards who I remembered from the Eurymedon campaign.

Eight hours later we had reached the border of Attica beyond Phyle and slept in a wood for the rest of the day. I dozed off quite quickly and then woke suddenly to the sound of a shouting match. There on the edge of the wood was none other than Cimon himself, wearing his usual red cloak. He had put on a bit of weight in exile and his complexion was even ruddier, but he still had that same proud stance. He was surrounded by his old companions and begging Pericles to be allowed to join our motley force, even as an ordinary ranker.

'Every man counts,' he was arguing. 'The Spartans are just a few miles ahead and in strength.'

'But you have shown yourself a friend of the Spartans and you have been voted into exile,' replied Pericles unsympathetically.

'I still believe the Spartans could be our allies, but if they invade Athenian soil, I will fight them,' retorted Cimon. 'We should not turn them into our enemies.'

'If they want to fight then Tolmides is confident we can defeat them,' went on Pericles. 'We have cavalry reinforcements on the way.'

'But Nikomedes has the pick of the Spartan guard,' pleaded Cimon. 'Crack troops.'

'For goodness sake forget the ostracism,' intervened Euthippos, stepping forward to support his old chief. 'We are all ready to die for Athens and so is Cimon.'

I could see that Tolmides would have welcomed even one extra experienced soldier, but Pericles was adamant.

'I cannot flout the votes of a democracy,' he said, a phrase he only used when the voters happened to agree with him.

Cimon looked almost apoplectic with rage, but like a true professional he accepted his orders, saluted and rode off towards the north.

'You can never trust these closet oligarchs,' muttered Pericles. 'What will the Tanagra set get up to next? By the way, have the Thessalian cavalry reported yet?'

That afternoon we moved down towards the plain of Tanagra which was covered with late corn. In the distance we could see the little city itself,[4] its walls creeping over the low hills with more turrets and gates than a city the size of Athens. Tanagra was after all where the god Hermes was born, but now it was better known for its breed of fighting cocks and workshops that turned out little statues of belly-dancers. To its left was a cloud of dust where the Spartan army was breaking camp and standing by to receive us.

'Let them come and get us,' growled Tolmides. So we waited in the shade of the forest by the main road to Thebes. There was an owl sitting on the branch above me, so I thought it was a sign of good luck. Athena always looks after her owls.

As I have previously confessed, I prefer ramming triremes to close combat with sharp metal, so infantry warfare is not my favourite activity, particularly if faced by opponents as fit and well-trained as the average Spartan. I could see too that Pericles was more worried than he admitted, for though Tolmides was in command of the troops, it was because of the great man's aggressive policies in Megara and Naupaktos that the Spartans now wanted to confront us. At least he had the courage to come out and fight despite the fact that as a politician he could easily have stayed behind. I felt a bit better once I'd put on my breastplate, my bronze-studded kilt and my helmet. Although they would not keep out a well-aimed spear they did give me a slight sense of security.

The battle, when it began, was desperate. The Spartans came at us uphill, but were very well-drilled and precise in their attack. It soon degenerated into a thousand tiny fights to the death, and I was very lucky to have two particularly good swordsmen on either side of me or I doubt I would have survived. As it was I had a fortunate early strike with my spear which boosted my confidence and after that managed to fend off a few Spartans for long enough to be left behind by the crowd. Then I could, without fear of disgrace, succumb to my total exhaustion. By this time I had heard that the long awaited Thessalian cavalry had turned up and would no doubt help turn the tide, but my head was swirling with fever and I felt I could do no more.

At this point as I lay behind a small bush I saw a figure crouched low over a horse cantering across the field where the cavalry appeared to be operating. I recognised the profile of the enigmatic Aristodikos of Tanagra, apparently on his home ground and carrying a heavy leather pouch. I thought little of this at the time, but having recovered after my rest, I rejoined the battle where things had begun to go against us again. About fifty feet away I could see Cimon's friends putting up a desperate fight against the Spartan right. And poor old Euthippos fell with a spear in his chest. Our ranks were getting decidedly thin.

'Damn Spartans,' muttered my neighbour. 'It's because they get whipped to the bone when they're young that they keep coming for more.'

At that moment I saw the Thessalian cavalry which had been supporting us on the left suddenly wheel round and circle back to attack us on the right. Such behaviour was unheard of and their treachery was the last straw. Tolmides understandably sounded the retreat and I'm glad to say we managed an orderly withdrawal, leaving large numbers of our own and Spartan casualties lying dead or moaning in that wretched field. It was then that I also saw Aristodikos again, this time riding away from the cavalry without his big leather pouch and heading for Thebes, and my suspicions intensified.

The exhausted remnants of our force crept back into the woods and lay there for a long time, too tired to argue over what had gone wrong. Luckily the Spartans were also too tired or they'd have followed us.

'What happened to the cavalry?' someone asked at last.

'Somebody offered them more money than we did,' answered Pericles bitterly.

'I don't believe it was Cimon,' said Tolmides. 'All his friends fought to the last man.

'He would not have done it. Never,' said one of the others emphatically.

'I think I can guess," I said. 'Who is Aristodikos working for? I saw him riding towards the Thessalians with a pouch that could easily have been full of gold.'

'Did you indeed?' said Pericles, fixing me with his eyes. 'A very devious bunch the Tanagra oligarchs. Aristodikos, if his name means best judge then it's highly inappropriate.'

'Best judge,' I repeated slowly to myself and suddenly something stirred in my befuddled brain.

Meanwhile Tolmides had joined us again. 'Damned Thessalian cavalry' he muttered. 'Just the types to change sides for the sake of a few drachmas. And that Aristodikos is just the sort of man to have provided the cash.'

I was still thinking and turned to Pericles. 'You know I was close to Ephialtes as he lay wounded in the Assembly,' I said. 'As he lay there he muttered something that sounded like best judge or best justice, and it suddenly occurs to me that maybe he was meaning our friend over there.'

'You could be right,' Pericles answered quietly, but then surprised me totally by going on to say, 'I don't think we should dwell on that, Phori, should we? The past is better left alone,' and he went off.

So it seemed he had no real interest in bringing the murderer of his rival to justice even if that person was also acting as a Spartan agent. For a while I felt somewhat disillusioned in our great city, but I learned later that about this time a deputation came to us from a small town in Italy called Rome whose people had heard good reports of our constitution and wanted to learn from it.[5] I suppose it was a compliment and we should be proud to be pioneers of democracy.

1. Mount Pentelikos rises to 3,600 feet and is famous for its marble quarries. The stone is of particularly high quality, white with a faint yellow tint that glows in sunlight. It was extensively used in the Parthenon including the statues known as the Elgin Marbles, some of them now in the British Museum. The mountain is largely covered by forest which is prone to fires. A particularly disastrous one occurred in 1995.

2. Euphorion's mention of Socrates is the first surviving record of the great amateur philosopher and political rebel, who started life as a stonemason like his father, served as a citizen in the army, but in due course started to question everything and was forced to commit suicide by the Athenian courts in 399 BC, a few years after the end of this narrative, leaving Plato to proclaim his ideas to the world.

3. Tolmides had been a successful general and rival of Pericles. He led the campaign against Sparta in 455 BC and was in overall charge of Euphorion at Naupaktos.

4. The date of the battle of Tanagra was 457BC. Nothing now survives of the town which has been the site of a large air-force base.

5. This deputation came to Athens in 454 BC when Rome was already a public, but considering a change of constitution. Of course it stopped being a republic 400 years later when Julius Caesar staged a military coup. By that time all the little democracies of Greece had long since disappeared and been swallowed up by the Roman Empire.

CHAPTER TWENTY- TWO

THE TROUBLE WITH EGYPT

IN THE AFTERMATH OF THE Battle of Tanagra I learned that it had by no means been such a disaster as we thought on the day. It turned out that the young King Nikomedes of Sparta had been so shocked by the casualties sustained by his troops that he too had withdrawn, so the campaign to stage oligarch rebellions in all the cities of Boeotia had fizzled out. Instead the democratic parties survived and they all continued to support the Athenian alliance. The results of this were that Pericles came top in our next leadership contest, the islands continued to pay huge sums of money into the treasury at Delos, our extravagant building programme was able to continue and the Spartans had to admit that not only was Athens the leading naval power in Greece but also no slouch at land warfare either.

The one problem that never seemed to go away was our involvement with the rebels in Egypt.[1] In retrospect it had been a dangerous move: Egypt was a long way off, its people were not even Greeks and were unreliable as allies, whilst the determination of their Persian masters to put down any rebellion was much greater than had been expected. For Pericles to be so confident that he interfered in the affairs of Egypt meant that he ended up taking a huge risk

Thus about ten days after our return from Tanagra, just when I was beginning to tire of my wifeless home and of the clucking disapproval of my old nurse Psyche, I had another summons from Pericles and headed for his office near the Assembly. When I went in his secretary Lampon was writing some dispatches and a woman of striking beauty was hovering in the background. It was common gossip that Pericles had a new mistress, Aspasia, for despite his now high position he had been divorced by his wife, so that she could return to her much richer ex-husband. It was just one of those things that happened in Athenian society. Pericles was greedy enough for power, but personal wealth did not interest him at all.

'I want your help on a delicate mission, Euphorion,' he said, sweeping back his rather sparse hair, so that it covered rather more of his pointed head. 'I'm concerned about the stalemate in Egypt and I think perhaps we could make use of a siege specialist like yourself. I'm sure you heard the news that Charitimides has captured the main city of Memphis, but he's made no headway with the citadel. Unless we can drive out the Persian garrison there we remain vulnerable to counter-attack. I need this rebellion finished so that we can recall our troops.'

I of course knew a little already about the problem. The man behind the rebellion was King Inaros of Libya and some Egyptians regarded him as just about as evil as their current Persian overlords, so why should we support such a rebellion? Our objective was not so much to help Egypt or Libya as to damage the Persians and sell Athenian goods to the Egyptians, but as so often happens with what seems like a good military idea, it had not worked according to plan. A large portion of our army had now been tied up there for more than two years.

Pericles continued, 'I'm going to give you three triremes and I want you to take them to Memphis with a message that we must capture the citadel within three months or we pull out altogether.' He slapped the table with his hand as if to emphasise the importance of his orders.

I was momentarily staggered, for two weeks previously I had thought I would never set foot on a trireme again let alone be given command of three. Then Euangelos, Pericles' butler, came in with a small cup of wine which he handed to me.

'By the way I've recalled Cimon,' said Pericles. 'His sister Elpinike has been begging me to do so for months and his group fought very well at Tanagra. He has written to assure me that he has had no contact with Aristodikos since the Ithome fiasco and I believe him.'

'He wouldn't lie,' I said.

'Nor would his slaves. We put them on the rack for three days to make sure.'

I was reminded that it was best to keep on the right side of Pericles for his ruthlessness towards his enemies was chilling.

'You know the Eumolpids of Eleusis, don't you?' he went on, changing the subject. 'Delightful family. Psamos the high priest and his charming wife Gaia. Pity they have no son to take over. Just a daughter. She'll be high priestess for life. I suppose.'

'Yes,' I answered.

'How's Aeschylus? Someone was saying he wants to go back to Sicily? What's wrong with the man?'

'He's got it into his head that he's going to die soon,' I replied. 'I don't quite understand why.'

'Maybe he's afraid of the competition. Now we have a new up-and-coming dramatist as well as Sophocles. Young Euripides, a bit of an eccentric, lives in a cave near Sounion, but he writes exquisite poetry.'

I sensed somehow that Pericles was now just making polite conversation and this was a signal for me to depart.

My three triremes were not yet ready for the sea so I had two days to spare and decided to head over to Eleusis to check out the family estates. My mother Phasia was white-haired now and beginning to shrink visibly with age. I found it hard to communicate with her the way I once had, for the guilt over my marriage and the ups and downs of my career made me feel inhibited, whilst she, I am sure, found me difficult and moody. Thus after a brief, rather stilted reunion I headed off round the estate, grateful to be alone. The vines had all been well pruned and the grape crop looked promising, so I said a few words to the slaves who did the work and listened patiently to the steward as he detailed his problems, though really they did not interest me at all. This estate helped me to fund my empty house in Athens and paid for fitting out at least one trireme. Nothing else mattered to me.

I had lunch with my mother, who thought I looked thin. There was our own goats' cheese, stuffed vine leaves, bread with poppy seeds, some skewered lamb with wine and honey cakes to follow. That was the best bit of the countryside, the food.

Next day, as if drawn by some unacknowledged force, I set off again past the healing ward of the temple of Eleusis. There was a number of wounded soldiers with bandages or on crutches, some groaning in their misery. The smell of mandrake[2] hung in the air, and in their midst I could just see the cool figure of Princess Kore, but she did not look in my direction though she had doubtless heard that I was visiting my mother.

I moved closer and tried to attract her attention.

'Stand clear, Euphorion,' she said. 'You are whole in body, but not in spirit. You have no place here now.' Her dog, Poseidon, growled at me as if to endorse his mistress's disapproval.

She waved me away with no hint of the warmth I had half-expected or perhaps imagined that I deserved, so with a feeling of anger I turned away towards the Piraeus. This black mood persisted the following day when my small flotilla made its final preparations for sea. I checked the equipment and stores of the three ships before signing for them and chatted about the ten-day voyage with the three ship masters, none of them as experienced as my old friend Kleistes. Our route took us to Melos, an arid island with only one small town, then on to Thera which rises out of the sea with huge black cliffs but has one reasonable harbour. Cyprus we avoided since much of it was still in Persian hands, so we must head straight south to Marea,[3] a city near the west mouth of the biggest river in the world, the Nile. Before leaving I had briefly met the gossipy Herodotus for a short chat, and for a cup of wine he told me the Nile was like a moving sea, even bigger than the great rivers of Sardis.

We had our share of favourable winds and actually made it to Marea on the Nile in nine days. This was where the rebel king Inaros of Libya had his headquarters. With Athenian help he had scored an initial victory over the Persian overlords, much to their surprise and dismay. As a reward for our help he had agreed to supply corn, dates and gold to Athens, hence Pericles' enthusiasm for this venture. He was a big, swarthy man, darker than a Persian, wrapped like a satrap in exotic robes, surrounded by fawning eunuchs and a competitive throng of mistresses or harlots, I was not sure which.

Inaros gave us a splendid feast of tuna fish and wine flavoured with spruce seeds, followed by dates with curdled milk and we drank a lot of the bread beer which they seemed to prize very highly. We were then ushered onto his balcony to admire three dead traitors tied to stakes in his courtyard and look beyond at the flat fields cut at regular intervals by deep ditches leading from the banks of the river.

'Now it's time for entertainment,' announced Inaros. 'Do you prefer boys or girls?'

'Girls,' I replied uneasily, not wishing to offend such an important ally. The beer still flowed and some flautists came in with slaves carrying burning bowls of incense. My girl was brought to me, but she was decidedly small and could not speak a word of Greek, so I did not need huge reserves of self-control to leave her untouched. To our host I pleaded exhaustion and winking he offered me something from a jar, but I pretended not to understand and excused myself for the night.

Our voyage up the Nile was a tedious process for we were against the current and only occasionally had much advantage from the wind. In all it took five days, for the heat was so severe that our oarsmen could barely row for more than an hour at a time without stopping to rest and drink copious amounts of water. We met a number of barges and sailing boats, passed many strange-looking palaces and temples with vast statues looking down on us. Along the banks were thousands of slaves working strange water wheels to fill the irrigation ditches. Finding good water to drink was not easy and a number of the crew, including myself, had brief spells of dysentery. On the fifth day, by which time I had recovered, we saw a huge city ahead of us and our pilot indicated that this was

Memphis.[4] We also saw a number of bodies floating down the river, some of which, alarmingly, appeared to be Athenian.

The camp of our army under Charitimides was beside a huge temple with a massive statue standing over it, apparently one of their kings called Rameses II, but the names were all strange to me and the writing which covered the walls completely unintelligible.

'Good journey?' asked a disillusioned-looking trierarch who came to the jetty to greet us. 'Horrible place this. Everything stinks. The Egyptians hate the Persians, but I don't think they like us or the tyrant Inaros much better. You can't trust anybody. We've made very little progress since we first captured the city six months ago.'

'You've still not captured the citadel then?' I asked.

'Just look at it,' he replied, pointing to a high white-walled fortress which loomed over the city. 'The satrap's holed up in there with the best Persian archers in their entire empire and the deepest, purest supply of water within fifty miles.'

I decided not to let myself be depressed by these remarks and went to sort out quarters for my three crews. Certainly the city which seemed even bigger than Athens, and much grander despite Pericles's new building programme, gave a feeling of unfriendliness and such native inhabitants as were still there looked at us resentfully, not with the gratitude you'd expect from the newly liberated. Add to that it was hot, airless and smelt of death.

'This city's been here for twenty-five centuries already,' announced Zeno, the scholar who had come with our little fleet to chronicle its achievements. 'Even before Troy there were kings here. That temple over there is to the god they call Osiris, who is much the same as the god we call Hephaestos, the god of blacksmithing.'

'Why did they not rise up against Persian rule themselves?' I asked.

'They're decadent. They lost the will to fight centuries ago. They're totally obsessed with death. That's why they all look so miserable. Thousands of them are employed to embalm bodies, nothing else, and not just humans, animals as well. That huge hall over there is for embalming their famous bulls. Imagine worshipping a bull, however big.'

I followed his gaze and beyond the massive embalming table was a huge stone cat with a man's face.

'Carved out of solid alabaster,' said Zeno, reading my mind. 'The cemetery of this city is larger than the city itself and that's saying something. See that pyramid over there? That's just a small one compared with the ones further down the river. It's supposed to have the body and the treasure of a king inside, but the Persians managed to find their way inside to rob it, as they have nearly everything else round here. You can just see the huge door they've rolled aside and the statues they've smashed. Of course they disapprove of all these Egyptian gods, but not of the gold. Naturally it will all be back in Sardis by now, in the Persian king's treasury.'

Two days later under cover of darkness I took my scouting party with me up to the base of the white fortress, but with all my experience of sieges I could see no means of making any impression on its massive walls. They were far too high for ladders and the limestone was too hard for us to chip footholds. What's more the Persian archers on the parapet soon showed that they were both alert and deadly. I realised that though Pericles might think that Charitimides was overcautious there was no way that this fortress could be captured unless the garrison ran out of food and water.

'I know it all already,' said Charitimides to me irritably when I reported my findings. 'Pericles will just have to wait. It's just a matter of time. We'll capture it in the end, but it can't be rushed.'

'What if the Persians counter-attack?' I asked,

'They can't as long as our fleet is here and controls the river. We have to be careful though with all the rot floating in this tepid river. The slime grows on the ships' hulls everyday. So I'm going to pull rank and requisition your three triremes plus half your crews. You can go back in two of ours.'

I was hardly delighted with this suggestion, but I had no choice. Yet as I looked at his emaciated face with its feverish yellow eyes, I wondered just how long he would last in this pestilential place.

'Please give this list of my supply requirements to that bastard Inaros,' he added. 'He should be in Thebes by now. And tell him to be quick about it.'

Thus with my remaining men and two rather decrepit triremes, plus a bag of despatches and a bag of gold, I set off back down the Nile the following evening. It was cool and the moon shone enough for us to steer safely past the shoals and then glide northwards with the current. There were ibis squawking in the reeds and strange geese flying low over the river.

About fifty miles down from Memphis we moored at a jetty supposedly near Thebes and, leaving one crew in charge of the two triremes, I took the rest with me to search for King Inaros. We passed several groups of traders on camels and I think even at this point I had doubts about our Libyan guide. I also had huge doubts about Inaros taking any notice of Charitimides requests for extra supplies.

It was just as we were passing another huge roadside cemetery that we were ambushed by a troop of Persian archers on horseback. We had little protection from such an attack and about half my party was killed or wounded by the first volley, With a couple of hoplites I threw myself behind one of the big cat statues and so survived, but we now saw Persian infantry picking their way through the stones towards us and knew that we could not stay still. I was conscious that our situation was desperate, for we were hopelessly outnumbered, cut off from any hope of assistance and on top of everything suffering from the extreme heat and short of water,

I persuaded some of our less badly wounded men to follow me, but some I had no choice but to leave behind, a fact which then and later caused me great distress. We retreated up a narrow defile behind us which soon narrowed still further into a man-made tunnel whose stone door had been prized open by tomb-robbers. There were Persians still pursuing us so we had no alternative but to go on. The tunnel was dank and airless and went upwards in almost total darkness. The sounds of our pursuers were deadened but still persisted. Then our tunnel ended abruptly, but feeling around frantically I found the rungs of a stone ladder which rose vertically in front of us. We climbed about twenty feet and then found a new corridor which led us to a long chamber lit from a single beam of light high above us. The walls were covered with paintings of scenes in the most brilliant colours I had ever seen interspersed with their indecipherable writing. There were strange fish and birds, with brown slaves in loin cloths and women with snakes in their hair.

By this time there was no longer any sound of our pursuers, so we sat for a while gulping for air and sweating profusely. I felt somewhat claustrophobic and dreaded that we might never find a way out of this ghastly tomb.

'At least some of us are alive,' I said somewhat lamely to my surviving group, trying to bring some humour to our situation. 'But we can't afford to hang around here. Somehow we have to get back to the river.'

For about an hour we waited and the beam of light disappeared, leaving us in total darkness. Then slowly we traced our way back by feeling the walls until we found ourselves at the top of the ladder. It was harder going down than coming up so it seemed like hours before we edged our way out of the defile to see if there were still Persian troops searching for us. There were none, only bodies, mostly of my old crew lying amongst the strange monuments. Back at the jetty there was no sign of my two remaining triremes so we set off walking down the bank of the river.

It was slow work crossing the countless irrigation ditches and it took us two days before we found an empty sailing boat, which I requisitioned. By this time we had blistered feet and sunburnt backs, so the men mostly lay in the bottom of the boat and let the current take us northwards. We had luckily found a few water melons and date bunches, but we were still decidedly weak. After some sleep we managed to get the sail up and the next day were delighted to see one of our triremes just ahead of us. The news, however, when we caught up with it was far from good, for we heard that our two ships had both been ambushed, many of the crew killed and one of the triremes set on fire before the other managed to cast off down river.

That night we reached Marea again and I was horrified to hear that the wretched King Inaros had been there all the time, making no effort to send up supplies to the army at Memphis. Our disastrous attempt to meet up with him at Thebes had been pointless and possibly even a deliberate trap. As usual he tried to console us with generous hospitality and glib promises.

'Tell Pericles we are grateful for his help,' he told me. 'I will send eighteen shiploads of corn and ten gold bars to Athens before the autumn. The supplies for Charitimides will be despatched tomorrow.'

Even then I was not at all sure whether to believe him, but I was anxious to get my one remaining trireme back to Athens, so I did not wait to see what happened. A few months later I heard that he had been captured during a Persian counter-attack soon after our departure. Apparently they crucified him and I cannot say that I was too sorry for him.[5] Meanwhile I was just desperate to get myself and the surviving members of my expedition back to Athens.

---

1.   It seems to have been around 450 BC that Athens received a request for help from King Inaros of Libya who wanted to drive the Persians out of Egypt and offered us huge rewards for our cooperation. Pericles succumbed to the temptation, taking huge risks as always to bolster his career. It ended in disaster with the loss of 250 ships and many men.

2.   Mandrake belongs to the nightshade family and has long been known as a hallucinogenic.

3.   The ruins of the ancient port of Marea on Lake Maryut south of Alexandria are quite extensive.

4.   The ruins of the long-abandoned city of Memphis lie some ten miles south of Cairo and were treated as a quarry when the Arabs founded their new capital, Cairo. The famous White Fort was probably already 2,000 years old when visited by Euphorion as it was believed to have been built by the first pharaoh.

5.   Thucydides gives a bitter account of the disastrous intervention of the Athenians in the affairs of Egypt. When the Greeks were driven out of Memphis by a large Persian army the survivors fled to an island called Prosopitis in the Nile delta and held out there for eighteen months till the Persians diverted the river, thus marooning the Athenian ships and making the men easy to capture or kill. Very few of them made it back to Athens and a fleet of fifty triremes sent to rescue them was also destroyed.

CHAPTER TWENTY-THREE

REUNITED WITH AN OLD FRIEND

AS WE SAILED NORTHWARDS PAST Crete I began to recuperate and it dawned on me that for the second time I had lost another trireme and my career would certainly not survive such a double failure. The idea of submitting myself yet again to the sarcastic tongue of the fleet inspector was far from pleasant, as was the thought that I had forfeited all hope of further commands. The fact that Charitimides had requisitioned my three original ships which were fresh from the dockyard and instead left me with two in poor condition after months in the foetid waters of the Nile made me feel no better. The only good thing was that my surviving ship had a stern wind as we left the delta and our tired crew had a reasonably easy journey home. It was not too hot, we had big jars of cleanish drinking water and fresh fruit, so we should he half-fit by the time we got home. In conditions like this I loved the sea.

As I've grown older I've come to realise that for every piece of bad luck you suffer you are usually likely to get something better if you wait long enough. Whether it's the gods on Olympus or just fate or even mere coincidence I haven't yet found the answer. But as we headed homewards passing Aegina our look-out spotted a lone enemy trireme with a Corinthian pennant. We'd enjoyed such favourable winds that our crew was well-rested and had plenty of energy for a quick burst of speed. So I gave the order to increase to ramming speed and headed straight for the Corinthian's bows, reflecting briefly that my ship might be already so weakened by rot that we would do more damage to ourselves than to the enemy.

For whatever reason the Corinthian was slow to react to our manoeuvre and when he did at last do so he headed for shallow waters near the shore, then changed his mind and tried to double back. Thus instead of having to ram him I found myself at the right angle to crash into his starboard oars. Luckily I had a very experienced crew and they left shipping our port oars to the last few seconds before we thrust our way down his side from the stern. Having thus seriously disabled him and with a fresh crew all ready for a fight after our frustrating time in Egypt, we grappled onto his side and swarmed across to overpower those who had survived the crash unscathed. Surprisingly for a Corinthian ship they put up less resistance than usual, so in barely twenty minutes we had secured our victim. I had lost one trireme but replaced it with another, so my career might just survive.

As it turned out this was not the end of my good luck for as we started to sort out the oars and rigging of the captured ship I heard a familiar voice shout 'Euphorion.'

I turned and on the second level of oar benches saw the grimy and bedraggled but still recognisable face of my old ship-master, Kleistes.

'Unshackle that man,' I ordered, for Peloponnesian ships still have to chain all their oarsmen to the benches.

'By Aphrodite's buttocks am I glad to see you,' said Kleistes, staggering to his feet and embracing me.

'Glad to see you're still alive, you old rogue. How are you?'

'Back's a bit sore sitting on these god-forsaken benches all day. If I ever get to be a ship-master again I think I'll be easier on the oarsmen. Unless they're Spartans.'

'I'm sorry,' I said. 'It was my fault you were captured. I left you with too small a crew.'

'Nonsense. I was careless and paid for it with two years' rowing practice. Besides I have been thinking all this time that you were drowned.'

'I nearly was,' I said.

'As Perseus said to the Gorgons,[1] we always survive,' he replied. 'But I admit there were times when I wished I hadn't.'

'Anyway, you can get your own back now. You're in charge of getting this captured trireme and your prisoners back to the Piraeus. I just hope it doesn't leak too much,'

---

1.   As I'm sure most people know the three Gorgon sisters had skins like fish, teeth like boars, hands of brass and a number of other unattractive features including the ability to turn their enemies to stone. They were eventually eliminated by Perseus, one of several sons resulting from one night stands by Zeus, chief of the gods.

CHAPTER TWENTY-FOUR

THE ENEMY AT HOME

MY ARRIVAL BACK IN PORT WAS much less unpleasant than I had at one time expected, thanks to the capture of a Corinthian trireme. In fact so much of the fleet was involved with various campaigns and blockades that the inspectorate were more than glad to welcome a couple of reasonably maintained triremes to the docking area. Once we had signed off our ships Kleistes and I strolled back up to the city, my friend having cleaned himself up considerably for the expected reunion with his wife.

'She's probably taken in a lodger,' he said, winking. 'Who could blame her after two years?'

Now that I was back from the ordeal in Egypt my thoughts returned to the welcome I might have received from Zoe, but now I was coming back to an empty house.

Just as Kleistes and I were about to head off to different parts of the city a young messenger came chasing after me.

'Pericles wants to see you,' he said. 'Immediately.'

'More trouble,' I said to Kleistes and wrung his hands before turning to follow the messenger. 'Give my love to your family.'

'Time you got a new one,' he said with a wink. 'Too much time at sea and you'll start to fancy oarsmen. Or goats.'

Ten minutes later I was in the great man's ante-room and soon after that he called me in.

'Bring me up to speed on Egypt,' he said.

So I gave him a reasonably detailed account of the siege up the Nile and emphasised the hardships and difficulties of our troops.

'So not even you could get up the walls of the White Castle,' he said.

'No, the stones of the main walls are tight together and so hard and smooth that no dagger would make any impression. The Egyptians certainly know how to build.'

'And starving them out hasn't worked either.'

'No, it's so hot and humid that our troops are having a worse time than the garrison who at least have shade and clean water.'

'I don't like failures,' he said. 'How easy will it be to manage a dignified withdrawal without loss of face?'

'Very difficult. The triremes are nearly all rotten and their hulls are covered in river slime. Many of the men are sick or wounded and since I left many will have died. The Libyans never came to our aid, never delivered the food or money that they promised and might well change sides and hinder our escape.'

'So high casualties,' he said with a shrug.

I sensed that he was not too concerned with casualties, only with potential loss of face. Human lives did not matter too much, but the prestige of Athens did. As usual he would console all the widows with a superb funeral oration. That was his speciality and the crowds would weep with pride. Yet his ambitious plan to drive the Persians out of Egypt had come to nothing. We would be lucky if more than a few of the troops made it back home. We had spent a fortune of the League's money and our ships were unlikely to make it to the mouth of the Nile let alone back to Athens. But Pericles was too conscious of his many successes to worry for long over a failure which he was clever enough to persuade the Assembly had really been a success.

He changed the subject. 'Now, Euphorion, I want your expert knowledge on Aegina. We have a slight problem there.'

I knew of course that he had been determined to conquer Aegina as part of his master plan. Aegina is an island to the south of Salamis and slightly bigger, say about twelve miles round. It's rocky and mostly infertile, so the inhabitants have a few almond trees and olives but make their living mostly from sponges, fishing and trade.

However their island sits right in the middle of the main trading ,routes from Corinth and Megara as well as Athens to Egypt and the Black Sea. So they can do a lot of damage to all of those cities which they fear or dislike. They even try to undercut the Athens ceramics industry. Recently they seemed to favour Corinth and hate Athens.

Pericles went on, 'Tolmides is still blockading the city, but it's taking too long. We must have Aegina under our control, and I don't trust their people. Too much Phoenician blood, I think, and far too pro-Persian and pro-Corinth. So I'd like you to take a couple of ships across and let me know what you think of the siege.'

I didn't jump for joy at the suggestion and he sensed it.

'Your wife died, didn't she,' he said.

I said 'Yes' but felt deeply bitter both that he had introduced the subject with such cold practicality and because I still felt guilty about the way I had so much taken her for granted and neglected her so badly.

'Time you found a new one,' he said. 'Have a swift voyage and report back to me in a week.'

I was dismissed and as I had nothing better to do I went back to the fleet office and signed up for a couple of spare triremes. I didn't ask for Kleistes to join me as I thought he should have a well-deserved leave, but there was nothing at home to detain me. The following morning we headed due south from the Piraeus, passed Salamis to port and made the landing pier outside the city before dusk.

Most of the Aegina people had either got behind the wall of their city, which had the same name, or had sailed away from the island and were sheltering elsewhere until the blockade was over. I could see right away why the place had not been stormed for the town was built on a high rocky promontory with substantial walls and little cover for besiegers.

Tolmides was in a typically gruff mood as he clearly guessed that Pericles had sent me to snoop on his campaign.

'They'll soon be starving,' he said. 'Bloody Myrmidons.[1] Nothing to eat but almonds, olives and dried fish that you can smell two miles away. They'll surrender before the end of the month.'

The people of Aegina were known as Myrmidons because Zeus had annoyed his wife Hera by having one of his supposedly secret one-night stands on the island, so she wiped out the population with a plague. Only the ants survived the plague, so they were turned into humans by Zeus; hence the slightly odd habits of the current islanders.

I made a perfunctory inspection of the blockade, decided that Tolmides was doing a perfectly good job, left behind one of the triremes and took the other back to Athens to put Pericles out of his misery. Little did I then realise that Pericles in his lust for control would ruthlessly drive out all the inhabitants of the island and replace them with retired oarsmen from our slums.

Back in the Piraeus there was a lot of intense building activity. The hundreds of oarsmen's hovels tottering over narrow, winding streets were being demolished. Now the streets were to be straight and there were new tenement barracks for ships crews, big new warehouses for the fleet stores, granaries and stores for the merchants to keep their huge vats of olive oil alongside rows of decorated pots ready to export round the Mediterranean. The bread-sellers, fortune-tellers, sausage hawkers and naked prostitutes of both sexes and all ages had been relegated to the back streets.

I was soon clear of the port area and headed up the road to Athens between the long walls which were now all but finished. As I entered through the Melitian Gate there was a procession of young maidens dressed as our patron goddess Athena.[2] I meant to drop in on Kleistes so I pushed my way through the crowd and found him on his doorstep watching the proceedings.

'Pretty, aren't they,' he said.

'Their mothers must have spent days getting them all dressed up with their helmets and shields,' I said. 'Is this what we've been fighting for? Traditions and gods we're not even sure exist?'

'If you have a daughter it's one of the things you must do,' said Kleistes, who was not nearly such a rebel as he tried to make out. Then, as we had turned back into his house he said, 'Thank you my friend,' and there was a tear in his eye. 'You saved me. We'll meet again soon.'

I felt a pang of jealousy as I was conscious of the joy that had been awaiting him when he was reunited with his loved ones, whilst I returned to a house empty but for a grumpy old slave. As it turned out not even Psyche was there to greet me, so I washed and headed for a tavern. I soon found a group of fleet officers drinking near the market place and, as usual, they were trying to sharpen their wits with the loquacious but ever-thirsty Anaxagoras.

'Life cannot be fair,' the worthy philosopher was expounding as he allowed his substantial goblet to be filled to the brim at the expense of one of the crowd. 'Think of the virgin Kallisto. She was raped by Zeus[3] and then punished for losing her virginity by Athene who turned her into a pig. What's fair about that?'

Naturally no one answered.

I turned and found that Sophocles was there and he came over to me. 'Sorry to hear that your uncle Aeschylus has passed on,' he said, with just a hint of sincerity.

'I hadn't heard,' I said, dismayed to hear family news from anyone but a close relative. 'I'm just back from Egypt.'

'Rumour has it that an eagle dropped a tortoise on his head, thinking it was a stone, but that's perhaps just gossip. Anyway I must go. Nice to see you back,' and he rushed off in his usual way as if he had more important people to talk to. As it happened I learned later that my uncle had grown unhappy with his reception in Athens and had gone back to his patrons in Sicily where there were no back-biting rivals. It was there among strangers that he had died.[4]

At this point six young men wearing female clothes and bearing a gigantic phallus came past and I realised it must be time for the theatre festivals. Then I heard another familiar voice; it was my former trierarch Lakedaimonios, Cimon's son, addressing me with his usual hesitance.

'How are things?' he asked.

'Not bad,' I replied. 'Just the usual trouble with the fleet inspectors. I set out six months ago with three newish ships, but had them requisitioned in Egypt and replaced with two older, half-rotten ones. Then one of them was burned by the Persians, but by a lucky stroke we picked up a Corinthian replacement on the way home, yet all the inspectors can do is moan about the fact that I'm short of fifty oar-thongs and a starboard halyard. Paperwork. How's your father?'

'He's back here, ready for a new expedition,' he said, as if uncertain if it was good news or bad so far as he was concerned. 'Try some of this wine. It's Samian, quite sweet with just a touch of mastic resin. I think you'll find it quite pleasant[5].'

'Thank you,' I said, taking a swig. 'How's Pericles? In a good mood?'

'Old Squillhead? Same as usual. He's got fleets and armies out in about five places at the same time. We hardly get any shore leave and he expects us to cough up for a new trireme every couple of months. He doesn't know when to stop.'

'And what's it all for?'

'He says the glory of Athens. I say the glory of ruddy Squillhead. Now try some of this Attic red from one of my own estates. It's got just a touch of Hymettos' honey. You can catch the scent of thyme.'

'I agree,' interrupted Anaxagoras, holding out his now empty goblet for a refill. 'Pericles wants to liberate all Greeks, whether under Persian tyranny or that of their own aristocrats. But what is the point if we are all still enslaved by our appetites?' he added taking a large gulp of the Attic wine.[6]

'Indeed,' we replied, almost in unison.

'And our desires,' he added as a lightly clad prostitute drifted past our group swinging her hips.

'What else should we do?' asked one of the others. 'I'd still rather go and kill Persians than sit around watching my olive trees grow.'

'What about Spartans?' I asked. 'Do you enjoy killing them?'

'Not quite so easy, but much more rewarding,' he replied.

I was beginning to find this repartee tedious, so I offered no resistance when Lakedaimonios beckoned to his slave to come forward with yet another different jar of wine.

'From our Thasian vinery,' he said modestly. 'Try it. It's pleasantly dry.' The slave also produced a bowl of fresh olives soaked in vinegar and some dried anchovies.

'I enjoy the huge variety of the earth's produce,' announced Anaxagoras. 'It provides a wonderful test of our ability to resist the crude demands of pleasure. Delicious. But why did the gods create such variety for our benefit?' He paused, clearly not expecting an answer from a group of uncultured trierarchs.

'Let's go back to my place for some skewered lamb and a round or two of kottabos,' said Lakedaimonios. 'I've got a pretty new slave that I'll offer as a prize to anyone who can beat me.'

It wasn't far to the Cimon family home and the slave girl, dressed for the occasion in the skimpy costume of a Maenad, was indeed attractive. Anaxagoras was notoriously incompetent at all things physical, so we had some amusement while he flicked his wine all over the place except at the target. The rest of us didn't try too hard at the kottabos so that we could let the oenophile[7] Lakedaimonios win his own first prize, but we drank a great deal of his wine. When at last we rose to go I admit that my legs were much unsteadier than normal in these circumstances, perhaps due to my privations in Egypt.

'Good night, Axanagoras,' I said, stumbling over his name as we departed.

'Night is by its very nature good,' he replied sagely. 'It is natural and cannot be evil like humans.'

Thus reassured I headed in the direction of the ceramic quarter, my head swimming happily and my feet not quite in control, a dangerous tendency at night in Athens where the cart ruts and sewers are hard to tell apart. It was particularly unwise because I was still carrying twelve drachmas left over from the wages of my trireme crews and would have been better leaving it on deposit with a friendly merchant. There were still one or two brothels open for business, but mostly it was so dark that I had to feel my way along the walls.

Just as I was entering the main pottery area I came to a tavern regularly frequented by foreign merchants, mercenaries and minor diplomats. It had an upstairs area that served partly as a brothel for their convenience and partly as a dormitory. Despite the fact that it was well past midnight the lights were still bright. Two men came out brawling and cursing, then disappeared into the night. Then I heard a laugh which seemed vaguely familiar and a minute later, despite the fact that he was muffled in a cloak I recognised the sallow features of Aristodikos of Tanagra.

'Out late, Captain Euphorion?' he said with a sarcastic smile. 'Bad habit. And I've heard rumours that you've been spreading foul allegations about me. The ridiculous notion that I was involved in the plot to murder Ephialtes. Preposterous. You should guard your tongue. I am a professional diplomat and my reputation for integrity is important to me.'

'I'm sure it is,' I said. 'All I ever said was that as Ephialtes was dying he seemed to be saying your name. Why would that be?'

'Lots of people say my name. Perhaps he had a message for me. You should be careful about drawing dangerous conclusions.'

Unfortunately my wits were still somewhat befuddled by wine or I might have managed an intelligent reply, but for the moment I was non-plussed. Then I was aware that the two brawling men had reappeared and conscious of a sudden movement behind me.

'You should leave these matters alone,' said Aristodikos, twirling his swagger stick. 'I advise you strongly for your own good.'

And at that moment a flash of lightning seemed to go through my head, my body was on fire and I was lying in the gutter, helpless and frightened.

1. Myrmidons had been elite troops of Achilles, whose armour was reminiscent of ants, so when only the ants survived the old plague in Aegina and were turned into humans they were nicknamed Myrmidons

2. In Athens Pallas Athene, Goddess of Wisdom, and motherless daughter of Zeus, was more often portrayed as a warrior, dressed in full armour and ready to let fly with thunderbolts at the enemies of her city.

3. Kallisto was an Arcadian princess or nymph who attended the Goddess Artemis aka Diana. She was the victim of one of the chief god's one-night stands during which he had transformed himself into Artemis aka Diana as part of his harassment strategy. As punishment Zeus's jealous wife turned Kallisto into a bear, after which Zeus worried she might be shot by a hunter, so he transformed her into a constellation more often known as Ursa Major or the Big Bear or in Britain as the Plough Ursa Minor is named after her son.

4. Aeschylus left an epitaph which translates as:

   Here Aeschylus son of Euphorion bred

   In Athens, lies in Gela's corn land dead

   His fighting prowess Marathon could show

   And long-haired Medes who had good cause to know.

5. This was of course an early version of the popular Greek wine Retsina.

6. Some readers may be offended by the suggestion that the great man never bought a round of drinks, but as an astronomer and teacher he had no steady income and though he taught his students to despise all carnal appetites, wealth and honours he did need to quench his own thirst.

7. Oenophile (a connoisseur of wines) is a fake Greek word invented by the British as they did bibliophile, necrophilia, philomath, philoprogenitive and philatelist (after all the ancient

Greeks didn't do postage stamps) but at least philosophy and Philadelphia are genuine Greek.

CHAPTER TWENTY-FIVE

TO HELL AND BACK

I WOKE UP TO FIND a rat sniffing at my face. I was too weak to do more than brush it away. My head was hammering, I felt I was about to vomit and I was shivering uncontrollably. It was nearly dawn and a few tradesmen and some slave girls carrying pitchers of water passed me by, but they obviously thought that I was just a drunk and besides I was too proud to ask for their help. So eventually I pulled myself upright and managed to stumble the short remaining distance to my home. There I fell on my bed and passed out again.

I don't know how much time elapsed, but at one point I was vaguely aware of being scolded first by Psyche, then by Kleistes.

'Hit on the head with a blunt instrument,' I remember him saying. 'I suppose the door porter must have fetched him.'

Then I was on a different bed and my fever was getting worse. Then I was conscious of being on a cart covered with hay and then being in yet another bed and there was a lady in white.

I woke up properly about a week later, I'm told. To my horror, now that I had recovered some self-awareness, I found that my body was covered in suppurating red sores which seemed to produce some filthy liquid which mingled with my dank sweat. I could smell myself and there seemed to be a fog in front of my eyes.[1] My body was still burning and I had a huge urge to throw off the sheet that covered me, but I was naked and there were people in the room. I had an overwhelming thirst which made me think I could dive into a river and drink it all up before I was satisfied.

The lady in white reappeared.

'Not a pretty sight, Phori,' said Kore the priestess of Eleusis.

'I'm sorry,' I muttered.

'You can drink this water,' she said, handing me a cup. 'But not too much.'

I took the cup and she went away. I felt helpless and deeply ashamed. Then I woke up and found myself in a puddle of my own excrement.

Someone washed me and I was grateful that it was not Kore. Some time after that I suddenly vomited green fluid on the floor and I still kept sweating and burning. I couldn't bear any cloth on my body and I wanted to drink far, far more than they would let me.

One day Kore did come back, I don't know whether it was the first time or not, and she started to wipe the sores on my body one by one.

'Phori smells decidedly impure,' she said as if I was incapable of hearing. 'He always seems to come back here to be put together again. I think he drank too much Nile water in Egypt.'

I was conscious of the sickly smell of mandrake and I think it was dittany she was rubbing gently onto my sores.

'I'm sorry,' I said as usual. I was well aware that I must be more repulsive than the most noxious reptile or insect. Yet her hands kept working away at my festering sores. I couldn't help wincing but she ignored me and I hoped she hadn't noticed.

She went away eventually and I drifted off back to sleep again. When I awoke I was burning and threw off my covers. My sores were now so itchy that I could not stop myself from scratching them.

'Stop that at once, Phori,' came the angry voice of the priestess. 'You must let them heal.' And Poseidon who was standing by her growled to emphasise his support for her orders, then began to scratch himself as if to display his superiority.

I covered myself and lay gasping and ashamed. The thirst still tore at my mouth yet I was always wet with stale sweat. Days and nights passed. When Kore was there I was embarrassed, but when she wasn't I longed for her to come back, if only I could keep control of my feeble and rebellious body. Often she brought me cups of their special barley brew laced with minty pennyroyal[2] and I think it helped to build me up. Her parents Psamos and Gaia both visited me once or twice and were as courteous as ever. One day Kleistes came to see me and admitted that it was he who had decided to bring me to Eleusis.

'By the navel of Artemis I'm glad to see you a bit better,' he said, smiling ruefully. 'What were you drinking that night?'

'I did have too much wine,' I admitted, 'but then I was clubbed by one of Aristodikos' heavies.'

'I heard he'd been in Athens.' Kleistes scratched his beard thoughtfully. 'Another of these pro-Spartan plots, I expect. Thucydides and his crowd. They want rid of Pericles. But Aristodikos will have disappeared again long since. I don't know how you'd ever catch up with him again, even if you wanted to.'

' The day will come,' I said, and I vowed to myself that eventually I would seek some form of revenge.

About two days later the fever suddenly seemed to leave me and the scabs began to fall away from the remnants of my sores. Kore's visits became less frequent and then stopped altogether, although I thought I heard her strumming softly on her seven-stringed lyre. At the end of that week Gaia came to tell me that I was fit enough to leave.

'Demeter[3] take care of you,' she said.

'I'd like to thank the Princess Kore as well,' I said.

She shrugged her shoulders and smiled. 'As you know only too well,' she said, 'Kore is not always of this world. Try the Hall of Mysteries if you want to.'

With some trepidation I walked across the temple courtyard to the Hall and into its cool darkness. There was no sign of Kore and my miserable state of mind began to intensify as I thought yet again of the empty life ahead with little prospect of further commands in the fleet and little desire to enter politics, no wife and no children, not even basic respect let alone love from the woman I most admired in all the world.

I came to the huge door at the side of the Hall. It was shut, but there was a smaller door set in its centre where an old man sat keeping guard. When I showed the initiate's token hanging round my neck he motioned me to go through and held out his hand for a coin, so I obliged with a drachma. On the other side was the path that led down into the cavern which I had seen when I came here for initiation ten years earlier. No one but the goddess Persephone or her earthly representative, the Princess Kore, was allowed to go further on pain of death.

I stood for a while staring down into the darkness but there was no sign of Kore. A row of bats hung blinking from the roof but the only sound was the distant plop of dripping water. Even on a warm autumn day there was still a cool breeze coming up from below. I waited full of self-pity, thinking rather bitterly that Kore did not even consider it worth saying goodbye to me.

I was still weak in both mind and body, so it was not so much courage that made me think of going on but rather the thought that I might as well be dead. I knew well enough the awful penalties decreed for anyone who offended the priests of Eleusis, but in a moment of deep resentment against my fate I decided to do what I knew was wrong. Some of the new philosophers like the hard-drinking Anaxagoras had started fashionable gossip that some of the gods were make-believe, but the old laws against sacrilege were still very much in place and the punishments severe. I took a quick glance behind me to make sure no one was watching and strode down the forbidden staircase into the cavern.

After about a dozen steps the floor of the cave started to slope down steeply and in the dim light I could just make out the path winding down the side. Moving more slowly so that my eyes might get used to the darkness I carried on downwards. But for the trickle and froth of a small stream ahead of me I had no real sense of direction and the cave was now totally dark. The air however was fresh and pleasantly cool.

My route went on down for another hundred paces and I began to regret my stupidity in entering the forbidden area. The legends came back to me so that I expected at any second to fall into the icy waters of the river Styx or some fiery pit. Unlike our great hero Theseus, I had made no attempt to tie a piece of string when I left the entrance so I had no idea of how to get back up to the daylight. I had little choice but to go on. Then there seemed to be a blur of bluish light which might have been my imagination, but I briefly saw the shadow of my hands and found a dry wall along which I could feel my way. It still seemed easier to go on than to go back, but as my powers of reason revived so did my fear and I was now more terrified than I had been in the worst moments of my career in the fleet. Now the floor seemed to have almost levelled out and the sound of the stream was getting closer. My mind grew less perturbed and I accepted the fact that I might never escape yet somehow no longer cared. Then suddenly I felt the wet nose of a dog against my leg. Then a bare arm pushed against my chest and gently halted my progress.

'You're lost, Phori,' said a familiar, mocking voice.

'Maybe I am,' I answered, my masculine pride slightly offended by her tone. 'But I have been entombed before and managed to get out again.'

'But not from here.' She picked up a small oil lamp from a niche in the cavern wall and it threw some light over our faces, but the ceiling above remained invisible as did all the walls except the one beside us. 'You're still not looking very pretty,' she said.

'I'm sorry,' I said. It was becoming an unfortunate habit.

'I don't mind,' she moved closer. 'Why did you come down here against the law of the gods? You could be executed.'

'I just wanted to thank you for saving my miserable life again,' I said.

'You've taken a very big risk just to say thank you. Is that all?'

'Well,' I hesitated. 'I wanted to see you. I couldn't go away unless I saw you.'

'Then I should thank you,' she said and I saw there was a tear running down her brown face. 'You're the only person who's ever risked death to come down here to see me.'

Instinctively I put out both arms and joined them behind her back as she faced me. For a moment I remembered that she was a priestess and hesitated, but then her look of vulnerability gave me courage. I lent forward to kiss her and she did not object. For the first time in my life my mind felt totally at peace with itself and my body turned from a thing of ugliness to beauty. Also for the first time Poseidon the dog no longer growled when I touched his mistress.

Perhaps half an hour passed and we stood wrapped together in joy like Perseus and Andromeda after he had killed the Gorgons.

'You are my whole life,' I said. 'You keep saving it. It belongs to you.'

She pulled gently away from me, looking mischievous again. 'You'll never find your way out of this cavern without my help,' she said. 'And even if you did you'll be executed.'

'I don't care,' I answered, kissing her again.

'There is one solution. You have to agree to become part of the priestly family.'

'I'm not exactly qualified to be a priest.'

'Yes you are. You have love. That's all you need.'

'I have love and I want love. Put down the lamp a minute, Kore. Then we'll go back up as I want to ask Psamos a question.'

'I think he's half expecting you,' she said.

---

1.   It has been suggested that the plague which struck Athens at this time was either typhus or typhoid fever, two different diseases that have symptoms in common, including the visual fogginess which gave them both their name. Typhos is the Greek word for mist or cloud.

2. Pennyroyal or squaw mint (mentha pulegium) was in those days a popular cooking ingredient, but it is slightly toxic and is now rarely used except as a weak herbal tea or in aromatherapy.

3. Demeter the Earth Mother also had a one-night stand with Zeus which resulted in the birth of Persephone otherwise known as Kore. The god had no shame.

CHAPTER TWENTY-SIX

SHORE LEAVE

YOU MAY THINK THAT AFTER the adventures and trials of my early life and the erratic route by which I had at last found real love then the rest of my life would be an uneventful anti-climax. It is true that by becoming the husband of a priestess and the son-in-law of a high priest I was reducing my exposure to military call-up and to murderous scuffles in the back streets of Athens, but as things turned out the next few years were to be extremely eventful for the city of Athens and from time to time I played a significant, sometimes dangerous role. It is also true that whilst my new happiness seemed to justify the sufferings that went before it, they also gave me strength to face unexpected ordeals that still lay ahead.

I was married to Kore in my 29th year[1] and I was to be over fifty when Athens was finally embroiled in that dreadful war with Sparta that was to destroy so many hopes and ideals, but in the meantime there were to be a number of campaigns and incidents in which I was involved, albeit less frequently than had previously been the case. There was also for some years at the back of my mind an unresolved worry about the attempt of Aristodikos to murder me and the fact that his behaviour seemed to lend credence to the theory that he had also been guilty of the attack on Ephialtes. In a strange way I bore less of a grudge against him now because the injury inflicted on me by his thugs had been the reason for my hospitalisation in Eleusis and thus indirectly for me at long last finding the truth of both my own feelings for Kore and hers for me.

Meanwhile for a whole year I didn't go back to sea, but stayed in Eleusis with my beloved new wife. Unlike my wedding with Zoe which I could barely remember except as a minor formal interlude between cruises, the ceremonies with Kore were a source of real happiness and lasting memories. After some initial hesitation both my mother Phasia and my old nurse Psyche came to very much favour Kore and fussed around us happily for days alongside her mother Gaia.

The ritual bath, the wedding feast, our journey across Eleusis in a little cart, our kneeling together at the hearth, being showered with nuts by our mothers and then suffering the obscene jokes of friends like Kleistes and even Sophocles were all events which we enjoyed at the time and treasured as memories in later years. Then came our secret acting-out of the abduction of Persephone which was in our case more meaningful because Kore was the Persephone of our generation and in a sense I had rescued her from the evil arms of Hades, whilst in return she had saved me from execution. We knew of course that at the next Mysteries she would still have to perform her hereditary duties and return to her cavern beneath the temple, but it was now an underworld that we shared, for as a senior priest I had to mix the famous drink kykeon[2] which was served to all those who swore to keep the secrets of Eleusis so that they would be purified from the defilements of the material world.

If you think there was any element of hypocrisy in my supporting a ritual which seemed in some ways to be a sham, I recognised that it meant a great deal to many thousands of ordinary people, and I have learned from bitter experience that there is more to life than mere truth. After all it was not a deception, for spring does come again, the flowers do reappear exactly on time and the barley does grow each year to give us food.

The night of our wedding, Kore came shyly into our master bedroom and said, 'You've been through all this before, Phori. Haven't you? With Zoe.'

'This is a bit diff….' I began to stutter and patted Poseidon who had followed her into the room.

'It certainly is,' she replied. 'For this time you could be executed for violating a virgin priestess.'

'It would be worth it,' I said. 'But you said I'd be executed when I violated your cave a month ago and I survived.'

'I'm not used to this kind of thing.'

'I love you. Nothing else matters.'

'Every time I've seen you in bed before today you've either been in a raging fever or covered in sores. Never very pretty.'

'You're a wonderful nurse, a lovely princess and so far as I'm concerned a goddess.'

'That's sacrilegious talk,' she replied. 'Which goddess by the way?' she added with the hint of a grin.

'Aphrodite, of course,' I said.

'The goddess of sex, of course, I've seen more of your body than you have of mine.'

'I got a quick glimpse that day you saved my life on the beach.'

'You know how to make babies, then? That's how Zoe died.'

'I'll feel guilty for the rest of my life, but I think Demeter will look after you.'

'Right then,' she said, pulled her tunic over her head, and stretched out her arms. 'Go and lie down, Poseidon,' she added.

Often in the weeks that followed I would visit Kore deep down on the edge of Hades and we needed no lamp. Then spring and love were reborn and we were officially reunited, leaping happily into the cold spring waters of the River Ilissos to purify us from sin and encouraging new initiates to do the same. So when winter was over we had special joy in the flowery meadows and scampering streams which led down to the Bay of Eleusis where I had escaped from the watery clutches of Poseidon and my life had been saved by Kore for the first time. I may have had doubts about the powers of the gods, but if nothing else the pure beauty of my wife reassured me there was something divine in the world. To me it was extraordinary that a woman could be so spiritual one day, yet the next would be dusting a baby's bottom as if she was no more than a common slave.

In the early summer of the next year our first son Kynegiros was born, named after my gallant father. Kore endured a lot of pain with great fortitude and I found that both my love and respect for her deepened still further. Gaia her mother tended to fuss around quite a lot, which I admit was initially quite irritating, but I gradually came to understand her feelings and looked on her and Psamos as firm friends. Poseidon fussed around as well but was eventually becoming resigned to my presence.

My duties as a priest were relatively light except during the annual Mysteries so I began at this time to take a more responsible interest in the running of the family estate nearby, particularly since one of my two younger brothers had now gone off with the fleet reinforcements to Memphis and the other was on garrison duty at Phyle. Whereas Psamos's estates were almost entirely devoted to corn and barley, mine were all still in olive trees, vines and flax. I owned eleven slaves including my old nurse Psyche, the ancient door-man in our city house, three other house servants and five farm workers. They didn't need a huge amount of supervision as they knew their duties, but there was no doubt that a bit of encouragement on matters like vine pruning and cutting away dead wood did produce improved results. My income depended on a decent pressing of grapes and at least a dozen cartloads of olives, so it was worth letting my slaves hear that I could tell the difference when they made an effort.

I kept out of Athens most of that year and was relieved to get no summons for sea duty. So far as we heard the news it was mainly still of Athenian successes, but there was an unhealthy silence about what was happening in Memphis. As I learned later Charitimides had never captured the citadel and the Persians had cut off his fleet from the sea by blocking the River Nile. The triremes, including my three, had to be left stranded in the desert and our forces were lucky to escape on foot. The reinforcement troops with my brother amongst them sailed straight into a trap and suffered heavy casualties though he was one of the lucky ones who got back.

Surprisingly neither of these disasters seemed to dent the confidence of Pericles, who had a remarkable ability to suggest to the Assembly that defeats were really victories or at worst honourable failures due to exceptional circumstances beyond our control. And of course he was brilliant at funeral orations for our fallen heroes. So they kept on electing him as chief general though he left most of the actual campaigning to Tolmides and my former father-in-law Myronides. Needless to say Charitimides got no further commands, for he was the scapegoat for the disastrous campaign in Egypt.

Certainly we all felt confident at that time and really came to believe that we were masters of sea warfare and that our city was now invincible, the greatest and most beautiful city in the world.

As a family we had very great joy that summer as Kore and I would often take our baby son to some remote part of our estates where we would not be disturbed. I would watch as young Kynegiros sucked his milk, pushing his stubby feet into the sky as Kore sat in the long scented grass. Then we would all splash together in one of the deeper pools of the River Kephisos[3] where the sun shone straight down to the yellow pebbles on the bottom and the fish always darted away. Even Poseidon joined in the entertainment.

Kore also took some delight in teaching me to find herbs and flowers in the fields and woodlands that led up to Mount Aigaleo[4] where years before the Persian king Xerxes had sat on his throne to watch the battle of Salamis.

'Look, there's a squill,' she would say. 'We'll hang it over our door.'

'A nice reminder of Pericles,' said I, for as you know the great man's nickname was Squillhead on account of his pointed forehead.

'There's mandrake, belladonna, pennyroyal and cannabis,'[5] she continued. 'We use all these in small quantities for the sick.'

She also kept her own herb garden near our house where she grew fennel and lettuce, chicory and endives in big pots. Then she had a larger area where she had carrots, and asparagus beneath her pomegranate tree. Near the beach were agnus castus[6] bushes which had a pretty flower and the branches were good to make baskets and there was samphire. Always she liked to encourage the cooks to add extra leaves or berries to our meals and I must admit it made eating more enjoyable. Tending the herbs was the job now mainly given to Psyche who was getting very bent. She spoiled Kynegiros hopelessly whenever she was allowed near him.

'There are rumours of another big expedition against the Persians,' said Psamos one day when I dropped into the temple to see him. 'Perhaps this will be the last.

'I would hope so,' I said, hardly daring to admit even to myself the faint stirring of excitement and slightly hurt that I had not been sent for.

'Cimon is leading it,' added Psamos. 'I hope he knows what he's doing, going back to war after all these years.'

'Cimon is the toughest of all the generals,' I answered. 'The only things he doesn't like are long sieges.'

I returned home and was rather more aggressive than usual with my slaves, as I resigned myself to being redundant from the fleet. Kore asked what was wrong with me, but I did not have the courage to tell her the truth.

'You're really not content just to look after your estates and do your temple duties once or twice a year, are you?' she said perceptively. 'You quite enjoy having a little son, but it's not enough for you. You had too much excitement and now you miss it.' She looked at me with some disappointment in her eyes.

'I'm perfectly happy,' I protested.

'You're a liar, Phori. I can always tell. There's something you still have to get out of your system before you're completely pure,' and with these words she stomped off to attend to Kynegiros, followed by an equally indignant Poseidon.

I knew, unfortunately, that there was some truth in what she said. Whether I was still feeling the need to compete with the ghost of my father or whether I had become too obsessed with great heroes of the past or whether I still even wanted to prove something to Pericles, I don't know. And there was always the nagging feeling that I should settle my score with Aristodikos.

Whatever the reason I found myself in a gloomy mood and causing some misery to the kindest lady in the world. So the following day, as I was nagging the local carpenter to repair my olive presses, I was more than pleased to get a tap on the shoulder and hear a familiar voice from the past.

'I've been promoted, as Daphne said when she was turned into a laurel bush.' It was Kleistes.

'Congratulations,' I said.

'To ship-master of the flagship *Salaminia*, destination Cyprus,' he went on. 'But only so long as you take over as trierarch,' he added. 'It has to be a priest, you see. Only a member of a priestly family is qualified to be trierarch of the *Salaminia*.'

---

1. This places the year of Euphorion's marriage as 456 BC, about the same time that his old enemy King Xerxes was murdered.

2. For ancient Greek peasants and other workers the drink known as Kykeon was a strange mixture of barley, wine and a sprinkling of goats cheese. But for the Mysteries it also included pennyroyal and other herbs which some have argued had psychotropic qualities resulting in the drinkers having visions.

3. The River Kephisos became the Saranadapotamos and runs part of its course in a conduit under the M1 Motorway to Thessalonika.

4. Mount Aigaleo or Poikilos west of Athens is a limestone outcrop rising to 1,560 feet above sea level and commands a view over Salamis.

5. The use of medicinal herbs in ancient Greece is well recorded: pennyroyal, for example, as a slightly toxic kind of mint was used for digestive problems and to flavour wine or puddings. It is worth mentioning that Eleusis is for some reason one of the hottest places in the whole of Europe.

6. Agnus Castus or Chaste or Monk's Pepper or Vitex, a bush with pretty flowers, had this name in the Middle Ages because if was believed to be the opposite of an aphrodisiac, so it helped monks to avoid sin. It is still sold by herbalists as an antidote for irritability.

CHAPTER TWENTY-SEVEN

THE AFFAIR IN CYPRUS[1]

WHEN I SUMMONED UP THE courage to ask Kore if she would mind if I went back to sea one more time she surprised me as she so often did. Instead of annoyance or sulky resignation which I might have expected she hugged me warmly.

'Take good care of yourself,' she said. 'I'm very proud that you'll be the captain of the *Salaminia*, because only a priest can do that. And my father will be proud of you too, even if he doesn't admit it.' She turned to Kleistes who had stayed on for dinner and said to him, 'If I were a real goddess I'd turn you into a frog.'

Kleistes just grinned and carried on giving Kynegiros a swing from his vast hairy arms. 'Koax, koax,'[2] he said.

'You'll be fine without me, Kore,' I said when we had a moment alone.

'Just get it over with and come back quickly,' she replied. 'Kynegiros needs you and so do I.'

When we went back Kynegiros was sitting on his potty, a relatively new achievement, with Kleistes encouraging him with a rattle and Psyche singing one of her appropriate ditties. We laughed and I gave Kore a final hug before loading my armour onto my personal slave and taking once more to the Sacred Way, followed by Poseidon for the first hundred yards till he decided to turn back.

Kleistes, who was always a lady's man, whispered wholly inappropriate words to Psyche who blushed and giggled before slapping him hard. She was obviously very pleased.

The Piraeus was busier than ever and I must admit it revived some happy memories when I smelt again the familiar odours of fresh pitch, wet hemp, stale urine and rotten cabbage which always seemed to hang over a fleet of triremes. Even in the past year the docks had been further extended, and there were new sheds covering the slipways and more ships taking shape on the stocks.

The general in charge was none other than our old commander Cimon, now restored to popularity with a mission to free the Greeks on Cyprus from Persian control. I'm not sure that he really recognised me or knew my name, but he had a knack of pretending these things, which generals seem to acquire when they want to. He gave me a slight bow to acknowledge my priestly status and welcomed me to *Salaminia*, the largest, fastest and most ornate ship in the fleet.

'You're in command of the ship,' he said. 'I'm just a passenger who happens to be in charge of the whole fleet,' he grinned. 'So I say where the fleet goes, but you have control of what happens on this ship. Clear?'

I nodded agreement. 'When do we cast off?'

'Tomorrow morning. I'd like to make it to Keos by tomorrow night. Then Delos, Amorgos, Kos, Rhodes, Myra,[3] Paphos. Seven days rowing or sailing should do it.'

I nodded again and spoke briefly to Kleistes who was sorting out his specialist crew members ready to put the flagship to sea. It was both wider and longer than most triremes and unusually was fitted with two large cabins: one for the general's office along with his butler and his seer, the other for the priestly trierarch who if the omens were wrong had considerable powers to overrule even a general.

'I'll sacrifice a piglet at dawn,' I told my slave and asked Kleistes to make sure that all the other trierarchs were around when I gave the fleet my official blessing before setting sail. Killing a piglet has never been one of my favourite pastimes, but there are occasions when it has to be done to add solemnity in life, especially when people are about to face danger and depend on each other. It's not just what I believe that matters.

Luckily the next morning the sun was shining and the two hundred ships with *Salaminia* at their head made a fine show as they left harbour at half-minute intervals and then formed up in four columns of fifty for the first leg to Keos. I felt guilty pleasure with the gently rolling deck beneath my feet again and once more a trail of friendly dolphins keeping us company. Cimon asked me to keep *Salaminia* in the middle of the fleet so that he would have a chance to watch the performance of his various crews. In fact only two ships had problems and even they made it to Keos soon after the rest of us. The main town is high up to make it safer from pirates, but the fishing harbour below was adequate. I went ashore to see the huge stone lion which is their main claim to fame though the people were well known as worshippers of the dog star.

Next day we made the standard stop at Delos to pick up fresh oar-slaves and money for wages from the treasury. As it happened the winds were light so we had none of the problems I had met with on my last visit there with Pericles. At this point sixty of our ships were detached to head south for Egypt to support one last rebel stronghold which was still defying the Persians. The rest of us headed for Amorgos, an island I had not visited before. It turned out to be long and narrow with several bays offering good shelter from the wind and a massive temple to the Pythian Apollo which we duly admired. After a short overnight rest we had a good sail the next day to Kos where most of our fleet was able to moor in the harbour of Astypalea.

I like Kos, perhaps because its rich flat fields remind me of home and also like Eleusis because it is a place where they set great store by healing the sick and wounded. In fact in my later days I and my family had help from a renowned healer there called Hippocrates.[4]

Meanwhile I bought a roll of excellent local linen to take back for Kore.

Two days later we anchored in Lindos,[5] one of the great cities of Rhodes where I had never previously landed. Rhodes, of course, was the island that Zeus plucked out of the seabed because he'd forgotten to provide a home for Apollo. I wished Kore had seen it with me for she would have loved the roses which grew in profusion round the city. As fleet priest it was my duty to propitiate the gods in every port where we landed and Lindos was a special case as, like Athens, it had a special temple for Athena. It was up a steep path to the acropolis and was of a stylish modern design with splendid carvings.

We now headed east and after a two day rest at Myra near Phaselis, which I had helped recapture ten years earlier, we turned toward Paphos,[6] one of the cities on Cyprus that was still held by the Greeks. It's a strange island, Cyprus, for it seems to belong to neither one race or the other, Greeks or Persians. Despite the fact that our goddess of love, Aphrodite, was born here we never seemed to take it very seriously. We had four good cities there, but so did the Phoenicians and both races seemed equally at home. Three of the Greek cities had already been freed by us from Persian control, but had not been particularly loyal since then, and I suppose it was mainly because of the copper mines that we wanted to keep at least a foothold, but the Phoenician fleet was of course pro-Persian and a constant menace.

Cimon's objective was to free the Greek city of Kition[7] from Persian control and then head down to Egypt to breathe some life into the stuttering campaign there now that Charitimides had retired. Kition was quite a substantial city with its acropolis set well back from the sea. The harbour was too small for us except for quick dashes in to unload men and equipment. Nor did we dare beach our ships on the long stretches of sand for fear of a surprise attack by the Phoenician fleet hired by the Persians and based in Salamis[8] on the east coast of the island. We did make some use of the huge salt lagoon on the west of Kition, but it tended to be too shallow and hard to navigate for our triremes. However, the rubber-necked flamingos provided considerable entertainment.

Despite my new priestly status some people still looked on me as a siege specialist, so Cimon consulted me as we set up the blockade and looked for ways to storm the city. Regrettably the Phoenicians are very well-drilled archers, so surprise attacks seemed out of the question. We thus decided to concentrate our efforts on the western part of the walls nearest to the sea where they were relatively low and faced ground with good cover.

'Unless we can find a quick way over that wall this is going to last the best part of a year,' said Cimon bluntly, when we met in his tent.

'I'm sorry, I don't think there's a way,' I said, 'Unless the garrison start to get sloppy.'

'There has to be,' said Cimon with an aggression that made his face seem even redder than usual. 'I will give you senior officers twenty-four hours to come up with some better ideas or I will hand over the job to the junior trierarchs.'

We suffered his rebuke with some embarrassment. I know it is normal enough for generals to use threats of humiliation to even their most trusted officers, so that they feel goaded into some crazily heroic action which may, by a fluke, produce results or just as likely lead to their deaths. That's generals for you and Cimon was a highly successful one, even if it was pitched battles rather than sieges that had made his name, so he was entitled to try the bully role if he wanted to. For myself I didn't much like that kind of pressure and spent the afternoon inspecting every foot of those walls as dispassionately as I could and without going within range of Phoenician archers.

That evening we gathered again in Cimon's tent and for my part I could still see no way of storming the city that would not be suicidal for those involved. Cimon had not been sleeping well and was more than usually irritable.

'I thought I could expect more from such a group of supposedly competent officers,' he said and then suddenly, without any warning, his speech became slurred and almost unintelligible. Then his face began to twitch and his left hand shot out, rigid like a wooden doll's.

None of us knew what to do, though everyone looked at me because I was a priest.

'Get him to lie on the ground,' I said. We did so, but I saw that he could not move his left arm and he could no longer speak. His face had gone a palish colour and his expression was somehow like that of a sulky child who just stared at us as if he no longer knew who we were.

He died later that night and we buried him with full military honours near a small temple by the salt lagoon. His second-in-command, Phasicles, hated sieges anyway and a month later we gave up the blockade of Kition. But, fired up by the emotion created by our great general's funeral, we sailed the fleet round to Salamis and challenged the Phoenician navy to chase us. They tried and in Cimon's honour we rammed fifty of their ships, boarded around twenty and chased the stragglers onto the shore and up into the hills beyond.

So at least they didn't pester the Greeks of Cyprus for many years to follow.

The one person whose attitude I found odd after the death of Cimon was his son, Lakedaimonios. Gone was the rather truculent and hesitant trireme commander, gone was the over-generous buyer of drinks. Instead he became an apparently more relaxed and assured man, happy with his environment and no longer needing to impress.[9]

---

1.   The Cyprus campaign began in 449 BC when Euphorion was in his mid- thirties.

2.   The words Koax, koax are used in Aristophanes' comedy 'The Frogs' first performed in 405BC some time after Kleistes.

3.   Myra was another of those Greek ports on the now Turkish coast which were silted up by their own rivers and left high and dry.

4.   At this time the famous doctor and author of the even more famous oath was about seven years old so it was still his father in charge of the Kos medical school at this time.

5.   At Lindos on Rhodes the ruins of the temple of Athena are still visible but incorporated in a more recent structure.

6,   Paphos is still a thriving city with an international airport, is on the UNESCO list for its historical and environmental attributes and was joint Cultural Capital of Europe in 2007.

7.   Kition was later renamed Larnaka and a statue of Cimon still graces the seafront

8.   The ruins of ancient Salamis lie near modern Famagusta.

9.   Lakedaimonios did in fact later rise to the rank of general like his father, though not quite so successful.

CHAPTER TWENTY-EIGHT

ON THE TRAIL OF ARISTODIKOS

I ENJOYED OUR VICTORIOUS HOMECOMING from Cyprus more than I had ever done in the past. Kynegiros had grown several inches in my absence and so had Kore for she was now expecting our second child. It was a fairly mild winter that followed and her sojourns in the cavern of Hades were kept brief, for even without my interference her father Psamos, the high priest of Eleusis, enjoyed his new role as a grandfather too much to risk any kind of threat to his daughter's health.

So in the spring of the next year our first daughter, young Gaia, was born, a little dark thing who gave us great joy. The harvests that autumn were good and now that there was peace with Persia there was no more talk of naval expeditions.

You may think that I showed great ingratitude to the gods in not totally appreciating the life of peace and prosperity that I could now enjoy. I really did feel many moments of absolute contentment with my little family and wonderful wife, but I have to admit that after the first year or so I began to find my priestly and agricultural duties a little too tame.

It was towards the end of that year[1] that Kleistes reappeared in my life to provide at least one alternative interest which was to prove very significant for me a few years later.

'I've come to ask a favour, Phori,' he said. 'As Zeus said to Leda before she started parting his feathers,' he added softly with a wink, for Kore was hovering nearby with some dried figs and plums.

'You're just an old trouble-maker, Kleistes,' she said, smiling without having heard a word of his proposal. 'Don't let it be another expedition or I really will turn you into a frog.'

'Koax, koax,' he said and started hopping around with some agility for a man of his age. The children loved it.

'No,' he said. 'It's just a business venture. As you know I've been a seaman all my life, mostly in triremes, but there's no work for us any more. So I'm wanting to buy a small merchant vessel to ply from Piraeus to Sicily and Italy, but I need to borrow a couple of hundred drachmas. I wondered if you'd consider taking a half share in the venture. At least you know that I can point a ship the right way to get to Sicily.'

I liked the whole idea very much, but even with Kleistes I didn't want to show enthusiasm too readily.

'Why Italy?' I asked.

'They're building a new city at Sybaris[2] to help develop trade. They're very keen on our red figure vases and we have a market here for their metalwork, plus cushion covers from Carthage and even some of that Sicilian cheese that's very popular with the rich. We'll have full cargoes in both directions, I reckon.'

I looked at Kore and she shrugged her shoulders, probably relieved that Kleistes had suggested nothing more potentially dangerous. Certainly I had surplus cash and to be honest needed a new stimulus for my mind.

'Well, I still have cousins on Gela,' I said. 'Two of Aeschylus' sons are there. It would be good to keep in touch.'

'We get half the profit of each voyage split between us,' said Kleistes.

'Just pay me back when you're ready,' I said. 'I'm not a usurer.'

So we sealed our bargain and I became, I suppose, a kind of merchant. As I said, I'm not desperately excited by business, but it was a new interest and at least it had to do with the sea. Psyche came into the room with cups of wine and as usual attempted to avoid Kleistes' wandering hands.

'You're looking lovelier than ever,' he said, and she nearly dropped one of the cups, but she laughed as she steered out of the way. 'You sailors are all the same,' she said, beaming.

Before I saw him again a year or so later Kleistes managed three successful trips across the Adriatic and kept in touch, so for a period the whole project provided a useful outlet for my mind. In that time we had our second daughter, little Phasia, who was quite different in character from her sister Gaia. Whereas Gaia was serious and thoughtful, Phasia was for ever laughing and up to tricks. Kore and I still shared most of our inner thoughts with each other and I could say that our relationship was perfect, though now that we had three children I suppose she did not have quite so much time for me, and in the quiet of Eleusis there were times when I still missed the excitement of war, however much I persuaded myself that it was hateful. Occasionally also I still had a nagging desire to get my own back on Aristodikos and to find proof once and for all that he was really guilty of killing Ephialtes. At least I was quite convinced that his thugs had tried to kill me in the ceramic quarter and that made the theory more than credible.

It was about two years after my return from Cyprus when I once more got a summons to visit Pericles.

'Surely he can't have soldiering for you to do,' said Kore, looking serene that day in the full yellow robe of a priestess.

'I don't suppose so,' I said. 'Though there are rumours of oligarchic plots in Thebes again. More likely he wants an ambassador. Kallias is getting past it.'

'Well don't stay away too long. We need you here,' she said firmly and we stood, in each other's arms, for several minutes.

It is a terrible thing to admit, but as I rode off up the Sacred Way to Athens I almost sang with a sense of freedom, though I was still deeply in love with the prison behind me.

I reached Athens in less than two hours and was greeted by Lampon who soon afterwards showed me into Pericles' office. 'Squillhead' I thought to myself, but bit the smile on my lips as I faced the great man once more. In fact I thought he had aged and looked worried. While he still had that serene self-control, even when surrounded by disaster, there were more lines round his face and his hands moved constantly on his desk.

'Welcome back, Euphorion,' he said. 'The Princess Kore is well, I hope?' He always had that politician's knack of remembering your wife's name.

'Yes,' I said. 'And your family?'

He smiled and then without answering moved quickly to the business in hand. 'We have a slight siege problem again and I thought you might be willing to help.'

'I really think...' I began.

'You'll have heard there's been a coup in Thebes and the democratic party has been replaced by an oligarchy. One of the chief plotters was an old acquaintance of yours, Aristodikos of Tanagra. He's getting on a bit now, so this must be his last try. Tanagra itself is still in ruins, but as a second choice he has seized the city of Chaeronea[3] about forty miles to the west. He's killed all the leading democrats and set himself up there as a dictator with the help of Thebes.'

He paused and saw that my interest had been aroused, as no doubt he had calculated.

'Anyway,' he continued, 'we can't do anything about Thebes without causing another war with Sparta. Chaeronea is not important enough to do that and, besides, not even the Spartans trust Aristodikos. On the other hand if we can save Chaeronea it means at least one democracy left in that area.'

Whether it was just coincidence or whether Pericles had used the bait of Aristodikos to get my aid in this little ploy I shall never know, but I consented to help the siege without any hesitation.

'There is another side to this whole business,' Pericles went on, 'but I'd like you to keep this to yourself. There are still one or two dissident oligarchs in Athens itself. Thucydides is one of them and an able leader. Now that they no longer have Cimon as their figurehead they have less need to appear moderates. Watch out for any signs of contact between them and Chaeronea for it could spell real danger for Athens.'

I did not much like these underhand aspects of campaigning, but I nodded and was given papers of authority by Lampon as I left.

An hour later after dropping in to my town house to pick up my armour I met Tolmides by the Assembly. He was in charge of the main force of around a thousand reservists being sent to help the democrats in Boeotia. The grizzled old general, for whom I had considerable respect, gave me the nearest he could manage to a warm welcome.

'We don't need a priest,' he said, half-smiling. 'This will be easy.'

I think this bravado was for the benefit of some of his officers standing nearby, many of whom looked as if they were just out of school. I doubted if Chaeronea would be all that easy a nut to crack. Anyway, as Kleistes was away in Sicily, I went to round up some of my other old siege assistants who had been with me at Ithome and Naupaktos. It took me another day to collect equipment and mules to carry it.

Two days later we passed the frontier post at Phyle and went on down into the plain of Tanagra where, as Pericles had said, the city was still in ruins from our last visit. We kept clear of Thebes as ordered and headed west past the reedy swamps of Lake Kopais[4] and the ancient capital Orchomenos where the Three Graces once lived. That evening we saw Chaeronea ahead of us, set on the foothills of Mount Parnassos where the road from the north crosses over to Delphi. The town itself was on a small hill by Mount Thourion with a deep ravine to the north and strong walls surrounding the town on all sides.

'Let's pitch camp out of sight behind this knoll,' I said to Oloros, my deputy, when we had reached a sheltered spot without being spotted from the ramparts, so far as I could tell. 'We can do our scouting in the morning.'

We ate quite well that night despite my refusal to let the men light fires, but for some reason I found it hard to sleep. I was worried now that I had not explained properly to Kore what I was doing and might never see her again. I was also concerned about once more confronting Aristodikos, one of the few men on earth that I really thought deserved death, yet as a priest or even as myself for that matter, I knew I could not kill him in cold blood.

The next morning I got up at dawn and the early sun was rapidly burning off the dew from the long grass on the hillside. I beckoned to Oloros to join me and we dressed our troop in rough cloaks to look like local peasants. I told the men to keep as quiet as possible and we set off to reconnoitre the most likely weak points of the city walls.

Previous experience had taught me that the walls of cities are usually at their most vulnerable in the places where nature has done most of the work. The ravine north of Chaeronea was its most obvious natural defence, but real cliffs are usually easier to climb than man-made walls. Luckily there were hundreds of goats scattered just below the city, so taking advantage of this, Oloros and I made a great show of herding them for half an hour so that our activities would be ignored by the look-outs. Then we gradually edged our way into the ravine where the rock and scrub gave good cover from the walls above.

The river Kephisos running through the ravine was a modest stream, probably because it was dammed higher up the hill to provide water for the city, but the rocks were slippery so we had to take great care climbing. Further up it was easier because so many small trees had taken root in the cracks that they gave us useful hand-holds. An efficient city ruler would have made sure these trees were destroyed, but perhaps there had been no feeling of danger here since the Persians captured it thirty years earlier.

By this time Oloros and I were no more than twenty feet below the walls and to my right there was a cleft in the rock where I knew we could push ourselves up using the two sides. At its top we found that the actual wall was of fairly rough masonry at this point. I had brought a few pegs which I eased into the cracks and threaded some dyed string between them so that we could find our way back up in poor light. Having thus prepared our route we headed back down to join the rest of my troop and wait for nightfall.

Though our main force under Tolmides had still not arrived I decided that it was better to chance a surprise attack without him, for as soon as the Chaeroneans saw an army approaching they would strengthen their guards. For once the weather was ideal for our purpose, a strong evening breeze to muffle the sound of our approach, enough moon for us to see our own feet, but not for us to be easily spotted by look-outs. We took ropes, pegs, some raw meat to toss over the wall for any dogs that might start barking and an assortment of weapons.

It is harder to climb silently with fifty men than with two and I wanted to be on the parapet at least four hours before dawn. Each man was told to test every foothold twice before moving, for even if one out of our fifty men fell it would cause enough noise to ruin my plan. I went first, following the route we had already tried and Oloros brought up the rear. My aim was for at least twelve men to be over the parapet in the first few seconds, enough to hold off any sentries until the other forty or so were able to follow. I doubted if the Chaeronians would have more than about twenty men on guard at night and they would be at intervals round the perimeter of the walls, with perhaps about fifty or sixty off duty in the various turrets. The rest of the garrison would be asleep in their homes.

I must admit to a deep sense of pride in the conduct of my troops that night. Not one of them made a mistake and we slithered over the wall exactly on time. Two of their sentries were about seventy feet on either side of our point of entry and shouted the alarm, but only once before my men overpowered or killed them. The next important step was to capture the turrets, including the main gatehouse where more off-duty guards would be resting. Luckily the city had been carelessly built with the craftsmen's hovels backing onto the fortifications and so close together that we could run across the roofs, so avoiding the longer trek round the perimeter wall.

I told Oloros to take charge of the gatehouse party and detailed six other groups to deal with the turrets. Then I took ten men to look for the headquarters of the people in charge, for they were the key to achieving a surrender. Oligarchs are by nature elitist, so I guessed that Aristodikos and his friends would have taken over the most impressive houses that Chaeronea had to offer, and there were not many to chose from in such a poor mountain stronghold. Even in the obviously rich quarter the houses were so close together that we could jump from roof to roof and dropping from above into their central courtyards was much easier than having to batter down the doors.

There were, as it turned out, only four houses that looked imposing enough to attract a man like Aristodikos and I took three men to the largest of them. Then we slid down from the roof into the neat central cloister. Posting one of my men to guard the door from the slaves' quarters and the other outside the men's sleeping area I headed for the master bedroom. Some instinct told me that this was to be the last chapter of a long epic and as I pulled open the door, I was certain that Aristodikos would be there.

I was wrong. The room was empty. Then I felt the tip of a sword pushed into my back and heard a familiar sneering voice.

'I heard you were still alive, Euphorion,' said Aristodikos.' Now you have the effrontery[5] to sneak into this peace-loving city. If the gods won't punish you, then I suppose that I'll have to do it for them.'

I managed to sneak a glance over my shoulder and I saw that my two men had both been overpowered. There must have been around half a dozen of the senior oligarchs camping out in that house. It is a tradition for well-born men from the Thebes area to live together unmarried and swear lifetime loyalty to each other. To be fair there were times when it did seem to add to their courage.

'The rest of your troops will soon be killed off,' went on Aristodikos calmly. 'We have a hundred excellent men here. I admit it was careless to let you scale the ramparts, but that is the only success I will allow you today.'

My memory of the next few moments is somewhat hazy, but I do remember that I was furious at so easily falling into a trap and once again being at the mercy of a man who was deeply corrupt yet always seemed to survive. I suppose there must be some good in him as he had devoted his life to the oligarchic cause, but that was a cause I despised. For moments I stood unable to move, thinking how badly I had let my family down, dying to save this small town from the oligarchs. It would be a poor tale for someone to tell Kore and the children.

There was further shouting from the ramparts that an army was in sight and I remember thinking that it might be Tolmides. Then there was the noise of a small riot in the working quarter of the city and I learned later that a group of local democrats had heard of our entry over the walls and had taken on some of the garrison to help us. Then out of the corner of my eye I saw Oloros on the roof above and his spear took Aristodikos between the shoulder blades. The Tanagran stared at me for a second and then slumped forward.

I had behaved with great stupidity but had been saved from certain death by the skill and courage of a friend. As we mopped up the remaining garrison with the help of the local democrats I took time to express my extreme gratitude to Oloros, both for saving my life and avenging Ephialtes, but he shrugged it off as of no consequence.

---

1.   This makes the year still 449BC.

2.   Sybaris aka Thurii became a famously wealthy Greek city in Italy; hence our word sybaritic meaning extremely luxurious. It was eventually buried under a sea of mud, so its ruins were not discovered till modern drilling techniques in the 1960s. Its site lies near the River Crati in the Gulf of Taranto, right under the heel of Italy.

3.   There is still a small village called Chaeronea on the site of the old city which was the scene of many battles. The great lion

monument put up in honour of the Sacred Band of Thebes was dug up here, and ruins of the acropolis survive.

4. Lake Kopais was drained in the 19th century so the River Kephisos which flowed into it was diverted to flow into Lake Yliki which provides most of the water supply for modern Athens.

5. The translator notes that the Greek word used here is hubris, which has also found its way into the English language, usually to refer to politicians who have become too arrogant and are likely to fall. The Greek concept of pride was that this was self-confidence taken a step too far and likely to lead to disaster.

CHAPTER TWENTY-NINE

DANGER NEARER HOME

WITH THE CAPTURE OF CHAERONEA I had done all that Pericles had asked of me and the killing of Aristodikos had closed another episode in my life. Oloros had done it to save my life and neither of us needed to feel guilty about it, so my specialist troop headed back to Athens leaving Tolmides and the main army to consolidate our gains. However, from that moment the campaign turned into a complete disaster and I was soon to discover that even my own family was in great danger.

Our success in Chaeronea turned out to have been extremely short-lived for despite losing Aristodikos the Boeotian oligarchs were still very numerous and well-armed. They ambushed an Athenian army at Koronea,[1] severely mauling our troops and killing the gallant old Tolmides. Then to add to our troubles it emerged that the Spartans had upset the calculations of Pericles, for they had been much more alarmed by the Chaeronea campaign than we expected, so they sent an army to attack Athens itself. To make matters even worse there had been several anti-democratic coups on the islands, and many of our reserve soldiers had been called out to deal with them. Thus when I got back to the city I found the place in a panic, which was quickly transmitted to my own brain when I heard that the Spartans had passed Megara and were heading for Eleusis.

I had already been feeling guilty that I had gone off to Chaeronea without sending any message to Kore about my mission, nor had I known myself how long I would be away from home, but I had never remotely imagined that Eleusis itself might be attacked from the other direction whilst I was away. The moment I heard the news I ignored the city by-laws and galloped through the streets to the Sacred Gate.

An hour and a half later, sweating more from fear than exertion, I was on the hill that looks down on Eleusis. I could see the Spartan army quite clearly, encamped outside the north wall of the town and there were small scouting parties scattered over the plain barring every entrance. The one good bit of news was that the town still seemed to be intact and there were no obvious signs of looting, fires or storming of the walls. Perhaps the reputation of Eleusis as sacred to the gods was deterring the Spartans from frontal assault, or they were just trying to challenge the Athenians to come out and fight in the open. There was supposed to be a small Athenian army operating near Megara, but it was far too weak to take on the substantial Spartan force under its impetuous young King Pleistoanax.

I felt acutely frustrated. I had to keep out of sight or I would easily be captured by one of the patrols yet I needed to get into the town to find my family, so I decided to edge down the gulley to the beach.

This was the same place where I had swum ashore ten years before after being shipwrecked and I had often subsequently walked along this stretch with Kore and the children, so I knew every rock and pool. Leaving my horse out of sight I crouched low as I descended the last section of the gully and used the cover of rough gorse and tamarisk, edging in close to the base of the cliffs as I got nearer so that I was less likely to be seen from above. At last I came to the narrow path which I knew led up from the harbour to the temple. The town gates would be barred and there were too many Spartans close by for me to dare shout for someone to let me in, but I remembered a place where the olive trees had been allowed to grow close to the walls. These might offer me both cover and some help in climbing the wall. However there were several Spartans exercising themselves ostentatiously nearby and Spartans have eyes like cats, so I had to wait for dark.

It was lucky there was no moon or I might have been spotted when at last I made my move. I sprinted across to the little olive grove, clambered up the tree nearest the wall and reached a foothold about six feet below the parapet. Then with a huge effort I hauled myself up and slithered over into the town. As I jumped down beside the temple I swore to have those trees cut down as soon as the Spartans had gone. For once in his life Poseidon did not bark at my arrival which was a huge blessing, but he was on the elderly side now and did not take guard duties so seriously.

When I reached our home I found Kore was just preparing for bed and the children were already asleep.'

'You vile, wicked man,' she said by way of greeting. 'Going off for months without a word.' And she slapped my head with some force.

'You're right,' I admitted contritely, but I couldn't help smiling for her anger was a truer expression of love than many may hear. But she bounced away when I tried to put my arm around her.

' You're not fit to be a father,' added the ageing Psyche, our family slave, who was supposed to dote on me, but on these occasions always stood up for Kore.

I followed Kore through to the children's room where little Gaia had been wakened by the noise. She sat on her potty rubbing her eyes, while Kore knelt beside her, hiding her face from me.

'I'm sorry ,' I said. 'I was under orders, but I should somehow have sent you a message. I came back as fast as I could.'

'Sorry indeed,' huffed Psyche. 'So you should be.' And at long last Kore burst out laughing, stood up and put her arms round me.

'Don't do it again,' she said. 'You can make the army wait the next time. We might all have been slaughtered by the Spartans. We still might,' she added.

I smiled. The master plans of Pericles for dominating Greece took little account of domestic arrangements and meant nothing to a mother with small children to look after. Meanwhile our three were all being tucked up again with a great deal of hugging and it seemed a long time before Kore came back to our bedroom, as if she was deliberately provoking my patience and taking some revenge for having been kept waiting for five weeks by me. Then she slipped off her gown, lay with her back to me but pushed back her hips against my stomach to get warm and held the hand which I put round her waist.

The next morning I consulted with Psamos, my father-in-law, about a possible plan to avoid the capture of Eleusis.

'I've warned the Spartans that it would be sacrilege to attack this holy city,' he said. 'But that young king doesn't understand such matters, and anyway he claims the Athenians have burned one of his holy sites.'

I looked across from the top point of our acropolis to the Spartan camp and it certainly looked as if they were preparing to attack. I knew that Pericles was too busy with the revolt in Euboea to send us help.

'We need to buy time. Let me go out and talk to them,' I said.

Psamos was beginning to look quite old and frail so he agreed with little hesitation to my suggestion. So I put on my priestly robes, said goodbye to Kore with a certain show of affected dignity and she confessed to having a slight pride in me that morning. Then I called for a horn player to sound some loud notes as they opened the town gates and I stepped out to face the Spartans.

The short walk seemed to last for ever as I bowed to the red-cloaked Spartan officers on either side and made my way to the king's tent. Pleistoanax was little more than a schoolboy, trained no doubt like all Spartan leaders to a perfection of physical fitness and superficial confidence, yet unsure of himself as soon as the conversation veered away from what he expected. He was the son of the wretched Prince Pausanias who had gloriously defeated the Persians at Plataea but then succumbed to greed and lust. His military adviser, Kleandrides, was double his age, thin, nearly bald and with very shrewd eyes.

'How extraordinary,' he said sarcastically. 'Two ambassadors in one day. We have just heard that Kallias has passed our outposts on the Sacred Way.'

'Of course,' I said, pretending that this was all part of a plan and in some ways much relieved. Kallias, the wealthy sometime husband of Cimon's unpredictable half-sister, Elpinike, was now the senior diplomat in Athens. To make matters more complicated his son had married his own other ex-wife who had meantime been married and divorced again by Pericles, so he was in a peculiar way very well-connected and should be bringing something useful, money or the surrender of a colony say, to help him bargain with the Spartans.

'Eleusis is a holy city,' I said, to gain some time. 'We have no quarrel with Sparta.'

' Your troops have been attacking our allies in Boeotia,' said the young king, his lip twitching very slightly. 'When I capture Eleusis I will spare the temple and other sacred areas, only destroy the rest. A holy city should not need fortified walls.'

At this point Kallias arrived with his entourage and I was pleased that for all his years and despite only a passing acquaintance with me, he instantly acknowledged my presence and treated me as part of his embassy as if that had been prearranged. We were all served with some of that dreadful black soup which was the standard diet for Spartans, mostly bits of pork cooked in pig's blood.

Then King Pleistoanax, speaking like a well-rehearsed automaton, launched into a verbal attack on the aggressive policies of Athens, particularly the way we had encouraged his helots to fight for their freedom. Luckily I think he was unaware of my role in that activity or he might have had me executed on the spot.

Kallias showed every sign of listening attentively and I give him full credit for his supreme patience and good manners in responding to the pre-scripted and highly repetitive litanies of the Spartans. He muttered occasional platitudes about Greeks not fighting Greeks and the respect which Athens had for Sparta, then he asked for a private word with me.

'Awkward,' he said. 'We need time. Too many of our troops are busy elsewhere and there aren't enough in Athens to come and help us here. So I'm afraid bribery is the only solution. What do you think is his weakness? Little girls, boys or money?'

He didn't wait for a reply but went on, 'I think money is the most likely and I've come prepared.' He tapped a large pouch hanging from his waist, then turned back to the king. 'Will you and Kleandrides join us in a toast to the liberty of Greece? This is a particularly pleasant red wine from Samos which we had specially stored under the Temple of Poseidon for the last twenty years.'

One of Kallias' retinue produced some fine gold goblets and a superb jar of wine followed by an impressive picnic of rare delicacies. This was spread on a huge carpet of exotic eastern rugs which appeared off the back of one of his horses. The skill with which Kallias set about creating an atmosphere of extreme luxury where shortly before there had been nothing but a camp fire was amazing, but no less was the constant stream of flattery and subtle allusions with which he set about captivating the young king. For an hour or more we sat there discussing the glories of former battles while our goblets were discreetly refilled by a startlingly beautiful couple from the Kallias entourage. Kallias winked at me to concentrate on Kleandidres while he worked on the king, but all the emphasis was on the pleasures and luxuries of peace as opposed to the austerities of a Spartan army on manoeuvres. Even Kleandrides began to mellow and Pleistoanax had clearly never seen or tasted most of the delicacies before.

Thus the right atmosphere was achieved for Kallias to make his final move. 'Some of our Athenian policies have been a trifle inconsiderate to our old allies,' he said contritely. 'So we should make amends.' And he produced twenty glistening gold talents from his pouch, then put them back and placed them loosely between himself and the young king.

'Kleandidres, I appreciate the courteous and wise way you have facilitated these negotiations,'he said. 'I appreciate that you have no interest in gold, but perhaps you would not mind taking back some of this to your wife. Say ten?'

Then he turned to the king. 'Here is enough[2] to build twenty triremes and two walled towns, whatever you please. We salute your bravery and the great traditions of the Spartan army. Let us make peace.'

We did not wait for an answer nor give any sign of expecting one but saluted the two men and marched gravely back to the town gates, as if we had just completed a solemn religious ceremony.

The following morning the Spartan army broke up their camp and headed west. The town of Eleusis was safe. Psamos and my colleagues were impressed and so, even though I confessed how little I had really done, was Kore.

So far as Athens and her armies were concerned it had been a disastrous summer. We had lost control of Boeotia where all the cities went back to oligarchies. Tolmides and his troops had been badly defeated. The revolt of Euboea[3] had been put down with difficulty by Pericles and we had only saved Eleusis and the rest of Attica by bribery. I heard later that Kallias had gone on to Sparta to negotiate a peace treaty between the Spartans and the Athenians that involved a considerable climb-down by our city and further loss of face for our remaining armies. Pericles had been to blame for us trying to be too dominant too fast, but he talked his way into continued popularity.

This was not the fate of the unfortunate Spartan King Pleistonax. He was convicted of bribery, dethroned and sent into a long exile, much of which according to rumour he spent in a cave on Mount Lykaion living like a wild wolf with his hair uncut and his hands like claws.[4] Kleandidres simply disappeared; perhaps he made good use of his gold, perhaps he was just quietly executed by his fellow Spartiates.[5]

1. The village of Koronea survives some 80 miles north west of Athens and it was there that the battle took place in 447 BC when Euphorion was thirty-eight.

2. There is an unexplained expenditure of ten talents noted in the Athenian accounts at this period, which many people regard as proof of the bribe.

3. Euboea is a long thin island close to the east coast (at one point only 150 yards away) with its own rugged mountain chain. In ancient times it was a fertile source of foodstuffs: grapes, figs, olives, goats and pigs. It also had marble quarries, as well as iron and copper mines, so it was rich and resented exploitation by Athens. Chalcis was a prosperous city producing high quality ceramics and metalwork.

4. Perhaps Pleistoanax had some kind of nervous breakdown rather like King Nebuchadnezzar in the Old Testament and suffered from lycanthropy (a form of delusion when a person thinks he is a wolf or other animal), but he seems to have recovered and engineered his own restoration nearly 20 years later by bribing the Delphic Oracle to advise Sparta to reinstate him. He died in 409 BC when he must have been nearly seventy. Mount Lykaion east of Sparta is over 4,000 feet high, sacred to Zeus, and every four years games were held on its slope like those of Olympia. The foundations of its hippodrome survive.

5. Spartiates were the military elite of Sparta.

CHAPTER THIRTY

PEACE FOR A WHILE

SOME READERS MAY FEEL THAT I should have written no further at this point, for I was approaching middle age,[1] there was peace and no requirement for me as a trierarch or siege specialist and it might be expected that my life after this would be of little interest. Nevertheless there were to be new adventures and crises in my life as the Athenians slowly recovered confidence and once more attempted to dominate the whole of Greece. Besides, my aim is not just to give an account of my own life, but also to record the remarkable achievements of our great city and perhaps hint at the reasons for its ultimate downfall.

Naturally the peace that Kallias had negotiated to last for thirty years between Athens and Sparta had a much shorter lifespan than he expected, but at least for the next five years life was happy and incident-free for Kore and myself. Our second son, the mischievous Psamos, was born and gave us both great joy, as did our other three children with their different laughs, tantrums, loves and hates. It was a time when I had no great adventures yet found that all of life was still an adventure.

My shared business with Kleistes was proving a great success. Between us we now owned five merchant ships, mostly still trading with Sicily or the Greek colonies in Italy. Kleistes was now himself quite a rich man but hadn't changed his character.

'By the hairs of Demeter's oxters,' he would say, but not when Kore was within earshot, 'we've brought enough pillows from Syracuse to cover the Acropolis. And a cargo of fresh whores from Tuscany.'

'I'm not sure we should take a profit from that,' I said a fraction pompously.

'Why not?' he replied. 'They're no different from slaves or any other cargo. Someone's got to give them transport. Why not us?'

'You should become a philosopher,' I smiled. Since slavery was a natural condition for large numbers of human beings I supposed whoredom was not really different. And there was nothing in the legends of our gods to suggest anything else.

At that time I used to go to Athens three or four times a year, once at least to preside over the Mysteries and occasionally on jury duty or to attend the Assembly. Certainly it was a period of great change in the city. The huge new temple of Athena the Virgin[2] on the Acropolis was rising perceptibly each time I paid a visit. Iktinos was the architect chosen by Pericles and I struck up a friendship with him since he was also doing some designs for an extension at Eleusis. The cost was massive and mostly came from funds paid in by our allies as part of their defence budget, easier now that the treasury had been moved from Delos to Athens. This was a point of dissension for the opposition party in Athens led by Thucydides who accused Pericles of misappropriating funds, but Pericles' golden tongue still held sway and Thucydides was ostracised for his pains.

As for the temple itself I was fascinated by its size and complexity, almost as large as some of the ruins I'd seen in Egypt but even more elaborate. There were nearly fifty massive columns round the outside, each forty feet high and each made out of twenty massive lumps of Pentelic marble. Every piece required a large cart drawn by oxen to drag it down from Mount Pentelikos to the masons' yards. Then it took more than a year's work to carve the flutings which each had to match precisely the flutings on the blocks above and beneath. But it was even more cunning than that, for Iktinos had calculated the need for a slight bulge in each column to trick the eyes of those who looked up at them. Iktinos himself was short, wiry and quick-tempered with just a few wisps of hair round his bald pate, and he drove even his best masons to despair with his insistence on perfection. For seven years he hardly ever left the Acropolis as he supervised every inch of the building. My old acquaintance Sophronikos, the mason from Eleusis, had been brought in to help and I noticed his son was no longer with him.

'Where's that young boy of yours?' I asked.

'Socrates? Good question,' answered the mason. 'Like all youngsters he did a spell in the army and came back unsettled. He could be a foreman mason by now if he wanted, but instead he's wasting his time with those foreign teachers who hang around the market place like beggars.'

'Bright lad,' I said. 'I remember him. Never mind, I expect he'll want to settle down again soon.' I moved on and came to the inner part of the temple where work was more advanced. Pheidias the sculptor whom I'd known from years before was fussing over his statue of Athena the Defender. These days he was famous throughout Greece, not just for his bronze Athena standing on the Acropolis which you could see from miles away but for many statues in other cities.

'The whole point is to get the dawn sun coming through the door on festival day,' he was arguing. 'The positioning has to be absolutely precise or the light won't focus on the statue that morning. What's the point in using real gold unless it gets the light?'

Pericles, I knew, was obsessive about getting nothing but the best. He had given Pheidias as much gold as would have bought fifty new warships just to provide the armour of the goddess, and her skin was of African ivory also bought in at huge cost.

Kallikrates the chief builder was a less eccentric character and invited me to see the carvings being completed ready for the pediment. They were in a large wooden shed and I had never seen such life-like and beautiful statues:[3] giants, centaurs, Amazons and Athenian heroes all cunningly designed to fit the triangular space of the pediment and waiting to be hoisted high above our heads.

I stared at the hundreds of figures, mentally calculating the wage bill in my head and wondering at the huge funds that Pericles must still be collecting for our supposed defence budget. Yet although I was beginning to think like a trader I still felt immensely proud to belong to a city which had achieved such huge strides in human endeavour.

On one of my visits when the temple was nearly finished I met Pericles by chance near the Assembly. As ever he was perfectly poised and in total control, but the receding hairline accentuated his squill-shaped head and there were now deep lines on his face. He was accompanied to my surprise by a young woman, for Athenian gentlemen did not normally walk in public with their daughters.

'It's a while since we've needed your skills in siege-work,' he said lightly. 'This is Aspasia, a teacher from Miletos.'

'A delightful city,' I replied in some confusion, as I had never heard of a woman being a teacher before and was puzzled as to why they were walking together. Then I realised my stupidity, for this had to be his new mistress. He was actually indulging in some personal pleasure after all this time. He was human after all, a man over fifty besotted with a woman half his age. Pericles who was renowned for his personal austerity and never going to parties or brothels was behaving like an ordinary hoplite.

' Euphorion is a priest as well as a resourceful naval officer,' he explained to her, then turning to me, 'I'm afraid Aspasia doesn't entirely believe in priests. Perhaps you can convince her.'

'I don't know that I believe in them either,' I said. ' All I know is that human beings are inadequate.'

Aspasia smiled at my comment and I thought that with the exception of Kore I had never seen a more beautiful woman.

'Very fair, Euphorion,' she said. 'I look forward to seeing you again.'

I bowed to her as they moved off and wondered if our great leader might make a fool of himself, a man who could manipulate fifty thousand might himself be easily manipulated by one clever young woman. I remembered hearing a rumour that they'd had a baby together, so while he was turning Athens into the most beautiful city in the world and attracting all the best brains to come here from other cities, all that philosophy might come down to his feelings for one little bastard child.

Meanwhile back in Eleusis my elder son Kynosargos was finished with his first school and ready to move on to the gymnasion. He was a good runner, as I had been at that age, perhaps a little introverted on occasion, but nice to his mother and with no sign of rebellion against the Mysteries. Our two girls were now nine and seven, just beginning to copy Kore's work on the loom and taking an interest in the kitchen and the animals. Young Psamos was still a toddler, chasing the hens through the dust and trying to climb the olive trees. Sadly, however, at this time we had lost one old friend, for our dog Poseidon had become extremely frail and laid down for his last sleep on the steps of the temple. Luckily a replacement dog appeared as if from nowhere bearing an uncanny resemblance to his predecessor, so we named him Poseidon II.

We would still have great afternoons stealing away in the summer up the river to the deep round pool where we could splash and dive, all of us playing together like children and then cooking skewered lamb on an open fire, even strumming a few discordant notes on Kore's lyre. After a suitable amount of begging by the children I would agree to recite a book or two from the Odyssey, much of which I still knew by heart. Kore's favourite bit was Odysseus returning to Penelope at the very end, especially the welcome he got from his aged dog.

In my mid forties I had to go to Athens again for a stint at the Assembly. I sensed the atmosphere had soured somewhat since my last visit, and this was confirmed by a trip to the theatre where the latest comedy by Kratinos was crammed with the most scurrilous jokes that I had ever heard, many of them poking fun at Pericles. There was no mistaking the actor with a squill head besotted with a whore of twenty. Every kind of phallos innuendo was brought in to mock the middle-aged lover obsessed with building temples while his mistress played around elsewhere.

That evening I went down to the Piraeus to meet Kleistes who had just arrived home in our largest merchant ship with a huge cargo of exotic fabrics from North Africa. As I approached the port I was amazed yet again by the changes in the town. Most of the old twisting streets I knew so well had been demolished and neat straight ones put in their place.

'It's that crazy Milesian builder,' said Kleistes when I mentioned it to him. 'Hippodamos. Pericles invited him here to make all the streets straight and all the warehouses square. There's nothing round in here, as the Amazon said to the randy centaur.'

It came back to me then how I'd taken a message from Pericles to the man in a tavern in Miletos, the man who was now redesigning our city and its port like a board game.

'I've heard he believes the whole of life should be symmetrical,' I said.

'Well I prefer life without too many straight lines,' said Kleistes. 'The best things in life are round. Including coins.' He winked and gave me a tally of my share in the latest voyage. It was worth more to me than my wine and olive harvests put together.

I wished him well and set off back to Eleusis. When I arrived I was met by Kore rushing out in tears. 'It's father,' she said. 'I think he's dying.'

---

1.   These events date from 445BC when Euphorion was forty.

2.   There was special respect for Athena's virginity for she had fought off the unsavoury god Hephaistos, patron of blacksmiths, as well as all the other men and gods who had tried to have their way with her. An American sculptor built a replica of the Parthenon in Nashville Tennessee.

3.   British readers will be aware that many of these statues were, for their own protection, taken to London from Athens by the Earl of Elgin in 1801, and are still in the British Museum despite frequent requests for them to be taken back to Greece.

CHAPTER THIRTY-ONE

BACK TO SEA

OVER THE YEARS I HAD grown quite close to my father-in-law Psamos who was a man of great sincerity and whose regard for the traditions of the priesthood was so unaffected that it was impossible not to respect him. But when I first saw him after my return from Athens I was shocked by the great change in him, for he was half-paralysed on one side and seemed unable to recognise anyone except little Psamos, his youngest grandchild. Mercifully his death was easy and he wasn't helpless for long enough to lose his dignity. I was there when Gaia and Kore closed his eyes and pulled his priestly robe tight over his shrunken shoulders. The ladies were strangely calm, but talked about him a lot in later months, endlessly retelling the main events of his life and the nice things he had done or said.

Gaia herself was never quite the same again. From being a chubby, cheery lady she became thin and round-shouldered. Just under a year later she had a severe cold and died quietly without complaint in her sleep. Of course they say bad things happen in threes and indeed a month after that there was a third death, this time my old nurse Psyche who had been a slave all her life, but had the spirit of a free woman. She just went out one day to the big olive grove and lay down to die.

After this sad period with only my mother Phasia left from the old generation of our families both Kore and I had increased duties in the new Hall of Mysteries. Not that I had ever had any vocation to be a priest: in fact I had been quite tempted by the views of men like Protagoras who said there were no gods at all on the top of

Mount Olympos, only clouds. But I recognised the power of the Mysteries to help many thousands of people to lead better lives than they otherwise would, so I was happy enough to devote a portion of my time to keep the tradition going.

Two or maybe three years later[1] I got my first summons from Pericles for many years and this was to result in one of my strangest adventures. It was the time of the Festival of Dionysos, so the night before I was due to meet him I went to the theatre to see Sophocles' latest play, a tragedy set in Thebes called Antigone. Though he was never a real favourite of mine, either as a man or as a writer, I have to admit it was powerful stuff, and naturally the main character reminded me of my wife, a strong woman who stands up for what she believes. There was another new play on the following day, this one by the mad new poet Euripides, who according to gossip, lived alone in a cave. He too wrote plays about women but I found them hard to understand.

'Welcome, Phori,' said Pericles affably, when I went into his office next morning. 'You look well.'

'So do you,' I said, and it was true. Pericles did seem to be thriving on having a young mistress, despite the jibes of Kratinos.

'You'll have heard we have a problem with Samos,' he went on, wasting no time as usual. 'It has attacked Miletos because it wants control of Priene.[2] We cannot allow one member of the League, especially a big one, to defy the rules. So we need a major fleet exercise. I'll be in charge, Sophocles will act as paymaster, Phormio as admiral of the reserve, but I'd like you as commander of the *Salaminia* again. Not this time because of your siege experience, but because Kallias says you're turning into quite a diplomat and priestly robes suit that job.'

'What about—?' I began.

'Kleistes? I've already checked and he's in the harbour ready to act as your shipmaster.'

I shrugged my shoulders and two hours later was on board the *Salaminia*, but I took care this time to send a messenger back to Kore with the news of my voyage. The next day, with Kleistes at the steering oars the noble *Salaminia* edged out of the Munychia harbour and we turned east as the dawn sun glinted on her two hundred oars moving almost perfectly in time together across what Homer called the wine-dark sea.

Samos had always been one of my favourite islands, but I found the people hard to understand: they sometimes seemed to be more Asians than Greeks, for the strait between them and mainland Asia is after all very narrow. They are, however, excellent sailors and skilled in many other matters. Long ago when the tyrant Polykrates was in charge they'd built the remarkable tunnel through the mountain to bring fresh water to their city. Amazingly they started at opposite ends and managed to meet in the middle.[3] He was a lucky man, Polykrates, for once he wanted to impress a visiting Egyptian pharaoh so much that he threw his jewels into the sea, but the very next day, according to the story, he was presented with a large tuna fish and in its stomach were the jewels that he'd tossed overboard. Eventually he went too far, as all tyrants do, and was murdered by a jealous Persian.

It took our fleet only five days to reach Samos and most of the Samian trouble-makers, oligarchs as usual, fled the island at the mere sight of our ships, so we occupied their capital without any problems. As part of the celebrations I held a service at the temple of Hera which stood on the spot where the goddess was supposedly born, by a willow tree on the banks of the River Imbrasos. Pericles meanwhile rounded up all the children left behind by the oligarchs and took them as hostages to Lemnos. So after leaving a garrison in the city our fleet set off for home.

As it turned out we had grossly underestimated the resilience of the Samian opposition. No sooner were we out of sight than they recaptured their island with Persian help, rescued their hostages from Lemnos and sent our garrison in chains to the Persian city of Sardis.

We had reached Delos on our homeward journey before we heard the news and Pericles ordered an immediate return to Samos. Clearly he must have been aware that his judgement had been at fault, but I did not see him at the time for as part of his image he did not use the general's cabin on the *Salaminia*, but was sailing in one of the ordinary triremes.

Two days later we were back off the coast of Samos and this time were met by a fleet of around fifty triremes, much the same number as we had ourselves. Each side suffered a few losses in the ensuing battle but neither admiral was willing to risk all for a decisive result, so they got away and we had to recapture their city, this time meeting much more resistance. The one good bit of news was that Phormio arrived with reinforcements and I had never seen a flotilla of triremes handled with such panache. He must have spent a lot of time training them for all fifteen ships moved perfectly together in formation, turned at exactly the same moment and then feinted in a double cross-over at forty foot intervals. I was quite sure it would impress the Samians but the siege went no faster.

I must admit that my vanity was slightly dented when there was no request for my siege expertise during the blockade that followed. Without even apologising to me Pericles had called in a fashionable new engineer from one of the islands. This man Artemon had apparently promised to undermine the city's walls, but he failed entirely and I was secretly quite gratified. Meanwhile Pericles asked me to undertake a mission which was even more challenging, to cross the frontier into Persian territory and negotiate the release of our captured garrison from the gaols of Sardis. To assist me on my mission all I was given was a hollow leather belt inside which were sewn twenty one golden talents at regular intervals so that they would not be obvious. Otherwise I had no bargaining points and this was to prove a difficult and dangerous task.

Thus the *Salaminia* headed for the mouth of the River Meander and on Pericles' orders I made a courtesy visit to the city of Miletos, our ally. This of course had been the home of one of the seven sages, Thales, the man who said he thanked the gods for three things: that he was human, not an animal, that he was male not female, and that he was a Greek not a barbarian. He'd also coined the maxim 'KNOW THYSELF' which had been carved above the oracle at Delphi. Anyway there was no doubt that the people of Miletos were reassured by the Athenian support and they entertained us well before we headed off.

This was my first trip to the Meander since the time I'd met Themistocles and his priestess daughter many years earlier in Magnesia. As a first step we headed for Smyrna,[4] a city which I had always wanted to visit because it was the birthplace of my great hero the blind poet Homer. To add to its curiosity value for me the city had been built by the famous King Tantalos of Lydia, the man who kidnapped Ganymede, the boy favourite of Zeus, and was punished for his crime by being given an unquenchable thirst. After sampling the local wine which they apparently mix with honey, chalk or marble dust, I suspected that was how Tantalos got his thirst, for even when I drank the stuff diluted it left me with the need to have another cup to wet my mouth after the previous one.

'It tastes like the excrement of turtles,' commented Kleistes who knew most of the wines on the Lydian coast quite intimately.

Apart from its wines it was pleasant enough though the people looked rich and lazy, but to my great delight they pointed out to me the place where Homer[5] was buried and I bowed my head in respect.

Thus after a pleasant night in Smyrna we headed north to the mouth of the River Hermos[6] which was similar to the Meander but even shallower, so I took a small party ashore and reported to the Persian fort guarding its mouth.

'The Satrap Pissuthenes has no wish to receive you,' announced its commander through an interpreter.

'But I am here as the ambassador of Athens,' I protested, 'to negotiate an exchange of prisoners of war.'

'Negotiate?' the man scoffed. 'Why should Pissuthenes, a nephew of the Great King, negotiate with you? Men of honour should never surrender. Your garrison on Samos showed no moral fibre.'

I found it hard to disagree with him, but I had orders to follow, so I produced one gold talent from my belt.

'You're wasting your time,' he said. 'But I'll send you up the river by barge with one companion, if you must.'

'Anything to avoid having to drink more of that Smyrna wine,' offered Kleistes.

So Kleistes and I took the offered barge which reached a dozen miles or so up river before we had to transfer to horseback for the remainder of the journey, but as I had heard before, the Persian roads were excellent. Now we had an escort of gold-clad Persian bowmen to guide us the remaining forty or so miles to the regional capital. I had been expecting a city unlike any I had previously seen and was not disappointed, for Sardis rose dramatically on a high rock above the River Paktolos which joined the Hermos nearby. This was the fabled city built by King Kroesos, the richest man who ever lived, for here the people dipped fleeces in the river and collected pure gold dust in the wool, which is why the Lydians were so rich. To its east stretched a wide straight road which I was told led all the way to the Great King's capital at Susa, with a change of horses available every twenty miles to help speed up the royal postal service.

Kleistes and I were now guided up a steep, stone-cobbled street past gorgeous mansions to the palace of the satrap himself. The huge temple of Artemis was in ruins but there was a strange new temple where the fires of the great magician Zoroaster burned day and night.

Pissuthenes himself was a small man dressed in the most exotic robes. Because he was a nephew of the Great King he lived in perpetual fear of being murdered by one of his siblings, for there was constant competition between the junior members of the royal dynasty. He made it pretty clear that it was well beneath his dignity even to speak to a Greek ambassador, a mere commoner, let alone negotiate and we were removed from his presence to spend the next two days in a small, dank cell beneath the palace. We were both searched for weapons and I was extremely grateful for the ingenuity of my hollow belt which looked too scruffy to be worth stealing.

'I don't suppose twenty talents will be much of an enticement to this arrogant ape,' I said to Kleistes.

'Maybe not,' he replied. 'But I've heard one of the things they're best at here is counting money and the Great King doesn't let his relations keep much of it, even if they are plucking golden fleeces out the river every day.'

'It's our only chance,' I said, not for the first time appreciating the shrewdness of my partner.

That afternoon we were summoned up to the satrap's anteroom for the customary two hour wait designed by the Persians to intensify visitor intimidation and frustration. Beforehand I had extracted one of the talents from my belt. When at last we were ushered into the great man's presence he told us through his interpreter that our visit was pointless, but as a favour we would be allowed to walk back to the coast in our bare feet.

'Wait,' I said. 'Give me ten barefoot Athenian prisoners and I will give you this golden talent.'

Clearly he was annoyed and mystified that I had managed to keep a talent hidden on my body despite the vigorous search, but I could see a hint of interest in his face.

'Give me twenty barefoot prisoners and I will give you two golden talents,' I went on. 'A hundred and I will give you ten, but I will need an hour alone in my cell to make the gold.'

It was poor stuff, but the best I could manage in the circumstances.

The satrap laughed and muttered to the interpreter, who said to me 'Prince Pissuthenes says that he will give you two hundred prisoners if you can produce twenty gold coins in one hour from now.'

I indulged in some excruciating acting to demonstrate just how difficult the task would be before I was escorted moaning piteously back to my cell. After that everything was surprisingly straightforward, though I admit to sweating all the time until the satrap took the gold and ordered the release of the prisoners. It then took Kleistes and myself eight days to march those two hundred half-starved, shoeless Athenians down the River Paktolos,[7] then the Hermos back to Smyrna. I think they were grateful, but they were so tired and weak that they could think of nothing but their feet until they lay on the smooth warm decks of the *Salaminia*.

A month or so after our return the city of Samos surrendered for the second time. I saw the rebel oligarchs taken away in chains and dumped on a deserted part of the coast near the Persian fort. Pericles exacted a huge fine from the islanders, adding to it the twenty-one talents which I had spent buying back our captured garrison from the satrap. As a general he was not much better than ordinary, but as a book-keeper and a politician he was little short of a genius. He had, however, convinced both himself and many others that violence and massive self-sacrifice were essential so that Athens could be the richest, most beautiful and most powerful city in Greece and that all consequential suffering was justified.

---

1. The accepted date for the revolt of Samos is 441BC when Euphorion was forty four.

2. The ruins of the ancient Greek port of Priene are now in Turkey some 20 miles north of the Meander and due to silting they are now a few miles inland.

3. Polykrates (d.522 BC), the Tyrant of Samos, organised the building of this remarkable tunnel which was a mile long, with opposite ends dug separately yet meeting exactly in the middle due to geometric and other extraordinary skills of the 6th century, and the tunnel still be visited. This and other ruins on the island are now part of a World Heritage Site that includes the Pythagorean Fortress named in honour of the locally born Pythagoras, inventor of the well-known theorem.

4. Smyrna, now known as Izmir, still has ancient Greek ruins and was the birthplace of the author of this book and probably also of Homer.

5. Some scholars think that because Homer's Iliad and Odyssey are such long epic poems, it was impossible for one man to have written them, especially a blind man, who perhaps never really existed. In the same way some experts think Shakespeare could not have written all those plays.

6. The River Hermos is now known as the Yediz. The great city of Sardis was destroyed many times, finally by the Mongols, but the modern village of Sart stands on its site.

7. This Turkish river, then known as the Paktolos, was once famous for bearing sediment of electrum, sometimes known as green gold, a natural alloy of gold and silver. Hence the legend of the Golden Fleece.

CHAPTER THIRTY-TWO

THE WORST WAR

I WILL NOT BORE YOU with an account of the next six years[1] for in many ways they were the easiest and least eventful in my life. I had a happy marriage and growing family with just occasional rows which were soon patched up, usually when I came round to admitting that Kore had been right in the first place. We had enough money, thanks mainly to Kleistes, though our estates most years also brought in a reasonable return. There were no serious wars to induce me to go back to the fleet and on the whole I steered clear of Athenian politics. The only real stress we had was the normal need for parents to accept that our children were becoming adults and had unpredictable minds of their own. And by this time Poseidon II had been replaced by Poseidon III who had somehow inherited the habit of growling at me whenever I seemed about to touch dear Kore.

Our eldest child, Kynegiros named after my father, had given us great pride when he passed out of the gymnasion and served in his first trireme under the admiral Phormio. Yet I have to admit that there were many aspects of his attitude to life which I found hard to tolerate. He had mixed with a very arrogant bunch of youths on his first garrison duties, all of whom seemed to think that they were invincible warriors who needed a good war to make their fortunes. For myself I had seen too much misery to want a new war started. I knew the futility of ambitious expeditions like the one to Egypt where so many unnecessary deaths had been inflicted on us.

To make matters worse these youngsters were hungry for war for its own sake, not in a worthwhile cause like defending our freedom or our great traditions, because in fact they seemed to question all of these. That lad Socrates, the stonemason's son, had turned into a real troublemaker who influenced my son and many others of his generation. Whenever Kynegiros came home in an argumentative mood, disagreeing with everything that Kore and I had ever stood for, we guessed that he had been listening to Socrates again. Yet despite all this I was sure that basically he was a decent enough son and better than many.

Young Gaia gave me great joy for many years because she so reminded me of Kore at the same age, but even she became quite hard to handle when she came to marriageable age. I was saddened that she chose to object to my first choice of husband for her after I had gone to considerable bother to negotiate an excellent match. Young Phasia was innocent and fun-loving, the easiest of our children to understand, but even her escapades caused me some worry. As I will tell you shortly all these difficulties seemed totally petty once the war started, for then death was everywhere and none of us had time for personal whims any more.

Young Psamos was different from the rest of our children, for though he was the youngest and Kore tended to spoil him, he was from an early age more interested in the world of the spirits than in normal boyish activities. Not that he was the least effeminate, but he seemed to inherit some of the deeper feelings from his priestly ancestors which were beyond anything I could understand, and while to be honest I did not totally welcome it, neither would I think of opposing it.

Of the two main occasions when I involved myself in Athenian affairs at that time the first was when the hard-liners launched an attack on Pericles about two years after the Samos rebellion. He was too powerful a figure for them to attack directly so they got at him through his mistress Aspasia, accusing her of atheism, a piece of hypocrisy if ever there was one, for these men were always making crude jokes about the gods in private. I gave evidence in her defence and as I was a priest it carried some weight, so Pericles was pathetically grateful to me after her acquittal. I had told the court that most intelligent Athenians no longer took literally the legends of gods on Mount Olympos, that if Aspasia was an atheist then she should be condemned to death, but in that case so should I be along with most of the senior magistrates in Athens. They then tried to concoct a charge against Pericles of raping his own son's wife, but that luckily went nowhere. The problem was that he had been in power for a long time and his mistakes were becoming more obvious than his achievements.

The only other person who did not approve of my defence of Aspasia was my wife, for though she was usually the most tolerant of people Kore nursed a strong disapproval of young mistresses with middle-aged lovers. She was also suspicious of intellectuals, especially female ones. Anyway I had to understand that Aspasia was much younger than either of us and had an air of confidence that was quite alien to the typical Athenian matron.

The second occasion when I intervened in Athenian politics was about seven years later and was very different because this time instead of supporting Pericles I did the opposite. That was when the issue of Megara came before the Assembly and one of the rare times that I chose to make a speech. By that time the atmosphere between Athens and Sparta had grown seriously poisonous again, but I still believed that war between the two cities should be avoided. Pericles on the other hand was determined to make Athens the leading city in Greece and spread democracy to other cities that didn't want it. I think he regarded war with Sparta as inevitable and presumably was convinced that we would win, the delusion of all politicians who start wars.

The Megara problem just happened to be the issue that finally proved too much for the Spartans to bear. I argued fiercely that we had no need to punish the Megarians as severely as Pericles wanted for I knew many of them personally and they came to the Mysteries in Eleusis. The allegation that they had trespassed on the lands sacred to Demeter was quite preposterous. Pericles was being vindictive just because Megara was disputing his authority and his proposal was that we should ban all their woollens from Athens and the cities in the Delian League. So since wool and cheap clothing were their main source of wealth this would be an economic disaster for their city. I thought it would probably make them even keener to join the Spartan side than they already were. So I made my speech and got a few votes, but Pericles got his way as usual and the embargo went ahead.

As I left the city that evening I looked up at the wonderful temple which now dominated the skyline and worried about the cost of all this magnificence and the way we had lost friends everywhere. We used to be liked but not so much admired. Now it was the other way round, and that, it seemed, was all that Pericles cared about.

I believe that young Thucydides is working on a history of our dreadful war but I doubt if I will live to see the end of it, so I will say frankly what I think caused it. Certainly the Megarian embargo was a step too far, but so was the help we sent for the Corcyrans[2] in their quarrel with Corinth. You should never interfere between a colony and its mother city, or between a husband and wife, however just the cause may seem. Mostly I think the war started because we levied such heavy taxes from our allies to pay for our ships, our new temples and the golden statues. To make matters worse, when they objected to the taxes we punished them too severely. We also kept trying to encourage populist coups by democrats in cities that really preferred oligarchs. That made many of them look to Sparta for help and the more we interfered the more alarmed Sparta became.

It was all very well Athens having the finest architects and sculptors, the best dramatists, the cleverest philosophers, but what was the point if we just destroyed ourselves? Of course Pericles was a very persuasive man who had by this time dominated all our lives for the past twenty-five years, but perhaps he had become too confident in his own powers and too obsessed with making Athens the greatest city on earth. He felt strong enough to destroy Sparta and he made others believe him.

I knew in my heart that the war would be much more difficult than the youngsters could possibly imagine and was worried that we might lose it, but not even for one moment did I think that it would be quite so long and disastrous as has proved to be the case.[3] Nor could I foresee the difficulties and dangers which I myself would have to overcome because of it. But as war approached I was horrified that the Greeks who had once fought so bravely against Persian invasions were now going to fight each other to the death.

It was heart-breaking that two great cities, Athens and Sparta, had grown to hate each other despite having so many things in common. Even worse every other city state in Greece and Asia Minor was forced to take sides whether they had any grievance or not. Sadly it was just one brilliant man who had devoted his life to enhancing the most spectacular city in the world, but become so vain that he now risked destroying everything he had achieved, causing thousands of unnecessary deaths yet still believed himself to be indestructible.

---

1. This would be from 439 BC (when Euphorion was forty-six) to 432 BC when a major war seemed unavoidable because of stubbornness and stupidity on both sides, together with a naïve belief on both sides that they would win it.

2. The struggle in Corcyra between the supporters of Corinth who were all oligarchs and the supporters of Athens who were democrats had caused trouble for many years and Euphorion's involvement is dealt with in the next chapter.

3. The historian A.R.Burns makes the point that the year 431BC in Greek history has many similarities to 1914 AD in European history and that little was learned by humanity in the intervening 2,345 years.

CHAPTER THIRTY-THREE

RESCUE MISSION

WHEN THE GREAT WAR, SOMETIMEs called the Peloponnesian War or Wars began I was aged fifty-four[1] and really only fit to be a general or a priest, but surprisingly I was to be called on in both capacities on a number of occasions. Kore was two years younger but still slim and energetic though the worry about our two sons was to try her sorely. Young Kynegiros had won his first command of a trireme and was serving with Phormio, by far the best of our admirals. He had married the daughter of Hagnon, another admiral, and our first grandchild was named after me. They made their home in Aegina after Pericles had organised its capture and the expulsion of all its original inhabitants, an act of cruelty of which I totally disapproved. It meant we saw little of our grandson which was a disappointment to Kore who loved small children, but at least we did not suffer the worry of staring at the horizon wondering if our son's trireme would make it home from each campaign.

Both our daughters married men from the cavalry just before the war started, so they too had an anxious time when the invasions started. Pericles never let the infantry out of the city gates if he could help it, but he often sent the cavalry out on hit-and-run missions against the Spartans and these were quite risky. However, everyone in our family survived the first year of the war, both the girls produced little daughters and young Psamos became an assistant high priest of the Mysteries in Eleusis.

Yet if I sound grateful now that we had survived that first year I didn't feel that way at the time. For from the walls of Eleusis we had to watch the new king of Sparta burning all our crops, our carefully trained vines and our ancient olive trees. All my family estates were ruined and still are, so if it had not been for my second career as a merchant I would be almost a beggar.

As usual Pericles gave me no advance warning of my first wartime mission which came soon after the main attacks began.

'I need an ambassador who also knows about sieges,' he said when I entered his office. He had aged a little but still had that amazing calm which seemed unaffected by the stresses of war. 'It's Plataea,' he went on. 'As you perhaps know a Theban force attempted to capture the city but they were captured themselves instead. The Plataeans apparently want to execute all the captives, which I think most unwise, for Thebes will have no choice but to retaliate in force and Plataea stands no chance. Get there as fast as you can, stop the executions and give them advice on how to survive a long siege.'

Plataea is a small city on a three-sided hill[2] about eight miles from Thebes on the main road south to Sparta. For the huge bravery of its people during the Persian Wars the city had been declared a sacred site, but this hadn't stopped the Thebans from attacking it. Apparently their plot to capture it had almost succeeded but the resourceful Plataeans had burrowed through their own house walls to join up without being seen, and then surrounded their attackers, the same two hundred men whom they had now condemned to death.

I took two horses for myself and set off right away with a cavalry escort, one of them little Phasia's husband. We hardly stopped on that thirty-five mile journey, the last stretch through the Pass of Kithairon where Hercules famously killed a lion. But sadly when we arrived I saw two hundred bodies stretched out on the rocks beneath the city gate. Such is the bitter hatred that seems to persist between Thebes and Plataea, despite or perhaps because the two cities are so close to each other. I put on my priestly robes to harangue the city leaders and put a stop to any further violence, but I knew the Thebans would soon be back for revenge.

'I can understand how you feel,' I said, ' but frankly your action was most ill-advised. Now the Thebans will throw everything at you, so you can expect no mercy. You must hold out or die. Athens may send you reinforcements, but that might be too late.'

As it turned out the help from Athens was far too little as well as too late. And I should have guessed that Pericles would do little to help, for why should he waste his precious infantry on a lost cause? In the meantime I spent the next month advising the Plataeans how to strengthen their walls, how to stock up with grain and live animals, check the water wells, flatten all the trees and undergrowth for half a mile outside the walls. I showed them how to build watch towers and fill in any tunnels which the besiegers might try to dig under the walls, then how to tunnel back again if they tried to build up ramps of earth outside the walls.

After that I rode back to Athens to look for reinforcements, for Plataea could muster a bare thousand men of fighting age to man its battlements, but it was a waste of time. Pericles made polite noises, and I knew right away from his tone that we would get no more help. Any land troops that Pericles had available were needed to harass the marauding Spartans who were still busy burning crops and villages all round Attica. So I was quite despondent as I set off back to Plataea.

There are times when you know that whatever you do will be wrong. I could stay with my eighty men and a few thousand Plataeans, men women and children, waiting for the city to fall into the hands of the enemy, which would mean almost certain death for all of us. Or I could try to evacuate the non-combatants back to Athens, which meant leaving a small garrison to fight to the last man. Neither option was very attractive.

As I have mentioned before, perhaps more than once, I believe in the principle of having gods who know more about life than we do, but I find it harder to accept that they have special names and sip nectar on top of a mountain, let alone take the trouble to sort our problems even if we ask nicely. But on this particular occasion I confess that I risked looking up and asking Zeus or any other god that might be listening which course I should follow. Two flocks of geese flew over afterwards going south and I thought that might hint at an answer, but I wasn't sure. Even an evacuation was fraught with danger, for we might be ambushed by the Thebans during the first part of our journey or by the Spartans in the second. Then I asked myself what advice Kore would have given if she'd been there and I knew that she would vote for life not death for as many as possible, especially children, so I decided.

The details of that grim journey with nearly four thousand people and a few hundred asses to carry their bits of bedding and cooking pots are too painful to remember. To avoid ambush we had to travel at night and use the less frequented passes of Kithairon,[3] then keep away from roads through the scorched fields of Attica. I had no sense of achievement except defeat and dishonour, both for my own city and for our little ally. The fate of the five hundred gallant men whom I left to almost certain death will be with me till I see them again in Hades.

I was to learn later that a few did manage to escape whilst the remaining two hundred or so held out for over a year until the Spartans promised to spare their lives if they would surrender for a fair trial. There were no trials. All were executed and the little city was destroyed stone by stone a couple of years later by the vindictive Thebans.

---

1.   The Peloponnesian Wars started in 431 BC and lasted with a short break for twenty-seven years, bringing disaster to the two main participants almost as damaging for the winners as for the losers and were an act of wanton self-destruction almost unparalleled in history.

2.   The ruins of the plucky little city of Plataea can still be visited on its triangular hilltop site by Kithairon. It was destroyed in 427BC but rebuilt by the Macedonians.

3.   Kithairon has a range of mountains rising to over 4,000 feet and separates Attica from Boeotia. Sophocles described it as echoless and it was where the future King Oedipus was left to die as an unwanted baby.

CHAPTER THIRTY-FOUR

THE PLAGUE

WHEN I ARRIVED BACK IN Athens the only good thing was that I found that Kore had moved in from Eleusis to our town house, for Eleusis was becoming unsafe due to the regular Spartan invasions. In fact all the villagers of Attica had been moved into the city for their own safety. Every corner of Athens now seemed to have some makeshift shack or tent with whole families crammed into tiny spaces. Even the temples, the towers and gate houses of the city walls were packed with squatters from the villages. The derelict areas between the two long walls that ran down from the city to the Piraeus were similarly covered with shacks, tents, children and washing hanging from ropes.

By this time Pericles was far from popular with either the pro-war people or those against it. For the hotheads didn't like his tactics of keeping everybody walled-up in the city whilst the Spartans roamed around destroying our fields and villages. They wanted to sally forth and give the Spartans a good drubbing, but he restrained them knowing well enough that they would be no match for such highly trained warriors. Just to make life more embarrassing for him the Spartans rather ostentatiously refrained from destroying his family farm, thus making it look as if he had some hidden agenda. The anti-war people, with whom I had a lot of sympathy, just blamed him for everything.

It was during the following summer that we began to see the ill effects of all this overcrowding and lack of fresh food, plague. I recognised the symptoms[1] right away for they were the same as I had suffered after my beating up by Aristodikos, so I knew I could survive, and because she had nursed me I knew that Kore too had the power to survive. But for most others it was much harder. Though it only started like a bad cold with headaches most people soon had bloodshot eyes, sore throats and their breath stank like a pigsty. After a few days they became very weak and their skins were covered in red sores, they coughed day and night and their stomachs burned. All they wanted to do was tear off their clothes and dunk their heads in any pool of water they could find. They would rant and slither around in their own filth till they died.

Kore did what she could for many of our friends, but it made little difference. Most people who caught the plague died within two weeks and nothing could stop it. When we heard that Pericles himself was ill Kore and I went round to see him. They had just elected him general again and made his bastard son legitimate as recompense for their earlier loss of faith in his leadership. But it was too late. I noticed that his mistress Aspasia, who was above all a survivor, kept well away from him, and there was nothing much even Kore could do for him.

There was the great man plowtering around the courtyard of his villa, skin blotched, incontinent, naked and almost a skeleton, his eyes bright red and his beard dripping as he stuck his face time and again into a bucket of water. Luckily enough I don't think he recognised us. We did what we could and left. A week later I delivered the funeral oration for the greatest and perhaps most dangerous man I have ever known. Above us loomed the magnificent but hugely expensive temple that was his brainchild, yet now sick men and women were crawling on its cool marble floors, looking in vain for relief from their suffering from those expensive stone gods.

For the following month it was normal to see hundreds of bodies being tossed into pits each morning and the streets stank. But at last it came to an end and for the first time in two years the city was no longer overcrowded. Then at last came a piece of good news when Phormio sailed back into the Piraeus claiming a major victory over the Corinthians. So people began to think we might win the war after all. But for me personally there was no such feeling for I heard the long dreaded news that our friends in Plataea had at last surrendered and, as expected, not one of them was spared.

Perhaps it was because of my residual guilt over Plataea or perhaps just the typical frustration of an old man who watches helplessly as the young go out to fight, but I was now desperate for another mission. It was not that I even approved of the war against Sparta and her allies, even when my own son and two sons-in-law were out fighting it, but I hated feeling redundant and even my priestly duties were in abeyance. The up-and-coming trierarchs had tricks which were new to me and my siege experience was rapidly becoming out of date, but I felt the need to do something.

'There's plenty for you to do here,' said Kore sensibly, but I found her advice hard to take.

Then quite suddenly an opportunity did arise. For a month or two there had been rumours that the islanders of Lesbos were plotting yet again to leave our alliance, just as Samos had tried to do ten years earlier. The Lesbian capital at Mytilene[2] had been refortified and it was pretty obvious that they intended to declare independence with the promise of Spartan help. Kleon, the new leader who had dominated the Athens Assembly since the death of Pericles, was quick to take action. I try not to be a snob, but most people would accept that Kleon did not have the background of men like Cimon and Pericles. He had made a lot of money in the leather trade and now wanted to make a name for himself in politics, but he had little military experience. When it came to making speeches, however, he had the common touch and soon became popular.

On this occasion his quick actions proved initially successful for the fleet that he sent not only captured Mytilene, but also the entire Spartan garrison that had been sent to help the Lesbians. At this point, however, Kleon showed very poor judgement and a nasty streak of ruthlessness for he recommended to the Assembly that all the women and children should be sold as slaves and all the male rebels should be executed. The assemblymen were easily led and agreed. I tried to make a speech, but was shouted down by the mob. It was typical of how years of war had turned the Athenian voters into callous thugs.

I was so shocked that I felt impelled to try again and make what was only my second speech to the Assembly, for I thought the decision was stupid as well as cruel. That evening I rounded up every sane acquaintance and demanded an emergency recall of the Assembly to countermand the order. Then I made my speech in which I was so angry that I stumbled over my words, but in the end common sense prevailed and the instructions were revoked. However the problem was far from solved, for a trireme had already set off for Lesbos carrying the warrant for the mass execution. Kleon, who was in a foul temper after losing the vote shouted at me 'You're too late anyway,' as if he still hoped that his original instruction would be carried out. 'The trireme sailed ten hours ago,' he added.

I was furious now too, but then I remembered something.

'As a high priest I have the right to take out the *Salaminia*,' I said, conscious that I sounded a little pompous, but knowing that I had to use every trick at my disposal.

'You haven't got a crew,' said Kleon.

Luckily Kleistes was among the friends whom I had called on for help in the Assembly, and he stuck up his thumb.

'I can find a hundred from my own crews,' he said, 'And we could call for volunteers.'

I knew that if we wasted too much time rounding up a full crew the other trireme would get even further in front of us, but with the help of Kore and Gaia's husband we managed to get our two hundred in two hours, made it to the Piraeus in three and were loaded with food and water after five, so that meant we were fifteen hours behind. I reckoned that we could make up at least six of those by sailing or rowing all night, for by luck there was a full moon.

'The others will probably have stopped for the night on Andros,' suggested Kleistes, and I agreed. 'It'll be as tight as Ganymede's backside,' he added.

Luckily there was some good wind off Sounion and our oarsmen had a reasonable rest before we had to use them again. We then alternated watches whenever the wind was unfavourable and thus kept moving almost non-stop for three days. Kleistes used all his experience to catch useful breezes and currents, which helped us keep up a good speed. I made sure we passed round flagons of diluted wine to the oarsmen and we had two men permanently mixing a porridge of barley, olive oil and wine for extra sustenance.

'It's ironic,' I said to Kleistes, 'that the flagship of the Athenian navy is putting up this superb chase not to catch an enemy ship but to overtake one of our own. This is all a huge waste of effort just to undo the damage caused by a stupid decision.'

I don't really think that Kleistes cared much whether the thousand men of Mytilene were executed or not; he simply saw the voyage as a challenge to his seamanship and accepted my judgement on the rights and wrongs of punishment.

'I'm going to rest for an hour,' he said. 'Give me a shake when the look-out sees the first rocks off Chios.[3] We should pick up some more wind there.' Then he went to relieve himself over the side. 'I'm passing my wine on to Poseidon,' he added.

We kept going all that day and the following night helped by a south-west wind but we had to slow down past the rocky reefs off Chios for it was too dark to see clearly.

For the first time in two days I dozed off, then wakened suddenly when someone shouted, 'Oars.' It was Kleistes, striding over the deck in the half light, getting the crews awake and ready to row. 'Halyards,' he yelled, for he was also standing by to hoist the sail. I felt ashamed that I had succumbed to sleep but grateful that I had such a reliable colleague.

For the next fourteen hours we rowed or sailed without stopping and there was still no sign of the other trireme, not even as we approached Lesbos[4] itself and entered the ten mile strait that leads up to Mytilene. I became deeply depressed and tense during the two hours it took us to row up to the harbour. Then finally we passed the entrance light and there was the other trireme already tied up at the jetty. Despite all our efforts we had lost the race.

'Damn Kleon,' I said illogically, sweat trickling all over my body. 'Too late.'

I leapt across to the other trireme as soon as I could and shouted for her trierarch.

'Up there,' said her ship-master, pointing to a damaged gatehouse in what had until recently been the city walls. I ran stiffly up the pier but my legs seemed to be the weight of lead. Then to my huge relief I saw the trierarch and he was talking to our force commander, obviously telling him of Kleon's orders and obviously being met with some objections. We had made it after all.

In retrospect I was satisfied that I had helped save a thousand lives in a war that cost more than ten times that number, and will cost many more before it ends. Whether my intervention did harm or good to our war effort I have never been able to tell, but I think our men were relieved that they didn't have to carry out the mass execution. The Spartan general, however, was still executed as were the ringleaders of the rebellion, but the shame and embarrassment for our great city were not as dire as they might have been. I felt both exhausted and exhilarated with the result that on this occasion I consumed rather more wine than is usual for a high priest.

---

1. Typhus or typhoid fever have, as we have seen, been suggested by modern doctors as the cause of this plague. In recent times the two diseases have been shown to be quite different, but in those days were easily confused, both having red sores and both having the fogginess of brain which gives them both their name.

2. Mytilene was originally founded 3,000 years ago on a small island which was later joined to the rest of Lesbos and is still the capital city. It is recorded that the fast trireme which brought the cancellation of executions managed the 186 nautical miles in less than 24 hours, an average of 8 knots.

3. Chios was justly famous for its mastic resin, the original chewing gum and later an ingredient of Turkish Delight, perfumes and numerous other concoctions. Mastic is the Greek word for chew; hence our word masticate.

4.   Lesbos is these days known as Lesvos and there are few remains of ancient Mytiline, but it does have a petrified forest and an Ottoman mosque. The island itself is so close to Turkey that many asylum seekers crossed to Greek territory this way during the Syrian War.

CHAPTER THIRTY -FIVE

A RELUCTANT GENERAL

IT WAS THE YEAR AFTER Mytiline that I was for the one and only time elected one of the generals. Not because of any ambition or aptitude on my part, but probably because people thought that as a priest I might help bring the war to an end. For that and other reasons Kleon was far from pleased by my election.

I must admit that I did quite enjoy the trappings of power and even Kore was occasionally heard to admit that she was quite proud of me, but now that I have had a taste of high command and known the dreadful decisions which it can involve I would never wish to have it again. The more glamorous exploits of my year as a general were all achieved by Phormio who was now by far the best fleet-handler in Athens. I only led one expedition and it was to prove both dangerous and frustrating.

Before that, however, I had a pleasant interlude on leave at home with Kore and met our two latest grandchildren for the first time. By that year[1] I had begun to think of myself as less than potent, but could not complain that the god Hermes had given me less than a fair share of nuptial pleasure. Perhaps it was just the depressing atmosphere after the plague or my feelings of humiliation after my mission to Plataea, but when I became a general I found my desires in that direction restored. Kore was nearly white-haired and had put on a little weight, but to me she was just as beautiful as Aphrodite herself and when she was not preoccupied with grandchildren or the Mysteries she could still frolic like a sixteen year old. We both felt extremely grateful that none of our family had succumbed to the plague and that neither of our sons had been killed or seriously wounded in battle. Our one great sadness was that we were still cut off from our home in Eleusis by the marauding Spartans and our farms, our vines and olive trees had all been devastated.

Naturally Kleon still resented my defiance of his wishes over the Mytilene affair, and as the man who still dominated the Assembly with his sharp tongue he made sure that as general I would get the worst assignment on offer. This was another occasion when Athens chose to interfere between a colony and its mother city, this time Corcyra which had been founded by the Corinthians. There had been a love-hate relationship between parent and child for centuries and it was made worse by the usual hatred between democrats and oligarchs, as well as some nasty family feuds.

I expect money was at the root of it all, for Corcyra had been chosen as a colony because it was a useful overnight stop on the sea route to Italy and the Adriatic. Fine. But once they'd built their new harbour the Corcyrans thought they should take over some of the juicy trade routes and deprive Corinth of some of its huge profits. And the sort of people who would do such a thing were free-thinking democrats and preferred Athens as a friend rather than ultra-conservative Corinth. So Kleon gave me a miserable three triremes and sent me off to achieve miracles. He also deliberately failed to tell me that another general, Nikostratos, had been ordered ahead of me with a more impressive twelve triremes.

By the time I was handed this mission which can only be described as toxic, the oligarchs of Corcyra had staged a coup, murdered sixty of the main democrats and burned half their own city to stop their opponents reaching the arsenal. Despite this, however, the two sides were very evenly matched and neither was strong enough to keep the other subdued for long. Hence the usual interference by Athens to support the democrats and by Sparta or Corinth the oligarchs. This just made matters worse.

The situation when I arrived with my flotilla was extremely distressing. The ships of the pro-Athens Corcyrans had just been beaten by the pro-Corinth Corcyrans and Nikostratos, who was trying to avoid fighting, had kept a safe distance. He fancied himself as a diplomat and began to shuttle between the opposing sides to arrange a truce. Then panic set in as a Spartan fleet of sixty triremes was spotted on the horizon, so I stepped in with some half-true news that there were sixty Athenian ships on the way too. So at least I achieved my first objective which was to drive away the Spartans. So Nikostratos proceeded with his talks and organised four hundred of the pro-Corinth/oligarch side to be shipped safely to Athens, leaving behind a garrison to prevent further violence. The oligarchs, however, smelt a rat and refused to board the ships, so the democrats interpreted this as the prelude to another oligarch attack.

So both sides were now so paranoid that every word spoken was assumed to be a deception. If anything the intervention of Nikostratos had made things worse than before.

The democrats now having a slight edge pursued the oligarchs into a temple, then to a small island, then back to the temple, then persuaded fifty of them to accept a proper trial for their attempted coup. Naturally the trial was far from proper. All fifty were immediately executed. The remaining three hundred and fifty decided to help each other to commit suicide, either by hanging from sacred temple trees or whatever else came to hand. The now jubilant democrats began a feverish search for any surviving oligarchs and slaughtered them. And when they ran out of oligarchs they began to kill financial rivals, unpopular uncles, fathers, grandfathers or elder brothers. To speed up the inheritance process some were slaughtered in temples, others walled up and left to starve, then others cornered in an enclosure and pelted with tiles. Even the women joined in. Both sides were so desperate that they even offered their slaves freedom if they would fight on their side. Then people who owed money made the whole thing an excuse to murder their creditors and many old scores were settled including brothers getting rid of their own siblings and sons eliminating their unwanted fathers.

Gradually, however, it became evident that the democrats were coming out on top, the allies of Athens, so I had to applaud this whatever my personal feelings. My real feelings were that the human race had sunk so low that I was ashamed to be part of it.

Here we were on this beautiful island with its fine beaches and clear turquoise sea, its cool cypress trees, olives and fruit trees. How could these people not be content?

They had everything but were not happy.

'There's nothing much to choose between them,' I said to Sophocles who had come with the expedition as reserve general.

He shrugged his shoulders and pointed across to the island of Dionysos where some more oligarchs had been walled up by the democrats and would soon starve to death.

'This war could go on forever,' he said. 'Athens will always win at sea and Sparta on land. Impasse.'

'Maybe no-one wants the war to end,' I answered. 'Too many people are making money out of it. All the ordinary folk are getting their wages and the merchants are doing very nicely, never mind the war. If they ever really want peace we'll know about it.'

'It was just the same in Sicily,' said Sophocles, whom I had never much liked, but I had to admit he was a good judge of character. 'Athens supports Gela against Syracuse or the other way round depending on who's friendly with Sparta or Corinth. What's the point?'

This remark proved quite timely for once the Corcyrans had grown weary of killing each other we received orders to proceed to Sicily where we were supposed to stir up the same kind of conflict we'd just left behind in Corcyra. The one good thing was that I ran into Kleistes on the jetty at Gela.

'Apollo's backside if it's not Phori,' he shouted, dropping some African cushion covers which he'd been inspecting. 'I heard they'd elected you a general. I thought you'd be too intelligent to accept. But I can't be right about everything.'

'You were right. I should have refused,' I said. 'How's the family?'

'Scattered all over the Aegean,' he replied. 'Every time Athens gets a new colony one of my children gets a house there. So I hardly ever see them, nor my seventeen grandchildren at the last count. But at least they've been out of the way of the plague and the war, so why should I complain?'

We went up for a cup of wine together in a local tavern and spent a happy hour or so, but then we had to go our separate ways and sadly it was to be the last time I saw him. For in the autumn of that year there were terrible storms and his largest ship, in which I was still a shareholder, was sunk with all hands somewhere in the Adriatic. He was the best ship-master I'd ever sailed with and one of the finest friends a man could know.

The rest of my expedition passed without incident. I was glad enough when we rowed back into the Piraeus and though it slightly hurt my vanity that I was not re-elected for a second term as general, I was at the same time glad that I no longer had to obey the orders of the Assembly, for it was now full of bitter and aggressive men.

That autumn I reached my sixtieth year and shortly afterwards we suffered the worst misfortune of our married lives. Kore and I were in our Athens house when a messenger came from the temple of Eleusis to say that our younger son Psamos, the least self-seeking of all our children, had died in a new outbreak of the plague. It was a bad, bad year.

---

1. This was 427BC when the war was in its fifth year and had already caused thousands of deaths, many of which we would describe as collateral due to destruction of crops and spread of disease. Amongst them was the bibulous philosopher Anaxagoras, but he was swiftly replaced by young Socrates and later by Plato who at this time was one year old.

CHAPTER THIRTY-SIX

THE FINAL MYSTERY
MY UNDISCOVERED CRIME

FOR KORE AND MYSELF THERE followed a long and difficult winter as we wrestled with our grief. Though our other three children were well enough, both Kynegiros and my two sons-in-law were all very affected by the fashion of empire and hatred of our enemies, always wanting to pursue the war against Sparta whatever the cost, still believing that we could win. Like so many they seemed blind to the thousands of newly dug graves outside every city. They thought their own triremes would never be sunk, but all I could see were young men on both sides slaughtering each other with no end in sight.

Our great admiral Phormio[1] had won some famous victories, but now he was ill, worn out with the strain. However many minor triumphs we achieved against the Spartans they always seemed to recover, whilst we had fewer and fewer men left to renew the endless combat. Most of the time it was still not safe for us to visit our home in Eleusis, for Spartan bands still kept invading Attica and burning any crops they could find. Our own olive groves and vineyards were scarred with old fires and smothered in weeds, so Kore and I sometimes felt that at our age we would never have the time or energy to get them restored, even if the wretched politicians did at last decide to make peace.

As it turned out there was to be one final occasion when I was able to intervene in what had become the increasingly murky state of Athenian politics, and by that time I was over sixty years old. In the meantime I had made a lifelong enemy of Kleon since my interference in his punishment of the Lesbians, and Kleon was still our leading politician. I may be biased but he had built his political career on the money he made in the leather trade, mostly government contracts, so though he was an elected general he had not done much actual fighting and this made his rabid enthusiasm for the war slightly suspect. His big advantage was his ready wit and his ability to win over the Assembly with a clever speech. At least there had recently been some opposition, mainly led by Nikias, a totally different kind of leader, one of the old families and a lifelong soldier, no match for Kleon when it came to speaking, but much more cautious, conventional and superstitious but sensible when it came to waging war. The one thing they had in common was money, for Nikias had inherited a huge silver-mine with thousands of slaves to work it for him.

The bitter rivalry between these two came to a head when Nikias was in charge of the siege of Sphakteria,[2] a little island off the coast near Sparta which the Assembly had decided would make a good base for annoying the Spartans. This had worked quite well for years until the Spartans had retaliated by putting their own garrison on the island and held out for so long against Nikias that the Assembly grew impatient. Kleon made a rash attack on his rival saying that if Nikias could not capture the island he would do it himself.

He of course never expected that Nikias would agree to let him try, but to his amazement that is exactly what Nikias did. Then to the even greater amazement of Nikias and perhaps even of Kleon himself the tanner demagogue actually succeeded where the professional soldier had failed. Now it might seem that this victory and the surrender of several hundred crack Spartan troops would be good news for Athens, and in many respects it was, but to my mind it just made disaster more inevitable, for it made both Kleon and the Athenian rabble ridiculously overconfident so that they then undertook even more ambitious attacks on the Spartans.

The episode[3] which ended the career of Kleon came when he was now so convinced of his abilities as a general that he took on a much larger Spartan army under their latest top general, the brilliant Brasidas. Thus his second outing as a field commander was his last, for he was heavily defeated at Amphipolis and killed in the act of trying to escape. By coincidence the winning general was also killed, but not whilst trying to escape. The defeat cost six hundred Athenian lives including one of my sons-in-law, so it was not just a disaster for our city but for my family too.

Kleon of course, was no great loss and Nikias briefly became quite popular again, even making peace with Sparta for a while, but sadly he was soon superseded by an even more dangerous firebrand, Alkibiades, who was as good an orator as Pericles, as devious as Kleon and as rich as Nikias. I was convinced that he would bring ruin to Athens and for that reason I decided to do my best to bring about his downfall. I had stood aside long enough, joining half-heartedly in this wretched war when I felt like it instead of having the courage to demand its end. Now Athens was facing total disaster with yet another over-ambitious amateur trying to show off his brilliance at the expense of ordinary people.

Alkibiades was a professional playboy whose father had been killed in battle when the boy was quite young, so he'd been brought up by his uncle Pericles. Surprisingly, unlike the great man's own children, he always had the best of everything and seeing his uncle at work he grew up with enormous ambition and the expectation that high office would come to him without much effort. Not that he was lacking in ability, quite the reverse, for he was immensely gifted, extremely handsome, a quick-thinking officer, a charismatic speaker and married to one of the most beautiful women in Athens. Yet for all his qualities he had no ideal beyond self-promotion and though he certainly wanted to add to the glories of Athens it was really just so that he could enhance his own reputation. Like my son Kynegiros he had listened to the trouble-making teacher, Socrates, and like Narcissus he had a compulsion to admire himself.

In his early career he always had to be a winner. He hated losing at wrestling matches and hardly ever did. It was the same if he played with dice or entered a horse race. In fact for the Olympic games he entered seven of his chariots to make sure of winning, so he won the first, third and fourth prizes all in one year and became a national celebrity. He boasted that he was descended from the legendary warrior Ajax. He treated ordinary people[4] as if they were slaves and slaves as if they were lower than animals. He deliberately bought a huge dog whose tail he cut off so that people would talk about him. To be fair he also showed considerable physical courage during several battles but again he was so desperate for attention that risk-taking was no problem.

His domestic life was far from straightforward for not content with his beautiful wife he had affairs with numerous other women and even a few men, so that his wife left him in despair, but when she made an appearance to sue for divorce he seized the chance to kidnap her back again.

Thus no sooner had Nikias organised a peace with Sparta than Alkibiades wanted to restart the war. He wanted Athens to dominate half the Mediterranean with himself naturally as leader. So he devised new alliances and new expeditions to irritate the Spartans and bring matters to a head.

All this was enough for me to seek out kindred spirits who would join me in opposition to this man before he brought destruction to our city, but I would probably not have stooped to deceit and violence had he not committed an additional outrage, which hurt my own dear wife deeply and drove me over the edge into less rational methods for undermining his authority.

This all took place in my seventieth year, an age when I wouldn't have expected any longer to be listened to in the Assembly or had any major influence over events. Alkibiades had now filled the heads of the Athenians with the notion that we could capture Syracuse, the richest city in the west. Then Athens would be able to control all the trade from Africa and Italy and our entire population would be rich while Corinth and Sparta would become mere backwaters. I must admit that most of the young men including my son, Kynegiros, were taken in by all this, though I myself was convinced that if by some miracle the attack on Syracuse was successful then every other city in Greece would gang up against us until we were destroyed. Unfortunately no one was in the mood to listen to me, except perhaps Nikias and he was too busy looking for omens in the guts of sacrificial goats to stand up and sound convincing.

So peace was forgotten and a massive fleet assembled in the Piraeus with a large army and all the equipment needed for a difficult siege. Alkibiades having concocted this, in my view, disastrous plan strutted round the city, overdressed, flirting with both sexes and behaving like a rich playboy without a care in the world, humiliating anyone who dared stand in his way or express disapproval. Thus since I fitted into this category it was not surprising that he tried to do the same to me .

If Alkibiades hadn't used dirty tricks against me and my family it is highly probable that I would not have used underhand methods either and would not have succeeded in my objectives, but he went too far and I made him pay for it. By attacking me through my wife he stirred up feelings that made me react far more violently than would otherwise have been the case.

Kore was nearly two years my junior but, like me, she was beginning to suffer the odd twinges of age and the long nights down in Poseidon's dark cave had begun to take their toll. She also had a deep reverence for the long family tradition which she had inherited and which our daughter Gaia was now carrying on into the next generation. In her declining years the Mysteries perhaps meant even more to her than they had in her youth. Thus when Alkibiades made a public mockery of our faith it was especially offensive to her. He staged a bizarre imitation of the Mysteries at his villa with a well-known whore playing the part of Kore and a bunch of drunks acting as chorus. It was a typical Alkibiades stunt with the sole intention of gaining attention for himself, something that he could never have enough of, and done with absolutely no consideration for those who might be hurt. From his point of view the objective was to make mock of everyone else in the world, so that he would be unchallenged.

It reduced Kore to tears and me to extreme anger. It's not that I believed that any religion should be compulsory or above criticism, but such outrageous mockery was an insult to those who did believe and extremely hurtful for those who found comfort in what it had to offer. Thus quite unexpectedly I found myself plotting to use Alkibiades' own disreputable tactics to accomplish his downfall.

My behaviour was of course reprehensible, especially for a senior priest, but no one including my dear wife had any inkling about what I was up to and my confession in this memoir will only be read after both our deaths.

Two nights after the incident, when Kore was still deeply distressed but beginning to regain her normal good humour I heard that Alkibiades was planning another of his decadent parties to celebrate the departure of the fleet to Syracuse. So putting on a rough woollen cloak to disguise myself as an immigrant craftsman I went to his villa and told the slave on the door that I had been sent to repair the roof and needed access to his tool shed. There I picked up the largest stone hammer that I could find and after shifting a few tiles on his roof I hid myself till the early hours of the next morning. Then I crept out and headed first for the market place where I used his hammer to smash off the stone face and phallos of the four great Hermes statues[5] at each corner of the market. These Hermai, as they were called, often quite obscenely carved, are important still to many Athenian men as symbols of their ability to father a new generation.

As a religious cult, however, it was distinctly old-fashioned and only an act of wanton destruction like mine would have won any sympathy for a cult that had almost died out except as a lingering superstition. Anyway, to make the most of it, I smashed another streetful of Hermai, including a number outside the doors of several prominent citizens. Then making sure there was still plenty of the stone dust adhering to the hammer I returned it to Alkibiades' tool shed and crept back home to lie down beside Kore.

'Where have you been?' she asked a little testily, still half asleep.

'Sorting out Alkibiades,' I replied and went straight to sleep, quite gratified by my night's work. I had never understood the Athenian obsession with phallic statues. It was as if the men felt insecure about their masculinity, which perhaps many of them were.

What happened next is well enough known. Alkibiades sailed at dawn the next day with the fleet, but it soon became clear that there was huge popular outrage at the smashing of the Hermai and the rapid departure of Alkibiades a few hours afterwards helped encourage the idea that he had played a part. Rewards were offered for information about the culprits because amongst the superstitious it appeared to be a bad omen for the expedition to Sicily. Since Alkibiades was already known to have been guilty of mockery against the Mysteries of Eleusis it was not too hard to suggest that he might also have committed this latest sacrilege, and I made a point of discussing such behaviour within earshot of some immigrants in the market place. And as I was a priest my words, of course, carried no little weight.

'Go and look in his tool shed and see if his hammers are still there,' I said to some officials who came to seek my advice. 'Whoever did it must have used a hammer and none has been found so far.'

That was enough. The *Salaminia* was despatched to bring Alkibiades back for trial. My old ship did indeed catch up with the fleet, but as you may remember he jumped ashore somewhere before she reached home. Then he headed for Sparta to see if they would have him on their side for the rest of the war. I expect he will long outlive me and do more mischief[6] but I can do no more.

---

1. Phormio was indeed a brilliant admiral and also good on land, especially sieges, but he seems to have become ill or disillusioned shortly after this event.

2. The island of Sphakteria is now uninhabited and lies in the Gulf of Navarino where another even greater battle took place many centuries later in 1827 as a result of which the Turks lost control of Greece. Navarino is the modern name for the ancient Greek city of Pylos and is the starting point of Route 82 which crosses over to Sparta

3. In 422BC when Euphorion was sixty-five Aristophanes wrote the play 'Wasps' ridiculing Kleon and all other politicians over-confident in their abilities.

4. Alkibiades was undoubtedly a brilliant and charismatic leader but prone to changing sides when it suited him.

5. The incident known as the Mutilation of the Hermai is well authenticated in Greek history (see Thucydides, History of the Peloponnesian War Book VI 27) as is the fact that Alkibiades was blamed for it. He denied his guilt, but was not altogether believed. The confession here by Euphorion confirms that his denial was the truth.

6. After these events in 416BC Alkibiades sought revenge against his accusers and betrayed the Athenian plans for the attack on Syracuse to the Spartans, then sank even lower when he betrayed all Greeks for a while by helping the Persians. Later he did return to Athens and won some remarkable victories, but was murdered by a Spartan agent in 405BC whilst trying to persuade the Persians to aid Athens against Sparta. He thus outlived Euphorion by only eight years.

CHAPTER THIRTY-SEVEN

THE CAVE OF HADES

TWO YEARS HAVE PASSED SINCE the Mutilation of the Hermai[1] and now I sit writing what must be the final lines of these memoirs. Poor Kore is fading fast and I no longer have any purpose in this world without her. At least we are back at home in Eleusis and shortly we are both going to make our way back down into the deep cave where we first declared our love. There we will lie down beside each other and wait for the god Poseidon or Hades or whoever comes to escort us on the final short journey to the underworld.

I believe I should have no regrets about causing Alkibiades to lose command of the expedition to Syracuse. Without him Nikias was a dithering commander and the siege was a disastrous failure, but had it been a success it would have done even more damage than its failure did to our state. Nikias was captured and put to death with great cruelty and that I regret. We have heard news that our son, Kynegiros, who was serving there with him was not amongst those killed, but is a prisoner and has been kept as a slave working in those hell-hole quarries outside Syracuse.[2] I have faith in his strength of character and am sure that one day he will make his escape and come home to his family in Athens, though we will not be there to see him.

I am deeply saddened by the way our democratic state has been corrupted by vanity and greed and sometimes question whether ordinary human beings can ever run their own affairs without stupid bickering and succumbing to silly delusions. Under Pericles we came close to creating the perfect city but even at our very best we were not content and wanted more.

I am also ashamed of the fact that our city is still at war with Sparta and there seems no prospect of peace. It is madness for two great states to waste their strength fighting each other when they have so much in common and so much to lose by mutual self-destruction. Yet I am now too old to make anyone in the Assembly listen to my views and I have long since lost any capacity to make a difference in the war. All I can hope for is that my grandchildren will survive and that so too will some of the beauty that we helped create.

Kore is standing in the mouth of the cave waiting for me. She is wearing her yellow robe as high priestess of the Mysteries. I write these last words, then I will go to join her. I don't know what awaits us when our bodies stop functioning but I am fairly sure that whatever after-life we enjoy at least there will be peace.

As I struggle to the end of this narrative I must express gratitude that I found a quantity of half-used parchment in Demeter's Temple, otherwise I could not have afforded the cost of writing such a document. My objective was not so much to record the life of a fairly mediocre man who led a more or less happy and superficially quite successful life, but to draw the attention of future generations to the folly of political ambition, and how a brilliantly civilized city endowed with large numbers of very talented people could delude itself into believing that all other cities should be submissive to its demands for money, its self-aggrandisement and exploitation, its vindictive punishments and its greed. And with so many good leaders to chose from why did the world's first brilliant democracy keep on electing men who would be its ruination? You could of course ask why I did not make more effort myself to be an effective politician, but perhaps like the rest of them I might have succumbed to ambitious pride and done more harm than good. I see a flash of yellow down in the cave and Kore is still waiting for me. I can hear her telling Poseidon III to go home to his bed, but I don't think…

---

1. The date would be 413BC so Euphorion would be seventy-two.

2. The original Greek colony of Syracuse, now known as Siracusa was on Ortygia Island and remnants of the stone quarry or Latomie used as a prison for captured soldiers like Euphorion's son can still be seen.

3. The Temple of Eleusis was finally destroyed in 391AD after the cult of Demeter had been declared illegal by the Christian Emperor Theodoric I.

4. The Peloponnesian War carried on for another nine miserable years after the death of Euphorion, finally ending with the surrender of Athens in 404 BC. Athenian democracy was never the same again, nor did Athens ever again have an empire, but men like Euripides, Aristophanes and Plato survived and so did the Parthenon until it was accidentally blown up by the Venetians. Athens finally lost its independence in 3363C when it was absorbed into the Macedonian Empire, then the Roman Empire, then the Byzantine Empire, then the Ottoman Empire till after six further centuries of subjection it re-emerged as the capital of a liberated Greece.

> # *BRIEF BIOGRAPHICAL DETAILS*

OF THE PEOPLE MENTIONED IN THIS BOOK

'T' means that the person is a genuine historical figure and the deeds attributed can be verified from original sources whilst 'F' means fictitious although based on fact - the small number of characters in this category, including the hero and heroine of this saga, nearly all belonged to verified historical families.

Athenians or Athenian Supporters
Generals and Politicians

- Alkibiades 'T' (450–404 BC) brilliant but unscrupulous and scandal–prone general.

- Aristides 'T' (530–468 BC) known as the Just, efficient but uncharismatic general, fought at Marathon and Salamis.

- Charitimides 'T' (c 485–454BC) general in charge of failed Egyptian expedition during which he was killed.

- Cimon 'T' (c 495–449 BC) son of Miltiades, highly successful commander, rich but politically conservative: patron of Euphorion.

- Kallimachus 'T' (d. 490BC) official chief general at Marathon but left strategy to Miltiades

- Kleon 'T'(–422 BC) former leather worker turned populist war leader killed in battle against Sparta.

- Ephialtes 'T' (–457 BC) brilliant democrat and rival of Pericles murdered in 457 BC.

- Miltiades 'T' (550–489BC) the man who masterminded Athenian victory at Marathon in 490, but was disgraced soon afterwards and died of wound in prison.
- Myronides 'T' reasonably successful general, father-in-law of hero.
- Nikias 'T' (d.415BC) leader of failed attack on Syracuse.
- Pericles 'T' (490–429 BC) key architect of democratic reform in Athens, and of the Delian alliance which helped fund his signature projects such as the Parthenon. Died of plague caused by his own war policy.
- Themistocles 'T' (523–458) pioneer of naval development in Athens and hero of naval Battle of Salamis, later disgraced and exiled.
- Tolmides 'T' general killed at Coronea in 447 BC.
- Xanthippos 'T' respected Athenian general and father of Pericles.

Writers and Artists

- Aeschylus 'T' (525–456) born in Eleusis, known as father of Greek Tragedy, wounded at Marathon, uncle of our hero, author amongst other plays of the Oresteia trilogy.
- Herodotus 'T' (485–425 BC) born Halicarnassos, known as the 'Father of History' and author of the history of the Eastern Mediterranean which ends with the Persian Wars.
- Homer 'T' (8th century BC) great allegedly blind, probably illiterate epic poet born in Smyrna and affirmed by tradition to have composed both the Odyssey and the Illiad.
- Iktinos 'T' (d.c 430BC) architect of Parthenon.
- Phidias 'T' (d. 432BC) chief sculptor of Parthenon
- Polygnotos 'T'(470–420 BC) painter born in Thasos
- Sophocles 'T' (496–405BC) seven major plays of the great tragedian still survive including Antigone and Oedipus Rex –he won the theatrical first prize 18 times.

- Stesopoulos, Stavros 'F' (d.1922) writer based in Smyrna and killed during the Turkish massacre of 1922.
- Thucydides 'T' (460–400 BC) beast known as the historian of the Peloponnesian War and source of many of the facts in this book, but also served as a naval commander, was condemned to exile for failing to relieve Amphipolis in 424.

Priests

- Kallias 'T' known as the Torch-bearer, brother in law of Cimon and chief peace negotiator.
- Kore 'T/F' daughter of Psamos and Gaia, hereditary priestess and earthly personification of the earth goddess Persephone.
- Mnesiptolema 'T' daughter of Themistocles and priestess in exile.
- Psamos 'T' chief hereditary priest of Eleusis, father of Kore.
- Gaia 'T/F' wife of Psamos.

Others

- Aspasia 'T' mistress of Pericles came from Miletos.
- Elpinike 'T' half-sister of Cimon and wife of Kallias.
- Kynegiros 'T' d. 475, hero of Marathon, brother of Aeschylus and father of young Euphorion.
- Euphorion 'T' father of Kynegiros and Aeschylus, grandfather of Euphorion the Younger.
- Euphorion 'F' author of this account, son of Kynegiros, nephew of Aeschylus, trireme captain, general and priest.
- Kynegiros II 'F' son of Euphorion the Younger.
- Kleistes 'F' ship master and merchant.
- Lampon 'T' servant of Pericles.
- Phidippides 'T' (d.c 490) courier who ran with message to Sparta 152 miles in 2 days. Also ran first Marathon.

- Psyche 'F' family slave.
- Poseidon 'F' dog.

Spartans
Kings and Princes

- Leonidas 'T' (killed in battle 480BC) joint king of Sparta and hero of Thermopylae.

- Pausanias 'T' prince, nephew of Leonidas and successful general at Plataea but later disgraced and imprisoned without food till he starved to death.

- Pleistoanax 'T' young king suspected of accepting bribes and exiled for two decades.

- Kleandridas 'T' Spartan general during attack on Attica, later executed for bribery.

Other Greeks
Politicans and Soldiers

- Polykrates of Samos 'T' notorious tyrant.

- Aristodikos of Tanagra 'T' mentioned only by Aristotle as probable murderer of Ephialtes.

Scientists and Philosophers

- Anaxagoras 'T' (c498–428BC) philosopher and astronomer friendly with Pericles and admired by Aristotle.

- Euclid 'T' (fl 300 BC) mathematician born in Alexandria Egypt.

- Heracleitus 'T' (fl 500BC) philosopher born in Ephesus and known as the Riddler who argued that everything is in a state of flux –you can never step into the same river twice.

- Hippocrates 'T' (460–337BC) known as the father of medicine born on island of Kos.

- Plato 'T' (428–337BC)major Athenian philosopher, born just after start of Peloponnesian War., pupil of Socrates, founder of the Academy and originator of the utopian myth of Atlantis.

- Zeno 'T' (332–262BC) founder of Stoics

Persians and other non–Greeks

Kings and Princes

- Darius I 'T' (548–486 BC) Great King of Persia, supporter of the Magi and reorganiser of Persian Empire who lost at Marathon.
- Inaros – 'T' Libyan prince who led revolt of Egypt against Persia, defeated then crucified in Sardis in 454BC.
- Mardonios 'T' Persian general killed at Plataea in 479BC
- Pissuthenes 'T' Satrap of Lydia during Samos rebellion.
- Xerxes 'T' (–464BC) Great King of Persia, victor of Thermopylae but defeated by Themistocles at Salamis. Murdered by own body–guard.

Gods, demigods

- Aphrodite 'T/F' aka Venus, goddess of heterosexual love, of uncertain parentage though Uranus was involved and she was born on a beach somewhere with frothy waves as portrayed by Botticelli, on/off item with smooth–cheeked Apollo, patron of Delos and Delphi, mother of illegitimate transgender Hermaphroditus after fling with Hermes (see below).
- Apollo 'T/F?' aka Pythos, see above.
- Asclepios 'T/F?' god of medicine, one of more useful gods, born as a result of a fling of Apollo's with a woman called Colonis, whom he killed in a fit of jealousy before the baby was born,
- Athena 'T/F?' goddess of wisdom and patron goddess of Athens, known to the Romans as Minerva and referred to as a virgin as she sprang from the head of Zeus, hence the Parthenon.

- Bacchus 'T/F' god of alcohol, result probably of one night stand of Zeus and Semele, patron of orgies held by priestesses (Bacchantes or Maenads) of his cult.

- Demeter 'T/F?' earth or mother goddess known to Romans as Ceres, responsible for crops, harvest and fertility of all kinds including human. One of Zeus' spare wives and they had a daughter Persephone also known as Kore. Worshipped at Eleusis.

- Hercules 'T/F?' hyperactive action man and patron of games.

- Hermes or Mercury 'T/F?' also of uncertain parentage, but born in Arcadia acted as messenger for gods, patronised tradesmen, shepherds and thieves. Allegedly stole Poseidon's trident and Aphrodite's girdle amongst other things. Associated with phallic rites in ancient Athens–the Hermai.

- Pan 'T/F' another of Hermes' sons, fashionable new god during the Persian Wars and credited with inventing panic which is named after him. Also played pipes, had horns and legs of a goat. Patronised sex life of men.

- Perseus 'T/F' son of Zeus and one of his one–night–stands, slew Gorgons and rescued Andromeda.

- Poseidon 'T/F?' known to Romans as Neptune god of sea, was brother of Zeus

- Zeus 'T/F?' current chief god and father figure, had seized the position from his predecessor Chronos. Known to Romans as Jupiter, married to Hera (known to the Romans as Juno) but regularly unfaithful, serial abuser, life–long patron of Olympic Games.

Further Reading

The Promise
When promises can cost lives

Simon's Wife
Time is running out, and history is being
rewritten by a traitor's hand.

The Unforgiven King
A forgotten woman and the most vilified
king in history

American Goddess
Ancient powers
and new forces

L. M. Affrossman

Two Pups
What makes us different. What makes us
the same.

Seona Calder

Comics and Columbine
An outcast look at comics, bigotry and
school shootings

Tom Campbell

Science for Heretics
Why so much of science is wrong

The Tethered God
Punished for a crime he can't
remember

Barrie Condon

Pignut and Nuncle
When we are born, we cry that
we have come to this stage of fools
King Lear

Des Dillon

Drown for your Sins
DCI Grant McVicar: Book 1

Dress for Death
DCI Grant McVicar: Book 2

Diarmid MacArthur

www.sparsilebooks.com